Waiting at the *Crossroads*

Book 2
in the **Love is Hell** series

by Sonia Branchaud

ISBN-10: 1477643605
EAN-13: 9781477643600
Library of Congress Control Number: 2012910749
CreateSpace, North Charleston, SC

Books in the **Love is Hell** series:

*I dedicate this book to my wonderful children,
Nathaniel and Xavier Branchaud.*

ACKNOWLEDGEMENTS

Again I have a great many people to thank for their help on this book. My husband is first and foremost. Followed by the same list of wonderful friends who have supported me from the very beginning: Sherri Thompson, Sandra Houillier, and Felicia Staub Brassard. But this time I have new readers who have advised me on this book in particular. Firstly, I would like to thank my brother, Paul Bichler. Romance is not his preferred genre, but he inspired me to add more action and adventure to this story. Secondly, I would like to thank my long-time friend Rose Shuttleworth for overlooking the small errors, opening up her imagination, and focusing on the impractical. She brought a fresh perspective to the book. Another person who helped with the review process is Jennifer Shnaidman. I look forward to reading many of her novels in the near future.

I would also like to thank all of the new fans of the Love is Hell series and especially those who have written such encouraging words to me personally or as online reviews for all to see. My family and friends have been so supportive and I want to thank each and every one of them

Chapter 1

Emilie Latour stood in her apartment, daydreaming about her new boyfriend. Dante Ashton was very special and not just because he was as beautiful as an angel. It was because he was an angel. Well, not exactly. He was a descendant of fallen angels, but he was close enough to paradise for Emilie.

She was in her small but well-organized apartment kitchen, watching some pasta boil for her lunch. She hadn't seen Dante since Halloween, just after he had taken her to the art museum. It was still difficult to believe that one of his own kind had tried to shoot him with a fatal venom dart. Even though she was only a lowly human girl, she had saved him.

As terrifying as the whole experience had been, she was glad it had happened. It had made her realize that she wanted to be with Dante no matter what he was. He lived in a dark and dangerous world, and at first she didn't think there was a place in it for her. Now she knew better, and she couldn't be happier. Well, that wasn't exactly the truth. She would be happier if he didn't work out of the country for so many days of the week, or if she could at least speak to him on the phone for hours when he wasn't here in Montreal.

Dante was a messenger with the Beyowan council. That might not sound like a glamorous job, but he was truly special. He could travel in mesay or through inter-dimensional space, which meant that he could go from one place in the world to another almost instantly. This advantage made him a very popular messenger.

Keeping in touch was somewhat problematic for the couple. Dante had made it clear that his council-issued phone was not a safe way of communication because it was probably being monitored. All of their phone conversations had to be of the type shared between two regular people. She couldn't mention anything different about him, and he would be sure to do the same. It was imperative for them to keep their relationship a secret from as many people as possible, and she wasn't supposed to know the truth about what he was.

He had chosen to be honest with her about himself and his world; maybe a little too open. She was having a difficult time accepting that the world wasn't the same place she had always thought it was.

They'd had a couple of brief and insubstantial conversations since they'd last seen each other, just his way of touching base and letting her know that she was in his thoughts. He had also sent her a steady stream of text messages. He was behaving like any regular boyfriend, and she was becoming increasingly pleased with him, even if he was technically a demon.

Her phone rang, and she rushed to pick it up, hoping it was Dante. It was.

"Hello," she answered cheerfully.

"Hello," he replied, his voice hushed as though trying not to be overheard.

"How are you?"

"I'm lonely and bored," he answered, his magical voice switching to something more soft and sad.

Emilie felt a surge of hope. "Are you at home?"

"Well, sort of…I'm at my home in Bangkok." He sighed. "And I can't sleep."

She was hoping that the pace of their physical relationship would start picking up. They were both consenting adults with their own apartments and yet they had barely gotten to second base. "Why not?" she asked mischievously.

"Because I'm thinking about you too much."

His words were like music to her ears. "Well, I wish I was there to tuck you in," she murmured. When they had last been together, he had tucked her into bed, kissed her goodnight, and disappeared into thin air, even though she had been secretly entertaining ideas of inviting him to join her for the night.

"Hmmm…That would be nice, but somehow I don't think having you here would help me sleep."

The deep, sensual, almost resonating quality of his voice sent a shiver down her spine. "That would be fine with me," she admitted, hoping he would take the hint that she was ready for things to move to the next level between them. If he had been sitting next to her, she would have given him a sharp punch in the arm. In his world, that type of gesture was considered a sexual invitation.

"But you're supposed to help me sleep not keep me up."

She hadn't missed his little play on words. "I could tire you out a bit."

His voice lost its humor and became even huskier. "I don't think you have a clue what you're getting yourself into with me, little girl."

"Try me," she challenged.

His soft sniggering sounded almost diabolical. "I'd like to. You have no idea."

"Oh, I have a very good idea. I can assure you."

He paused for a few seconds and then whispered, "I miss you."

She smiled wistfully. Demon or not, he was the sweetest thing alive. She whispered back, "I miss you too. You have sweet dreams now, my angel."

"I'll try."

"Goodnight."

"Goodnight," he replied, then hung up.

Emilie put away the phone, smiling from ear to ear. She loved him way too much, and he had made her day by calling.

ॐ

Dante put his phone away and pretended to be sitting quietly with his book before heading off to bed. His bodyguard, Jude, dragged himself into the room and flopped down on the other side of the couch.

"Feeling OK?" Dante asked.

"I'm not looking forward to another night of getting up all the time to make sure you aren't sneaking off on me," Jude grumbled, glaring at Dante for good measure.

Dante chuckled. "I've been meaning to talk to you about that."

"I don't think I want to hear this," Jude muttered.

Dante laughed again but even more uncomfortably this time. His relationship with Emilie complicated his life on so many levels. As a Dark Angel, he was supposed to avoid any involvement with humans. Plus as a council messenger, he had a great deal of enemies who would be more than happy to use Emilie as bait for a trap.

He had applied for a hunting license to protect both Emilie and himself. It was the only way their relationship would be sanctioned. In a sense, he was purchasing her life from the council as well as from the humans. Once he held that permit, she would belong to him. If anything happened to her, the council and the human authorities would only feign concern and quickly find a way of covering everything up. It was a staggering responsibility, and Dante was determined to do everything in his power to protect her.

Owning a hunting permit for a human civilian seriously violated his religious beliefs, but it was their only option. As his official mistress, Emilie was protected by the council, and despite the seriousness of the situation, he was looking forward to exploring his relationship with the woman he suspected to be his soul mate.

But it was time for him to let Jude in on the secret. "I've done something I shouldn't have," he began with trepidation.

"Emilie's pregnant, right?" Jude asked, his eyes wide and his expression serious.

Dante snorted. "Would I be smiling if she was pregnant?"

"Knowing you, you'd be at least a little smug. Worried but smug."

Dante stretched himself out in his seat and put his feet on the coffee table. His species, the Beyowans, had serious fertility problems, and it was the responsibility of every member of the noble class to produce as many children as they possibly could. "I would be rather proud of myself, I suppose. But I don't want any illegitimate children."

"There's nothing wrong with illegitimate children," Jude stated, thumping himself proudly on the chest.

Dante looked his friend up and down carefully. "You're the best illegitimate child I know, but that's not my point. You have to admit that you would have preferred to be your father's legal heir and living the good life instead of following a spoiled, selfish brat like me around."

"My father looks after me in his own way. And you're not so bad. You're a bit of an idiot, but not so bad." Jude slapped Dante playfully on the arm. "I'm not as pretentious as you are, though. I don't think I'm cut out to be an arrogant, inbred heir out trying to reproduce. There's an incredible amount of freedom being illegitimate."

Dante narrowed his eyes and announced, "I'm not inbred."

Jude laughed, knowing Dante had accepted that he was both arrogant and pretentious.

Dante continued, "It would be quite a relief not having my entire family breathing down my neck, waiting for me to produce an heir of my own."

"I can have as many illegitimate children as I want."

"I can too," Dante responded with a snort. "No offense, but I just don't want that kind of life for any child of mine. Anyway, how many children do you have after over a century of trying?"

"I guess I'll just have to try harder, that's all." Jude sniggered and stretched out, his eyes peacefully closed. "I spend too much of my time following you around, remember?"

"That brings us back to our original topic of discussion."

Jude opened an eye and, seeing Dante's anxious face staring at him expectantly, opened the other. "OK...At least I'm sitting down."

Dante took a deep, hesitant breath. "I'm dating Emilie," he admitted, his eyes locked on the floor. There was a pause, and Dante lifted his gaze to assess his friend's reaction.

"What exactly do you mean by *dating*?" Jude asked, rubbing his hand across his face.

"She knows what I am," Dante whispered, bracing himself.

Jude's hand froze over his mouth but his eyes bugged out in surprise. "What do you mean, exactly?"

"She knows the truth."

Jude stood up and started pacing around the room. Dante tracked his friend's movements. He hoped that Jude would be understanding and supportive, but he expected a huge lecture.

"Is it too late for you to get out of this mess?" Jude asked, his voice uncharacteristically pleading.

"It is," Dante confessed. "I'm too attached to her." He wasn't comfortable emotionally exposing himself in this manner. His feelings and his dealings were always carefully guarded.

"Exactly how attached have you gotten to her?" Jude sneered, a wicked grin decorating his lips.

"It's not like that…At least not yet."

"She's a human civilian, Dante. You'd better be careful. Your money and your social position aren't going to protect you if you mess up. The rules apply to you even more. The council expects to be cleaning up after dirty little vampires, but they expect better from Beyowan nobility."

"I know. I know," Dante hissed. "Don't remind me. I can still fulfill my responsibilities to my family and be happy about it. Can't I?"

Jude stopped pacing and swung around to face Dante. "Not with a human civilian," he corrected harshly.

Dante returned his gaze to the floor. "What if she doesn't remain human?"

Jude gasped and jerked to another sudden stop. After taking a moment to process the magnitude of the question, he asked, "You would go against *everything* you believe to have this insignificant human girl?"

Emilie is far from insignificant, Dante thought. "Maybe…" he answered aloud.

"Even then. You would be dirtying your bloodline. Your family won't accept her."

Dante sighed deeply. "They won't have a choice. I'd be within my legal rights to take her as my wife."

"Colin's going to tear into you, and you're going to put your father into an early grave. Your cousin, the chairman, is going to make things difficult for you as well, not to mention many other inconveniences."

"I'm going to try to keep this quiet and move it along as quickly as possible."

"Does Emilie have any idea what you're setting her up for?"

"We haven't talked much about it yet. I want to give her time to adjust. If I rush this, I risk scaring her half to death. There's too much at stake to proceed flippantly."

Jude nodded. "I'm surprised it didn't scare her half to death to find out that you aren't human."

Dante chuckled, remembering. "She was scared. I was worried."

"You're making more than just your own life difficult, you know," Jude said as he came back to sit next to Dante.

"I know, I know. I'm sorry, but this is what I want."

"You always seem to get what you want," Jude grumbled, shaking his head.

Dante pointed his finger at Jude while knocking on the wooden table in front of him with his other hand. "Don't jinx me, you twit."

"If this is what you want, who am I to stop you?" Jude grumbled, looking hard into Dante's determined face. "Just remember that you're playing with fire."

"You only live once," Dante quipped.

"Yeah…But for how long?"

Chapter 2

Emilie finished stuffing books into her backpack. It was
Sunday afternoon and she was preparing to head over to the
school to study because she was too distracted in her apartment. A
change of scenery was the only solution.

She had gotten up late this morning and needed to get serious
about her schoolwork or she would be in trouble for final exams.
As she was about to leave, her phone rang in her purse, and she
stopped to check. It was Dante.

"Hello," she said eagerly.

"Hello."

"Are you home?"

"As a matter of fact I am."

She started jumping up and down in place. "Can I see you?"

"Well...I want to ask you something first."

The serious tone of his voice concerned her. "What?"

"Should I buy tickets for the ballet this Friday night?"

"You want to take me to the ballet?"

"You told me that you were a ballerina when you were younger,
and I thought it might be nice to go together."

"I don't have anything to wear!"

"Hmmm," he mused. "This is a one-night-only special event. I
really wanted to see it."

"I don't know what to say..."

"I have an idea," he interrupted. "Will you let me play dress up
with you today?"

"What are you talking about?"

"I want to take you shopping."

"Shopping...for a dress?"

"Exactly."

"Sure, if you want to," she replied. "It's just that most men don't like to shop with their girlfriends."

"I've told you before, I'm not like most men."

They made arrangements for him to pick her up and she went to change into something slightly less frumpy. She felt guilty for neglecting her school work, but getting to see Dante was more important.

A short time later, he called her from the car to say that he was waiting, double-parked, outside of her building. She ran downstairs to meet him. As she slid into the seat next to him, she leaned over to give him a quick kiss.

He looked really disappointed. "Come back here," he insisted, reaching for her.

She laughed and leaned back toward him. This time he slid his arm around her shoulders to prevent her from escaping before he was satisfied. "That's better," he murmured as he unlocked his lips from hers. He looked deeply into her eyes while brushing the hair gently out of her face.

"OK..." she replied. She wondered why he would want to sit double-parked in front of her building kissing for so long after telling her that they needed to keep their relationship a secret. "You're in a good mood."

"You sound surprised," he said, pulling out into traffic. "Am I normally grouchy?"

"No...That's not it. I was just expecting less of a public display of affection."

"I missed you...I have a hard time keeping my hands to myself."

"I'm not complaining," she clarified. "So how long will you be in Montreal?"

"I'm meeting my father later today. I haven't seen him in a while, and he's feeling neglected."

Emilie was disappointed. She had hoped to keep him to herself, but she couldn't be selfish. There were others in his life who deserved a portion of his time. It was just so difficult being away from him so much. Perhaps he wouldn't be leaving town right away. "Do you have to work all week?"

"I'm afraid so." He flashed her his sad puppy dog face. "Sorry."

"But I'll see you on Friday for the ballet," she replied, sighing in resignation.

"Yes. I bought the tickets, so we better get busy."

Dante parked the car in front of some very expensive-looking boutiques. "I don't think I can afford these stores," she whispered, flushing with embarrassment. She regretted neglecting to mention her budget to Dante before they had left.

He waved his hand dismissively. "Don't worry about it. You let me pick the dress, and I'll pay for it."

She was uncomfortable with that arrangement. "I don't know… You bought the tickets. I should at least be able to dress myself."

"I insist," he stated in tone that left no room for argument.

She got the impression that he was a man unaccustomed to taking no for an answer. She had never been comfortable with men spending money on her, but she didn't know what else to do, so she just got out of the car and walked through the shop door that he was holding open for her.

She looked around nervously as Dante flagged down a sales-person. A young, immaculately dressed blond with a polite smile approached, and he announced authoritatively, "We need a dress for the ballet this Friday night. I want to see a nice selection."

Emilie shot him an irritated glance as she was escorted toward a rack of dresses. He just grinned and walked to the back of the store where he found a chair on which to make himself comfortable while waiting for the fashion show to begin. As he folded his coat neatly on his lap, she had to smile. He was dressed like a runway model again. He wore a button-down shirt and tie, dress slacks, and a sports jacket cut to perfection. Unfortunately that meant she spent more time looking at him rather than the dresses she was being shown, although the sales girl seemed equally distracted.

Dante was busy poking his phone when Emilie walked by on her way to the dressing room. He looked up at her and smiled encouragingly. She crinkled up her face in annoyance, but he only laughed softly to himself and returned his attention to his toy.

She had a pile of dresses to show him and was beginning to feel self-conscious. She glanced at the price tags on a few of them and almost fainted. She assumed that Dante had no idea how expensive women's clothes could be and was concerned that he would balk at the cash register. Now she was filled with even more dread. *Good thing I have a reasonable credit card limit,* she thought.

After a few unsuccessful garments, she tried one made of some kind of smooth, shiny, bright red fabric. As she scanned her reflection in the cabin's mirror, she had to admit that the dress fit her body perfectly, and her figure was downright voluptuous in it.

Thus far Dante's reactions had not been particularly enthusiastic. She closed her eyes, took a deep breath, and stepped out of the dressing room. As he glanced up, she prepared herself for another tepid reaction, but then his mouth dropped open.

"Doesn't she look beautiful in that dress," the salesclerk declared in what could only be described as an awed whisper.

Dante snorted. "She looks beautiful in whatever she wears," he corrected.

He stood up and walked around Emilie, running his eyes over her as though checking every stitch of the garment. "It isn't that she looks beautiful in this dress. It's that the dress is beautiful on her."

Emilie's face flushed to the exact color of the gown. She was having difficulty meeting his gaze while he stood essentially undressing her with his eyes.

"You're absolutely right, sir," the salesclerk corrected, smiling enviously in Emilie's direction.

He leaned in and whispered, "I love red, but I don't think this is the one we're looking for." He walked back to his seat, and she thought she heard him whisper, "I might buy it anyway."

It took another half dozen dresses before Dante made his choice. The gown was elegantly seductive in a dark royal purple that went wonderfully with her skin tone and eye color. She was forced to admit that, for a man, he had excellent taste.

ஃ

Dante was in a fantastic mood. He had been preparing himself for an argument over the bill, but it appeared that Emilie was actually going to allow him to pay for the dress. Even so, he wanted to take care of the transaction before she emerged from the dressing room because, if given enough time, she might change her mind.

It was remarkable how much pleasure could be had from such a small gesture. She made it easy for him to want to spoil her. She had no financial expectations of him whatsoever. She knew he had money and yet never asked for anything but his time and attention.

He was so lost in thought that he didn't notice the woman smiling at him from behind the counter until she said, "Hello, Mr. Ashton."

His gaze snapped up to her face, but it took a moment for him to sort through his memories enough to identify her as Amber from the changeling club A Basement. He had met her on the day he'd been sent to meet with the human crime lord in charge of Montreal, Jordano Gomez. Dante had been so occupied with his delivery schedule for the upcoming week and Emilie's dresses that he hadn't noticed Amber in the shop. This was disastrous. "What are you doing here?" he demanded.

Amber laughed at his lack of manners. "This is just one of my jobs," she explained. "The money I earn at the club doesn't afford me the kind of lifestyle I desire."

Are you asking me for money in return for your silence? he wondered.

She held her hand out expectantly once the price of the dress had been rung up in the cash register. Dante was hesitant to give a woman who worked for human organized crime his credit card information, but he didn't have enough cash in his wallet to cover the cost of the dress. Reluctantly he handed her his card.

Amber looked it over carefully and slipped it into the machine for him to enter his security code. Dante resolved to pay particular attention to his statements from this point on.

"I thought humans were off limits," she whispered across the counter to him.

Dante had to suppress a snarl at the disrespectful sneer in her voice. This woman had no business prying into his personal life. "How do you know she's human?" he replied, flashing her with his eyes.

The confidence on Amber's face wavered, but by this time, Emilie was ready and making her way toward them. Dante held his hand out and she took it in hers, smiling cheerfully.

"Have a nice day," Dante said to Amber, turning immediately to leave.

"Thank you for shopping here, and please come back anytime," Amber replied.

Emilie had missed the suggestive glance that Amber had included with her parting remarks. Emilie thanked the salesclerks politely, and he rushed her toward the door, trying not to draw too much attention to his haste. He was beyond relieved that Amber had not asked to be introduced to Emilie. His good breeding would have forced him to comply, and then he would have had a great deal to explain to Emilie.

He had to assume the worst. Amber would report this meeting to Gomez. This could be valuable information, and the financial remuneration could be substantial if Amber also had photos on her phone of Emilie to back up her claim. Gomez wouldn't hesitate to use Emilie to his advantage if an opportunity presented itself.

Dante dashed to open the passenger door for her. He slipped the dress in the back seat and saw Amber peeking out of the door of the shop. *Damn*, he cursed to himself, *now she'll have my license plate number and Gomez will be able to track my movements around the city.* He had wanted to spend his day off relaxing with his girlfriend and visiting with his father. Now he would have to go to the council office and request a new license plate and possibly a new vehicle. *Damn*, he cursed again. *I love this car.*

He started the engine and glanced over to find Emilie smiling at him with a bewildered expression on her face, making him stop to ask, "What?"

She laughed. "You're a mystery to me."

He shook his head and pulled out into traffic, not sure whether or not she had picked up on his anxiety. "What did I do?"

"I'm still trying to figure you out, that's all."

He rolled his eyes. *I wish I could tell you everything, but there's too much at stake for me to be overly forthcoming at this point*, he thought, but said aloud, "I'd rather not look at shoes and handbags if that's OK with you."

"Fine. I'll go with Caroline later in the week, but I really should get some studying done. I don't think your father is going to pass me just because we're dating."

Dante coughed. How many problems would he have to deal with in one day? "Listen, I would rather not tell my father anything until things get more serious between us, OK? He's rather overprotective."

The cheerfulness in her eyes was replaced with doubt and pain, making him wince with regret. *How can I explain myself?* he thought. He wasn't ashamed of her, but she was human, and his father would never accept her as a daughter. As if Dante didn't have enough to worry about with Gomez, the council, Jude, and Colin, he couldn't risk getting his father involved in this relationship.

He looked over at her with concern. "Are you OK? You were gone there for a bit."

"I'm fine," she replied with a sigh, but then shot him a look filled with hope. "Do you want to come in for a while?"

They were approaching her apartment building, and he wished he had more spare time. He smiled devilishly. "I would love nothing more, but I have to meet my dad soon, and I have a hundred other things to take care of before I leave tomorrow." He pulled up in front of the apartment and leaned toward her.

"I don't know how to thank you for the dress," she admitted between kisses.

"Just wear it to the ballet on Friday," he replied graciously as she pulled him toward her by his tie. Her increasing desire, in combination with the sweet little sighs she made as they kissed, was causing him to reconsider his decision to leave.

"Are you sure you can't come in for a little while?" she asked breathlessly.

He smiled. After what just happened at the dress shop, he wouldn't leave this car outside this building for anything. "Sorry, but I have to go."

"I love you," she whispered as she ran her fingers through his hair.

"I love you too."

Emilie slid out of the car and took her dress out of the back. She waved to him with her free hand and closed the door. In his rearview mirror, he could see her standing on the sidewalk, watching him drive away. Now he had to figure out what to do about Gomez and his spies.

ψ

Dante held his new license plate in his lap and stared across the desk at his cousin, Purson Maxaviel, the chairman of the Montreal Council Office.

Purson said, "So you're really worried that Jordano Gomez is going to come after your mistress."

"Yes, I am," Dante replied. "He asked me outright if I was a family man. He's looking for a weakness to exploit."

"I doubt he would be that stupid." The chairman shook his head. "I have to say, it's bold of you to bring this information to my attention. I could decide it's easier to be rid of your mistress than to deal with Gomez."

Dante nodded. He was between a rock and a hard place. He didn't want to be presumptuous, but he was banking on the fact that it would be harder for the council to replace a messenger than a crime lord. A fact that should give him some leverage. "I felt that if you knew about the situation, we could deal with it together instead of having my concern distracting me from my duties."

The expression on Purson's face suggested that he understood the message behind the words. "Does this woman mean that much to you?"

"She's my first mistress, sir. You have to cut me some slack," Dante answered, flashing Purson a sad puppy dog look.

The chairman smiled nostalgically. "I guess I can understand, and I do appreciate your coming to me so quickly instead of flying off the handle and making a mess of everything. I have to give you credit, you're covering your tracks well and behaving responsibly, as usual."

"What do you recommend I do, besides killing my mistress?"

"I'll set up another meeting between you and Gomez," Purson suggested. "You might be able to get a sense of the seriousness of the threat, if any."

When Dante had last met with his cousin about the purchase of his hunting license, he had also arranged to have a discreet man watch over Emilie for him. It wasn't twenty-four hours a day, seven days a week, but it gave him a great deal of comfort to know that someone so skilled and meticulous was watching over her, just in case. "Do I have your permission to instruct Soeren to terminate any suspicious individuals found following her around?"

Purson's brows furrowed. "Your mistress is already causing trouble and your license hasn't even been issued yet."

"I know, sir," Dante muttered, uncertain what to say. Then he thought of something. One of the many benefits in his employment contract was being allowed to kill a quota of humans every year, but as a Dark Angel, he had never used it. He hadn't wanted to risk having his license for Emilie expensed through the regular channels. Too many eyes on the paperwork could only lead to disaster, so he had opted to pay out of pocket in order to preserve his secrecy as much as possible. "I don't want any human dictating what I can or can't do with my personal life. I'm a nobleman! I paid for this woman fair and square and deserve to maximize my enjoyment of her without any outside interference."

The chairman sprang forward and pointed his finger sternly across the desk at Dante. "You don't have a license yet, my boy. You better be careful just how much you're enjoying that civilian."

Dante nodded, scrambling to think of what to say to ease his cousin's mind.

Purson sniggered. "But you're absolutely right," he added, leaning back in his seat. "You've worked hard for us for almost a century and have asked the council for very little in return. You do deserve this. Why should we give them so much power? We are the superior species."

Dante furrowed his own brow in indignation and nodded his agreement, although he was disgusted with himself for speaking like such a bloodthirsty demon.

"Tell Soeren to send images of any suspicious characters to the office. If our security team can identify them as part of Gomez's crew then we might just send him a firm message."

"Thanks, sir," Dante said, reaching across the desk to shake the chairman's hand.

"No, thank you, Dante," Purson said. "We owe you this much."

Chapter 3

T he following evening, Dante found himself standing at the entrance of the changeling club A Basement with Jude and his favorite martial arts student, Rodney Saddan, dreading this meeting. He had always tried to avoid the human side of the venom industry. It was easier to reconcile his religious beliefs with his career by telling himself that all he did was move boxes from one city to another. He didn't kill humans, he didn't harm humans, and he didn't turn humans. What was in the boxes he carried and what was done with the contents was locked in his subconscious to be dealt with once he faced God at the time of his judgment.

As horrible as the venom business was, he couldn't bring himself to leave because, in the end, even more humans would end up dead. Other messengers allowed shipments to disappear or charged the council a percentage of the merchandise as part of their transportation fee. Having venom of different levels of purity being sold on the black market caused nothing but problems. The council made sure the venom they sold to civilians, either directly or through middlemen, was as safe as physically possible. Human criminals didn't care about the cost to their own species as long as there was good money to be made.

Now Dante found himself mired in dangerous ground, all because of his love for a human. He couldn't refuse Purson because Emilie's life hung in the balance, and he had to be watchful of Gomez for the same reason. *Man, that woman complicates my life*, he thought.

As Dante, Jude, and Rodney walked through the door, Amber greeted their party and smiled warmly at him but kept her distance from Jude, whose gaze didn't remain still for an instant. Even Rodney was affected by the tension radiating from Jude.

"Mr. Gomez is ready for you now, Mr. Ashton," Amber said, gesturing down the hall toward Gomez's office.

"Thank you, Amber," Dante replied and headed toward this inevitable confrontation. Hopefully everyone would put their cards on the table and the games could come to an end.

Gomez stood behind his desk with the illegal changelings Leonard and Sid on either side of him. "Mr. Ashton, it's a pleasure to see you again."

"Indeed," Dante replied, shaking Gomez's outstretched hand.

"Please, have a seat."

Dante sat, but Jude and Rodney remained standing, flanking him from behind. Dante's skin was crawling from the anxiety pouring off of his friend. "Jude," he scolded. "Enough."

Jude cleared his throat, took a deep breath and released it slowly. The tension lessened and Dante could finally relax enough to focus. Gomez stared at them across the desk as though trying to ascertain if the two men were communicating telepathically in some way.

"I'm sorry, Mr. Gomez," Dante soothed, leaning back in his seat and crossing his legs. "Now, how can I help you?"

"We need to talk, Mr. Ashton," Gomez explained. "Privately would be better."

Suddenly the tension in the room increased to an oppressive level. "Exactly how private?" Dante asked.

"How about just the two of us?"

Dante hesitated. In a way it would be better if fewer ears were listening to what Gomez had to say.

"Please tell me you're not actually considering this," Jude interjected.

"I said enough," Dante insisted. The grinding of Jude's teeth was still loud enough to interfere with Dante's thought process. "Fine," he announced with a heavy sigh.

"You've got to be kidding—" Jude began.

Dante sprang to his feet. "You two," he growled, pointing at Jude then Rodney. "Out!"

Rodney looked back and forth between his two companions then turned to leave without a word.

"Sid, Leonard, please take our guests to the bar and make them comfortable," Gomez instructed, a victorious grin stretching his lips.

Leonard walked to the door and opened it, gesturing to Jude. "After you, gentlemen."

Jude growled and flashed Leonard with his eyes but stepped outside, throwing Dante one last concerned glance as he disappeared. Dante watched Leonard close the door and hoped he wouldn't regret this decision. This was a risk. It would be most advantageous to Gomez to be rid of him quickly, but Dante wouldn't make it easy. He was determined to use his last breath of life to grab Gomez and launch himself into mesay, trapping his enemy and condemning him to a long and painful death.

Dante resumed his seat, stretched out, and rubbed his hands together as if about to say a prayer. "Now can you please get to the point?"

Gomez sat back down and made a show of rearranging some paperwork on his desk. "I'm having a bit of a problem, and I'm hoping you can help me."

"OK."

"I followed your advice and brought five men to the council for transformation, but four of them were refused."

Potential candidates were put through a rigorous set of trials to determine their suitability. Many applied and few were chosen. "Did you get any explanation for their rejection?" Dante asked.

"I was told that they failed the screening."

"Was it for physical or psychological reasons?"

"I'm not sure."

This was unusual. Normally the full report was given to each candidate regardless of the results. Either Gomez was lying or something was odd about the way his men had been screened. One way or another, Dante didn't care. "Well, I'd be happy to go over the paperwork for you, but I doubt there's much I can do. The council is very strict, both for you humans and for all of my kind. If your men are not strong enough to survive then you'll be wasting your money. But if the problems are psychological then the council doesn't want to shoulder the responsibility for them if they should become unmanageable after transformation."

"What if I agree to assume responsibility for them?"

Out of politeness, Dante suppressed his laughter. "Do you understand what that entails?"

"Absolutely."

Ridiculous, Dante thought. "Do you have enough connections through the police, the health care system, and government to cover-up any crimes committed by your men?"

"We have people we can turn to in case of emergency."

My cousin Purson comes to mind, Dante thought. He didn't believe Gomez for a second. What he wanted was to have dangerous changelings released into his custody and then appeal to the council if any problems arose. The council couldn't afford any security breaches and would be forced to use their influence in order to keep the peace with the humans. "My cousin might be persuaded to reconsider if you place some funds with the council as an insurance policy," Dante suggested. "Then if any problems arise, those funds could be used to pay your men out of trouble." Although, in most instances, the changeling in question would be exterminated. The council didn't believe in rehabilitating offenders.

"How much money are we talking about here?"

"I'm afraid I don't know. It would vary between individuals, and you would be charged for each of your changelings separately, not as a group."

Gomez sighed irritably. "Sounds expensive."

"I'm afraid so. Wouldn't it be easier for you to provide the council with some other candidates?"

"I wish the decision rested with me and me alone, but Mr. Marquez is adamant that certain men be transformed."

Mr. Marquez was Gomez's boss and a man of rising power and influence. "I really hate to mention this," Dante began and leaned forward. Montreal wasn't the only major city Marquez held. He had other options. "But has Mr. Marquez submitted a request at any other offices around the world?"

"Unfortunately these individuals have been refused before. We were hoping for a different answer this time."

"The North American and European offices often have stricter standards because the risk and expense is so much higher. You might be better off in South America or Africa. Many of their governments are so corrupt that it's easier to bribe your way out of trouble."

"We tried, Mr. Ashton. But we were told that the newly created changelings would not be allowed to leave their host country, and as you can assume, this did not suit Mr. Marquez's plans."

Dante nodded his understanding. If one office transformed a questionable individual, it would be held responsible for any crimes committed regardless of the country in which the crimes took place. In fact, it was not uncommon for many changelings to be forbidden to travel. Any of these individuals caught out of bounds were immediately exterminated. The council had a shoot-first-ask-questions-second policy in such cases. Conversely, those changelings who had scored well in the screening process had opportunities available all over the world and often led happy lives.

"I was wondering if there might be another way," Gomez began.

Dante didn't like where this was headed. "I don't see any."

"I've heard that some messengers take a cut of their shipments and sell to the highest bidders."

"I don't know where you heard that," Dante lied.

"I have some reliable sources."

"Really?" Dante would have to speak to Purson about this. Valued partners were given information over time, and Gomez was only newly established in Montreal. He hadn't earned many privileges yet. This was another reason many human crime lords ran changeling clubs—to keep a finger on the pulse of the Beyowan world.

"Is this not true?" Gomez asked.

"I'm not in a position to confirm or deny any speculation."

Gomez nodded, but looked disappointed. "You're a messenger, Mr. Ashton. Do you ever transport pure venom?"

Dante was one of the only messengers entrusted with pure venom, but he wasn't about to paint a target on himself. "Rarely, I'm afraid."

"That's too bad. I was hoping we could make a deal."

It was suddenly obvious to Dante that Gomez wanted the opportunity to bid on some pure venom. If he was spreading this information, his plea would eventually reach interested parties. This was another matter Dante would have to bring to his cousin's attention.

"You know the council's position on illegal changelings."

"I do, but again, this matter is out of my hands."

"I sympathize with your uncomfortable position, but I'm afraid there's nothing I can do to help you."

"If you should find yourself in the possession of any pure venom, I would be prepared to offer you a much higher than market price for it."

"I'll keep it in mind."

"Thank you, Mr. Ashton," Gomez said as he passed Dante a business card. "I look forward to hearing from you soon."

"Is there anything else or are we finished for today?"

"Unless there's something I can offer you in terms of entertainment, we're done here."

"I have other pressing matters to attend to today, but thank you for your generous hospitality." Dante rose to his feet, shook Gomez's hand, and hurried to find Jude and Rodney. He was relieved that there had been no mention of Emilie. One way or another, Dante had much to report back to the council.

Chapter 4

Standing in the entrance to her apartment building, Emilie awaited Dante's arrival. She and her best friend, Caroline Grissom, had managed to find some beautiful shoes and an elegant wrap to go with her dress. They had even found a necklace that was strung in such a way as to give the illusion of crystals floating against her skin.

Her long hair had been pinned up so that she could show off her dress to advantage. While at the salon, she'd even had her fingernails and makeup done. If she was going to walk in on Dante's arm, she wanted to look her best and make him proud.

An unfamiliar dark green car pulled up, but she recognized Dante in the driver's seat and dashed outside. She slid awkwardly into her seat and just gave him a quick kiss. He looked disappointed.

"You're not messing up my makeup tonight." She batted her eyelashes and fluffed her hair gently.

"You look very nice, but I can't see you very well," he complained, squinting. "How about you come over here a little closer?"

"Oh, no you don't!" she insisted. "I'm not falling for any of your smooth talk. You'll just have to wait until later."

He pretended to sulk as he put the car into gear. "Fine. Be that way," he grumbled, but a playful grin crept across his face.

"What happened to your red car?" she asked.

"This is the same car," he answered. "I've always loved British racing green, so I had it repainted. It was time for a change."

"I like it."

He smiled and patted her thigh. "I'm glad."

As they drove along in silence for a while, she glanced over at him a couple of times, hoping that he wouldn't catch her admiring him. He was particularly sharply dressed in a very stylish black suit. He was so handsome, and she had missed him horribly all week long.

Dante met her gaze and smiled self-consciously. "You can't change your mind now. I'm driving."

"I'm on my best behavior tonight. Your driving wouldn't normally deter me. You're just lucky that I'm all fancy." She stuck her nose in the air to stress her point.

"You really do look nice."

"Thank you," she said, blowing him a kiss. "So are you working all weekend again?" She was hoping to get a better answer than in the past.

"I work here in Montreal tomorrow, but I should be free at some point on Sunday." He paused. "Although I might have to bring Jude along."

Emilie clamped her teeth together and suppressed an irritated sigh. She would finally get a respectable amount of time with him and he had to drag along his bodyguard. Not that Jude was unpleasant to have around, but what she had in mind for Dante's body required more privacy.

"Is Jude feeling neglected too?" she asked facetiously.

"He's being very supportive of my...attachment to you. Keep in mind that it's his job to be worried about me. I'm relatively safe... normally. Travelling in mesay makes me difficult to track, and I'm unpredictable in my outings. The problem is that it won't be long before someone figures out that I'm spending a great deal of time with you. Then I'm not so unpredictable anymore."

"So are we going to Thailand together to see the crocodiles?" she teased.

"I don't know about that. Jude isn't the outdoorsy type. He would prefer to stay at home or go to some of our hangouts."

"Where do you guys hang out?"

"Mostly at the gym. But we go to some private clubs. No humans allowed, sorry. It wouldn't be possible for me to bring you along."

"So what did you have in mind then?" she asked. She was beginning to suspect that he was deliberately avoiding being alone with her.

"I haven't given it much thought. What do you want to do?"

She thought about what she wanted to do with him and a big dirty grin stretched across her face, but she kept silent. He didn't notice because he was so distracted, parking in the underground lot at Place des Arts. She would just have to see what happened between them after the ballet. Perhaps her concerns were unfounded.

Upstairs, as they checked their coats, she found that Dante really did look handsome in his black suit. He had bought a tie that was accented with the same color as her dress. They made a coordinated pair. He extended his arm to her and she slipped her hand through it, smiling. This promised to be an enjoyable evening. She felt like such a grown-up. He made her feel special, like a lady.

ॐ

At the intermission, Dante and Emilie waited at the bar for their wine. He slipped his arm around her back and allowed his hand a quick stroke of her bottom before bringing it innocently to rest on her hip. She looked up at him, her eyes sparkling with humor. He was smitten with her. She had such enthusiasm, and her sharp mind always kept the conversation interesting. He enjoyed her companionship, without any expectation of reward.

He had been out with many women for the thrill of the conquest. Beyowan women expected to be flattered and fawned over, and as a nobleman, he was expected to consider himself fortunate to be given the opportunity to vie for their attention.

"Mr. Ashton, how nice to see you again," a male voice said.

Dante hadn't noticed Jordano Gomez walk up behind them. Now he was stuck. He swallowed hard and put on a brave face, suppressing the urge to grab Emilie and dash into inter-dimensional space. He also said a silent prayer that she would follow his lead and not force him to reveal her true name.

"Mr. Gomez, what a surprise," he declared, although it wasn't. Amber had probably collected as much information as possible from her colleagues at the dress shop and had reported everything about Emilie and this outing to Gomez. What better way to size up an opportunity than to appraise it in person.

"Dante, this is my wife, Catherina," Gomez began, gesturing to the elegant middle-aged woman he was with. "My dear, this is a business associate of mine, Mr. Ashton."

"It's a pleasure," Catherina said, extending her hand to Dante.

"No, ma'am. The pleasure is all mine," he replied, smiling roguishly as he kissed her hand instead of shaking it. Catherina blushed, but seemed pleased with his attention.

Dante straightened and gestured to Emilie. "Mr. and Mrs. Gomez, this is my friend, Elizabeth Lachance." Dante's gaze snapped nervously to Emilie's face.

She didn't even bat an eyelash. "Nice to meet you both," she said, her voice calm and friendly.

"How long have you known Dante, Elizabeth?" Gomez asked.

She smiled up at Dante and replied, "We've known each other forever. Haven't we?"

He nodded his agreement.

"Do you work together?" Gomez added.

"Of course," she explained.

"Of course," Gomez repeated, examining her more closely.

Dante was fairly confident that Emilie's beauty would confuse Gomez enough that he wouldn't be able to tell if she was human or not. She was doing such a good job of throwing him off.

"What do you do, Mr. Ashton?" Catherina asked.

"I'm a messenger," Dante replied and smiled as Catherina ran her eyes over him as though she couldn't reconcile the title with the man.

"And you, Elizabeth?" Catherina asked politely. "Are you a messenger too?"

"No, I work in the morgue," Emilie explained.

"Oh, my!" Catherina exclaimed. "How gruesome."

"You get used to all the blood and guts," she explained with a dismissive wave of her hand. "It's incredibly interesting work. People can die in the most extraordinary ways."

Dante made every effort to swallow his laughter. He was so proud of her that he wanted to pick her up and swing her around. She was making Gomez visibly nervous. He was probably trying to figure out if there was a threat in her words and to ascertain if she was a council employee, planted in the human world to collect information.

The group made a polite amount of chitchat and then Mr. and Mrs. Gomez made their way back to their seats. Dante was so relieved to see them go that he thought he'd burst into song, until Emilie shot him an angry glare, took him by the hand, and towed him off to the side.

"What was that about?" she demanded.

"I'm so proud of you," he declared, reaching for her other hand.

"Really...I was getting the impression that you were embarrassed by me."

"God, no," he insisted. "You can't even begin to imagine how important you are to me."

"You have a strange way of showing it," she complained.

If you only knew, my dear, he thought.

"Elizabeth Lachance?" she asked with a chuckle.

"In my nervousness, I almost said Virginia Wolfington."

That got a smile out of her. "But why the lies?"

"That man is dangerous, and I didn't want him to have your real name."

She seemed taken aback. "Is he Beyowan?"

"No, he's human," Dante answered. "Listen, I have to ask you a couple of questions."

"OK..." she mumbled. "But be quick because we're gonna miss the ballet."

"Did you say anything about yourself to the salesgirls at the dress shop the other day?"

"I don't know. I didn't give anyone my name."

"Good," he said with a hearty sigh of relief.

"I might have said that I'm studying at McGill," she added.

Dante's heart sank into his shoes. Gomez had probably been searching for days now. His men could have been wandering around the campus with her picture, keeping an eye out. Gomez was obviously curious enough to show up at the ballet. His presence here was most likely not a coincidence. Hopefully he hadn't found anything yet. All of this misinformation could work to their advantage. If they were lucky, Gomez would believe that Emilie was protected by the council and turn his attention elsewhere.

"Dante, should I be worried?" she asked as they made their way back to their seats.

The fear in her eyes broke his heart. He didn't want her constantly looking over her shoulder. "No, my darling," he soothed. "I've got your back."

"Can I offer you a few other parts to go along with that?" she teased.

"Sounds tempting," he purred, squeezing her hand in his.

۵

After the ballet, they made their way toward the coat check. Emilie leaned against Dante and wrapped her arm around his waist. She felt relaxed and romantic, all thoughts of their earlier meeting forgotten. She had been soothed by the music, moved by the dancing, and was perfectly content.

Suddenly he slipped his arm off of her shoulders and took two steps away. She looked up at him in surprise to find him staring off at something, his expression tense. "What's wrong?" she asked, following his gaze through the crowd until she noticed two spectacularly gorgeous people walking toward them. He didn't look very happy to see them. *Now what?* she thought.

The young woman with long chestnut hair was wearing a fantastic black dress and she smiled at Dante in a very familiar manner. Emilie wasn't the slightest bit amused by the way this woman was leering at her boyfriend or in the way Dante was grinning so mysteriously as he watched the couple's approach.

"Elizabeth, this is Gavin and his wife, Tasia," Dante introduced. "This is my friend, Elizabeth."

"Nice to meet you," Tasia said politely as she looked Emilie up and down carefully. Then she shot Dante an accusatory glance.

*I'm his friend Elizabeth again, great...*she thought. "Nice to meet you too," Emilie answered, verifying Dante's reaction to Tasia's behavior. His expression had turned smooth and unreadable.

"Elizabeth, I need to have a word with Dante. In private," Tasia announced in a sweet but authoritative tone, taking Dante roughly by the arm and dragging him off in the direction of a more private spot.

"Gavin, you be nice now. OK?" Dante scolded the handsome man left staring silently at Emilie. He was about the same height and build as Dante, but he had much more rugged facial features. He had short brown hair and dark blue eyes. Like Dante, he had on a very stylish suit and looked really sharp. He stood quietly for a while, examining her as if confused about something.

"So…How long have you known Dante?" Gavin asked.

Emilie was certain that this person was Beyowan and was irritated to find him staring almost indecently. "Not long," she answered with exaggerated innocence. Gavin probably assumed that she was one of Dante's playthings, just like Ethan had. Dante had saved her life from a changeling who had worked as a bartender at one of her favorite dance clubs.

"You might want to reconsider getting involved with him," he explained. "There's a lot more to him than meets the eye."

"Really?" she replied, faking surprise. "Like what?"

Gavin's smile widened. He leaned toward her and said, "Dante's very charming and has a way with women. But watch out, he's a wild animal. Someone like you…might get seriously hurt."

Emilie had to laugh. She knew Gavin knew that she was human, but he must not have suspected that she knew Dante wasn't. "How do you know that he's so dangerous?"

Gavin laughed softly for a second or two, considering his answer carefully. His blue eyes sparkled when he finally replied, "I've known Dante for a long time. We share many things in common."

She saw him glance in Tasia's direction as he said this. She had expected a vague answer from him, but his words had baffled her more than she'd anticipated. "Does that make you dangerous as well?"

"In many ways, I'm far worse than him."

She glanced back at Dante and Tasia, who appeared to be engrossed in a rather serious conversation. "Well, I consider myself warned." Emilie wished she could understand what was going on here. "Your wife seems to know Dante very well," she sneered, trying to throw Gavin off the topic of her relationship with Dante.

He sniggered darkly. "He knows her very well indeed."

Emilie was surprised by his response. She wasn't expecting a confirmation of her personal fears about Dante's relationship with Tasia. She found it strange that Gavin would come right out and admit that Dante may have been intimate with his wife as if it were no big deal. Emilie was suddenly filled with questions, but doubted she would get many answers.

ॐ

Dante didn't want to talk to Tasia here in front of both Gavin and Emilie. In his opinion, they didn't have anything to say to one another.

"What the hell are you doing out with that human?" Tasia snarled, still holding tightly to his arm.

"What I do is none of your business. I'm not your husband," Dante replied, untangling himself from her grasp. He didn't appreciate her tone. She was being too presumptuous about her position in his life. She'd had her chance to marry him and now he only wanted Emilie. It was hard to believe that he had bedded Tasia only a couple of months ago, but she better not get any ideas about anything else ever happening between them.

"I sure hope you have a license for that...thing. You really need a proper wife. Does Colin know what you're up to?" Tasia lectured.

Again, none of your business, he thought. "I don't have the kind of relationship with her that requires a license," he retorted. *Not yet anyway.*

"Good!" she snarled, glancing over at Emilie.

Dante could feel his ego swell by what he suspected was a hint of jealousy on Tasia's face as she examined Emilie with a critical eye. *Go ahead,* he thought. *She's gorgeous.* "What did you want to talk to me about?" he asked.

"I'm pregnant," she blurted, staring him hard in the eyes in order to witness the full effect her words would have on him.

Dante's grip on reality faltered for a second. Any other time he would have been happier than a grizzly in a salmon run to hear such an announcement. But not today. "Congratulations. Gavin must be on cloud nine."

Tasia was obviously expecting a different response. "That's all you have to say about it?" she asked with a sly grin.

Dante swallowed hard. "How pregnant are you, exactly?"

"Not very," she replied evasively.

Dante tried not to betray the growing panic rising in his chest. He already had too many obstacles between him and Emilie. This would be the straw that broke the camel's back. He couldn't have them both. "When's your amnio?"

"The beginning of December."

He paused to make a few mental calculations and then said with confidence, "So you just wanted to tease me with this information because it couldn't be my baby."

"No, it's not. I must have already been pregnant when you and I..." She finished her sentence with a seductive look.

"You're evil," Dante murmured, smiling broadly.

"So are you disappointed?" she asked, eyes downcast.

Her demeanor seemed almost insecure. "Of course I am," he answered, and it wasn't even a complete lie. "I've always wanted to marry you." By Beyowan law, they would be forced to marry in order to legitimize their child, and he had actually hoped to impregnate her the last time they'd been together. Was it only a couple of months ago? He might live to be four hundred years old, but it still amazed him how quickly life could change. Today he was actually happier to hear that he wasn't the father of her baby. "Gavin must be very excited," he said, glancing over at his old friend. *As if I didn't already have enough reasons to be jealous of you*, he thought.

"He's over the moon about it. But he's looking forward to the paternity test results."

"I'm sure," Dante agreed. Knowing Tasia, he wasn't the only other man who had been in bed with her so close to her fertile time. "I bet Gavin's being very territorial with you now." *I would be if I was your baby's father and this child was my legal heir.*

"He's driving me crazy," Tasia hissed, but smiled in Gavin's direction with obvious pride. "But I guess I can't blame him. Our families are overjoyed for us both."

"You'll send me a copy of the paternity test results, won't you?"

She seemed amused by the fact that he didn't completely trust her. "Of course I will."

After everything they'd been through over the decades, she shouldn't expect any different. "Let's go then, shall we?" He gestured toward Emilie and Gavin. "I do sincerely wish you luck with everything."

"Thank you, Dante," Tasia replied, rubbing her abdomen.

ψ

Emilie was glad to see Dante and Tasia working their way back through the crowd. This was a very strange end to what had been a wonderful evening.

Dante stopped close to Emilie without touching her. "Has Gavin behaved himself?" he inquired.

"He's been a complete gentleman," she answered, smiling slyly at Gavin.

"You remember what I told you," he said through his own mischievous grin.

"I will," she replied. "It was nice meeting you both."

Gavin shot Dante a lewd grin. "It was a pleasure, Elizabeth."

"Goodnight." Tasia's voice was cold and dismissive, spoken over her shoulder, as Gavin helped her with her coat. He slipped his arm around his wife and smiled innocently back at Dante. Then they both turned and left without another word.

Dante retrieved their coats and helped Emilie with her wrap. "How did you like the ballet?" he asked on their way down to the parking lot.

"It was beautiful, but the ending was a bit confusing."

"The ending?" he muttered, obviously lost in thought. "I'm not sure what you mean."

"The ending where you left me with a strange demon while you went off and had a deep and meaningful conversation with his wife, with whom you've obviously been intimate."

He stopped in his tracks and stared at her. "What did you just say?"

"Nothing…" she mumbled, continuing on her way to the car, leaving him staring after her. She heard him sigh deeply and follow along behind, unlocking the car remotely so she could get in her side.

"What did Gavin say to make you so upset with me?" he asked as he sat down next to her.

She was trying not to be upset and desperately trying not to fidget. "You used a false name again. Who were those people?"

"They're Beyowan, and I don't trust either of them for an instant. Gavin and I essentially grew up together. He and Tasia have been married close to twenty years now," Dante answered. He still hadn't started the car. He just sat there, staring at the steering wheel.

"You've slept with Tasia," Emilie challenged, still unable to meet his gaze.

"How do you figure that?" he asked, laughing softly.

She felt dirty and confused. She didn't appreciate the fact that everyone of his species seemed to treat her like some nasty whore. She also didn't appreciate feeling like she was the only one in a group excluded from the jokes. "Much to my surprise her husband practically spelled it out for me," she snapped.

Dante snorted. "Did he?"

"Yes, he did," she grouched. "Plus she looks at you like you're all naked and covered in whipped cream."

He burst out laughing. "She does look at me rather indecently, but I've never thought of it quite like that before."

"You've managed to avoid my question."

He blinked in confusion. "What question?"

"The question about whether or not you've slept with Tasia," Emilie explained slowly, as if he didn't understand English.

He sighed. "I've been in bed with Tasia before, but we never did any sleeping."

You're just making everything worse for yourself, she thought. He was smiling rather broadly to himself as if remembering something that she didn't want to imagine. "I knew it," she grumbled. She tried desperately to understand why exactly this mattered so much. She knew he'd slept with other women. She shouldn't start taking inventory of them all. It wasn't relevant to their relationship. Unless..."Have you...not slept with her...recently?" she asked, almost afraid to get his answer.

Dante's smile slipped off his face. "Define recently."

She locked her eyes on him angrily. "While you and I have been together."

"Define together," he asked, looking guiltier as the seconds ticked by.

"While we've been dating."

"You mean *after* I told you the truth about myself?"

"Yes."

"OK…" Relief spread instantaneously across his face. "Based on those criteria, I have not—not slept—with her recently."

Emilie was still confused. At least his expression made it seem as if he hadn't done anything wrong. "Maybe I need to clear something up with you."

"Please," he encouraged.

She suddenly felt naive and foolish. "Are we a couple or are you seeing other people?"

"Is that what's gotten your knickers in a knot?" he exclaimed. He reached over and patted her hand gently.

She yanked it away. She wasn't going to let him distract her from the question.

"Listen…This whole dating thing is new to me. I've been trying to follow what I believe are the rules. I haven't had sex with any woman, at all, since the day I saved you from Ethan. I'm not seeing any other women except at work, for work related things. I've been yours, and only yours, body and soul, since that day."

Now she felt even more foolish. She had panicked and jumped to conclusions.

"Are you OK?"

"No…I don't think I am."

"What did Gavin say to you, sweetheart?"

"He said that I shouldn't get involved with you."

Dante laughed. "He's right, but I told you that myself."

"He tried to tell me there was more to you than meets the eye."

Dante nodded. "It's the truth."

Her anger was dissipating and she allowed herself a little chuckle. "He said you're an animal and that you were going to hurt me."

The smile vanished from Dante's face. He froze, fumbling for a response. "I don't want to hurt you. You have to believe me, but he's right to warn you. You have to understand, it's not just me. All of my species, we like…" He hesitated.

"What?"

"I don't know how to explain this to you properly."

"Just try…"

"Emilie…" he whispered, then groaned. "We're very instinctive and aggressive creatures, and we have bodies that heal quickly. We tend to get a bit rough with each other when we're…intimate."

"Are you trying to say, in a roundabout way, that you like rough sex?"

Dante smiled roguishly. "I like sex…It doesn't have to be rough."

"But you like it to be?" she pressed.

"Yes," he answered, his eyes locked on the steering wheel again.

"I see…" She wasn't sure how to process this information. *At least I know what to expect from him. If he gets rough with me, I'll have to understand it's just the way he likes it.* At least now she was prepared.

Dante seemed to be trying to assess her level of anger. "Are you OK?"

"Yes…I'm fine now. But for your information, I can handle you."

His eyebrows shot up his forehead and a devilish grin crept across his face. He started the car but kept silent until they came out of the parking garage, then he muttered, almost to himself, "Gavin shouldn't be talking about me being an animal."

"Why?"

"You're never going to believe this, but Gavin is a shape shifter. He can actually turn himself into an animal. It's really quite amazing."

He was right; she couldn't believe it. "You're kidding!"

"You know…Werewolves, mermaids, centaurs, minotaurs, and others were all created by people like Gavin mating with animals while in their animal forms."

She had a hard enough time accepting that she was dating a demon, but to have to accept that all of those other creatures actually existed was just too difficult to process. "You can't be serious."

"Oh, I'm serious. Many of them didn't exist for long, but they were all real. I don't know how many of them exist today. I've never met any hybrids, but I've heard rumors. I know for a fact that Gavin can change into an animal because I've seen it with my own eyes."

"What's Tasia's ability?"

The corner of his mouth twitched, but he managed to control himself. "She actually doesn't have one, which is unfortunate for someone with as pure blood as she has, but it happens more and more often these days."

Emilie was fuming. Dante seemed to sense the anger pouring off of her and tried to focus on the road, a guilty expression on his face. She wasn't pleased with him for alluding to how much fun he found Tasia sexually. Some information was best kept to yourself. He still had a lot to learn about girlfriends.

He absently flipped through the radio stations and suddenly started bouncing in his seat. "I love this song!" he shouted and began to sing. Her irritation melted away once his magical voice filled the car. She had always thought his voice had a musical quality, but the reality was that he could sing like an angel.

He was too distracted to notice her wide-eyed stare and her mouth dangling open. When the song ended, he resumed fiddling with the radio. He glanced over at her. "What?" he asked nervously.

"I didn't know you could sing," she answered, her voice trembling. She was a woman after all, and women were easily impressed by musical men; especially men as handsome as Dante.

"All of us angels can sing. I thought you knew that."

She shook her head back and forth, still staring at him as if she had just met him for the first time.

He went back to playing with the radio. "My species also has the ability to mimic accents as part of our camouflage," he added in a perfect British accent. "Although I should be able to speak with both a British and a South African accent, seeing that my father was born in South Africa to British parents," he continued in a melodic South African accent.

She hadn't expected a little thing like an accent to make him any sexier than he already was, but somehow…it did.

"I'm going to have to remember this," he said smugly.

"What?"

"How to make you look at me as though I was naked and covered in whipped cream," he teased.

Emilie could feel the color rush up her face and managed to exchange her dirty grin for a sheepish one. Unfortunately they were almost back to her apartment.

"Should I call you on Sunday so we can make plans?" he asked.

"I was hoping you'd stay for awhile," she purred.

He flashed her his sad puppy dog face. "I have to work early tomorrow, and I'm jet-lagged. I've hardly slept in the last couple of days."

Somehow she wasn't surprised by his excuses. *What's really going on here?* she wondered. But they had done enough bickering for one evening; better to finish on a positive note. "Thank you for taking me to the ballet. I had a good time," she said, leaning toward him as he stopped the car in front of her building.

"I'm glad," he replied. He wrapped his arms around her and kissed her gently, being careful not to smear lipstick all over them both. The gentleness and playfulness of his lips and tongue were making her even more eager to take him to bed. Just as she was about to run her fingers into his hair to get a firmer grip on him, he pulled away, grinning. He wiped his lips off on his hand with a chuckle. His brown eyes sparkled as he reached over to wipe her lip with his thumb. "Goodnight, beautiful."

"Goodnight, my angel," she replied and reluctantly got herself organized to exit the vehicle. She slid out as gracefully as she could but looked longingly into the car as she waved. As she closed the door, he waved back and put the car into gear. *Mister, I've got to get you alone*, she thought.

On her way up to her apartment, it occurred to her that he might be afraid of being alone with her because he was worried about hurting her physically. *We'll definitely have to discuss this situation. Although I would prefer to just try it out without any talking at all... and see how it goes.*

Chapter 5

On Sunday, Dante convinced Emilie to go on a double-date with Jude and Emilie's best friend, Caroline. They went out for a great dinner together, and Jude even behaved himself like a proper gentleman. Dante even suspected Caroline of nurturing romantic intentions toward him. *Poor Jude*, Dante thought. *I sure make his job difficult.*

Now they were at Emilie's apartment, watching a movie. Dante sat cross-legged on the living room floor with Emilie beside him, leaning her body against his, her head resting against his shoulder. He was glad that Jude and Caroline were on the couch behind them because it was getting more difficult to keep his hands off of Emilie. *It would be so much easier to be a demon*, Dante grumbled to himself. *Being forbidden from having sex with humans is extremely inconvenient at the moment.*

Everyone else's attention was fixed on the movie, but Dante was too distracted to watch some dull romantic comedy. He was far too aroused and was struggling with his instincts. He wasn't used to having access to a woman's body without being able to have sex with her. He had never been affectionate with anyone before. He had always been emotionally disconnected from the women of his kind that he had hooked up with. In his world, emotion didn't play a part in sex. As a nobleman and a council employee, he had access to a great many privileges and had spent decades working on his reputation as an eligible bachelor. With his tainted blood, how else was he supposed to secure himself a high-ranking wife and father a legal heir to his fortune?

The human world was totally different. Men and women formed emotionally charged pair bonds and built lives together, completely devoted to one another. *How odd...Well, I better learn to adapt.*

Dante decided to experiment with what he could and couldn't do within the physical boundaries of their current situation. He slipped his arm around Emilie, and she responded by snuggling against him, sighing contentedly. *I'm enjoying her warmth and closeness, but I really want to be free to touch her anywhere and any way I wish,* he thought. As he nuzzled his nose and lips into her hair, savoring her scent, he could sense her increasing arousal, which only encouraged him to expand the parameters of his experiment. He removed his hand from her shoulder and ran his fingers through her hair, then along her cheek and down her neck. She squirmed and snickered against him, looking over at him curiously. He just smirked and pretended to be watching the movie. She made a sweet little snort of irritation but returned her attention back to the TV.

As the minutes ticked by, he grew bored and restless. He wasn't interested in the movie. Suddenly Emilie slid down and lay on the floor next to him, resting her head against his thigh. He straightened up in surprise and stared down at her lying contentedly in his lap as if it were a common occurrence. He knew exactly what he'd like her to be doing while down there and had to hold his breath in order to rein in his rampaging hormones.

Jude kicked him gently from his seat on the couch, snapping Dante out of his fantasies. He glanced back to see Jude smiling crudely at him, gesturing toward Emilie with his chin. Jude understood where Dante's thoughts had wandered. He chuckled out his frustration and went back to watching the movie, but it was to no avail, he couldn't resist her. He leaned over on one arm and stroked her hair with his other hand. She just ignored him. He wanted a reaction from her so he ran his fingers along her shoulder and arm, even going so far as tracing his index finger along the inside of the neckline of her sweater from her shoulder around to the back of her neck. She squirmed in his lap and snickered. *I must be tickling her,* he hypothesized. Instead of following the sage advice being broadcast clearly inside his brain, he repeated the gesture, this time even more gently, trying to provoke a similar response. Emilie rolled onto her back, glaring up into his face, her aqua eyes sparkling. She wrinkled up her brows in mock irritation and waggled her index finger back and forth as if to say, "Stop it."

Dante fixed hungry eyes on her playful features. *How I crave you, you evil temptress,* he thought. *Having you wiggling around in my lap like this is a recipe for disaster. I'm already far too excited and now you're challenging me.* Before she could roll back onto her side, he leaned down, brought her head up on his thigh, and locked his lips to hers. There was nothing chaste about his kiss. He was determined to get a good taste of her and ran his tongue along her lips, fighting the urge to flip himself conveniently between her legs.

She opened her mouth with a sigh, making his pulse accelerate to an almost dangerous speed. He was losing what little remained of his self-control. She tasted so good and felt even better. *I'm going to take my time exploring your delectable body, you siren...*

Emilie pulled her lips from his, laughed, and rolled back onto her side. Dante was beyond annoyed and didn't know which feeling to address first, his anger or his arousal. Fortunately he was able to blink his eyes to erase the fire reflecting in them. He didn't want to frighten her with glowing red eyes. Once sufficiently calm, he sighed in irritation and tried to distract himself with mundane thoughts of work.

Jude kicked him again, necessitating another glance back. Jude shot him a disapproving glare, making Dante feel even more guilty for his bad behavior. He ignored his friend, but as he returned his attention to the screen, he noticed that Caroline had inched closer to Jude. *Let's see how you like having female attention you can do nothing about,* he thought with malevolent satisfaction.

Unfortunately he quickly got bored and uncomfortable. His current position was compromising the flow of blood in his legs. He put his arms straight back behind him and stretched out his legs, bouncing Emilie's head on his thigh in the process. She looked up at him curiously, but he just shrugged his shoulders, allowing his expression to convey his true feelings.

She sat up and crossed her own legs then gestured, not so subtly, that he should lie down in her lap. He hesitated for only a second, then stretched out on the floor and rested his head on her thigh. He shivered as she ran her fingers playfully into his hair. *I love it when she does that,* he thought as he closed his eyes. Almost every ounce of tension in his body melted away under her casual touch. Unfortunately he couldn't keep the fantasies, spurred by his ever increasing desire, from disrupting his tranquility.

He inhaled deeply and savored her scent as a wine expert would analyze the bouquet wafting from an excellent vintage. He wanted desperately to slip his face under the fabric of her skirt and kiss his way up her thigh. He practically choked on the growl bubbling up from his chest. Fortunately he was distracted by the need to remove the fire from his eyes before opening them again to look up at the source of his suffering.

Emilie had lost interest in petting him and was focused on the movie. He shifted his position slightly, hoping to draw her attention back, and was rewarded by her hand kneading his shoulder. He closed his eyes again and smiled. It was nice basking in her affection, but he also found it utterly confusing. He was almost painfully aroused, and yet he found it so satisfying just lying peacefully in her lap. He closed his eyes and allowed himself to drift off. *Despite my frustration, I've never been so happy in all my life*, he thought cheerfully.

Then Jude kicked him again, making Dante's eyes fly open. He picked his head up and glared over at Jude, who was passing his hand quickly back and forth in front of his neck in a "cut that out" motion. Dante didn't understand the message, and his irritation made him bark, "What!"

Everybody stopped what they were doing and stared at him. He suddenly remembered himself and his embarrassment only compounded his anger. He pointed at Jude and snarled, "Don't touch me again."

He lay back in Emilie's lap without even acknowledging the uncomfortable energy flowing from her or Caroline's wide-eyed stare. He heard Jude chuckle under his breath and knew he wasn't offended. Emilie leaned down and whispered, her voice soft and sultry, "Jude was worried because you were purring...my tiger."

Dante's eyes popped open in surprise. He hadn't realized. He rolled onto his back and stared up into her bewitching aqua eyes. "I like it when you pet me," he admitted, hoping she would continue.

She laughed, gently bouncing his head in her lap. "We're going to have to go into the other room if our petting gets any heavier," she replied with a seductive smile.

What an excellent idea, he thought. He lifted his head off of her lap, slipped his fingers into the back of her hair, and locked his lips onto hers. She made a sensual gasp of surprise at the intensity of his kiss. He was about to squeeze one of her breasts when Jude viciously kicked him. Dante was positively fuming and released Emilie to glare back at his bodyguard. "If you kick me again, I'm gonna rip your leg off! Understand!"

Silence...Everybody's eyes were fixed on Dante until Jude's laughter shifted their focus. "I'd like to see you try, little prince," he challenged.

"How dare you," Dante hissed as he sat up facing Jude, coiled and ready to spring. "Maybe I should put you in your place."

Jude snorted out his scepticism. "Bring it on...pussy cat!"

Dante launched himself upright. Jude was off the couch and glowering down at him in the same instant. Both women were up and trying to drag the men away from each other. Dante could hear the buzz of voices in his ears, but he wasn't listening. "Be careful what you wish for...you puffed up beach master," he growled to Jude. "I haven't been in better shape since I was twenty years old."

He burst out laughing. "You've been working out a great deal lately. Haven't you, you old dragon?"

Realization struck Dante like a ton of bricks. Jude was just trying to protect him from doing something that he would regret later. There was no denying that the only solution to this problem was to remove himself before he completely lost control. "I have to go," he sputtered as he fled to the hall closet to retrieve his coat.

"Maybe you need to release some energy," Jude suggested as he followed.

Jude meant that he should be unfaithful to Emilie. He glanced over at her. She was staring at him as if she wasn't sure what to expect from him next. He took a deep breath and let it out slowly. He couldn't do that if he wanted to remain her boyfriend. But if he wanted to remain a Dark Angel, he would just have to get used to being frustrated. *I can build a relationship with this woman without having sex with her. Can't I?* "I have to go," he repeated, swallowing hard.

"I'll come with you," Jude declared, patting Dante on the shoulder.

"Fine…" Dante began, then quickly added, "Oh…Sorry, Jude."

"No problem. I know when to take you seriously."

"What's going on here?" Emilie insisted as Dante stuffed his feet into shoes. "Do you really have to leave so soon?"

He couldn't afford to argue with her tonight. He was wound up too tightly. "I'm not feeling very well."

She took him by the hand and yanked him down so she could whisper into his ear. "I was hoping we could have a little time alone tonight."

You have no idea how wonderful those words are to my ears, he thought. *I'd be willing to give a great deal in order for it to be possible, but the price is too high.* "I love you so much," he whispered, planting his lips firmly on hers.

"Well…stay and show me just how much you love me," she managed to say through his determined kisses.

He wrapped his arms around her and squeezed her body against his. *You're so thin and curvy*, he thought as he ran his hands over her and deepened his kisses. *Damn it! I have to get out of here while I still can.* He released her and backed away, leaving her slightly unbalanced and glaring at him. "I…I have to go…" he stammered, his voice deep and gravelly.

He looked over at Jude, who was talking to Caroline off to the side. She stood very close to Jude, running her fingers lazily down his arm. He certainly seemed uncomfortable. Dante gestured toward the door with his chin, and Jude jumped at the opportunity to depart before Caroline got any fresher with him.

"I'll call you later," Dante mumbled over his shoulder as he opened the door.

"Mm-hmm…" Emilie grumbled, her disappointment obvious.

"Goodnight, everyone," Jude called as he rushed to catch up to Dante, who was practically sprinting down the hallway.

Dante felt sick inside.

"You need to take better care of yourself, my friend," Jude advised as he caught up.

"I did take care of myself before we left," Dante grumbled. "It doesn't help."

Jude burst out laughing, immediately recognizing what he had been implying.

It was going to be a long, cold, lonely night.

ॐ

Emilie closed the door, shaking her head angrily. Dante was such an unusual creature, and she didn't know what was wrong with him tonight. He was normally so smooth and controlled, but this evening he had been downright agitated, almost on edge. He couldn't sit still and had to be touching her or he wanted her to be touching him. She shivered, remembering the intensity of his kisses. He'd been on fire, and she wouldn't have been surprised if they'd had to excuse themselves during the movie.

She was unsure what to think of the interesting noises Dante had been making. He was going to be an animal in bed. He sure sounded like one. *If I can ever get him into bed, that is*, she complained to herself. *He likes rough sex. Maybe I'll have to get aggressive with him.*

"Wow...that was a weird evening," Caroline muttered, putting her hand on Emilie's shoulder.

She had almost forgotten that Caroline was still with her. "Dante and Jude are a bit different from your average guys."

Caroline appeared deeply concerned. "Dante's very uptight. Does he act all mean and bossy with you on a regular basis?"

"Dante's as gentle as a kitten. Don't look at me like that," Emilie grumbled.

"Like what?" Caroline asked innocently.

"Like you think he's beating me up when we're alone."

"Is he?"

"Far from it. As a matter of fact...I still haven't gotten him alone."

"Really? He was sure acting like a horny animal tonight," Caroline added and shot her an apologetic look.

She wasn't offended, she was relieved. "I thought so too. I'm glad to hear that I wasn't misreading the signs." She paused, shaking her head in confusion. "I don't understand what Dante wants from me. Does he just want to be friends? He seems to like kissing me...and touching me, but he won't let it go that little bit further."

"He wants you," Caroline soothed. "Men don't make noises like that with women they just want to be friends with."

Emilie sniggered. She was finally beginning to relax. She and Caroline made their way back into the living room and sat on the couch to finish their conversation. "I'm going to have to talk to him about this."

"You'd better, and soon." Caroline cleared her throat. "So what do you know about Jude?"

Oh no! Emilie almost said out loud. She shook her head back and forth with conviction. "Don't mess with him."

"Why do you say that?"

It was absolutely imperative to convince Caroline to remove any romantic ideas involving Jude from her mind, but her warning had done nothing but pique Caroline's interest. "He's nothing but trouble, and you'll only get hurt."

"What if I just wanna take him for a test drive?" Caroline inquired, bouncing her eyebrows suggestively.

Emilie snorted. "Good luck. You'll probably have even less success than I'm having with Dante."

"What's wrong with those guys?" Caroline complained. "They must not be normal men."

"They're men. They're just something else." Emilie had to make a conscious effort not to burst out laughing.

"Let's watch the rest of the movie," Caroline said as she picked up the remote.

Emilie sat back and began formulating a strategy to get Dante alone. If he was worried about hurting her, then she wished he would just be honest with her about it. They could work something out. *I'm not a delicate orchid. I can be a wild flower, if that's what he's craving. I want him, and I'm going to do everything in my power to get him into my bed...the sooner the better.*

Chapter 6

I t was Wednesday, and Emilie was waiting for a rare midweek visit from Dante. She hadn't seen him in over a week because his schedule had been so full that he hadn't had a chance to sneak away. Now he was off for a few days, and she was pleased to find herself on the top of his priority list.

There was a knock at the door and she jumped off the couch to let him in. He was leaning against the doorjamb, smiling mischievously. Her heart raced at the sight of him. Not only because he always managed to take her breath away, but because she'd given their situation a considerable amount of thought and had decided that tonight was the night she was going to seduce him. She couldn't afford to let her nervousness show. She had to be strong and focused. It was time to take their relationship to the next level, and she wasn't prepared to take no for an answer. *Step inside my web, little fly*, she thought as she leaped into his arms.

"I guess you're glad to see me then. I was worried you might have changed your mind about me."

It was one of those jokes with an underlying current of truth to it, and she knew the perfect way to reassure him about the strength of her love. They let go of each other slowly, and she stepped backward into her apartment, leading him through the door by the hand. Her confidence wavered as his face changed from smiling and friendly to smooth and expressionless. *Not a good sign.*

As soon as the door clicked shut, he pulled her hard to him, catching her up in his embrace. "There's something different about you," he muttered.

His voice was deeper than usual and had an uncomfortable edge to it. Despite his intensity, she was eager to snuggle into his arms. He bent down and rubbed his face up the side of her neck and along her cheek, breathing deeply. His five o'clock shadow and his snuffling breaths tickled her. She struggled to get free of his grip, but instead of letting her go, he tightened his hold on her.

"You smell wonderful," he purred into her ear, still inhaling deeply.

"You're tickling me!" she squealed and intensified her attempts to be free of him. "This isn't funny anymore. Let me go!" She had goose bumps running wild all over her skin, and her natural fight or flight responses were beginning to kick in. Out of sheer giggling necessity she shoved hard against his chest, trying to break out of his arms.

Before she knew what was happening, he had swept her off of her feet and carried her into the bedroom. "Oomph," Emilie grunted as she found herself flat on her back, on the bed, with Dante's full weight on top of her. He had both of her hands held high over her head in one iron fist, and he proceeded to force her legs wider apart with his knees.

"I've warned you about playing rough with me, woman," he rumbled into her ear. "I'm having a hard time with my control right now."

There was something of a growl emanating from him and she could feel it vibrating through his ribs, which were pressing down on her breasts. *Well, this is different!* she thought helplessly. *Somehow I'd expected it to take a little longer to get him into bed, but now that we're here, I don't know if I want to stay.* Her eyes were wide and staring up at the ceiling, and she was making every effort not to move a muscle. She could only breathe in short, uneven gasps, mostly out of necessity. He had her pinned down hard under him and was heavier than she had anticipated.

Dante ran his tongue slowly up her neck from her shoulder to her ear, almost in the same way a predator licks his prey before he tears into it. Unfortunately that tickled her even more. Her body rebelled against all of her efforts, and she involuntarily wiggled under his iron grip.

Big mistake...He pushed her down harder onto the bed. She had chosen to wear a sexy little skirt, but was regretting her choice as he ground the bulge in his pants firmly into the thin fabric of her panties, making his need as well as his intentions crystal clear. She held her breath and went back to staring wide-eyed at the ceiling. She didn't want to believe the situation was headed in the direction it seemed, but fear was creeping into her heart.

Dante kissed Emilie's shoulder and slowly made his way up her neck to nibble her ear. He lifted himself up slightly and brought his mouth to hers. His kiss was firm and gentle. He rubbed the tip of his tongue sensuously over her sealed lips, teasing them open for him.

She decided to give him the benefit of the doubt. After all, he had warned her that he liked things rough. She let go of her anxiety and began to relax in his arms. She closed her eyes and opened her mouth with a sigh.

As Emilie's tension eased, Dante's seemed to increase. He kissed her so passionately that it sent shivers all over her body. His mouth became rough and demanding, but he released her hands. He adjusted himself more carefully on top of her, taking some of his weight off by propping himself up on one arm. None of his minor physical adjustments interrupted his kisses, though they gentled again and became much sweeter.

She decided against moving and just lay quietly under him, planning to follow his lead. Dante seemed very pleased with her decision and ran his free hand down the length of her arm to her ribs, and kept going. But he surprised her when he gave the fabric of her blouse, which had become tangled beneath her, a ferocious yank. His face hovered above hers as he struggled with her bra, his eyes glowing dangerously, which only served to remind her of what he was—a child of Satan—a demon.

Emilie's uncertainty threatened her composure. Dante was such a large creature, and he was so much more powerful than she had imagined. He had always been so sweet, gentle, and protective. *Wait a second,* she thought. *I've wanted him for so long, and I've been prepared for things to be different between us. I love him despite what he is, and I have to trust him.*

The sexual energy pouring off of him was intoxicating. She had been afraid that he didn't want her in the same way; now she was certain she had nothing to fear on that score. Granted he was being a bit rough, but he wasn't hurting her, just scaring her, and she was enjoying him even through her fear.

She was determined to turn this situation to her advantage. Slowly she wrapped her arms around his neck. He had successfully dealt with her bra and was smiling smugly to himself as ran his hand under her shirt. He cupped her breast and brought his lips back down to hers. He tensed up and started breathing hard again, as if fighting for control. He was making every effort to be gentle and didn't seem to want to cause her any pain.

His fingers were warm as he stroked her breast, her nipple hardening in response to his touch. The pleasure his hand and mouth were giving her was spreading quickly throughout her body, causing control problems of her own. He gave her nipple a tiny squeeze and that was it, she was undone. Emilie arched her back and ground her pelvis against his. "Oh, Dante..." she gasped into his ear.

She didn't get the reaction she wanted or expected. He untangled himself from her embrace and leaped off of the bed as though she had somehow caught fire and was burning him alive. "Oh, God help me, I've got to get out of here!" he exclaimed, casting desperately around as if about to disappear.

Before he could, she screamed at the top of her lungs, "Stop!"

He stood frozen in place, staring at her with his mouth hanging open, momentarily startled out of his panic. She had to act fast before he remembered what he was doing. She sat up quickly, pointed her finger at him, and snarled, "If you leave me now, like this, don't bother coming back!"

He looked into her hard, angry face and realized that he was trapped. He threw his arms up, stomped over to the chair at the far side of the room, thumped himself down, and crossed his arms over his chest. He stared coldly at her with his beautiful lips in a thin, tight line. "I'll stay for a minute if you promise to remain over there."

Everything that had just happened was tumbling around in her mind, and she was having trouble deciding where to begin. She sat sulking on her bed, shaking her head back and forth, trying to regain her composure.

"Any time now!" he barked.

That did it. All of her fear, arousal, and anger erupted at once into tears of frustration. She sank her head into her hands and roared, "I don't understand what the hell is going on here!"

Dante snarled something in another language but was back on the bed in an instant, wrapping her up in his arms. "I'm sorry, Emilie...Please stop crying, my love," he pleaded, kissing her hair and rubbing her gently in his arms. "God, I'm such a rabid animal. Please, darling."

Once the flood gates were opened, there was no holding back, and she just let the tide wash over her as he held her patiently while she sobbed onto his shirt. She slowly felt her composure return and got up in search of a tissue, adjusting and fastening her clothing as she went.

His concerned eyes followed her every step. "Are you feeling any better?"

"No!" she grumbled, embarrassed by her crying.

He just sat there dejectedly, wringing his hands as he waited for her to finish blowing her nose. "You'll have to try to forgive me, my love," he whispered, his eyes locked on the bed. "This is all new to me. I guess I have some explaining to do."

"No kidding," she replied tersely.

Still staring at the bed he added, "Where should I start?"

"Whatever works for you," she answered. She settled back down on the bed, watching him carefully.

He finally brought his eyes up to hers. Looking into his anguished face, Emilie felt her anger and embarrassment evaporating fast. For some reason, she wanted to comfort him, to tell him that everything was going to be fine, but it was better to give him time to organize his thoughts.

"I don't deserve you," he mumbled, peeking at her tentatively from under long lashes.

"Not tonight anyway," she stated, but couldn't help letting a laugh escape her lips.

ॐ

Dante had resumed his seat in the chair across the room from Emilie. He couldn't believe that he was still here after coming so close to losing complete control of himself. *Why does this human have to make life so difficult for me?* he thought. *She's precious to me and I don't want to hurt her.*

Her scent was intoxicating. *Damn it, I should have been watching for this.* It was all he could do to focus his thoughts. His heart pounded, and his muscles twitched. He felt as if he had been running at full speed for an hour already. *What is Emilie expecting of me? Reason? Manners? She's lucky she's still conscious or, for that matter, breathing. Does she think that if I sit here long enough in torment, I'll eventually give in to my instincts? Damn her! She's probably right, the evil little temptress.*

He was desperate to flee the scene. He didn't feel confident about his ability to maintain control for an extended conversation. Talking required thinking and breathing, and today breathing was going to inhibit thinking. *Why am I still here? Why am I letting her control me like this? Love is Hell!* "Are you sure we have to talk about this right now?" he pleaded, his suffering plain on his face.

"You started this. You'll finish it," she commanded.

He started to take a deep breath but let it out quickly as her intoxicating scent flooded his nose. "I'm never going to be able to think straight with you in that condition!" he growled.

"What condition?" she asked, rolling her eyes at him in annoyance.

"It never ceases to amaze me how out of touch you humans are with your bodies and your instincts."

"What are you talking about?"

"Don't you realize what time of the month it is?"

"What? How exactly do you know?" she responded with scepticism.

"You must have an irregular cycle, and you've had me so distracted that I haven't been paying enough attention."

"What?"

"You're giving off the most subtly delightful bouquet of pheromones I've ever had the pleasure to smell."

Emilie burst out laughing, and Dante sat back in his chair, his arms crossed over his chest. *This isn't funny,* he thought, glaring at her. "I don't think human males are as sensitive to body chemistry. It's my suspicion that you're ovulating today or very soon will be. This makes you even more attractive to me...which is saying quite a lot, actually."

She got herself under control again and asked, almost resentfully, "So tell me...Why did you stop?"

He smiled. He could hardly believe it himself. "How can I explain this to you in a way you'll understand?" He paused and shifted restlessly around in his chair. "I'm sorry, I'm still having trouble thinking straight. Just because I look like you doesn't mean I am like you. It can be very bothersome being so instinctive. Trust me. I may be more of an animal than you are, but I'm trying to behave like a…gentleman."

She stared at him incredulously for a moment. "What if I want you to be an animal?" she suggested, throwing him a sultry glance.

He couldn't believe his ears. How could he make her understand how serious this was without scaring her half to death? He brought both of his hands up and covered his face in frustration. "I'm trying to do what's right here, not what I want!"

"What do you want?" she urged, her voice suggestive.

I want to pin you to the bed, sink my teeth and nails into your delicious skin, and completely abandoned myself to the absolute pleasure of the experience, he fantasized. *But it would mean the end of our relationship and probably your life. And a hunting without a license conviction would be an irremovable brand of sin on my very soul.* He pulled his face out of his hands and barked, "It doesn't matter!"

"It does to me!" she snapped back with equal ferocity.

Before he realized what was happening, he had exploded out of his chair, sprung gracefully onto the bed, and had her by the wrists, flat on her back again. He secured her hips between his knees and then looked into her face, the heat of his passion burning in his eyes. She seemed to finally recognize the danger of her situation. She stared up at him uncertainly, forcing Dante to renew his battle for control. He didn't want the woman he loved covered in bruises, so he loosened his grip on her wrists. Her body was so much more delicate than his, and he needed to take that into consideration, no matter how loud his instincts were shrieking in his ears.

"I want you, Dante. I won't fight you," Emilie whispered in a honeyed voice.

Stupid girl, he cursed. *Struggling with me now would only seal your fate.* "Fighting with me wouldn't be in your best interest," he muttered aloud, but he was losing this battle. Despite his efforts, he slid her hands farther up the bed, bringing his face closer to hers. Her scent rushed his nostrils, making his eyes burn even brighter.

He could sense her desire as well as the undercurrent of fear running through her. Unfortunately that only made her all the more difficult to resist.

He had hoped the harshness of his voice would deter her, but she brought her face up and kissed him hard on the mouth. A ripple of pleasure ran through him as her lips locked onto his. He responded fast as lightning and laid himself out on top of her, spreading her legs out under him without even severing his lips from hers. She tasted so good and smelled even better. His instincts were pounding in his brain, and he knew exactly what he wanted. He ground his pelvis against hers and stopped. He positively ached to be inside her body.

There's too much clothing in the way, he cursed as he slid partway off. He released her wrists and ran a trembling hand up her thigh. A low, rumbling growl escaped his lips as his fingers reached the top of her stockings. They were crotchless and held in place at the top of each thigh by a thin layer of elastic under a strip of lace. *How convenient.* His fingers resumed their inspection of the lingerie with which she had chosen to tantalize him. Her panties were satiny smooth and decorated with lace. *My little devil,* he thought. *You certainly know how to seduce a man.* He hooked his nails into the soft fabric of her panties and was toying with the idea of ripping them off her when she picked up her body, making it easier for him to remove them.

As he was busy sliding her panties down her thighs, she reached for the belt of his pants. In the process, her fingers brushed against his erection, uncomfortably compressed within. Dante teetered on the brink of absolute surrender. Then he looked into her lovely face and knew he couldn't do anything to hurt her, no matter how much it cost him.

With a sudden burst of determination, he leaped off of the bed. "I can't do this to you," he croaked, trying to swallow the urge to growl. As he backed quickly away from the bed, he did up his pants with shaking hands.

Emilie smiled devilishly and crooked her finger at him.

"You've been sent here straight from Hell to torture me, haven't you!"

"I don't want to torture you," she soothed, her voice smooth as silk. "I have something else in mind."

He closed his eyes and growled quietly to himself, his jaws tightly clamped shut. "You're an evil temptress," he mumbled through gritted teeth. "I thought I was supposed to be one of Satan's children, but there's something dark in your soul."

"If you want me then come and take me. I'm all yours, baby."

He couldn't believe his ears. She must have an incredibly strong instinct to breed. Most human girls would be terrified by now. "Oh man…are you ever asking for trouble," he murmured. "If I want you…If…"

"You're starting to hurt my feelings now," she grumbled.

He was hit with an unstable shock wave of conflicted emotion radiating from her. "It's not your feelings that I'm worried about hurting, you silly girl!"

"What's your problem then?"

"I don't want you to get pregnant, for one thing."

"I thought you said that your species has fertility problems?"

"My last sperm count was as high as any average human," he grumbled under his breath. He replied more clearly, "I might not have fertility problems."

"Really? How many children do you have?"

"None…"

"So how do you even know that you can?"

"I was tested. We're all tested at puberty and then periodically throughout our lives," he admitted, staring at her as if it was the most obvious thing in the world.

She seemed surprised. Probably because most humans didn't know their fertility status until they started trying to have children. "We can be careful," she suggested, a crooked grin on her face.

"Yes…We can be careful by not having sex," Dante corrected. Today was not the day to propose an experiment with birth control.

"Why does it have to be that way?"

"For a lot of reasons I'd rather avoid talking about right this minute," he explained, throwing his hands up in the air and resuming his seat in the chair.

"Why not now?"

"Because I'd like us to have a rational conversation, and I'm only two breaths away from attacking you again."

Emilie straightened herself and adjusted her bra and panties. "If I promise to keep my hands to myself, can we talk about this? It's really important to me."

"Could you keep your pheromones to yourself?" he scolded. "It would be much more helpful." She laughed, and in spite of himself, so did he. "You do understand that I want more from you than just your body, don't you?" he asked, admiring her from the safety of his seat.

She smiled broadly. She seemed to be fumbling for a response. Perhaps she hadn't been expecting him to be so charming after behaving like such a brute. "You're very sweet," she replied with a little chuckle. "This is going to be a cultural thing, isn't it?"

He nodded. *I can't bring myself to admit that I'm forbidden from having sex with you because of my religion, so how should I phrase this?* "We have a different class system than you do. It's extremely complicated. I don't even know where to begin."

"Why don't you just tell me why you won't have sex with me?" she demanded with surprising intensity.

Her fire only fuelled his own. "Fine!" he snapped. "Because you're human!"

She seemed shocked. "So why did you get involved with me in the first place?"

"You know how I feel about you," he grumbled, his exasperation clear on his face. "But my species, my religion, and my social position have very strict rules about intimate relationships, especially with humans, and I fully intend to do things properly, for both of our sakes. Even in your own history, if the earl's son impregnates one of his serving staff, he doesn't marry her. She gets a bag of money and is discreetly sent off to another country. Then the earl's son marries a rich, well-connected girl of noble blood."

"Am I the serving wench in this scenario, your lordship?" she sniped, glaring at him so angrily that he actually expected her eyes to start glowing.

"Please try to understand," he soothed. "In my world, men like me don't get seriously involved with humans. That's why I tried to keep from getting involved with you in the first place. Yet here I am...in love with you. And even more shocking is the fact that I'm actually arguing with you about why I'm...*not*...having sex with you.

I can't believe it myself." He had to pause and chuckle. "I'm not just looking for a little frolic with you here. I want something more, and somehow I thought you understood my intentions."

"Are you telling me that you've never been intimately involved with a human?" she asked, the tone of her voice daring him to give her an answer other than the one she obviously expected.

"That's not exactly what I'm saying at all," he replied, sensing a trap.

"So you have then?"

His sexual escapades with humans were not something he was prepared to share. "Do I have to answer that?"

"Why wouldn't you? Do you have something to hide?"

"Emilie, I've spent my whole life hiding! It's all I know," he snapped. "The look on your face scares me, and I'm having trouble remembering that I'm the dangerous creature here. Aren't you torturing me enough with your scent? Now you intend to stretch me over the rack for interrogation."

"If you don't answer, you'll be leaving it up to my imagination."

"That would be dangerous," he sneered, imagining the possibilities. "Listen…I'm rich and spoiled, plus I'm curious to a fault. I like to try things out for myself. What else do I need to say?"

"You can tell me where this leaves us."

"Couldn't we just wait?" he pleaded.

"Wait for what?"

"Marriage…maybe?" he mumbled, almost under his breath.

Emilie was shocked again. "So are you saying that it's against your religion to have sex before you're married?"

He stared blankly then burst out laughing. He laughed for a long time, trying desperately to get control of himself. *That's not what's against my religion*, he thought. Finally he managed to say, "That would never, and I mean *never*, work. In my world you can have sex with whomever you choose, but you marry for blood and money."

"So why do we have to be married?" she asked nervously.

"Mostly because I don't want to have any illegitimate children," Dante whispered, almost too quietly for her to hear.

"We could get married if I got pregnant."

Her reply suddenly made him very curious. "Are you ready to get married?"

"Not yet...Are you?"

He paused, thinking carefully about his answer. They didn't know each other well enough to marry, but he had a feeling deep in his soul that they were meant to be together. Otherwise, he wouldn't be putting himself, or her for that matter, through all of this trouble. The problem was that marriages to humans were not legally recognized by the council, and therefore any child born of the union would be illegitimate. It was far too soon to bring up the fact that Emilie would have to transform herself in order to become his bride. "It's about time for me to marry. But it doesn't matter, because we couldn't get married if you got pregnant."

"I've known a couple people who have," she said with a silly grin.

Dante rolled his eyes. "I'm not talking about getting married in *your* world. We could do that today if you wanted to."

"Could we now?" she purred, staring at him as if she might actually be interested in that option.

"It would change nothing for me," he mumbled disdainfully. Then he shot her a guilty look, realizing that he needed to make more of an effort to think before he spoke. He kept putting his foot in his mouth. "It would mean more for you, I suppose, so I should have been more...sensitive to your feelings. I'm sorry," he added quickly.

She seemed satisfied with his backpedalling. "Why couldn't we get married in your world if I was pregnant?"

"Mostly because you'd be unlikely to survive," he answered evasively, hoping to avoid this subject as well.

"Really?"

"I'm afraid so."

"Why is that?"

"Beyowan women have a hard enough time carrying and delivering children. Human women are simply too delicate. For them, it's almost always fatal. For this reason, pregnancy and childbirth are actually covered under the conditions of our hunting permits. Which I still don't have, by the way."

"There are other ways of dealing with unwanted pregnancies."

Dante jumped out of his chair and stood staring at her in confusion. What a despicable thing to imply. "You could do that to...

to *my* child?" he squeaked pitifully. He felt nauseous at the very thought.

Emilie appeared annoyed by his response. "Don't tell me that your God thinks that sex is for procreation and that every pregnancy is a precious gift!"

Now it was his turn to be angry and indignant. "My God, as you say, cursed us with infertility! We're the ones facing extinction here! Procreation was not high on His list of priorities for us. I believe that sex is a basic need, like hunger or thirst. As for babies, every Beyowan baby is rare and special, but babies sometimes die for many different reasons I don't pretend to understand. I can't bring myself to believe it's God's will that you humans breed like...insects!"

"OK...let's have a time out here!" Emilie shouted, throwing her hands into the air. She patted the spot next to her on the bed and crooked her finger at him. "I promise to behave," she said and put her hands up as though surrendering to an enemy soldier.

Dante eyes were slightly glowing red. He had let his irritation get out of hand. He was just too volatile and wanted nothing more than to escape before he said or did something to ruin everything they had worked so hard to build. "Aren't we done yet?" he grumbled as he reluctantly went over to sit beside her.

"Why are your eyes glowing like that?" she asked. "I've seen it happen before."

She leaned forward, determined to inspect him more closely. He put his hand out to stop her, then started laughing, and the glow was instantly gone. "You sure are easily distracted," he muttered. "Doesn't it scare you when my eyes do that?"

"No...Well, maybe a little."

"I didn't realize it happened so often. I'll have to make more of an effort to keep it under control. My eyes glow when I get aroused or angry." He laughed again, watching her curious face examining him as if he were on display at some sort of strange exhibit.

"You're really trying hard to do what you believe is the right thing," she began diplomatically, patting him gently on the knee.

"OK..." he urged. *Where's the but?* he asked himself.

"I need to clear a few things up. I'm trying hard to understand what you want and expect from our relationship. I think you might need to understand what I want and expect from it too. Fair?"

Dante rolled his eyes but held his tongue. Emilie fumbled for the words to express herself. "Now are you saying that we're more than friends but we're not going to have a physical relationship unless we get married first?"

He sat, blinking, then rubbed his hand across his face in frustration. "I don't know what I'm saying." He had to tread lightly over the subject of his religious restrictions. "I just know that I'm not having sex with you...today."

"I have a pretty strict policy myself," she said. "Marriage is like shopping. If something is on final sale, it's best to try it on before you buy it. Once you've taken it home, you can't return it if you don't like it."

What an incredible analogy, he thought. *It's hilarious.* But he had every confidence that he could make her scream in ecstasy. She had much to look forward to as far as he was concerned. He shot her a dazzling smile and purred, "Tell me now...Are you really worried that you won't like it?"

Emilie blushed up, down, and sideways. It was a delicious flush of color, and he had to resist the urge to jump on top of her to get a little taste.

"I think the possibility exists that I'm going to like it...quite a bit." Her color deepened. "But I have a few concerns about how it will work...between us...with you being different from me."

Dante couldn't help sniggering at her obvious discomfort. "I know what I'm doing, usually. Today is an exception, not the rule. So don't worry."

"There are other mutually satisfying things that we could try today," she suggested with exaggerated innocence.

He burst out laughing but managed to choke out, "What am I going to do with you?"

She tried to snuggle up closer to him and murmured, "I can think of a few things."

Oh no you don't, you siren, he thought. He was tempted to allow her to pleasure him with her hands or mouth. He desperately needed the release, but he was positive that he would never be able to reciprocate while she was in this condition. His appetite was too large, and one way or another he would end up inside her. It wasn't worth the risk.

He jumped off the bed and backed toward the door. As he jammed his feet into his shoes, he said, "You promised to behave. Anyway, today is a bad idea, but I'll definitely take a rain check on that offer. OK?"

She followed him seductively to the door, crooking her finger at him again. "Come back here. I'm not done with you."

Oh baby, he thought as he stood transfixed, watching her approach. *You keep away from me.*

She managed to pin him up against the door with some very interesting parts of her body.

"I have a hundred things to do today," he explained, and it wasn't even a lie. "Maybe I'll see you tomorrow. In a public place." He brought his face down to her cheek and filled his lungs with her scent. His eyes rolled back into his head and a diabolical grin crossed his face. *How exquisite...*He exhaled slowly, as though he had inhaled some intoxicating substance. "Hmmm...Maybe the day after that...or later."

"Now who's torturing who?" Emilie whined, tracing her finger down the front of his shirt.

Her fingers didn't seem to want to stop at his belt, forcing him to take her in his arms. He spun around so that she had her back against the door instead. Then he brought his lips to hers and kissed her. She tasted so good that he almost reconsidered. Perhaps if he tried with all his might, he could muster enough control to make it satisfying for them both. The chances of a pregnancy were, in reality, rather slim. Maybe it was worth the risk. *God, she has so much power over me.* Dante whispered into her ear in his lowest, silkiest voice, "You are pure evil, you know?"

He opened a mesay doorway and quickly walked through before she could entice him any further. He stood in the threshold, watching her slide down the door, a euphoric expression on her lovely face. He couldn't help but laugh. She was something else. She *had* to be mixed blooded. For a human, she was just too instinctive, but it was too early in their relationship to ask for blood. She would think he wanted to eat it, not test it, but he was curious to have a look at her genetic profile because he was certain there would be something interesting hidden in there somewhere.

He left her sitting on the floor and headed home. Thankfully Colin was gone today. Dante didn't want to have to look him in the eyes tonight. Emilie's scent probably lingered on his clothes, and Colin would never believe that he had resisted her. He could barely believe it himself.

He came out in the entrance to the condo. Jude jumped up, an anxious expression on his face. Jude knew it was only a matter of time before Dante slipped.

"That was a lucky escape," he announced.

"What do you mean?" Jude asked nervously.

"I think we better start packing," Dante mumbled, almost under his breath.

"Why do you insist on playing with fire?"

Dante plunked himself down in his favorite chair. "That little one is fertile today."

Jude seemed genuinely impressed. He leaned over and sucked in a huge breath through his nose. "Wow…And you didn't put her in the hospital?"

"Oh, I came close," Dante admitted. "If you'll excuse the pun," he added with a chuckle. "But luckily I got a grip in time."

"No kidding?" Jude asked, obviously even more impressed, and not at all shy about having another sample of Emilie's scent.

"That evil thing is just too willing," Dante whimpered.

Jude laughed unsympathetically. "And that's something to complain about?"

"On second thought, I was lucky that she didn't fight me."

Jude had understanding written all over his face. "Maybe you should have let yourself go wild with her. Then she wouldn't ever want to see you again."

"Great! As if I don't have enough guilt. Let's go to the council office and check on my hunting license."

Jude cleared his throat. "There are other more satisfying things that we could look into while we're there."

Dante shook his head sadly and said, "I have to practice being monogamous."

"You've got to be kidding me!"

Dante glared at him angrily. "Emilie is human, remember? I made this choice. I have enough guilt. I can't explain to her that, although I can't have sex with her, I can go skipping off to the council and get my jollies any time I want. Plus I wouldn't hesitate to kill any other man who dares to touch her."

"You don't have to tell Emilie anything," Jude sneered.

"She would know, and I would feel guilty. It would be bad enough to betray her in that way, but then to lie to her on top of it. Why add insult to injury? I'm not an idiot. I'm just a horny devil."

Dante needed to change his clothes. He had to get Emilie's scent off of him before he changed his mind and returned to her welcoming embrace. "Ugh…I've had enough talking for one day. Let's go. I'll check my license and you can do whatever you want. I can go to the gym and train while you're…busy." Dante added snidely, "I know you won't take long."

Jude just laughed off the slight. "You can make all the jokes you want, stud. At least I'll be getting some." He paused, growing more serious. "Are you sure you really want this human girl? Think of everything you'll have to go through and everything you'll have to give up."

"Believe it or not, I'm more sure than ever," Dante replied. A sense of relief wash over him, but the full extent of his commitment to Emilie took him by surprise. He had never felt this strongly for any woman before. "She's worth it," he added with heartfelt conviction.

Chapter 7

E milie was annoyed that Dante had been true to his word about keeping his distance. It was rare for him to be home during the week and it irritated her that he refused to see her until he was certain that she was no longer fertile.

While she walked to the restaurant where they were to meet, she mused about their relationship. She was coming to accept the fact that, in many ways, he really was more of an animal than he was human. He growled, snarled, and even purred like an animal. He also occasionally displayed problems with his emotional controls and instinctive drives. He had explained that Beyowans actually took pride in their animal nature and considered themselves better than humans, the best of both worlds.

In her opinion, his little quirks just made him all the more special. She was totally besotted, but dating a demon was a confusing and frustrating process. He didn't share much about himself, his family, or his world. Information seemed to be doled out on a need to know basis. She was having trouble piecing everything together on her own. She wanted to be understanding for his sake, but it was difficult for her to absorb all of the cultural and physiological differences between them. Still, he was making an effort, and she had to admit, after a hundred years of being on his own, he would need time to open himself up to her. Their relationship was worth her patience.

Dante was waiting outside the restaurant and opened the door for her as she drew nearer. He was such a gentleman. A waiter brought them to a table in the corner. Dante snatched up the menu as if he was going to slip into a coma if he didn't get something to eat fast.

"I've never seen anyone eat like you do," she teased, shaking her head at his obvious discomfort.

"You've seen Jude eat," he argued without looking up from the menu. He leaned closer and whispered, "My species needs more energy than humans. That's why we're always hungry. It takes so much energy for our bodies to perform at these levels. Our cell regeneration and camouflage alone require more calories than a normal human consumes in a day, not to mention everything else. We also need huge quantities of protein for muscle strength and iron for our blood. That's why we're almost exclusively carnivorous." He started scanning the restaurant for a free waiter. "Are you ready to order?" he asked, waving his hand up in the air, trying desperately to get someone's attention.

"Sure," she answered, giving the menu a quick scan.

Somebody came and resentfully took their order, allowing Dante to lean back and relax. "Would you like me to tell you a story while we wait for our food?" he asked.

She reached across the table and took his hand in hers. "Is it a happy story?" He had divulged some very disturbing things so far and she didn't want to ruin her appetite.

"Yes."

"Sounds interesting."

"It's my parents' story."

She nodded encouragingly, pleased that he was going to share something about his family.

"In 1889 my dad was in Madagascar living with and studying a tribe of people. He was already in his forties at the time and had been living with them for two years, trying to learn their language and understand their complex religion and culture.

"One day he was out for a walk, gathering medicinal plants, when he met my mother. She was the most beautiful person my father had ever imagined, and he was convinced he was hallucinating. Of course, it was love at first sight. My mother's name was Delilah—"

"Like the biblical Delilah?" Emilie interrupted.

Dante smiled. "Delilah means 'desired' in Hebrew. And trust me—men wanted her with a hunger. She was a member of the noble class, like a princess, and could trace her blood back farther than the first pharaohs of Egypt."

Emilie thought, *Dante's whole face lights up with pride when he talks about his mother. How sweet.*

"My father asked her what she was doing in the middle of the jungle all by herself. You know the old expression, 'What's a girl like you doing in a place like this?' She told him that she was hiding from her fiancé. My father was crushed to find out she was engaged, but he invited her to stay with his tribe for as long as she wanted.

"Later, my mother admitted to him that when they shook hands for the first time, something magical happened, and she knew right away that she'd found her true soul mate. She felt she could trust him completely and would have followed him to the edge of the world itself if he'd asked her to go. But it took a while for my mother to tell him that she wasn't human. She was so afraid of losing him, but in the end, my father found it all fascinating instead of terrifying."

Emilie had to smile. She had never heard Dante talk about anything with so much feeling. It was obvious that he was proud of his parents and loved them both very much.

"My mother wanted them to marry, but she didn't know what to do about her fiancé. She was engaged to a very powerful Beyowan from an ancient and influential family, but he didn't love her in the slightest. He just wanted to marry her for her bloodline and her ability. You see, my mother was incredibly lucky to be venomous.

"As you already know, venom is a rare gift, and when she hit puberty, it was discovered that she produced the venom for transforming humans. It's the most valuable of the two and the most desirable ability to have. The other type kills my kind instantly, but it also causes heart attacks and brain hemorrhages in humans."

How interesting, she thought. *Many untimely deaths in normal healthy people might be explained by Beyowan venom poisoning.*

"Beyowans are usually only allowed to legally marry other Beyowans, but in some cases it's acceptable to marry a changeling."

Emilie was surprised to hear this part of the story. She wondered if he was trying to give her a subtle hint or if he had let the fact slip unintentionally. The subject of marriage had already been broached between them, but he had never mentioned anything about her having to change herself first. She resolved to return to this topic at a later date. For now, she would take advantage of his willingness to share his life.

"My father agreed to be transformed, but my parents couldn't risk being discovered by going through the council. After much painful deliberation, it was decided that my mother would use her own venom for his transformation. It was a huge leap of faith because it was so dangerous. She had no idea what to do, yet my father survived. They believed it to be a sign from God, confirming the fact that they were soul mates and were destined to be together. My mother had been following the Dark Angel's line of religious thinking and practice for almost her entire life, so my parents travelled to the Angel's Temple in Thailand to be married.

"My parents went into hiding for six years until my mother's fiancé finally tracked them down and dragged them before the council in Bangkok to answer for what had happened. In my world, religious marriages are acceptable but not legally binding. Their marriage was going to be annulled and my mother was going to be forced to marry Galen Habbara, her fiancé."

His expression got much angrier when talking about his mother's fiancé. *He must not be a very good guy,* Emilie thought, and in Dante's world, that was saying a great deal.

"But what they didn't know was that my mother was already pregnant with me. Conception of a child between a religiously married couple makes the marriage much more likely to be legally sanctioned by the council if any contentious issues should arise. Plus she had an ace up her sleeve. My grandfather was on the Bangkok council. She was his only child, and next to money, children are everything to Beyowans.

"Although my grandfather was ashamed that my mother had eloped with an illegal changeling and brought disgrace to our family bloodline, he loved her more than anything and was excited about being a grandfather. My mother told the councillors that she couldn't live without my father and if they forced her to marry, she would kill herself and her unborn child. My grandfather knew her well enough to recognize the seriousness of the threat, so he pressed the council to make my parents' marriage legal and to dissolve her engagement agreement with Galen Habbara. Of course, my grandfather got his way, but he must have spent a fortune in order to make it possible."

The waiter finally arrived with their food. It seemed to Emilie that Dante's eyes were softly glowing red when he started devouring his food. "Thank you for sharing your parents' story. It was romantic," she said tenderly. She hoped that this was just the beginning of his willingness to open up to her about his past, his family, and his feelings.

He was soon done with his meal and was wiping up every last drop of his rare rack of lamb. She actually expected him to pick up his plate and lick it, but he contented himself with picking at the fish left on her plate. She decided to ask, "Is there anymore to your parents' story?"

A pained expression crossed his face as he said, "My mother died giving birth to me."

She remembered him telling her that his mother had died when he was very young, but she hadn't realized he'd never even met her. Dante's physical intimacy issues were probably more complicated than she had first suspected. "I'm so, so sorry…that's horrible," she soothed, stroking his fingers and giving his hand a gentle squeeze. "What happened to her, if you don't mind my asking?"

He brought her hand to his lips. "You're very sweet." He sighed heavily but continued, "Being pregnant for a Beyowan is far from easy. Many die before they give birth. You see, because we have to blend in with you humans as best we can, we have adapted a similar gestation period to yourselves. In order to accelerate growth and development, our babies consume an enormous amount of energy. Expectant mothers have to eat constantly just to save their own lives. Then comes the tricky part: the birth. Our babies are much larger than humans so they almost always have to be delivered by C-section. Beyowans invented C-sections, though we don't get credit for it."

She didn't miss the resentment in his voice.

"Also, it's not uncommon for our babies to become stressed during labor, and they have sharp teeth and nails with which to cause an alarming amount of damage, so a speedy delivery is essential. Luckily our bodies heal at an accelerated rate and it's fairly easy for a woman to recover from the birth if it's monitored properly.

Humans, on the other hand…" He shook his head, avoiding her gaze.

A chill ran through her blood. He had warned her that pregnancy was dangerous, but she had never fully appreciated the risks until now.

"Anyway…All of this is simply to set the stage for my mother's story. She and my father had moved into a home in Bangkok, close to the council office. My parents lived in constant fear of retaliation from Galen and his family. My father believes that my mother's death was not as accidental as it seemed, but he has never been able to prove anything.

"Here's what my father thinks happened. Galen organized a messenger, like me, to sneak some kind of poison into my mother's food, inducing her labor prematurely. Now my parents were prepared for that possibility, but they hadn't planned on Galen sabotaging their transit route.

"Telephones were still uncommon in Thailand at that time, so my parents sent one of their servants ahead to notify the council office to have medical staff ready for their arrival. Then my father loaded my mother into the carriage and set out for the office. There were only a few roads that were easily traversable between their house and the hospital, and Thailand has always been crowded. What they discovered was an overturned cart full of merchandise in the middle of the main road, forcing my father to turn back and take an alternate route.

"He believes that Galen's hired messenger also bled out their carriage horse because the animal died halfway to the hospital. My poor father had to arrange other transportation, but all of this was taking too much time. My mother, meanwhile, had fallen into semi-conscious hibernation due to the excruciating pain and blood loss."

Dante sighed deeply and stared off into the distance for a moment. "My father and their bodyguards had to carry my mother on foot the last leg of their journey to the hospital. Their servant had successfully organized the medical staff for their arrival, and my grandfather had sent out aides to make sure my parents got in safely, but in the chaos, the aides couldn't find my parents. The doctors managed to save me, but my mother's body had suffered too much damage and she was in shock from the experience and also, my father believes, from the poison. Her body was unable to heal itself quickly enough and she passed away, right there in the delivery room."

"That's awful," Emilie croaked, fighting back tears. She wanted to say something more intelligent and comforting, but she couldn't because her throat had closed shut, making speech impossible. She was trying not to cry and embarrass herself, but the pain she saw in Dante's eyes was heart wrenching. She loved him deeply and she understood the magnitude of his loss.

He smiled tenderly and reached over to wipe a stray tear from her cheek. "Let's get out of here," he said, hailing a waiter and making a "let's have the bill" motion with his hands.

On their way out of the restaurant, she felt sufficiently composed to ask, "What happened after your mother died? Didn't your father or grandfather press charges or something?"

He shook his head sadly. "There wasn't anything they could do. My father was so overcome with grief that everyone feared he would find some way to kill himself. My grandfather blamed my father for my mother's death. He had wanted them to live in the council office for the duration of the pregnancy, but my parents had insisted on their privacy and independence. Plus my father's carriage and horse were stolen after they had been abandoned. So no one could prove that anything suspicious had happened to the horse. They couldn't find any poisons in my mother's blood because my species turns to dust when we die, making autopsies impossible. Plus we are talking about the eighteen-hundreds here. Medicine just wasn't as advanced as it is today. To make matters worse, Galen has a special ability. He can, to a certain degree, control peoples' minds, which makes him immune to invasive mind probing. There just wasn't enough evidence."

"That must have been so frustrating for everyone," Emilie soothed, putting her arm around his waist as they walked back toward her apartment. His world was a very dangerous place indeed.

Dante held her tightly and snuggled his cheek against hers. "I love you so much, you know," he whispered into her ear.

"I love you too," she whispered back, squeezing him. She still wasn't used to him being so emotional with her, especially in public. He obviously needed this hug, so they stood quietly, holding each other for a while longer, even though they were blocking the side-walk. People wove angrily around them, but they didn't care. Dante finally let her go, but kept his arm wrapped around her shoulders. She kept hers around his waist, and they started off again.

"You don't blame yourself for your mother's death, do you?" she asked.

His face grew troubled, but he said with confidence, "For a long time I did, but as I got older, I understood that my mother gave her life for me, and I chose to honor her sacrifice by trying to live my life in a way that would have made her proud, instead of wasting my life in sorrow and regret."

"That's incredibly mature of you. Many people wouldn't feel the way you do."

"Don't be too impressed," he muttered. "It doesn't mean that I'm not still angry about it."

Dante's expression was that unreadable mask he used when trying to hide his feelings. She couldn't blame him. He had shared a great deal with her and she wasn't going to push her luck. They had all the time in the world for sharing. She rested her head against his shoulder as they made their way back to her apartment.

Chapter 8

Emilie was surprised when Dante called on Sunday and said that he wanted to see her again so soon. Normally she had to wait a whole week to see him. Whatever the reason for his unexpected visit, she was grateful.

As she opened the door, she was taken aback. He looked like he was dressed to go on a hike. "What are we doing tonight?" she asked as she held the door open for him.

"We're going for a walk," he answered cryptically.

"But it's night...and it's cold out," she complained, looking into his smiling face.

"It's not night where we're going," he said. "I don't know exactly what the weather will be, so dress warm, in layers. If it's warmer then we can take off our coats, but it's early there and it might be cold and windy. It's late November there too."

Emilie was over-dressed for a walk. "I'm going to have to change. You should have told me what to wear in the first place," she said, slapping him on the arm as she turned and marched into her room to change.

"You're evil," she heard him growl from the entrance.

"Why do you say that?" she hollered from her bedroom as she stripped off her clothes.

"You slap me and then go off and get naked," he grumbled.

"You're welcome to watch," she taunted.

"Great...I can look but I can't touch."

She didn't understand what he wanted from her. "I didn't say that."

"You heard me, did you?" he asked nervously. "You have good hearing, for a human."

"Thanks," she replied. She had almost gotten on all of her clothes. "I have a lot of other nice parts, for a human. Are you sure that you don't want to see?" She was fairly confident that he would keep his distance.

"Thanks..." he griped from the entrance.

Being from Vancouver, she understood the importance of dressing in layers. She was well prepared for whatever weather they encountered on their walk, but she wanted to be sure to go to the bathroom before they left. She didn't want to be doing any embarrassing dancing for Dante to see.

"Are you ready?" he cheered as she came out of the bedroom.

"Almost."

Once she was done with all of her preparations, she walked over to him. "Should I bring anything?"

"I think I have everything we'll need. I don't expect to be gone for too long. It's late, and I have to work tomorrow."

"OK then, I'm ready."

"You know the drill. Hold my hand and don't let go." Dante took Emilie's hand in his. His other hand gripped a black sports bag swung over his shoulder.

They walked for quite a while through inter-dimensional space. Suddenly Dante stopped. He was checking something that Emilie was unable to see. She really tried, as much as possible, to keep her eyes closed while in these corridors.

He walked out and she followed obediently behind him. She couldn't believe her eyes. "Are we on the Great Wall of China?" she squealed as she jumped up and down like a child.

He looked rather proud of himself for doing such a good job of surprising her. "Yes, we are. I think we're in what would be considered Inner Mongolia."

She jumped into his arms and hugged him. He put his free arm around her and laughed.

They were standing in a little stone room, looking out over endless golden fields of windblown grass. "Let's walk to the next watchtower," he suggested, pointing at another little stone shelter far off in the distance.

She was amazed at how beautiful the wall looked as it weaved all over the landscape. The air was quite cool. She thought that it must be early to mid-morning. Because of the barrenness of the landscape it was a bit windy as well. It wasn't horrible weather, just not nice and warm. At least it was sunny.

They walked along in silence for a while, admiring the view together. "We should have a reasonable amount of privacy out here," he announced, looking around peacefully. "We're way out in no-man's land. Not very touristy."

"What do we need privacy for?" she grumbled under her breath.

He looked down at her and shook his head. "You're still fuming about the other night, aren't you?"

Emilie felt guilty. Here they were walking along the Great Wall of China and she was griping about the fact that he wouldn't have sex with her. "I guess I still don't completely understand why you're trying so hard not to be alone with me," she answered, looking down at her feet as she walked along.

He put his hands in the air and turned around. "It seems to me that we're alone right now." He stopped and leaned against the wall. "Watch your step. You have to be very careful. Out here in the less touristy areas the wall is not always in great shape."

She slipped her arms around his waist. He really was a sweet creature. She did love him with all of her heart and didn't want to fight. "I haven't kissed you yet tonight—or should I say this morning?" She smiled, stood on her tiptoes, and raised her face to him. He smiled back at her and brought his lips to hers...briefly. She looked up at him in disappointment.

Dante sighed. "So you feel that I've been deliberately trying to avoid being alone with you."

"Aren't you?"

"Yes...I am." He started walking again, and she followed.

"I knew it."

"You don't seem to want to accept the seriousness of our situation."

"I don't see what the big deal is if we have sex," she said bluntly. "We're both consenting adults."

"It's against the law for me to do it!" he insisted. "I've applied for my license, and technically I could probably get away with it in advance, but the council puts the fear of Heaven and Hell into all of us Beyowan men from an early age. It could be extremely expensive for me."

"So this is about money?" she accused.

He stopped walking and growled in frustration. "How can I put this to you so you can understand the comparison?" He paused, cogitating. "I can do as much heroin in my world as I could possibly want. It's not illegal. If I brought a bag of heroin over to your apartment and wanted to sit out in front of your building and shoot up with you, how would you feel?"

"I would think that you were completely insane!" she exclaimed, glaring at him as if he were.

"Well," he hissed. "For a Beyowan heir like me to have unlicensed sex with my human civilian girlfriend is just as nuts. Mind you, heroin is very bad for your health. My body can process it more efficiently, although I'm not really a big fan of needles."

"You're a strange creature," she announced. "You could just put on a condom."

He rolled his eyes and grimaced. "This isn't just about the pregnancy risks. We're not allowed to have sex with civilians. Period. The council offers all kinds of services to both men and women in order to avoid having these problems. It doesn't make any sense for us to be out and about, looking to get lucky in your world. Did you know Beyowan women need licenses too, even though the risks to human men are significantly less than you unfortunate women?"

"I didn't know that."

"It isn't even about sex. It's about the security risk of having our world exposed. The council has to make it inconvenient and expensive for us to get involved with you. It reduces the chances that somebody will make a mistake."

She felt foolish for not figuring it out on her own. It made perfect sense for the council to keep everyone happy by satisfying all of their needs easily and conveniently in order to prevent people from getting themselves into trouble in the human world. "OK, I'm starting to understand. Involvement is discouraged between your kind and mine."

"That's right," he confirmed. "I'm lucky I have money. I can pay my way out of trouble. For a changeling to be hunting without a license is almost certain death. And I've mentioned before that in my world, death can come in many unpleasant ways." He shuddered. "Do you have any idea how much trouble I could get into just for what we already have? As it is, they could easily see you as a risk and have you killed. You'd be just another missing girl in your world. I'm sure they're only tolerating my behavior because I'm a Dark Angel."

"I understand," she acquiesced. "But I'm not happy about it."

He marched off, shaking his head. "By the way, it's against my religion to have sex with humans."

"Why did you get involved with me in the first place?" she demanded as she caught up with him.

"I ask myself that on a daily basis!" he answered, skidding to a halt. He cupped her face in his hands and kissed her deeply.

She felt warm all over, standing there on the Great Wall of China, kissing her angel. What an incredible dream. Once they had resumed their journey to the watchtower, she asked, "I thought you just couldn't harm humans and drink blood?"

"It's just better for our two species to stay separate."

"How do you drink blood, exactly?" she asked, looking curiously into his face.

"Do you want me to show you?"

She hesitated. The tone of his voice had been threatening, but she knew him too well. "Yeah, like you would," she taunted.

Dante stepped closer to her with a dark and determined look.

She backed away from him but kept her smile intact. She knew he wouldn't. "You don't have a license for that either," she stated, pointing her finger at him.

He smiled and grabbed her, wrapping her up in his arms. He stuck his face into her neck and pretended to bite her, making all sorts of slurping noises. He was tickling her something awful and she giggled and struggled with him, but he was just too strong.

"You're going to make me pee myself!" she warned. "Cut it out!"

He finally let her go and stood back, watching with amusement as she recovered herself, but the smile suddenly slipped off of his face and his expression changed to something more austere. "Now you've stimulated both of my appetites," he scolded. "You really are an evil little temptress."

Emilie finally recovered enough to notice him watching her in a way that made her feel uncomfortable. But that didn't make her any less curious. "Seriously," she said, attempting to mirror the way he was staring at her. "How do you drink blood?"

He had to laugh. He took her hand in his and started walking again. "We're never going to get to the other watchtower if we keep stopping," he complained as he quickened their pace.

"Do you have fangs?" she asked, struggling to keep up with him. She wasn't going to let him change the subject.

"Yes, of course."

"Where?" She grabbed his arm and tried to look into his mouth. "Can I see?"

"No!" He backed away from her. "Absolutely not!"

"Why not?" she whined.

"Because I don't want to scare you."

"I won't be scared of you. You wouldn't bite me if your life depended on it."

"Oh yes I would!"

"I don't believe you," she announced with conviction.

"You be careful taking too many things for granted. I almost had sex with you the other day, and I could be in a position at some time or another where I might bite you. I run on instinct, and it can be difficult for me to think first and act second."

"You're just trying to scare me," she sneered.

"I'm just trying to warn you," he replied darkly.

"OK...OK, Mr. Scary Vampire. I've been warned."

Dante rolled his eyes. "I guess I deserved that," he conceded.

"So...Tell me where you hide your fangs."

He laughed at her persistence. "They retract like cats' claws."

"Are they hollow?"

"They are, but not for drinking blood. We all used to have venom."

"So how do you do it?"

"We puncture our prey with our fangs. They also work well to subdue our prey. It would be painful to struggle with sharp teeth deeply embedded in your neck. You see, the fangs are grooved in the back like some arrowheads in order for the wound to bleed more freely. We just swallow the blood that leaks out. Also our healing ability is transferred in our saliva and our fangs help to keep the wound open until we're done feeding, but we don't have to leave them in.

It depends on how much blood you want to drain from a victim. The wound closes quickly after we let go. That's why it's best to choose a spot with a major artery like the neck, wrist, or the thigh. We aren't mosquitoes; we don't suck blood through our teeth. We're more like…vampire bats."

Emilie was fascinated—sickened, but fascinated.

He started walking again and called over his shoulder, "Did you satisfy your curiosity, my little kitten?"

"Almost," she answered, taking him by the hand in order to slow down his pace.

"What?"

"Do you like it?"

He was taken aback. Then he vigorously shook his head. "I'm not answering that one," he snarled "For—get—it!"

"What? I know you've done it before," she insisted.

"I don't want to talk about this anymore," he grumbled, resuming his previous pace.

"Why?"

He stopped and spun around to face her, a sickened expression on his face. "Are you asking about human blood or just any blood?"

"Fresh human blood," she specified slowly and clearly so that there would be no misunderstanding.

He started walking again. "I haven't done that very often, and I was very young, so it was a long time ago."

"Did you like it?" she repeated, struggling to keep up with him.

"It's complicated."

"Why?"

"Because I had both of my appetites engaged at the same time," he answered, turning toward her as though waiting for her to scream.

She understood at once. "I guess it was hard not to like it then."

He just took a deep breath and let it out slowly. "I can't believe I'm having this conversation with you."

"What? I'm just curious." She was also curious about something else. "Would you do that to me?"

He stopped and stared at her in disbelief. "Did I hear you properly?"

"I'm just curious," she repeated with exaggerated innocence.

"No...No! Absolutely not," he answered, practically jumping up and down. Then he stopped. "Would you actually let me?"

"No, absolutely not," she assured him, but she wondered. "Would I like it?"

He paused. "If I did it, you would," he answered smugly. "But I'm not going to do it. So forget it."

"I wouldn't let you, so you forget it."

"OK, can we change the subject?" he whimpered. "I'm starting to feel weird...again."

"OK. What do you want to talk about?"

"I'm having a difficult time thinking right now. Distract me," he pleaded, swallowing hard.

"So tell me why your father is allowed to be a teacher? With all those tempting, tasty human girls running around him all day?"

"You're not doing a very good job of distracting me." He laughed softly and she could tell that he was avoiding her gaze. "But seriously," he continued. "He's allowed to teach because he does a lot of work for the council covering up anthropological evidence of our existence."

"Really?"

"We have all sorts of people, in various different fields, around the world, working to cover up our existence. It's a serious effort. Just think for a moment about all the religious cults throughout history that worshipped bloodthirsty gods or gods that were human-animal hybrids.

"Take witch hunting in Europe. That was our fault. The Middle Ages were hard on everyone. Many people sold their souls and were changed. The council had very poor control at the time and there were too many dirty vampires running around getting into trouble. The human population panicked and started burning everyone. Fire is an excellent way to kill one of my kind. We can't regenerate fast enough from that extensive damage. Unfortunately, you silly humans burned more of your own kind in the process."

"Wow!" When Emilie thought about it, she realized that all sorts of events throughout history might be tied to Beyowans.

They walked along in silence for a while, each lost in their own thoughts. The temperature seemed to be warming slightly and the breeze was gentling.

They finally reached their destination and entered the watch-tower. "Thirsty?" he asked, pulling a large water bottle out of his pack and handing it to her. She took it from him gratefully. As she drank, she admired the view through a window. The wind was making whimsical patterns in the golden grass.

When she turned around again, he was opening the plastic cover around a brand-new blanket. "What are you doing?" she asked, surprised.

"What?" he answered, looking around him in confusion.

"You bought a new blanket just to put on the floor?"

He shrugged. "I don't have stuff lying around my apartment. I don't think Jude would appreciate giving us his blanket. It's not like I have any overnight guests that require extra supplies."

"You really don't picnic much do you?"

He shook his head as he spread out his new blanket. "I don't usually go out much, especially without Jude, and he hates open air public places."

"Didn't you do any fun and carefree things as a child?"

He threw his head back and laughed. "I had a horrible childhood. I barely saw the light of day until I was thirteen. I started working at sixteen, so there you go—my childhood."

"That's boring," she teased. "I'm going to have to spice up your life a bit."

"You already have, you little devil," he murmured, taking the water bottle back. "In many ways, I've had more fun with you in the last couple of months than I've had in over a hundred years."

"Don't you do anything in your spare time?" she asked, watching him drink.

He replaced the cap on the water bottle as he considered his answer. "I don't get a lot of time off. I've been working five to seven days a week my whole life and don't know anything else."

"Don't you have any hobbies?" she asked as she tried to peek into his bag to see what else he had brought.

"I read. I listen to music. I train in martial arts. I scuba dive, sky dive, race cars, and travel, of course."

"Well…that's better," she acknowledged. "What else is in your bag?"

"I didn't bring much. I wasn't planning on staying for long," he apologized as he rummaged around in the bag. He pulled out a bottle of red wine and handed it to her. Then he took out a piece of hard cheese wrapped in plastic and a large bar of dark chocolate.

"I wanted to show you that I don't just eat raw things," he said, smiling. He played with a Swiss army knife, searching for the cork screw. "I'm so glad I don't have to take airplanes. I would never get anything useful through security. I don't know how everybody else puts up with it."

He was lucky. She handed the bottle back to him so he could open it.

"I would have brought some foam cups," he said. "But I didn't want to be a copy-cat. I have to admit, that was the best wine I've ever tasted out of a foam cup."

He smiled, took out two glasses wrapped securely in a dish towel, and poured the wine. She took her glass from him and sniffed it disdainfully. "I don't know if I can drink this if it isn't in a foam cup. It's just too classy for me."

Dante chuckled as he unwrapped the cheese and cut a piece off for them both.

"I can't believe that I'm sitting here in China having wine and cheese with a…Beyowan." Color raced up her neck as she realized that she'd almost called him a demon to his face. She had to be more careful. He was awfully touchy about it considering, by his own admission, that was what he was.

They sat in silence for a while, enjoying their wine. After she had finished her first glass, he filled it again. Afterward he seemed to be staring off at something unseen.

"What are you thinking about?" she asked.

He laughed self-consciously and looked away. "Nothing…"

"What?" she insisted.

"I was thinking about birth control," he admitted sheepishly.

"You're a man. You would be thinking about sex."

He rolled his eyes. "You'd be surprised how much a man thinks about sex when he can't have any."

She snickered unsympathetically. "So what about birth control interests you?"

He snorted. "Nothing."

"You've never used any birth control?"

"Never. You humans are lucky that you have to worry about these things."

"Really? The face you're making suggests otherwise."

He was trying hard to contain his laughter. "I would be happy to use birth control if I was human," he replied. "Well, some of it anyway," he corrected quickly, grimacing.

"So your species doesn't use birth control at all?"

"I don't think so. Most of us spend our entire lives trying to have a child. Many try really, really hard and still can't have one; even with access to all of the same reproductive technologies as you. We have a different mentality about reproduction than you humans do. It's more instinctive for us. You humans think more about the pleasure of sex. Reproduction is just an unfortunate by-product. We get pleasure from the whole experience. Having a baby is a big deal. You'd be surprised how popular a fertile woman is in my world."

He took her half empty glass and filled it again. "Now you have to try the wine with the chocolate; same wine different effect. I like to chew the chocolate a bit first and then drink the wine before I swallow the chocolate."

He broke a piece off of the bar and held it in front of her lips. She smiled and opened her mouth for him to put the chocolate on her tongue. The chocolate was quite bitter. She took a sip of wine and was surprised how interesting the flavors were together. She had expected the chocolate to make the wine taste sour, but it didn't.

He popped a piece of chocolate into his own mouth as he watched her reaction. Emilie sniggered and snuggled up to him on the blanket. She looked into his big brown eyes as she leaned in to kiss him. As she pulled slightly away, she brushed her lips against his seductively. He tasted like wine. "We're all alone here. No one will know. I won't tell if you don't," she whispered in a silky voice as she slid her hand up the front of his pants. His eyes popped open in surprise.

"Hmmm…You are an evil little temptress," he purred. "I like that about you."

She kissed him harder, running her tongue along his parted lips. "You know you want to," she murmured, stroking the front of his pants again. "And I know you want to," she added, pleased that there was more to rub this time.

"You have no idea what a dangerous game you're playing here," Dante said huskily as he drew in a ragged breath.

"Show me," she challenged. She kissed him again and rubbed the bulge in his pants more firmly this time.

He pulled his lips away and groaned. "Oh God! You complicate my life," he hissed, backing out of reach. "Listen to me, I really... really...don't want to hurt you."

Emilie had a good feeling from the sound of his voice and the expression on his face that his self-control was wavering. She either had to back off now or go for it all the way. She made her choice and slid away from him, then jumped to her feet. She unzipped her coat and took it off. He sat still as a statue, watching her with hard, hungry eyes that were beginning to glow. She grabbed all of the layers of her clothing at once and yanked them up over her head. When she was free of them and returned her eyes to his face, he was shaking his head back and forth, his body tense and coiled to spring.

"You need to remember that I'm not human before you go and do something you might not be able to stop." He swallowed hard. "That I might not be able to stop."

She undid her hiking boots, kicked them off, untied the lacing on her exercise pants, unhooked her bra, and tossed it casually aside. She cupped her breasts, rubbed her thumbs over her nipples, then slid her hands down her abdomen, hooking them into her pants.

His jaw was clamped shut, a snarl twitching his lips. His intensity should have made her hesitate. He was a demon, and she didn't know what to expect from him, but his desire was radiating off of him in powerful waves, encouraging her to continue. She slid her exercise pants and panties off, kicking them in front of him on the blanket. She stood smiling at him completely naked, then put a more alluring expression on her face and started to move her body more seductively for his viewing pleasure. She knew some very captivating dance moves he might enjoy, but before she got very far into her demonstration, he stood up. The November air was nothing compared to the icy hands he placed on her shoulders. He slowly ran them down her arms, drawing her closer to him. She shivered under his touch but looked forward to the warmth of his body.

"You're so beautiful," he whispered, his voice deep and resonating, like something other-worldly.

She cuddled against him, using his body as a shield against the breeze blowing through the windows of the watchtower. She slipped her arms around his neck and brought her face up in invitation. His normally golden skin had lost some of its color, and he was panting as if he'd just returned from a jog. His eyes glowed bright red, and she almost felt afraid by what she saw in them. Almost...She trusted him.

She closed her eyes as he brought his lips to hers. His cold hands travelled down her back and forced her hips hard against him. She held him tighter, her body beginning to tremble from the combination of longing and cold. She wove her hands into his hair and kissed him more passionately, picking her foot off of the ground and running her thigh up the outside of his leg. His hand had warmed on her skin and felt wonderful as it passed over her bottom. His fingers splayed out and brushed inquisitively between her legs on their way up the back of her thigh.

In a flash, Emilie's back slammed into the freezing stone of the wall. She gasped as the cold raced over her skin, flushed with the heat of desire. His hungry mouth covered hers and kissed her with a fire that threatened to engulf them both. Suddenly he released one of the thighs she had wrapped around his body and adjusted her weight on his other arm, keeping her firmly in place in front of him. His strength and agility were impressive. He was basically holding her up one-handed while the other hand fumbled with the front of his pants. She felt his fingers between her legs and gasped again as he sheathed himself to the hilt in one quick thrust.

He brought his hand back under her hip, jostling her body into a more convenient position. She wrapped her arms and legs around him as he wasted no time in plunging into her again, a ragged growl emanating from his chest.

She hadn't expected things to move this quickly but was pleased to finally have him inside of her. She tried to relax into the steady rhythm of his movements, but he had a merciless grip on her with his hands, and his lips were demanding more than she could give. Each thrust was grinding her lower back into the stone wall, wearing at her skin as they increased in strength and speed.

"I've wanted you for so long," his deep and shaky voice whispered into her ear.

He was hurting her, and as he embedded himself fully, her vertebrae were pressed between him and the stone. Emilie made a whimpering groan, but instead of being deterred by her pain, he seemed aroused by it. His response was to dig his nails into her thighs and ram himself into to her with a ferocity that frightened her.

"Dante, you're hurting me," she pleaded in between his rough kisses.

But he didn't seem to be listening. He just buried his face against her neck and continued to plunge into her, groaning contentedly to himself. "Oh God...you feel soooo good," he panted.

She tried to take a deep breath and relax her body. She was tensing and tightening in response to his movements. A strange tenderness was building deep inside of her with each impact of his body. Tears filled her eyes. This had to stop. "Dante, please..." she begged, but she didn't get the response she wanted. He adjusted her body in his hands, curving her back and pelvis toward him, thereby giving him better access to her. Then he thrust deeply, raking her shoulders up the wall with the force of his entry.

Emilie gasped, but not for the reason she was expecting. A ripple of absolute pleasure spread through her, radiating out from the point where their bodies connected. The tenderness inside of her was transforming into a pulsing ache, demanding his immediate attention. She found herself trembling in eager anticipation of his next move.

He started rocking himself more gently in and out of her body, breathing hard into her neck as if he was exerting himself more instead of less.

"Dante—" she began, feeling a completely different kind of desperation building inside of her.

"I'm trying, baby," he interrupted through gritted teeth.

She could feel his whole body quivering with the effort of keeping himself in check. "No...Dante, please don't stop now."

He seemed confused, so she locked her lips to his, pressed her shoulders into the stone, and forced her pelvis into his with a moan of delight. He was more than happy to resume his previous pace, and she couldn't believe the sensations that coursed through her. She had never experienced anything like it before. This was building unlike any orgasm she'd ever had. The rougher he was, the better it felt, and she didn't know how far it would climb before reaching the pinnacle. She arched herself, trying to get as much of him as she could. Her breath became nothing but ragged gasps, and she cried out with each impact.

Finally he couldn't hold himself back any longer and squashed her against the wall as he shuddered, lost in his own gratification. Right on cue, the ache inside of her detonated spectacularly. As the waves of pleasure slowed, she realized that tears were running freely down her cheeks, her throat was sore, and her heart was pounding at a breakneck pace. She couldn't feel the cold anymore even though, all over her skin, her nerves were tingling.

He just held her for a while, breathlessly groaning into her neck. Then he looked with horror into her tear-streaked face. "Emilie..." he started, but he was having trouble with his voice and had to stop to clear his throat. "I'm so...so sorry...I...I don't know what to say."

She blinked a few times and stared into his anxious eyes.

"Are you OK, baby?" he asked.

She smirked and replied in her own hoarse and husky voice, "I'm fantastic."

She watched as relief spread across his face and a smug smile replaced his worried frown. He brought his lips to hers and kissed her tenderly. He pulled away and said, "I hope this hasn't changed the way you feel about me."

The worry was back in his eyes, but she couldn't believe how wonderful it was to look into his handsome face while their bodies were still so pleasantly attached. "I think it has," she answered.

His eyes fluttered closed and he sighed.

"I don't think I'll ever be able to look at you again without remembering how wonderful you can make me feel," she murmured. She removed her hands from his broad shoulders and slipped her fingers into his hair, pulling his face closer to hers.

Dante smiled. "I can live with that."

ψ

When they arrived back at Emilie's apartment, Dante wrapped her up in his arms and kissed her on the forehead. *What have I done?*

he demanded of himself. "I'm going to have to ask you something embarrassing," he announced with obvious discomfort.

She didn't look enthusiastic. "Yes?"

"Could you make sure to wash your pants and underwear right away, please?" he asked sheepishly.

"What for?"

"I'd like to destroy any genetic evidence of the crime I just committed," he muttered, rubbing his hand across his face. *Thank God I applied for that damned license. Otherwise, I'd be screwed.* He had to laugh at the irony in that statement. "I'm not horribly worried about getting caught, but I want to be safe," he said out loud.

"Being safe is good reason for condoms, you know," she began, shooting him a judgmental glare. "I bet a lot of Beyowan men, out hunting without licenses, use them for that reason."

He grimaced at the thought of having to use birth control. Then he contemplated the reasons most noblemen hunted humans and snorted out his disagreement. "I wish it were true." He paused, making a quick mental tally of all the men he knew with hunting without a license convictions. "Most of them act rather spontaneously, if you understand my meaning." He bounced his eyebrows suggestively. "I suspect it has to do with how fertile you humans are. Too many tempting pheromones wafting around."

He had tried not to allow his tone to be too sympathetic because he could see anger creeping onto her face. There was no way for her to understand that some men had little self-control when it came to their instinctive drives, especially with humans. "Plus for many of them, being able to father a child is well worth the penalty. It's a matter of personal pride to prove one's virility. Others are just too stupid to realize how easy it is to get caught." He snorted again. "Like me."

"Fine. I'll be right back with a bag full of evidence for *you* to wash, you naughty boy," she declared, pointing her finger at him.

"Hey! That's not fair!" he exclaimed. "I wanted to be good. You're the naughty one, you evil little temptress." But he had already accepted the wisdom of her words and was prepared to deal with the evidence himself.

"Did you want to watch this time?" she called seductively from her bedroom.

*Oh you…*he thought to himself. *I wish you hadn't said that.* She had no idea of the magnitude of a young Beyowan man's sexual appetite. He would love to take this opportunity to prove that he actually had some skill as a lover. *I'm already up to my neck in trouble. I may as well maximize my enjoyment.* They had taken the edge off his hunger. He had every confidence he could take his time and make her scream in ecstasy all over again. He quickly came to his senses and remembered that she was human, and in his struggle for control, he had been rather rough with her, not to mention the abrasions she'd suffered. She might be trying to spare his feelings by playing down her physical discomfort.

"You have to understand," he called back to her. "I'm like a starving man who's been brought into a five-star restaurant and given one of those tasty appetizers. I've enjoyed it thoroughly, but it's just made me hungry for more. Umm…Aren't you sore?"

He could hear Emilie laughing as she fumbled with her clothes. "Yes…" she answered. "But I'm sure you could be gentle this time. And wear a condom."

He snorted. *I'd rather not, in that case.*

She rejoined him in the hall and handed him a bag containing all of her soiled garments. He took it and then wrapped her up in his arms. "By the way, don't leave these lying around either, OK?" He snapped her underwear elastic against the skin of her lower back. "Just to be safe."

She winced and nodded her head. "I'll keep them for you too."

He sniggered. "This is part of the reason I wanted to wait. Not very romantic, eh?"

"We can make love another time. Sometimes you just need a little something quick and dirty."

He didn't want what he shared with her to be quick and dirty. "As long as you don't think it has to be that way every time. I'm normally under better control, so I don't want you to be afraid of me touching you."

She squeezed him tighter. "Does it seem like I'm afraid of you?" she teased. He smiled and stroked her hair. "Don't worry about me," she soothed. "You just get your license because I have big plans for you now, mister."

He laughed softly but held his tongue. He should never have done this and had no intention of making it a regular habit. He wanted a life with her, but he still wanted to be a Dark Angel. While she was human, he would have to be careful.

Emilie snuggled her face into his coat. "I love you, my angel."

Her words made him wince with guilt, but fortunately she was looking away. "I love you too…my little devil."

෯

Back at his condo, Dante locked his bathroom door, turned on the shower, and stripped off his clothes. He hoped that Colin was out for the night. Dante dreaded a confrontation about what he had done this evening. He picked up his underwear and stared at them for a moment, shaking his head sadly. There were bloodstains on them; not his blood either. He dropped them on the floor, climbed into the shower, and stood there for a few minutes, letting the warm water run soothingly over him. He felt dirty and ashamed.

How could he have lost control of himself like that? He should have refused Emilie's advances. If only he had stopped her before she had removed her coat. After that point, the animal inside of him had taken over. He sighed heavily. *What on Earth was I thinking?*

She had looked up at him with her trusting eyes filled with love, and he had pounded the stuffing out of her. *Poor little human girl!*

Oh…when did I become such a horny devil? He rubbed both of his hands over his face, trying to wipe the memory out of his eyes. He knew it had been wrong. She was human and forbidden. He had little experience with humans. He had also been very young when he had strayed from the path. His demon of a grandfather had encouraged him to experiment with the lifestyle available to young men of noble blood. Dante had never been a perfect angel, but he had kept himself pure for a long time, and this slip hurt him more than he cared to admit.

To make matters worse, he'd hurt the woman he loved. He should have stopped at the first sign of her discomfort, but he had been so despicably weak. He had been completely swept away by the pleasure her body had given him that he had suspended all reason. *But it could have been so much worse*, he consoled himself. *I could have gone completely animal on her.*

He had fought a ferocious battle with his instincts and was beyond relieved that Emilie had enjoyed herself in the end. He smiled, remembering the satisfied grin on her face. She could have easily changed her mind about dating him, and he would have been heartbroken. He was far too attached to her.

He wasn't used to feeling like this. For the most part when he had sex with a girl, as soon as he was done with her, he wanted to leave. Quickly...He laughed, thinking that he was like a cat. When he wanted to be petted, he could be all purring and friendly, but when he was satisfied, he could be downright nasty. Today, he had been terrified that he would have the same reaction with Emilie. In the end, he had felt quite the opposite. He had become even more attached to her.

He finished washing and walked out to dry off. He winced as the towel rubbed over the knuckles of one hand. The backs of both of his hands had gotten rubbed raw against the wall of the watch-tower. He had kneaded his fingers into Emilie's bottom and thighs, but had done his best to protect her delicate skin from the rough stone wall. He was lucky he hadn't broken any bones, but the pain had helped him focus.

He had never, in his life, done anything like this. *Hunting without a license...What kind of Angel am I?*

He would have to wash all of their clothes, plus the blanket. He might even have to dispose of his underwear and maybe his pants. He took a deep breath. Having her blood in his underwear would be difficult to explain.

He would check on the status of his license first thing in the morning. If only he could get his hands on that license, then he could get his hands on Emilie without worrying about all of these hassles. The only remaining hassle would be religious. God would have to forgive him because he was even more determined to marry her.

He walked into his bedroom to change. Then he gathered up his soiled clothes, the blanket, and Emilie's things and went to figure out the washing machine.

On his way back, he found Jude sitting in the living room flipping angrily through the channels on the television.

"Back for a while or just passing through?" Jude grouched.

"I have to get some rest if I'm going to work in the morning," Dante answered, walking toward his room. Jude wouldn't be talking like this if Colin was here, so at least he had dodged that particular bullet.

"You seem very relaxed tonight," Jude commented, the accusation undisguised.

Dante stopped and smiled devilishly, knowing Jude couldn't see his face. "What are you implying?"

"Did you pick up your license, by any chance?"

Dante turned around and went to sit in his favorite chair. "No. Not yet."

Jude's attention was drawn to Dante's hands.

"What did you do to yourself?" Jude asked, genuinely concerned.

"It's a long story..." Dante said with a crude grin.

"Don't you have enough trouble with the humans?" Jude snapped. "Now you want to take on the wrath of the council."

"What makes you think I've done anything wrong?"

Jude shot him an angry glare. "Don't insult my intelligence!" he hissed, followed by a snort of disgust. "Normally when you come home from seeing Emilie, you have energy to burn. You work out and then you shower. Showering as soon as you come home suggests that you have...evidence to wash off. And since when do you do the laundry around here? Did you fire Claudia?"

Dante laughed uncomfortably. "No, I didn't fire anyone." *Time to stop this conversation.* "I'm going to bed. I'll see you in the morning."

"You're going to get into so much trouble, my friend. I hope she's worth it," Jude grumbled as Dante got up from his chair and headed for his room.

"She is," he answered with a contended sigh.

ॐ

Emilie and Caroline were walking to the library together. Emilie had research to do for a paper. She was having trouble keeping pace with Caroline's determined stride. Emilie's thigh muscles were sore and stiff, as if she had recently been horseback riding. Plus her lower back and shoulders ached and were covered in scratches. She'd had a rather powerful animal between her legs this weekend. She laughed out loud, remembering.

"What's the matter with you?" Caroline asked, looking Emilie over with concern.

She blushed. "I had a rather vigorous workout this weekend and my muscles are sore," she replied sheepishly.

"What were you doing?"

She couldn't tell Caroline the truth, not yet at least. She wanted to keep everything about her and Dante private, at least for a little while. "I was practically doing the splits. I'm not as flexible as I once was. I'll have to be careful to warm up a bit better next time."

Caroline shook her head. "Whatever…"

They stopped for coffee at the cafeteria in the library. Emilie needed to fish her wallet out of her backpack in order to pay for her snack.

Once they were sitting with their cups, Caroline leaned over and whispered, "Why do you have underwear in a ziplock bag in your backpack?"

Emilie closed her eyes and sniggered to herself. *What can I possibly say?* "It's a long story."

Caroline blinked her eyes expectantly and leaned in closer.

"Basically, I'm doing laundry as soon as I get home tonight," Emilie added. She couldn't say that she had taken off her underwear before soaking herself in the bath and couldn't leave them in the apartment because they might contain traces of Dante's semen.

Caroline shook her head. "You're a strange woman. You know?"

Emilie chuckled. "I know."

"So what else did you do this weekend?" Caroline asked between sips of her coffee.

Emilie closed her eyes. She really wanted to divulge all of the tantalizing details about her walk on the Great Wall of China and how she'd had the best orgasm of her life from having unprotected and illegal sex with her fallen angel. "Not too much. Dante and I hung out a bit. What about you?"

She smiled, running the details through her mind as she tried to pay attention to Caroline's list of activities.

Chapter 9

Dante had been surprised to find a message from Jordano Gomez on his cell, requesting another meeting. His phone number was private and shouldn't be that easily accessible.

After the last meeting, Dante had reported directly to the council office. The chairman had been quite upset to hear of Marquez's intentions. Now Purson was hesitant to proceed with the transformation of the only man to pass the screening. The council provided a number of services to their changelings, and this man would be well instructed in his new world as well as his place in it. Perhaps both Marquez and Gomez were not ready to have such a powerful tool in their possession.

Human business partners were broken in and trained in the same way as horses, with a gentle but firm hand. Some relationships grew into mutually profitable arrangements and some did not. Both parties needed to work together to benefit the whole, but each also needed to remember their place.

Dante dialed the chairman's office and his assistant put him right through.

"Hello," Purson said.

"Sir, I just got a message from Gomez on my private line requesting a meeting."

"Interesting…" the chairman mused.

"Shouldn't all meetings be scheduled through the office?"

"I would say so."

"What should I do?"

"Did Gomez say what he wanted?"

"No, sir. He just said that he wanted to meet with me."

"Well, son, go ahead and do whatever you think is best. Just keep me in the loop."

"Yes, sir."

Dante put his phone away and tried to figure out how he should handle this situation. He could ignore the call, forcing Gomez to go through the proper channels. He could call Gomez and suggest that he schedule a meeting through the chairman's office. Or he could meet with Gomez, but on his own terms.

Dante came to a decision. He took out his phone again and dialed the number Gomez had left.

"Hello," Gomez answered.

Dante was taken aback because he had expected to reach the club, not Gomez's personal line. "You called, Mr. Gomez."

"Mr. Ashton," Gomez cheered. "I'm glad to hear from you."

"How did you get this number?"

"I told you I had reliable sources."

Somebody was leaking information. Purson would want this person silenced before he or she sold the wrong information to the wrong individual. Dante was irritated enough to have his privacy invaded by this human, but humans could be far more irritating.

"You do realize that you should be making requests through the council?" Dante explained.

"Yes, I know. I just wanted to speak to you privately."

"Why?"

"Why don't we set up a meeting and I'll explain everything?"

"Fine. Meet me at the café around the corner from your club in ten minutes."

"Couldn't we meet at the club a bit later?" Gomez inquired, sounding very put out.

"No," Dante answered in a commanding tone. He didn't want Gomez to have time to make any arrangements to have the café secured or install any surveillance equipment prior to his arrival.

"OK, I'll be there."

Dante put away his phone and headed right for the café. He and Jude were done with their deliveries for the day, and now Jude was at the gym. They were to meet up with Colin later in the evening to get a bite to eat at one of their favorite restaurants. Dante didn't have long before his absence would be noticed, so he couldn't afford to give Gomez much time.

Dante came out of mesay beside a garbage dumpster in the alley behind the building, then headed into the café to secure a private table. The shop was crowded, which would help to keep Gomez in line. He wouldn't want to draw the human authorities to this place. Dante could easily disappear in a chaotic crowd, leaving Gomez to face the humans on his own.

It didn't take long for Gomez to arrive with Sid and Leonard in tow. They took seats within watching distance as Gomez joined Dante. The two men shook hands and quickly took their seats.

Dante had a partially devoured sandwich in front of him and asked, "Did you want to get anything for yourself before we begin?"

"No, thanks," Gomez replied. "I'll be brief, Mr. Maxaviel."

Dante had to rein in his temper. How dare this human address him by that name. "Maxaviel is the name of my noble mother," he explained. "I use my father's name in the human world."

"I have to admit," Gomez began, "I was quite offended to find out that we had been introduced under those terms."

Tough! Dante thought. *Emilie has yet to call me by that name and you don't outrank her in my life.* All people of noble blood used aliases in the human world. Gomez should understand this. He had been introduced to Purson Maxaviel at the council office and was only allowed to use that name out of professional courtesy. "I reserve my noble name for others of my kind, Mr. Gomez. It wasn't meant as a slight to your personally."

"I see," Gomez replied, obviously unmoved.

"What do you want?" Dante growled.

"No need to get hostile," Gomez soothed.

"Perhaps if you had wanted a different response, you shouldn't have provoked me."

"I've obtained a great deal of information," Gomez said. "It would seem your name is not the only thing I was misinformed about."

Dante gestured impatiently for Gomez to continue.

"You told me that you rarely transport pure venom," he added. "I've since learned that you're the primary transporter."

"Are you so confident in your sources that you would risk offending me?" Dante growled. "I am a nobleman and deserve to be treated as such."

Dante was tempted to remove Gomez's sources personally. On rare occasions Dante had served the council as an assassin. He was so effective that they had been encouraging him for decades to expand these services, but it wasn't something he took lightly. Venom was one thing, murder another.

For someone to risk the wrath of the council was foolish. No Beyowan would divulge information about the venom trade to humans. The council didn't exempt anyone from the rules, regardless of bloodlines. Many council offices had Beyowans with other abilities in their employ. There were those who could read minds, making criminal activity less profitable. Most changelings would rather die at the hands of humans than at the hands of the council. Whoever this source was must be absolutely desperate or completely delusional; either way they were treading on dangerous ground.

"From what I've gathered, there are two key families, the Maxaviels out of Bangkok and the Enasvants out of Beijing."

This information was true, but Dante made no move to confirm or deny anything for Gomez.

"We've also learned that you're the messenger in charge of the bulk of the shipments from both of those cities."

Again nothing from Dante, much to the frustration of Gomez.

Dante leaned forward and glared at Gomez. "Are we ever going to get to the point?"

"Most messengers take a portion of their shipments as part of their fee, correct?"

"Some do."

"Mr. Marquez would like to bid on your portion of your next shipment."

"I see," Dante mumbled. "Let me explain something. I get paid very well for what I do, and I've been running venom for almost a century. My grandfather was a Maxaviel and my grandmother was an Enasvant. Who do you think owns my loyalty?"

Gomez nodded, leaning back in his own seat. "So much is falling into place now," he began. "They trust you because you're family. You must be the only messenger with blood ties to the supply."

Dante didn't answer. He was seething. How dare this human ask him to lighten a shipment in order to line his pocket? He didn't even need the money. He'd inherited all that was his grandfather's and grandmother's, as well as his mother's. He had more money than he could spend, even with his extended life.

"So are you saying that you don't charge any fees?" Gomez asked.

"I haven't the time or the inclination to deal in black market venom."

"Perhaps you would consider charging the occasional fee, and we would be happy to offer you an above market price for the product? It would take little of your time and would benefit all concerned."

"Don't you think my family would notice the shift?" Dante demanded. "Not to mention the council."

"I didn't say *every* shipment," Gomez explained.

"I understand what's in it for you, but what's in it for me?"

"Money," Gomez answered as though nothing else needed to be said.

"I don't need money."

"Drugs?"

"I can afford my own. Plus the council offers far superior products than I can get on the streets. No offense."

Gomez shrugged. "None taken. What about women?"

Dante laughed. "Humans are off limits to me."

"You must sneak a little something once in a while."

Dante sniggered, thinking of Emilie. "No, sir. Off limits entirely."

"Really?" Gomez asked, incredulous.

"I can get humans through the council as well."

"Of course," Gomez muttered. "What about men?"

Dante shook his head, smiling.

"What about changelings?"

Now Dante was intrigued. "Do you know someone who would give herself to any man?" he asked. "You do understand that it's very difficult to rape a changeling woman. She could easily tear a man to shreds. Not to mention the fact that I'm an animal, Mr. Gomez. I don't find any thrill in unconscious or incapacitated partners."

"I see your point," Gomez agreed. "But I do have a few options."

"Technically, changelings are humans that have become servants of the Devil."

"Problematic," Gomez conceded.

"I'm an unmarried nobleman with a fortune to leave to my heir. Do you think I lack feminine attention?"

Gomez burst out laughing. "I guess not. You certainly don't lack confidence, Mr. Ashton."

At least they were back to using respectful titles.

"What about blood sport?"

Many Beyowans craved the hunt and paid high prices to kill particular prey. "No, sir. I can't eat a human...in any way."

Gomez chuckled, catching Dante's play on words. "There has to be something."

"I'm a spoiled creature," Dante explained. "I already have everything I could ever want."

"You know I've looked all over Montreal for Elizabeth Lachance," Gomez began. "There isn't anyone who meets the description of the young woman you were with at the ballet."

Dante couldn't allow his composure to betray his anger. "I travel in mesay. Who says she's from Montreal?"

"I did consider that possibility, and I'm still looking. At one point or another, I'll find her."

"Whatever..." Dante muttered, glancing at his watch.

"This woman is important to you."

"I took her to the ballet. I didn't submit her family an offer of marriage. If you abduct every woman I've ever been out in public with, you'll be a busy man."

"You're not a very good actor, Mr. Ashton. I've seen the two of you together. She's more than a bed warmer to you."

Dante came one split second from ripping Gomez's head off his shoulders. Emilie was far more important than he could ever know. "You go ahead and find Elizabeth," Dante said with as much disinterest as he could manage. "I'm not going to aid you in releasing monsters into the human population. It goes against everything I believe." He stood up. "I'm leaving."

"Are you a gambling man?" Mr. Gomez called.

"No."

"I am," Gomez explained. "As I've said before, you're not a good actor. I know a bluff when I see one."

Dante left the café without another word. *I may not be a gambler, but I know you're just trying to rattle me so I cave or make a mistake. I won't give you the satisfaction,* he thought. Gomez didn't have anything yet, but it might not take him long. As Dante ducked into the alley, he wondered how much Emilie would object to relocating to another city. He sighed heavily. His plans to woo his soul mate would have to be accelerated. Their wedding would be the solution to all of his problems, as well as the realization of all of his dreams.

Chapter 10

Dante hvad reconciled himself to the fact that he was going to have a sexual relationship with a human civilian. Emilie was his soul mate, of that he was fairly certain. Even his religious master, Michael Enasvant, had said that if God meant them to be together then it would come to pass. Dante needed to focus less on her humanity and more on the life they could build together in his world once her humanity was no longer an issue. Once he could protect her with his Beyowan name, he could shed the threat of the council as well as the threat from human criminals.

I have a girlfriend, he thought. It still felt weird.

Unfortunately, instead of feeling carefree and happy, he had an uncomfortable lump of fear in the pit of his stomach. As if this relationship wasn't complicated enough, there were some daunting hurtles yet to leap before they crossed the finish line and seized their prize. He sighed deeply. There was so much at stake. He had to make every effort to be honest with her, but there was much to divulge, and some of it would be difficult for her to accept. It was essential that he ease her into his life with patience and understanding. After all, she was only human.

That fact seemed to complicate his life to no end. The safe back at the condo contained a copy of his hunting permit for Emilie. He had committed himself to this relationship in the most serious way possible. He had, for all intents and purposes, bought her life. The weight of that responsibility was a heavy one, but he was determined to do everything in his power to protect her and guide her into his world.

Yet these wonderful thoughts brought him back to his fear. There were some important issues that needed resolving before they could take their relationship to the next level. If she balked, he would be in big trouble.

He couldn't afford any mistakes, so he would make every effort to be considerate of her feelings. He wanted to be optimistic about the outcome of this conversation, but he had to be prepared for the worst. Was her love for him strong enough to see her through this challenge?

Dante had always looked forward to his time off from work, but now everything had been intensified. His constant yearning to be with Emilie was sometimes disconcerting and made the week drag by so much more slowly, but he had something worthwhile to look forward to.

He came out of mesay in the stairwell of her apartment building and walked down the hall. He smiled broadly as he knocked.

"Are you finally here?" she barked as she ripped open the door.

"I'm not late. Did you miss me?"

She jumped into his arms. He caught her easily, picked her up, and swung her back and forth like a rag doll. Once he put her feet back on the ground, he finally got to kiss her.

She was very enthusiastic in her greeting. "You definitely missed me," he managed to say. "Aren't you even going to let me in before you start molesting me?" he joked, trying to peel her off of him. Emilie let go long enough for him to come in, take off his jacket, and kick off his shoes. Then she jumped back into his arms.

"If we get any more serious, I'm going to have to get a new job," he said between kisses. Something he fully intended to do if they were to build a life together.

"How was your day, dear?" she asked pleasantly, leading him by the hand into the living room. She sat on the couch and he sat down next to her, smiling.

"Boring, as usual. And you, my darling?" he answered, playing along.

"Excruciating. I spent the entire day counting the minutes until you got here."

She looked almost embarrassed by her admission, but he found it heartwarming. "This is really nice. I could get used to this," he said, laughing softly. "I've never had anyone miss me like this before. Colin misses me when I'm gone, but he refuses to kiss me when I get home."

"His loss is my gain," she replied. She leaned forward, grabbed him by the front of the shirt, and pulled him on top of her on the couch.

He wanted to rip the clothes from her body and savor every square inch of her, but he knew better than to get himself too worked up before they had a chance to talk. His lips brushed gently against hers, but he couldn't allow himself too much of a taste.

"Let's stay here tonight," she murmured, running her hands down his back and patting him firmly on the behind.

He stopped nibbling her ear and looked into her eyes. "What do you want to do here? As if I don't already know."

"We could see if anything interesting pops up," she suggested, wiggling under him provocatively.

"Oh, you're awful," he moaned in disgust, but climbed quickly off of her because it wouldn't take too much persuasion on her part to convince him to start something intimate before they had a chance to have the unpleasant conversation he was dreading. "Listen, I want to talk to you about something important for a minute."

"OK," she answered nervously and sat cross-legged on the couch facing him.

"Our relationship has started to get a bit more serious, and it's come to a point where we have to talk about some things before we can go any further," he began soberly.

"OK."

Here goes nothing, he thought. "In my world, a Beyowan heir like me normally looks forward to a financially driven, heavily negotiated, and usually loveless marriage based on the understanding that the ultimate goal of the union is to produce the next generation of Beyowan heir."

"What are you talking about?" she asked, looking at him in confusion.

"In my world we still have arranged marriages that are basically financial contracts brokered between families and negotiated down to the smallest detail."

"What are you trying to say here? Can't you pick your own wife?"

This is where it starts to get tricky, he thought. "I can have more than one wife, technically," Dante answered, watching for her reaction.

"Can you now?" Emilie replied in a velvety tone. Her expression suggested that he was completely out of his mind if he actually expected her to go along with that option.

"It's not as if we would all live together or anything. Don't look at me like that! Women have more than one husband. It's fair…"

"Really?" she sneered. "Sounds rough."

Her level of agitation was rapidly escalating and he was beginning to fear that things would quickly get out of hand. The last thing he wanted was a heated argument. "Listen, I'm not suggesting that you become part of my harem. I'm just warning you about what kind of world I live in and what's expected of me by my family."

She stared at him for a moment. "You're right, I'm sorry. I'm just having a hard time with my objectivity while discussing your future wife, especially with her being somebody other than me."

"Fair enough," he conceded as he uncrossed his arms and made more of an effort to relax. "I'm sorry if I sound upset. I don't mean to provoke you, it's just that this is already unpleasant for me because it's an unavoidable part of my reality, but I need to share it with you and I'm afraid of your reaction."

"Go on then. I'm listening."

"A while ago we talked a bit about illegitimate children, but I never explained why I didn't want any." He waited for her to nod. "You see, money and property are inherited through bloodlines alone. Legal bloodlines, meaning that any illegitimate children don't inherit estates. Whoever is your closest blood relative will inherit your estate. This is the main reason I don't want to have any illegitimate children, because they would financially mean nothing to me no matter how much they meant to me emotionally.

"Also the council takes all illegitimate children from their parents at the age of thirteen, so they are given very little time together, even though the parents are financially responsible for their care and upbringing. Illegitimate children don't sit well on our social ladder either. They're considered nephilim or half bloods. I guess it comes down to a matter of personal pride on my part because I wouldn't want any child of mine in that position."

She seemed to be listening attentively and was nodding her understanding.

"Jude is an illegitimate child," Dante stated matter-of-factly.

"Really?"

"Jude's father is a very lucky man. He's over three hundred years old and has three children. Jude has a legal sister who is about a hundred years older than him and a hot-shot legal little brother who is only twenty-two. Jude was a...a surprise."

"It always sounds nicer to call somebody's birth a surprise rather than an accident," she began cheerfully. "Accidents are negative things that you try to avoid, but a surprise has a more positive connotation. I myself am a surprise because my mother was told that she couldn't have any children. She was forty-two when I was conceived."

"Jude prefers the term 'act of God,' but maybe I should call him an accident."

"Really? Why would Jude's birth be something negative?"

He hesitated. Hunting licenses were a dangerous subject. "Jude was an expensive mistake for his father. He was caught hunting without a license."

"So Jude's mother was human?"

"Yes. Jude's father had taken an interest in her and kept her as one of his mistresses. He was surprised when she became pregnant. Unfortunately she didn't know what he was and he didn't have enough interest in her to make sure that she survived the pregnancy," Dante explained, avoiding Emilie's gaze. He didn't want to scare her too much, but she needed to see how serious the situation actually was.

"That's awful..."

"Jude was brought up in the illegitimate child care program provided by the council in Cairo. He has a reasonable relationship with his father, but it's not the same as if he were a legal child. He won't inherit anything, but he's still Beyowan and his father has a good social standing. It's a complicated system."

"Well, I can understand why you don't want any illegitimate children," she acknowledged, patting his knee.

Dante allowed himself a little smile. *So far so good*, he thought. "Having children is a big deal for Beyowans. It's the main reason why we're allowed to marry as many partners as we want. We have to increase our chances of having a legal child. Monogamy would never work because unsuccessful couples would be forced to divorce each other or they would have to resort to cheating. In our system you only divorce someone if you really don't like them, and you take as many spouses as it takes to produce an heir."

"Doesn't that get ugly?"

"You have no idea," he replied and sighed heavily, thinking of all the dramas that had unfolded in his lifetime alone. "It can get very ugly. So spouses usually have contracts brokering any further additions to the family. It works out more peacefully that way. Everything is done by making deals, and you can have almost anything you want if you can work out a deal for it."

"So Beyowans just get married to have children and pass along their money?"

He paused, uncertain how to answer. "Keep in mind we take pride in the fact that we're more like animals in many ways than humans. We aren't as social. You humans are more dependent on each other for your happiness. In nature, male and female creatures often only come together to mate. Other than that, they live fairly solitary lives, or else they live in tight groups with a strict social pecking order. It's easier to have more than one spouse if you aren't emotionally attached. Your spouse is more of a financial asset, a statement of social class, and a means to a reproductive end. In most cases married Beyowans have perfectly healthy, functional relationships with one another. They have mutual respect and work within their respective family frameworks to benefit everyone concerned. Take Colin. He has four wives with whom he maintains reasonable relationships. I think he's even looking for a fifth."

Emilie was shocked. "Colin's married? Why does he live with you?"

"He doesn't live with me, all of the time. He has his own homes around the world. Plus he visits his wives and his mother, and he often studies at the temple in Thailand. He has a life. He just needs to keep an eye on me to make sure I'm not off chasing any human civilians."

"He's doing a great job. Isn't he?"

Dante felt a stab of guilt. Colin was such a good friend and mentor. Dante was betraying him in the worst way. "He'd be furious if he found out about us."

"Why does he care so much about what you do?"

He paused. He wasn't sure if he should say anything about this sensitive subject, but he wanted to put her more at ease. "Can you keep a secret?"

"You know I can."

"I believe that Colin has taken me on as a pet project mostly because he was in love with my mother." Dante smiled introspectively. He had little fact on which to base his theory, but over the years, he'd heard enough rumors. Even Colin himself had let enough slip to make Dante feel fairly confident in his assumptions.

"Really? Colin's as old as your mother would have been?"

"No, he's younger, but when you live up to four hundred years what's a decade or two? Beyowan women are serious cougars. Many older, childless women prefer taking young, virile men as husbands."

Emilie chuckled and shook her head contemplatively. "How did Colin know your mother?"

"Mostly through family connections, like all Beyowans. But my mother and he studied at the temple in Thailand at the same time," he explained. In a drunken stupor, Colin had once let slip what a tigress Dante's mother had been in bed. Dante was never sure if he had been speaking about her reputation or from actual experience. He'd never had the stomach to ask Colin outright what he'd meant. Dante added, with an involuntary shiver, "I wouldn't be surprised if they knew each other…very well indeed."

"Really?" she asked, shaking her head incredulously. "Doesn't that creep you out?"

"I try not to think about it, really. Colin's a good guy overall, and he would have made my mother a good husband if she hadn't met my father. She was young to have a child. Normally we don't get married before we come of age at forty, but getting pregnant guarantees marriage for Beyowans, no matter how young you are. My mother was only forty-seven when she had me. Colin was thirty-one when I was born. Jude's only eight years older than I am, for that matter."

"Beyowan life sounds a bit like a soap opera in many ways," she teased.

"You have no idea!" he exclaimed. "We have few secrets from each other. I'm sure the expression 'having skeletons in your closet' comes from us Beyowans. Plus, because we turn to dust when we die, we use the expression 'brushing dirty secrets under the carpet.'"

"Wow…" she said with a hint of sarcasm. "What a mess."

"That's why I'm not married." He paused and took a deep breath, letting it out slowly. "But I'll have to be at some point. It's my responsibility." He dropped his gaze to the floor. He didn't want to frighten Emilie away, but he wanted her to know that he was serious about their relationship. "I'm like my mother in many ways. She wasn't happy with the marriage brokered for her and snuck off to marry my father out of love. I'm also a romantic fool and would like to marry for love."

"How unreasonable of you," she teased, patting him on the knee.

He smiled and ran his eyes over her longingly. "My family is still going to pressure me to marry for blood and money. To us, marriage is about inheritance and not about legitimizing your relationship with another person. Human monogamy is different. Your one spouse is everything to you legally and sexually."

"Don't get me started about monogamy," she warned.

He laughed sheepishly. "I'm not complaining, just pointing out facts. Anyway, I'm considered tarnished because my father wasn't even born into our world because he's a changeling. Already many families don't consider me as a match for their daughters, no matter how much money I have. For many families blood is more important than money, but some are willing to dirty themselves to improve their bottom lines. If I was to marry below myself socially, I would be dirtying my bloodline even further. Hatred toward humans is always a factor, but I think it's becoming a realistic fear that we'll become more and more human over the generations until we're completely extinct."

She appeared taken aback. "Do you think your species will go extinct?"

"Maybe, but it'll take time. We still live a lot longer than you humans," he answered. "Reproductive technologies are shifting the odds in our favor, so there's still hope."

"Why don't they just change the rules of inheritance?"

"Families with money want to keep it all in the family. They'd never be willing to risk money that has been amassed, sometimes over thousands of years, to the foolish whims of their children. Look at your own system. Don't you have people leaving millions of dollars to their dogs? That's what we're afraid will happen." Dante punctuated his statement with a snort of disgust to make his opinion quite clear.

"What about illegitimate children?" she asked. "Couldn't they inherit?"

"It's tricky. The fear is that no one would get married, and we'd all just run around trying to have children with whomever. We might irrevocably sully our bloodlines, plus fortunes get diluted when they're split into too many pieces. Historically speaking, it's the people with money and power who make the rules, and having illegitimate children inheriting wouldn't be in anyone's best interest over the long term."

"Doesn't anyone in your world marry for love?" she asked shyly, her eyes downcast.

"Don't get me wrong, it happens. It doesn't usually last for long because I don't think anyone of my species trusts anyone enough to love them—or loves them enough to trust them, for that matter. I also think that love and lust are often confused. Lust is a good reason to get married in my world. If you have good sexual chemistry then you're more likely to have a child together. Love tends to make you jealous and possessive, two things that don't work well for us."

"So you can't choose your own wife?"

Dante needed to reassure her without divulging too much. "I can have anything I want, if I can make a deal for it," he answered. "That's what I need to work on."

He stood up and started pacing around the room. Emilie watched him closely. She appeared to be calm and handling everything reasonably well, considering. Dante stopped pacing and just stared at her. He had something difficult to admit and was anticipating an angry outburst. Worst case scenario, she would become so upset that she would terminate their relationship. But he had to tell her. If she found out through any other means, she'd be furious. They'd reached the point where it had to be said. He took a deep breath and readied himself. "I have something important to tell you, but I'm afraid of your reaction."

"Chances are good that I'll get upset, but I can try to hear you out before I jump down your throat," she offered with a smirk.

"That's...comforting," he replied sarcastically. He was seriously reconsidering his decision. Maybe this wasn't the best time.

"OK. OK. I'll try to be understanding to promote honesty in our relationship."

He plucked up enough courage to speak. "There's no way to say this nicely so I'll just say it. When I was a baby, my grandfather brokered a marriage for me, and I was forced to sign a contract when I entered adulthood at thirteen, so I'm technically engaged." He waited with bated breath to see how she would react.

She remained composed, but he could detect the slight glistening of tears in her bewitching eyes. He suddenly felt like such a cad. What was he doing, courting a human girl when he already had a fiancée? Emilie must feel that he had no respect for her at all.

"So I'm your mistress, technically speaking," she remarked acidly, wiping away a stray tear.

He winced. He hated that term being applied to her, and it sounded far worse spoken from her lips. "Technically, yes," he muttered. It was difficult for him to gauge the severity of her anger because it was well blended with pain. "But you must know that I didn't want to be engaged, and I don't want to marry her. I've been stalling, at great personal expense, for over fifty years."

When she opened her mouth to speak again, he expected her to order him from the apartment never to return, but instead she said, "Thank you for telling me the truth. It was very brave of you. But tell me, where does this leave us?"

He couldn't believe his ears. She seemed to be accepting his engagement. He tried not to nurture his optimism as he walked over to sit next to her on the couch. He wanted more than anything to hold her, but he was unfamiliar with protocol in such situations. Would she be more angry if he touched her or more angry if he didn't? Hesitantly he slipped his arm around her shoulders and pulled her toward him so she could lean her head against him. "Remember I told you that I can have anything I want if I'm able to make a deal for it? Well, I'm working on a plan to get out of my marriage agreement."

Perhaps he had said the wrong thing because her level of agitation increased.

"A lot of cheating dogs tell their mistresses that kind of thing, and nine out of ten times, they're just lying through their teeth," she said crisply.

"I know, I know…" he replied. He gently took her shoulders in his hands and looked her hard in the eyes. "I can't blame you if you don't believe me, but if I wanted to lie to you, I wouldn't have told you the truth about this, and I'd be filling your head with ideas about how easy this will be for us. I'm going to prove myself to you. Talk is cheap after all."

Emilie looked like she wanted to believe him.

He quickly added, "You do understand that this is part of the reason I've been trying not to take advantage of you…physically."

"You do score bonus points, I guess," she replied, punching him playfully in the arm.

Dante shot her an irritated glance. "You have to stop doing that to me."

"OK," she purred. "I'll be careful. But you better watch out or I might try negotiating a deal in order to get my evil way with you."

"You've already had your way with me, you little devil," he declared, his voice smooth as silk.

"Only once…" she retorted with a pout.

Dante wanted so badly to kiss those lips. "You got to try me on. Didn't you like it?" he inquired, referring to her "marriage is like shopping" analogy from a previous conversation.

"Yes…but I think I need another sample, just to be sure."

He was more than happy to oblige. Taking her by the shoulders again, he laid her back on the couch, locked his lips to hers, and adjusted himself comfortably between her legs. Propping himself up on one elbow allowed his other hand the freedom to explore, particularly under her blouse.

"Aren't we cooperative tonight," she whispered, pulling his shirt out of his jeans and sneaking her hands up the tense muscles of his back.

"Would you like me to play hard to get?" he asked, rubbing her with his hips at a key point in the question.

"Oh, man," she mumbled. "Now which one of us is awful?"

He couldn't help sniggering. Sex wasn't supposed to be funny, was it? She seemed undeterred and began unbuttoning his shirt. By the time she reached the bottom, she seemed to be having trouble so he pushed himself up into a kneeling position to finish off the buttons, then shrugged out of the shirt and yanked the undershirt over his head.

The view his eyes returned to was spectacular. Emilie's long, dark hair was spread out around her face and over her shoulders, contrasting with the porcelain beauty of her skin. Her blouse was open, her breasts bulging out of a red lace bra with every breath. Her legs were bent at the knee and pulled up close to her body with her skirt falling down her thighs, allowing him a tantalizing glimpse of the matching panties peeking through the folds of fabric. He had never wanted anything as much as he wanted her.

"Your favorite color," she whispered, obviously pleased with the grin he was wearing.

"You look good enough to eat," he purred.

"Help yourself."

Don't mind if I do, he thought as he leaned over and slowly kissed his way up her abdomen, stopping only to feel the fabric of her bra on his face. Having given the garment the attention it deserved, he was eager to see it removed. She must have read his mind because she reached behind her to unclasp it for him.

"You have your license, don't you?" she asked.

Oh, no. Mood killer, he thought. Seeing how it was impolite to talk with a full mouth, he closed his around her nipple. Perhaps she would forget about the question. To be sure she would be sufficiently distracted, he ran his hand up her thigh and stroked the smooth fabric of her panties.

As he finished a thorough sampling of the first breast and made his way over the other, she whispered, "You are an animal, aren't you?"

Dante hadn't realized he'd been purring so hard with every breath. It was just a natural response to his feelings of relaxation and contentment. "I'm going to make every effort to be tame with you tonight."

"I like you a little wild," she murmured, unzipping the back of her skirt.

Music to my ears. Seeing how she would need to close her legs in order to remove her clothes, he got up off the couch to rid himself of what remained of his.

One rule he had always tried to instill in his martial arts students was to ensure that they had adequate space in which to move freely. Looking down on Emilie, he decided they needed more room for the activities he had in mind. He reached down, swept her off the couch, and carried her into the bedroom, planning out the meandering route he would take on his exploration of her delectable body.

Chapter 11

Emilie was physically spent. Where their first time together had been rushed and rough, their second had been slow and teasing, as was their third and fourth. Dante had successfully incorporated both romance and passion into this endurance race of theirs in which he was the undisputed victor.

She was almost afraid to move in case he took it as an invitation to begin anew. It was getting late and her body was sated, her eyelids heavy. She just wanted to snuggle up to him and drift into sleep.

"I'd like to take you away for the weekend," he announced as her consciousness was about to escape her.

She rolled onto her side and looked into his brown eyes. "Really? Right this minute?"

He glanced at his watch and nodded. "If we hurry, we won't miss it."

"Miss what?" she asked.

"It's a surprise," he purred, drawing her closer to him.

Oh, no you don't, mister, she thought. She kissed him quickly and rolled toward the edge of the bed. "So what do I need to pack?"

"Not too much. We can pick up anything you're missing there, but plan for warm weather."

It wasn't long before they were dressed and ready to leave. She took his hand and followed him carefully through mesay. Even though she hated being in this cramped and confusing place, it was always worth it. Wherever they were going this time, she would be spending the night in the arms of her angel.

She stepped through the mesay portal behind Dante with her eyes still closed. The smell was her first clue to their new location, followed quickly by the sounding of an alarm. Her eyes flew open and she found herself in another bedroom. *Oh, no,* she thought. *Here we go again.*

As he dealt with the alarm, she scanned the room. The dominant feature was a queen-sized bed equipped with a massive, almost gothic, dark wooden headboard centered in the middle of the wall opposite the door. Decorating the bed was a simple yet masculine comforter in a solid coffee-cream color, with white sheets and beige, black, and red accent pillows. There was a night stand with a small lamp and a clock. The wall with the headboard was a deep blood red; the others were a darker coffee-cream color. A tall dresser was against the wall to the right of the door. On the other side next to the door to the ensuite bathroom was a large black leather chair with a foot rest. Hanging on the wall behind the chair was a familiar floral painting and, not surprisingly, it was the perfect accent for this room.

"Come on," he urged, taking her by the hand. He led them down the hall to the living room and to the sliding door leading out to the terrace. When Dante drew back the curtain and opened the door, Emilie couldn't believe what she saw. They stepped out onto a patio-style balcony overlooking paradise.

The air was hot and humid but sweet and tropical. The light breeze was scented with salt, fruit, and flowers. The view was unbelievable. Stretching above the ocean was a blue sky with the occasional white puffy cloud drifting by, but the sun was beginning to set, staining the blue with a reddish hue.

His quiet laughter drew her attention back to the balcony. She squeezed his hand in hers as she advanced to the black railing at the edge of the balcony. They were in the highest apartment of this building and there were other tall buildings on either side of them as well. Below them an aqua pool glittered, full of people laughing and playing. A beautiful landscape consisting of mostly tropical trees and some low buildings of different shapes and sizes stretched out in front of them. Where the land met the ocean, she could just make out the sand of a beach. *I can't wait to lay in the sun,* she thought cheerfully.

Emilie turned to Dante. He had a mischievous grin on his face. "Do you like it?" he asked.

"Where are we?"

"This is my apartment in Maui," he explained, putting his free hand on the railing and then leaning forward to take in the view for himself. "Beautiful, isn't it?" he added, sighing deeply.

"Unbelievable…" was all she could manage.

"I'll get us a drink," he announced and walked back into the apartment.

There was an elegant patio set of stainless steel and slate tile in a shaded corner. She walked over, pulled out one of the four chairs, and sat down to inspect her surroundings better. It was difficult to wrap her mind around the fact that she had gone from lying in her bed to sitting here, watching the sunset in Hawaii.

She was so absorbed in the view that she didn't even notice him come back out. "Here you go," he said, handing her a glass of white wine. He put his own glass down on the table and pulled out the chair next to hers. "I think I made the right choice," he whispered, almost to himself.

"What do you mean?"

"I own property all over the world and I had to decide which location you would enjoy the most," he answered, reaching for her hand. "I wanted you to be happy."

"I would have been happy with you back in my apartment, on my couch. You didn't have to do this for me."

"I'm romantic. What can I say?"

"Why did you pick this place?" she asked. "I thought you didn't like being out in the sun."

"Who said we're going out in the sun?" he replied, looking very serious. Too serious…

She punched him hard in the arm. "You can't possibly expect me to spend a weekend in Hawaii and not go outside!"

His eyes glowed red and a low growl escaped his snarling lips. "Are you starting something with me, my little devil?"

"Easy, boy…" she soothed, but that reminded her of an unanswered question. "Do you have your license?"

He growled again, but this one had an altogether different tone. "Do we have to talk about this?"

"I have a right to know, don't I?"

"Yes…and yes."

"OK..." She paused but didn't want to ruin the mood. "So tell me why you chose Hawaii."

Dante seemed to appreciate the change of subject. "I brought you here because I realized that it would be six hours earlier, so we would get more time together. Plus the sunset is the reason I bought this apartment in the first place. If we went to Paris or London, we would be losing time together and the jet lag would probably be too much for you as well."

While he had been explaining, she had realized just how unprepared she actually was. "I didn't pack a bathing suit, and I don't have anything nice to wear." He looked completely unapologetic, which only fuelled her frustration. "You're such a man! You should have told me what you were up to!"

"Don't get all upset," he soothed. "I'll buy you anything you need, and I was just going to pick you up and carry you off without saying anything at all. Would you have preferred that instead?"

"No," she conceded. She could easily imagine him doing exactly that. She was glad to have been given the chance to pack a few essentials because she doubted they would have a chance to go shopping until morning.

The possibilities available for their weekend were endless. "What are we going to do tomorrow?" she asked eagerly.

His elbow was resting on the table with his chin cradled in the palm of his hand. He looked at her flirtatiously and replied, "Guess."

"I'm serious...you!" she scolded, and in her annoyance, she punched him in the arm again.

His face popped out of his hand and he glared at her intently, his eyes glowing softly. She would have to think fast if she was going to diffuse this situation. He looked like a predator with prey in his sights, preparing to pounce. "Can I have some more wine, please?" she asked, gulping the last of it and shoving her empty glass at him. After all, he had seen the sun set before and she hadn't.

He snatched her glass out of her hand and got up, smiling wickedly down at her.

She tried to act innocent and sat smirking. "Thank you," she managed to say politely before she started to giggle under her breath.

He rolled his eyes but left without another word.

Emilie stood up and returned to the railing again in order to take in the entire view. The sun was setting faster now and the sky was becoming more brilliant.

After a while, she walked over to the sliding doors and peeked into the apartment. She had never seen how Dante lived and was overcome with curiosity. She opened the door and stepped in to look around more closely. The living room, like the bedroom, was very masculine and decorated neutrally in beige, black, and brown.

He was pouring their wine in the open concept kitchen-dining area, and as she watched him, many familiar insecurities began creeping unbidden into her mind. She tried to dismiss them but they gnawed away at her tranquility.

He walked over and handed back her wine glass, then they headed out to the balcony together. When they were standing by the railing, she asked, "How many other girls have you had out here with you, watching the sun set?"

He cocked his head and replied, "I thought you knew you were my first girlfriend."

"What?" She stared at him incredulously for a moment. "You haven't mentioned anything of the sort! You haven't had *any* girlfriends? You can't be serious."

He shrugged helplessly.

"What do you mean?" She ran her eyes over him, dressed like a rock star in black jeans and a long-sleeved black shirt with a tattered-winged, weeping angel airbrushed on the back. All he needed to complete the look was an electric guitar and his dark sunglasses. "Just look at you. You must have women throwing themselves at you every day of your life."

He was sporting a particularly uncomfortable expression. "I don't spend much time with humans," he muttered.

Now this makes more sense, she thought. "So I'm just your first *human* girlfriend?"

"Definitely...But I've never had a changeling girlfriend, and I've only been serious about one Beyowan girl. Even then, nothing ever came of that relationship."

"What about Tasia?"

"She's the Beyowan girl. I actually asked her to marry me."

Emilie's teeth snapped together and she could feel a growl boiling in her chest. "And she said no."

"No, she said yes. Her father said no."

Why did I have to open this can of worms, she chastised herself. *I'm going to ruin what could have been an amazingly romantic weekend by indulging my stupid insecurities.* "Sorry, I didn't mean to grill you."

"As you said before, you have the right to know. That said we don't have the same system in place that you humans do. We don't date. We're free to hook up with whomever we choose, whenever we choose. Sex is easy, but marriage is serious business, and we only marry for blood and money."

"So you must be serious about me because you've already mentioned marriage," she teased.

"I've never been more serious about anyone in my entire life."

Emilie's insecurities evaporated quickly. "I'll drink to that," she declared, and they both sipped from their glasses.

They sat together engrossed in conversation until the sky was completely dark and the air was beginning to cool.

"I'm so tired," she complained.

"Well, for you it's late."

"Aren't you tired?" she asked.

"Beyowans can sleep anytime of the day or night, plus I'm so accustomed to being in different time zones that I don't even notice anymore."

The jet lag and the wine were affecting her more than she wanted to admit. "It's too early for bed, isn't it?"

He glanced at his watch and shook his head. "You'll be up at the crack of dawn."

"OK. We'll have more of the day together."

He stood up and looked over the railing. "There's something I'd like to do."

She was afraid to ask. Being romantically involved with a demon was going to require a lot of energy, on her part at least. He didn't seem to tire out. She remembered a phone conversation where she had suggested that she would like to tire Dante out so he could fall asleep. He hadn't been kidding when he'd implied that she would have a difficult time of it.

"What do you want to do?" she asked in a guarded voice.

He seemed to pick up on her tone right away and laughed smugly. "Have I worn you out already?"

He had every reason to be proud of himself. He was going to give her a heart attack if he continued at the same pace. "I'm not tired of you, my love. I'm just tired."

Her answer seemed to satisfy him enough to make him stop laughing. "I want to go swimming, you silly girl," he explained, snickering again. "Because of my camouflage, I can't expose my skin to the tropical sun for long. I'd burn something fierce and probably break out in a rash. Plus my eyes don't handle the bright light very well. I actually have better night vision. I like to swim, so I usually go at night."

Emilie felt badly for being so presumptuous. There was one major problem with his plan. "I don't have a bathing suit."

"Would you consider going in your underwear and a t-shirt? There isn't anyone out there right now."

"OK. But I don't want to get caught, all right?"

He made no effort to disguise his gratitude. "Let's go get ready."

They locked the balcony door and made their way back into the bedroom. She put on a clean pair of panties and slipped into the t-shirt he had found for her in one of the drawers of his dresser. While she waited for him to return from the bathroom with towels, she stretched up tall and yawned drowsily.

He threw the towels on the bed and wrapped her up in a big bear hug. "When we come up to bed again, I'll keep my hands off of you until you wake up on your own in the morning. Deal?"

"Sounds good to me, because I don't want to be a grouchy old bear this weekend," she half-joked.

He just laughed and threw her a towel. "As long as I get to wrestle with you, you can be as grouchy as you like."

"Even if I scratch and bite?"

The shape of his bathing suit gave away his feelings on the matter even before he said, "Especially if you scratch and bite."

"Fine, then. Let's get going before you change your mind. I'll just have to trust that you'll keep your hands to yourself."

They left the apartment and waited together at the elevator. He leaned over and whispered, "Is it that easy for you to trust someone?"

The way he was looking at her made her think that trust was not something overly familiar to him.

Before she could answer, he continued, "You know what I am and you hardly know me. I've taken you to another country and you have little money, no documentation, and no plane tickets. I don't think many women of my kind would make themselves so vulnerable, unless they stood to gain something of great value. You must really love me."

She wasn't sure how to respond. "Trust is something that's earned, not just given. I didn't trust you when we first went for lunch together. Remember? I came close to refusing to get into the car with you."

"I would have been so disappointed, you know. But I would have thought of somewhere within walking distance."

"Somehow I'm not surprised," she replied. "So far, you haven't given me any reasons not to trust you, and I do love you. I guess it makes it easier for me to…to want to trust you." He seemed to be pleased with her answer, but that only made her curious about his own feelings. "Do you trust me?"

They walked out of the elevator on the ground floor and headed for the pool. The whole building was quiet, but she wrapped her towel around her shoulders so if anyone saw her they would just assume she had a bathing suit underneath.

Dante cleared his throat. "I don't know what to say. I do love you, and I guess I want to trust you. Let's leave it at that for now."

He put his towel down on the concrete, near the stairs into the pool. He stepped in and whispered, "I can't stay in here for long. The chlorine isn't good for my skin or eyes either." Then he dove in and disappeared under the water.

Emilie put her towel next to his and stepped in tentatively. The water was cold. He swam over, watching her gradual progress. He had that predatory look again so she whispered to him in her sternest voice, "Don't you do anything stupid or I'll scream."

He laughed darkly to himself, sunk under the water, and swam away. She finally submerged herself up to her neck, hissing and cringing all the way. When she swam out to meet him, he took her in his arms. His body was surprisingly warm compared to the water so she brought her own arms around his neck and wrapped her legs around his waist, cuddling as close to him as possible.

He brought his cool lips to hers. She tried to discreetly scan the area to see if anyone could see them, but it seemed that they were all alone. He carried her over to the edge, backed her up against the wall of the pool, and started kissing her more deeply. His lips were beginning to make her feel much warmer all over.

He kissed along her neck, and then he whispered seductively into her ear, "I said that I wouldn't touch you when we got back upstairs, but can I touch you out here?"

She rubbed her cheek against his and gently brushed his ear with her lips. "You're already touching me. What other kind of touching do you have in mind, my naughty angel?"

One of his hands snuck under her t-shirt and ran delicately over her skin. His fingers were like ice, making her wiggle and twitch away from them.

His seductive voice was back in her ear. "I like it when you struggle with me, baby."

"Dante, your fingers are cold," she whimpered.

He ran them along the inside of the elastic waistband of her panties. "Why don't I put them somewhere to warm up?"

"Don't you dare or I'll scream for sure," she hissed.

He tightened his grip. "But I enjoy making you scream."

He slowly ran his lips down her neck from her ear to her shoulder, sniggering darkly. Emilie snuggled herself closer to him. He was such a naughty angel, but he was irresistible. "Aren't you worried about getting caught out here in the water?"

"It would do wonders for my reputation at work if I got arrested for having sex in public with my human mistress. They might insist I take a seat on the council," he teased.

She didn't find it quite as funny as he did. "OK, I think I've had enough touching for now. I don't think I could...anyway. I'm worn out, remember?" She let go of him and tried to slip away, but he was already too committed to his purpose to be that easily deterred.

"I love a challenge," he purred, trying to get his hands back under her shirt.

"You're going to scorch your skin in here and then we'll be trapped inside all day tomorrow until you heal. Let's go back to bed and I'll make it up to you later, I promise."

He seemed to be in a reasonable mood and let her swim away from him but followed closely behind. Emilie wondered if he had ever been refused. He was a wealthy nobleman and was accustomed to certain privileges.

They swam together for a while longer and then went back upstairs. He was a true gentleman and tucked her into his bed, kissed her goodnight, then went off to read, allowing her to fall asleep unmolested.

⚙

Dante leaned on the doorframe, admiring Emilie's peaceful form asleep in his bed. He could easily get used to that sight. Having her around all the time was convenient, and he could use a few years of rest and relaxation to make up for the decades of constant work. *I could build a very comfortable life for myself with this woman by my side,* he thought.

He had just towelled off from a shower in the guest bathroom. It was his first time using that one. Washing in the comfort and familiarity of his master bathroom wasn't worth the risk of waking Emilie. As he walked back into the living room to sit on the couch, he thought, *How odd. I'm willing to sacrifice my own comfort for hers.*

He took out his phone and dialed Jude.

"There you are," Jude growled. "I was seriously considering dropping into your little love nest with Colin."

"I would make sure you got stuck protecting some spoiled Enasvant princess if you did," Dante replied and wasn't even joking. The last thing he wanted was for Emilie to be caught in the middle of a fight between the three of them. Things could be said and disclosed that would be disastrous to the budding relationship he was trying to nurture.

"We've got trouble here in Montreal," Jude warned.

"Really?" Dante asked. "What kind of trouble?"

"Jim told me that he's been approached about information and access to the condo."

James Robertson and his wife, Eliza, managed the building in which Dante lived. James was common blood, meaning that he'd been born to two changelings. He was Beyowan and had a higher status than his changeling wife and parents. People of noble blood didn't live in buildings that were not managed by their own kind. It was just too dangerous.

"Did Jim get security footage of this person?" Dante asked.

"Yeah," Jude replied. "It was Sid, from the club."

Gomez would have had to send a changeling. People of common blood wouldn't talk to humans. Deals would only be made with their own kind—one of the reasons human crime lords were so eager to create their own changelings. It paid to have people loyal only to you and to other humans instead of their own kind and their council offices. Changelings managed through the council learned quickly that any number of career opportunities were available all over the world, many of which were quite rewarding. Human crime lords often treated their changelings rather contemptuously and found them difficult to afford as well as to manage.

"What did Sid have to say to Jim?"

"He asked whether or not you were in the habit of bringing women home with you, in particular our little Miss Elizabeth. He wanted to know if he could buy his way into the condo to have a look around and plant a few bugs."

"Make sure Jim is properly compensated for his loyalty," Dante insisted. "I'll make sure to let Purson know that if anything remotely frightening befalls anyone close to me in Montreal, I'll handle it personally."

Many people of common blood as well as changelings chose to serve certain noble families because they would fall under the protective umbrella of their master's households. Dante had never had a problem staffing any position available in any of his homes and had no shortage of people willing to work with him on any project he undertook. He had always tried to surround himself with loyal people and rewarded everyone for their hard work. Treating people with respect and consideration went further toward earning their loyalty than financial incentives, and Dante was fiercely protective of all of the people in his employment. He involved himself in their lives and made sure that they were safe and comfortable.

Jim and Eliza had been carefully chosen among a great many applicants when Dante had decided to take up a more permanent residence in Montreal.

Dante's housekeeper, Claudia Borsov, was also common blood. She had been one of his grandfather's servants and was at least three hundred years old. She had begged to come to Montreal to make sure Dante was well cared for in his home away from home. He trusted her with his life and had been more than happy to set her up with her own apartment close to the condo so she could have her independence while she managed everything in the condo from the laundry to the groceries. She even had a set of keys to his Jaguar and was insured as one of the drivers.

"What about Claudia? Is she OK?" Dante asked, concerned.

"I've spoken to her and she knows who to watch out for."

"Thanks, Jude."

"How's it going with Elizabeth anyway?"

Dante smiled. "She's the light of my life."

"Oh, don't make me puke," Jude snarled.

Dante didn't expect Jude to understand, but things would be easier if he could get his bodyguard on board with his girlfriend. "Anything else?" Dante asked through gritted teeth.

"No," Jude answered, equally brusque.

"Fine. Bye then." Dante put his phone away and went to the fridge. Nothing but wine. Not a crumb of food was in the apartment. He and his friends didn't often stay for long. They would come to watch the sun rise or set, eat at a restaurant or go to a club, and then leave. In the morning, he would have to speak to the management service he dealt with in Maui to have the apartment properly stocked for the weekend.

Until then, he was stuck. He wasn't overly concerned about his level of hunger, but it never paid to go too long without eating. He didn't want his instincts getting in the way of his relationship. Emilie was accepting the differences between them thus far but probably wouldn't find his moodiness amusing.

How many hours do humans need to rest? he wondered. He would find out soon enough, although he was fairly confident that she would be jet lagged and up early.

He walked back to the bedroom and sat on the edge of the bed. She was so lovely and he wanted to wake her up again, but his promise held him back. *Emilie trusts me...How strange,* he mused. *I don't want to betray her trust, even if it means that I don't get what I want. Words can be powerful.*

He slid carefully into the bed and laid next to her, fantasizing about what he would like to be doing to her. He could wait. Sometimes the anticipation was part of the enjoyment. He took a deep breath and smiled. This was something he could definitely get used to. As Dante closed his eyes and relaxed his body, he wondered if he would ever stop wanting to touch her every minute of the day or night. *I hope I never do.*

Chapter 12

Emilie was up early in the morning, which was fortunate for Dante because he was so eager to go out to eat that he didn't even want what most men want first thing in the morning. As soon as her eyes had opened, he had rushed her to get dressed so they could go out. Somehow she had expected a different need to be his priority, but she had to remind herself that he wasn't like other men.

At breakfast, Dante consumed enough food to feed at least two adults and barely seemed satisfied with the amount. After they were done, they did a little shopping on their way back to the car. Emilie needed a few items for her weekend wardrobe, plus they picked up other necessities like sunscreen, magazines, drinks, and snacks.

Once well supplied, they headed back to the apartment to change and get ready for the beach. Dante planned to sit in the shade and read while she soaked up the sun.

As he pulled the car out into traffic, she had a naughty idea. She innocently placed her hand on his thigh. He looked over at her curiously, but she pretended not to notice. When he seemed satisfied that she wasn't up to anything, she slid her fingers between his legs and started stroking him. He shot her a more surprised look this time. She just winked at him mischievously from under her sunglasses.

"Hey, I'm driving here!" he declared, taking one hand off the wheel to chase her hand away from his lap.

"Dante, the light is red," Emilie announced and laughed as they screeched to a stop.

Her hand found its way back, and she could tell that he was both tempted and irritated by her persistence. He was breathing hard and making little groans as she got a better hold on him, but he kept both hands on the wheel.

"Dante…" There was a loud honk from behind them. "The light is green."

He snarled something in a foreign language and stomped on the gas pedal. The car was a stick shift and he was revving the engine far more than necessary before changing gears. Emilie giggled devilishly to herself.

"We're going to have an accident if you don't stop this right now," he grumbled, again chasing her pertinacious hand away.

"Don't Beyowans have better reflexes?" she inquired, slipping her fingers through the unzipped fly of his slacks.

He glared at her, his eyes flashing red. "You've got to be kidding me…" He paused to groan again before continuing, "…Come on."

She had to laugh. "You come on, baby."

"Oh, man…" he grumbled. "I'm not in the mood for this."

"I beg to differ," she countered, giving him a squeeze. "Dante… Stop sign," she warned as she tittered behind her other hand.

More foreign language and another jerky stop. He closed his eyes and started growling, then turned to her and muttered, "You're pure evil, you know."

There was another honk behind them and she took advantage of his focus on the road to slip her hand into his underwear.

He groaned again but fast as lightning had the car pulled over to the side of the road. He slammed it into park, grabbed her by both wrists, shoved her way over onto her side, and leaned in closer. "You little devil…Maybe human males are so desensitized that they can do these two things at the same time, but I can't focus on anything else while you're doing that to me. I'll probably be able to get up out of this car no matter how badly I crash it. You, on the other hand, will not. I don't have time to sit here in Maui waiting for you to get out of traction. So cut it out! Or I'm going to make you walk. Am I making myself clear?"

She tried to keep a straight face throughout his rant. She wanted to appear to be taking him seriously but couldn't help chuckling under her breath.

A grin twitched at the corners of his mouth. He released her arms and did up his slacks, glaring at her all the while. "Aren't you even a little afraid of me?"

She shrugged. "Nope."

"I *am* a descendant of Satan," he argued.

"The son is not responsible for the sins of the father."

He sat growling to himself for a second or two. "You sure are an unusual creature. Are you sure you don't have a vampire in your family history somewhere?"

His eyes were sparkling with humor, so she decided not to be insulted by his use of the "V" word.

They were back at the apartment in a matter of minutes. She had barely gotten her legs out of the vehicle before he swept her off of her feet and into mesay, reappearing almost instantly in his bedroom. He wrapped her in his arms and kissed her with enthusiasm. The bags she had retrieved from the back seat on her way out of the car were still in her hands and she brought them up between them, forcing him away from her. His kisses never stopped, but his hands went from around her body to trying to relieve her of her burdens.

Emilie laughed but wouldn't let go.

"What?" he asked, obviously agitated. "Is there something in those bags that's going to be ruined if it sits on the floor for a while?"

"Easy, boy," she soothed. "I want to show you something."

"Oh, good," he purred, trying to capture her again. "I was getting worried."

She dropped all but one bag. The one remaining contained her purchases from the drugstore. She rifled through it and withdrew one particular item, setting the rest on the floor.

Dante reacted like an archetypal vampire splashed with holy water. He leapt back and hissed, his face expressing his utter disgust. "Oh, no, no, no," he complained.

Emilie examined the box of condoms in her hand and burst out laughing. Once she regained enough of her composure, she launched her strongest argument. "You said you didn't want me to get pregnant."

"You won't," he whined. "You've already been fertile this cycle and I can tell if you come back into season." He leaned toward her and slowly filled his nostrils. "Nothing but your normal tantalizing scent."

"Dante…" she scolded.

"You're pure evil," he complained. "First you give me the stink-eye every time I so much as glance in the direction of another woman."

"You were giving that waitress your dazzling grin," she corrected.

"She started it," he insisted. "I was only being polite."

"My ass—"

"Is lovely," he interrupted. "Then you tease me mercilessly in the car," he continued on his original train of thought. "And now you want to numb me with one of those torture devices."

"Don't be such a baby."

He snorted out his objection. "What if I refuse?"

"Your choice. I won't force you."

"I would love to see you try," he muttered, then stopped short as the hidden meaning behind her words was finally deciphered. "You're going to refuse me, aren't you?"

Emilie nodded.

"You know what I am, don't you?" His eyes started glowing brightly and his body language became much more menacing. "And what I'm capable of."

"You're my angel, and you love me."

He snorted again, but the red was gone from his eyes. "I do."

She opened the box, pulling out a strip of condoms. "This probably won't be enough for today, knowing you."

He sniggered but looked pleased with her compliment about his stamina. "We'll see. If I don't like it, we'll both be cold and bored in this bed."

"You won't even notice the difference."

"Are you sure you don't have a vampire somewhere in your lineage?" he asked, this time more seriously.

"Should I be insulted?" she replied, raising her eyebrows speculatively.

"I don't mean to be insulting," he insisted. "Beyowan men and women are watched very carefully and are held accountable for any of their illicit dealings. Changelings are more difficult to keep track of. They're also much sneakier about their behavior, because it's so much more dangerous for them to get caught. The council offices are always cleaning up after changelings with a taste for humans. But there are exceptions. For example, a changeling woman impregnated by a human man might be able to hide her pregnancy and put the baby up for adoption in the human world. Also, these mixed children marry humans and continue breeding undetected. So in reality, you're more likely to have a vampire in the family than a Beyowan."

She found the whole idea incredibly amusing and decided to string him along. "Well, now that you mention it, my mom was adopted," she teased, although she was telling the truth.

He gasped as though he was considering her answer even more seriously than she had intended. "Are you serious?"

"Honest to God."

"How much did you weigh at birth?"

"I was a big baby, almost ten and a half pounds."

"Hmmm…Were you a C-section delivery?"

"As a matter of fact I was."

"Really? What did your mother feed you?"

"She said that I was a miserable, colicky baby until she put me on solids."

There was a most amusing look creeping across his face. Then he smiled and said, "Our babies are born with teeth because they need blood with their milk, which makes them very easy to identify, but I've heard of some exceptions. I'm going to have to watch you more closely. I'm starting to get worried. You smell like a human, but I don't know…" He stepped closer and examined her with a critical eye. "Open your mouth and let me check your teeth."

Emilie shrieked and bolted away from him, but he had her pinned down on the tile floor in a heartbeat.

"Open wide."

She clamped her jaws shut as he tried to stick his fingers into her mouth. She snapped out like a vicious animal and managed to bite his finger, then clamped her jaws shut again. He winced and put his finger into his smiling mouth. "You are nasty, aren't you?" he mumbled, then shook his wounded hand back and forth. "I like that in a woman."

"Want me to kiss it better?"

He flashed her his sad puppy dog face and held his finger out for her. She took his hand in hers and kissed the injured digit, then ran it along her parted lips. His eyes began to glow and the grin slid off his face as she slipped the finger into her mouth, circling it with her tongue.

Dante had the sexiest growling purr when he was aroused. The sound of it sent shivers over her skin.

"You are evil, and I wouldn't have you any other way."

She removed his finger and wrapped her arms around his head, drawing him in for a kiss.

ψ

Dante and Emilie spent their afternoon at the beach. Emilie's time was about equally divided between the ocean and sun bathing. Dante kept a watchful eye on her from the shade of the copse of trees at the top of the beach near the parking lot. As the hours passed, lying in the sun made her sleepy, but she didn't want to fry her pale skin to a crisp, asleep in the sand. It was time to pack up and head back to the apartment for a nap.

When Emilie woke, she was surprised to find Dante still with her. This weekend had allowed her to discover just how restless he was. Beyowans never seemed to let their guard down all the way and didn't need to rest for long periods at a time.

He was lying on his side, facing away from her. She admired the sculpted perfection that was his naked upper body, draped like a Roman with the white sheet across his backside. She inched over to his side of the bed, slipped her arm around him, and kissed her way up his spine into the loose curls at the nape of his neck.

He rolled onto his back and wrapped his arm around her so she could rest her face against his chest. She draped her arm over him and threw her leg over for good measure. She felt so languorous.

He was the first to break the silence between them. "I've never been so happy in my entire life. I had no idea people could be this happy."

The depth of feeling that he was sharing with her was touching, and she was moved by the sincerity in his voice. He was normally more guarded with his emotions.

"I don't want this weekend to end," he continued wistfully, drawing her closer to him. "I want to stay here with you forever."

He had been alive for a lot longer than she, so his words carried more weight. She kissed his chest and whispered, "I'm happy here with you too, but we don't have to stay. I'll be happy with you anywhere."

"I have so much I want to share with you. We can travel all over the world together. It will take years to show you everything that I want you to see."

Dante wasn't the only one unaccustomed to making themselves emotionally vulnerable to a partner. For reasons unknown, Emilie blurted, "Maybe you're secretly hoping that I do get pregnant."

"No!" he snapped. "Not now anyway," he added more softly. "I'll be happier if I can have this weekend with you and still get what I want in the long run."

"You're used to getting what you want, aren't you?"

"I try," he purred.

"So tell me again, what exactly is it that you want?" she asked, running her lips absently along his skin.

She could tell that he was uncomfortable with her question. Obviously he wasn't used to sharing his hopes and dreams with anyone else. Being truly intimate with someone was a complicated, multi-layered endeavour. He had mastered some areas of intimacy, but in others he definitely lacked confidence. She was not one to judge so she just lay quietly, allowing him a moment to sort through his thoughts.

"I want to have you...as my wife," he whispered. "I want us to be together, always."

He couldn't look her in the eyes as he spoke the words. She could tell that it was difficult for him to open up on such a personal level. He had been implying that he wanted to marry her for a while, but he had never come right out and said anything as definitive, until now.

"Are you asking me to marry you?" she teased, hoping to break the tension between them.

He cleared his throat. "I'm not exactly in a position to ask you to marry me. Yet..."

He was taking her a bit too seriously. She needed to reassure him that she wasn't pressuring him to do anything. "I'm not in any hurry, by the way. After all, we hardly know each other. We still have lots of time."

But she suspected that if he had been in a better position, he might actually have asked her to marry him right then and there.

He looked at his watch. "If we don't want to miss the sunset, we should move this conversation outside."

She was happy to change the subject as well as the scenery, so she leaped from the bed and chose some clothes for the evening.

As they sat out on the patio sipping wine and watching the sunset together, Dante asked, "Do you remember when we went to that coffee place and you asked me about my definitions of Heaven and Hell?"

"Yes."

"I wanted to tell you that love is Hell."

Emilie looked over at him in surprise. "Really? Why do you say that?"

He smiled. "I was in love with you, and I knew that I couldn't have you. But I couldn't keep away from you." His facial expression darkened suddenly and almost seemed angry. He pointed his finger at her and barked, "By the way, you were fertile that night. You were lucky you had an exam and didn't invite me in, or you and I would currently be expecting a child. I was in absolute Hell!"

"You wouldn't have done anything," she stated with confidence, knowing full well how difficult it had been seducing him, even after they were dating.

"Oh, yes I would have," he insisted. "You might not have enjoyed it as much as I would have, though."

She had to laugh. "What about now? Is love still Hell?"

"Yes."

"Really?"

"Being with you sometimes feels like the most enjoyable and yet the most frustrating torture. You're always in my thoughts, and I crave you physically. You're my addiction, so you see, it's Hell." He sighed and looked at his watch. "We should start getting ready for dinner."

The sun had disappeared and they had reservations for sushi. Emilie was looking forward to it. To the casual observer he wouldn't seem any different, but she had become more sensitive to Dante's moods and could tell that he was getting hungry.

They ate a huge meal, of course. She was worried that she would start gaining weight, eating with him on a regular basis. He didn't have an inch of fat to be pinched anywhere on his body, and she had done an extensive search. Her metabolism was not as efficient in comparison.

After dinner they went window shopping for a while, enjoying the tropical evening. They walked hand in hand and talked about this and that. She enjoyed just spending time with him.

They decided to catch a late movie together. It was great knowing that she would be able to cuddle up with him during the movie. She was wearing a splendid lavender sun dress that she had bought earlier that day and in combination with the fantastic sandals she had also acquired, she felt her figure was shown off advantageously. Dante, being himself, always looked like he was ready for a photo shoot and was dressed all in black again.

On their way into the theatre, she noticed some girls watching them and whispering behind their hands. They could look all they wanted, but they couldn't touch. She slipped her arm proudly around his waist. He just smiled and squeezed her closer, kissing her on the forehead. Being with him made it the best movie she had ever seen, though she could barely remember what it had been about.

On the way back in the car, she thought about how odd it was being involved with a man who was so sensitive to everyone's reproductive status. It had been difficult finding the perfect seat in the theatre because of Dante's delicate sense of smell. He had refused to sit anywhere near any women that were fertile or bleeding too heavily.

He drew her out of her musing with a question. "You don't trust me around other women, do you?"

He was right. He was drop-dead gorgeous and she, well…she just wasn't. Plus it didn't help that monogamy was a foreign concept to him. One way or another, he deserved an honest answer, but she didn't want to come across as insecure and over-possessive—not great qualities in a girlfriend. "I guess I sometimes feel inadequate," she admitted.

His eyebrows furrowed. "I don't understand. In what way are you inadequate?"

"Look at yourself! And look at me…"

"I never get tired of looking at you. I still don't understand."

He wasn't just playing dumb with her. He seemed confused and almost embarrassed by his miscomprehension.

"How can I put this to you?" She paused. "You're my beautiful angel and you attract attention from women of all ages, wherever you are. You may love looking at me, but I'm just a regular human woman."

"Do you really believe that about yourself?"

Again, she couldn't detect any maliciousness in his tone. He was genuinely surprised by her answer. "I'm just a regular woman."

"Perhaps you need glasses," he joked. Before she could think of a witty come-back he continued, "There's nothing regular about you, and I need you to understand something important here. You're beautiful. So much so that men of my species would feel obliged to come over and verify your scent just to be absolutely certain." He paused to let her digest this information.

"You're just saying that because you're my boyfriend and it's your responsibility to make me feel better about myself. And I appreciate your efforts. Really I do…"

"You obviously don't know what kind of power you have," he interrupted. "I know I'm beautiful, and I use that to my advantage whenever I want because I'm vain and selfish. When we're together, you must be paying too much attention to what other women are doing to notice the other men. Do you know how many men turn their heads in your direction when you laugh? And it's not because you're silly and annoying, as you once described, but because you're enchanting. When you lean across the table toward me with a seductive grin, I notice others watching with desire written all over their faces. Or when you walk, your body flows with confidence. It's enticing."

"You're sweet," she said, but didn't want to stray too far from the original question. "Remember when I said that trust is earned?"

"Yes."

"I guess I'm so possessive with you because I'm concerned that you don't really understand monogamy. I hope you realize that I won't ever share you with another woman." She was shocked at how much emotion flooded through her as she admitted these feelings out loud. He was from a different world, and she was worried about his reaction. This could be a deal breaker for them both.

He laughed. "I know...I've known from the beginning. I also know that whatever words I speak will do nothing to alleviate your fears."

"Dante...you're an incorrigible flirt."

He nodded. "I like the attention."

"That's exactly why my trust is weak on this issue."

"I never thought for one minute that you would share me. I may be pretty, but I'm not stupid. You're the type of woman who accepts nothing less than one hundred percent of a man's attention. I can't even look at other women without being marked by you. Remember that this is new for me. I've been unattached for a long time. I'm still figuring out the rules."

"The rules with women are pretty simple. Don't for any reason, or at any time, make the woman you're with think that you want to be with any other woman. It doesn't take a genius to understand that." She should be making more of an effort to be understanding, but she could sense her tentative control over her emotions slipping away.

Dante slipped his hand onto her knee. "I don't want anyone else."

Emilie had to give him credit. He was a good listener and it was easy to talk to him. He didn't get all nasty and hurtful. Plus he didn't shut down like some men. Although his honesty and bluntness could sometimes be painful.

"What if you get bored?" she asked.

He laughed, and not just a little silly laugh but a real laugh, as if he couldn't believe how ridiculous the idea was. "I'm not the slightest bit worried about getting bored with you, you little devil."

When they got back to the apartment, they went for a quick swim, where they relaxed and enjoyed each other's company. But later, as they showered off the chlorine in Dante's master bathroom, he started to get very persistent with her physically. She enjoyed his advances, but found she enjoyed his reactions even more. If she changed positions or took his hands away, he would become somewhat inflamed until he could get himself under control again. She knew that he was having fun playing with her, but she had become much more aware of the amount of control he used with her body.

She wondered what sex was like between two of his own kind. Things probably got quite rough. Being the child of wildlife photographers, she had watched many documentaries about animals in the wild. Some creatures had fierce mating practices. She could imagine allowing your instincts free rein with bodies that were stronger, more pain resistant, and healed quickly. It would be very different indeed.

She decided to conduct a little experiment of her own to see if they could find an acceptable compromise between what she liked physically and what she guessed Dante liked. She already knew that he was stronger than she was, and not just in terms of the normal difference between men and women. He was much stronger. She didn't want to do anything foolish, but she felt it was a matter of trust. He wouldn't do anything to hurt her; not too much, anyway.

After teasing him in the shower just enough to keep him interested, she stepped out, dried off, and put her plan into action. He followed her into the bedroom, looking her up and down suspiciously before saying, "What's going on here? You're sending me mixed messages."

It was her turn to examine him. Even completely relaxed he was an impressive sight. The slightest movement of his body proved that he was well muscled and tight as a spring. She would have to be careful.

As she was pondering how insane she must be for wanting to do this with him, she found herself blurting, "You might have to get rough with me tonight." Then she smiled and laid herself seductively on the bed, crooking her finger at him.

He stood at the foot of the bed, looking a bit uncertain. She could see by the serious line of his lips that this was not going to be as easy as she had first imagined. He sighed heavily. "Emilie, I don't think I understand what you want here. If it's what I think..." He paused, shaking his head, "...Then perhaps you should reconsider. You don't fully appreciate the fact that, if I get too excited, I could potentially...hurt you."

His magical voice was soft and gentle and she could tell that he was trying not to frighten her. He didn't want her being impulsive and starting something that she would quickly regret.

He gave her a moment to think about what he had said before going on. "I want what we share together to be mutually satisfying. I don't want to use you physically for my amusement. I need it to be crystal clear that I don't want you to feel obligated in any way to do things for me just because I'm different from you."

His concern for her safety and satisfaction only strengthened her resolve and made her even more confident that he would behave himself. It wasn't as if he had been denying himself lately, so he shouldn't have too much pent-up sexual energy.

She rolled her eyes at him and said, "You're thinking too much. Come here…" As he walked around the bed she continued, "We can play a bit rough. I'm not as delicate as you think. I'll tell you if things get out of hand."

He sat on the bed next to her with his uncertainty showing in his brown eyes.

"Come here!" She crooked her finger at him again. "Or am I going to have to chase you around and scare you stiff?"

Dante laughed and shook his head. He took in the sight of her naked body laid out so temptingly on his bed. Lost in his own thoughts, he unconsciously reached out his hand to touch her. She seized her chance to get his attention back by slapping his hand away, and not just a teasing little tap, but a stinging "get your hands off" slap.

Instantly his gaze snapped back to her face. His eyes narrowed and his expression became much more intense. She just smiled and raised an eyebrow at him suggestively. He glared at her for a second or two, and she could feel the electricity building between them. Then he closed his eyes, took a deep breath, and when he opened his glowing eyes again, he had a very powerful and determined look on his face. Her smile grew wider and she shivered at the intensity of his stare. She quickly slid away from him, and he made a playful swipe at her. They were now each standing on opposites sides of the bed.

"You be sure to let me know if this goes too far," he insisted.

"OK, but you have to let me know how far you want me to go."

"Remember the scratching and biting you mentioned yesterday?"

She nodded. "You let me know if I get too rough."

"I'll let you know if I want more," he answered with a confident smirk.

He lunged across the bed with lightning speed, making Emilie squeal in surprise. She had frozen like a deer in the headlights for

just a second and it was that critical hesitation that was her undo-
ing. She jumped back and twisted her body to run, but he must
have anticipated this and snatched her wrist just as she bolted. She
was jerked backwards and felt her skin burn under his iron grip. All
of the muscles in her arm stretched out until she snapped back and
came face to face with him. He was kneeling on the edge of the bed
and she still had both feet on the floor; his arms wrapped around
her torso, locking the top of hers to her sides.

"Gotcha," he whispered, planting a kiss on her cheek.

Bending her arms at the elbow, she reached around his back
and raked her nails into his skin. By the euphoric grin spreading
across his face and the deep sigh accompanying it, she could tell
that this was exactly what he had hoped for. He was distracted as he
savored the effects of her actions and his grip loosened. This time
she didn't hesitate. She threw herself backwards and dropped to
the floor, dragging him off of the bed.

As she had expected, he twisted his body so as to protect hers.
He could have dropped his full weight onto her and had her pinned
to the cold tile floor, but he toppled beside her instead.

In order to retain enough of his balance to control his fall,
he had released her arms. Now she was free to move and quickly
scrambled away from him. He could have fallen on her other side,
trapping her in the corner of the room, but he had generously
allowed her this opportunity to escape. As she passed the footboard
of his bed, she stood up and planned to make a run for it.

Before she had a second to react, she found herself back on the
floor. She had mistakenly thought that he would have to round the
footboard himself before continuing with his pursuit, but he had
simply reached under the bed and grabbed her ankle as she stood
up. She realized that he could have easily dragged her under the
bed toward him, making any struggle almost impossible in such
a confined space, but he mercifully released her. In one graceful
move, he bounded up onto the bed and vaulted to the other side.
She only had time to roll into a defensive ball like a turtle, her arms
and legs tucked tightly under her body.

As she felt his warm skin cover hers, his teeth ran rather firmly
from the top of her shoulder up to her ear. "Gotcha again," he
boasted, his voice deep and eerily resonating.

With her bottom propped up on her feet, this position was most convenient for him and he seemed to be adjusting himself to take full advantage. "Let's get back on the bed," she suggested. "It's not comfortable down here."

"Oh, I can assure you, I'm perfectly comfortable."

"I promise to give you more scratching and biting," she pleaded.

"OK, in that case, I can wait," he purred and scooped her up in his strong arms.

Chapter 13

T he next morning, Dante and Emilie had a later breakfast, and then he surprised her with a helicopter tour of the island followed by a drive along the coast, searching for the best beach for snorkelling. He had rented her some gear from a little surf shop so she could maximize her time in the ocean.

Once they had made their choice of a spot for the afternoon, she headed directly into the water. He regretted that he couldn't join her, but the salt and the sun would scorch his sensitive skin. So he lay on a towel in the sand with his hands behind his head, staring up at the sky through the leaves of the palms, lost in self-reflection. He was growing concerned that he was giving too much of himself to Emilie. These thoughts were most distressing. He enjoyed loving her. He especially enjoyed making love to her, but he didn't enjoy feeling like he couldn't live without her. *Why can't I control my emotions?* he chastised himself. *I spend so much of my energy trying to please her in any way that she needs. It's strange and it's weak.*

He sighed heavily. Instead of being angry, he just found himself filled with contentment. Emilie seemed to be putting a lot of her own energy and imagination into pleasing him. He had been terrified of playing rough with her. It wasn't something he'd encourage with a human partner. His instincts to hunt and kill tended to mix with his instincts for sexual satisfaction. Combined with his strength, healing ability, and pain tolerance, it was a recipe for disaster.

But she had been much stronger than he had given her credit for. It had almost been like having sex with one of his kind, except that he didn't get to scratch and bite her. *She's going to be wild when she's transformed,* he mused. *Maybe I won't be able to handle her. I'm looking forward to finding out.*

The wind shifted suddenly and he was torn out of his fantasies by a familiar scent. He popped upright and cast about for its source. He found it at the top of the ridge pointing a camera at Emilie, who was facing away from them, waiting for a large enough wave to carry her to the shore.

Dante recognized the changeling scout as Carter Murphy. Dante took this opportunity to stalk his distracted prey. Keeping downwind of the scout, he planned his path carefully. Hidden by the trees, he walked directly below Carter and quickly made his way up through the wild guavas to where the man was standing. Carter had chosen his vantage point carefully and had done well to stay out of sight. But in his eagerness, he had strayed too close to a fellow hunter.

Carter had left his camera hanging around his neck by its strap and was craning his neck, trying to locate Dante through the foliage.

"Your camera, please," Dante purred, his hand outstretched.

The man was so taken off guard that he practically fell down the ridge. "M-Mr. M-Maxaviel," he stammered. "I didn't see you there."

"Obviously," Dante growled. "Kindly refrain from using that name out here."

"Sorry, sir. But that's an interesting choice of companion for a Dark Angel," he added, shifting his gaze back in Emilie's direction.

"She's none of your business."

"Perhaps we could work out a deal with her...and no one would have to find out."

Dante growled. "She's not a civilian, she's mine."

"Is she?" he asked. "Mind if I confirm that claim?"

"I could just yank you into mesay and leave you to starve."

Carter nodded, but swallowed hard. "Just doing my job, sir."

"Your camera," Dante repeated, his hand out again.

The scout sighed heavily but removed the camera from around his neck and handed it to Dante.

He turned it on and flipped through the pictures, stopping at one in particular. It had been taken from behind. He had his arm around Emilie's shoulders and her arm was around his waist. He was kissing her cheek and his profile was clearly identifiable. "Now this is an excellent shot," Dante said, showing the screen to other man, who seemed flattered by the remark.

"Do you want to make some real money?" Dante asked.

"Are you offering me a bribe, Mr. Max...I mean Mr. Ashton?"

"No, I mean you could sell this photo to someone else."

"And make more money than finding evidence against a nobleman out with his trophy?"

Dante laughed. The council paid very well for this type of information. "You can confirm my claim with my cousin Purson Maxaviel of the Montreal Office, but there won't be much money in it for you, and you'll make an enemy of me," he explained. "I know someone who will pay dearly for this photo, and I'd love to get him all excited for nothing."

"Really?"

"I'll give you his name and number if you promise to keep quiet about my being here."

"What if he doesn't pay me?"

"Oh, he will. But be sure to tell him that Elizabeth..." Dante began, then stopped as if he'd said something he shouldn't have. "The girl," he continued more guardedly, "is not human."

"Really," Carter said, furrowing his brow. "Unless my nose is deceiving me, she's human."

"Yes, but I don't want...my friend...to know that. Understand?"

"I don't know about this."

Dante reached into his trousers for his wallet. There wasn't much American cash to be found. "How about I sweeten the deal?"

Carter perked up and smiled hopefully.

"I'll set you up an account with the council office here that will be paid off for as long as I need your silence. But if I see any of these pictures on any gossip sites or get any questions from Purson, I'll be back, and you won't see me coming."

Carter shot one last look in Emilie's direction, but extended his hand for Dante to shake. "Deal."

Dante returned the camera and gave the man Gomez's number. "You can send as many pictures of me as you want, but no pictures of her face, clear?"

The scout nodded.

"By the way, we're leaving the island soon, and if I see your face again today, I may get violent."

"I'm sure I can find something else to do with my time."

"I'll call the office and have them set something up for you right away."

"Thanks," Carter said, looking as if he might want to add something but thought better of it.

As Carter walked off, Dante turned back to the beach. Emilie had emerged from the sea and was searching for him from the comfort of her towel.

Once he felt confident that the scout was gone for good, he headed back to his shady spot. On his way he purchased a tall, thin, blue-and-white-and-red popsicle from a merchant. He was feeling possessive and wanted to mark his territory.

Emilie looked pleased to see him with a cool treat for her. It also explained where he had been. She took the popsicle from him with a smirk. "Thank you," she said.

"My pleasure," he purred and walked back into the shade to watch her eat it. She understood his intentions perfectly and put on a phenomenal show. Many other masculine eyes watched her running her tongue over the phallic-shaped object with porn star enthusiasm. Dante sniggered to himself, but his reaction to her performance was stronger than he had anticipated. Hopefully she would tire of the beach soon so he could get her back into bed.

⚘

On their way back to the apartment, they dropped off the snorkel gear. They were going to watch the sun set for the last time this weekend, then go out to one of Dante's favorite Thai restaurants before spending the night at Emilie's apartment.

As they got off the elevator, she realized that she had yet to try Dante's jet tub in the master bathroom. A quick bath after an afternoon at the beach was a wonderful idea. She had actually bought some bubble bath at the grocery store just for this occasion.

Emilie was soaking happily when Dante appeared with a glass of wine for her. She took it from him as he admired her bubble outfit. She asked, "Why don't you join me?"

He looked at her incredulously and replied, "There isn't enough room for the two of us in there."

"Sure there is. It'll be cozy."

He smiled mischievously as he made up his mind. "OK," he announced as he stripped, leaving his clothes on the tile floor in a heap.

She stood up and let him step in with her.

"Wow, you take hot baths," he complained, but grabbed her and pressed her sudsy body against his. "Hmmm…You're nice and warm." He ran his hands over her, trying to wipe off some of the bubbles.

"You sit down first and I'll try to fit between your legs so I can lean back against your chest," she suggested, feeling the chill of the air-conditioned room seeping through the rather poor insulation of the suds.

"I would rather be between your legs," he purred, running his hands over her skin more firmly.

"Fine, you naughty boy," she said, shaking her head in mock frustration. She sat down and patted the water between her legs. He turned around and gingerly took his seat. It was a tight fit, but with a few minor adjustments, they were in. She gently splashed some water up Dante's chest. It was funny to see his big knees poking up out of the water. He wasn't very well submerged, but he wasn't complaining.

Emilie had an urge for a little mischief. She started building an elaborate hat out of bubbles on the top of his head. He laughed quietly to himself. "What on earth are you doing, you silly woman?" he asked, shaking his head back and forth.

"Hold still!" she scolded. "I'm making you a hat."

He laughed again but stopped struggling. After some creative sculpting, she managed to get a respectable pointy hat to stand up stiffly on his head. Now all he needed was a pointy beard to go with it. She peeked over his shoulder and began sticking handfuls of bubbles to his chin.

"Now what?" he demanded suspiciously, spitting bubbles away from his mouth.

"You need a beard," she said as if it was completely obvious.

"I can grow one for you if you like."

"Can you grow one right away?" she asked curiously. She wouldn't be surprised if he could.

"No." He laughed as though it was completely ridiculous, but how was she supposed to know? He could do all sorts of other special things.

Emilie burst out laughing, but for a different reason altogether. She had been hoping for more of a garden gnome look, but Dante was beginning to resemble Santa Claus instead.

"Stand up carefully and look at yourself in the mirror," she ordered, trying to suppress her laughter.

He was far too curious to refuse, so he stood up and admired her work in the mirror above the sink across the room. He burst out laughing, shaking off all of her hard work.

Some bubbles had inadvertently been transferred from his face to hers as she had worked on his beard, and it had given her an idea. She started building industriously on her own head and face. "You look like Santa Claus," she teased while he stood, admiring himself.

"Oh! Great!" he grumbled, scooping huge handfuls off of himself and flapping bubbles all over the bathroom. Then he knelt back in the water facing her. "Hey, little girl, why don't you come over here and sit on my lap?" he purred. He was trying to be serious but was having trouble keeping a straight face as her beard grew bigger.

She stared him right in the eye as she brought her index finger up to her chin. She made a buzzing noise and pretended to be shaving herself with an electric razor. He laughed so hard that she was worried he might slip and hurt himself.

"My turn!" he said, kneeling between her legs. He reached around himself and gathered up all of the remaining bubbles.

She held still so he could create his own bubble masterpiece. She felt very sentimental, gazing into his beautiful, playful face. She wanted to reach out and hold him. *Must be PMS*, she thought hopefully to herself. "I love you," she whispered, her new beard flopping around on her chin as she spoke.

Dante smirked at her as though she was the strangest thing he had ever seen. "I'm afraid I can't possibly take you seriously with your hat and beard."

She just laughed.

He continued, "You know...I've never been attracted to men before, but there's something irresistible about you."

Emilie spoke in her deepest, raunchiest voice, "Come over here and give me a kiss, big boy."

He started laughing too hard to respond to her, so she crept forward and kissed him. Bubbles squished all over their faces and into their mouths. His lips felt so good. The bath jets had stopped bubbling, and Emilie was ready to get out of the tub and into his bed.

She drank the rest of the wine out of her glass. "You stand up and I'll rinse the bubbles off of you. I don't want you to get all itchy later with soap dried to your skin."

He looked at her oddly but complied. She proceeded to pour wine glasses full of warm water from the tap over him.

"Penny for your thoughts," she said as she shooed him out of the bathtub and started rinsing herself.

Dante wrapped himself in a towel and replied in a petulant tone, "My thoughts are worth more than that."

"OK then...Are we going to haggle?"

He looked her over oddly again and shook his head. "I find it strange that you're trying to take care of me."

She was distracted with her rinsing. "What are you talking about?"

"You're always thinking about me. I mean, about what I want and what I need. You're worried about my skin, or whether or not I'm too hot or too hungry. You pay attention to everything and you fuss. I find it strange."

"Am I getting on your nerves?" she asked, stepping out of the tub and into the towel he was holding open for her.

"You might eventually, but for now I find it really sweet. I'm not used to anyone paying so much attention to me. I'm going to get spoiled."

"What do you mean, *going* to get spoiled?" she teased.

"You can pay people to do anything for you, but you can't pay them to care about you, that's something very different. Maybe I just need therapy because my mother died when I was a baby and I now have 'issues' because no one mothered me as a child."

Dante pretended to sniff and sob, but Emilie could tell that he was just trying to escape from the conversation before it got any more emotional. She let him walk out of the bathroom. He was new to this whole relationship thing and she didn't want him to feel emotionally invaded. He could share what he wanted, when he wanted to, and she would pick her battles. The important thing was that he was happy, and that made her happy too.

Chapter 14

The first thing Dante did after he said good-bye to Emilie at her apartment was to go see Jim and Eliza Robertson, the managers of his building. Once he had reviewed the security footage, asked all the questions he needed to have answered, and reassured the couple of their safety, he returned to his condo.

"I'm back!" he called.

Jude poked his head out of his room and said, "So how'd it go."

"It was fantastic." Dante headed for his bedroom to change. He was wearing something from his wardrobe in Hawaii, and it wasn't appropriate for late November in Montreal. "Did Colin show up?"

"No, as you predicted, he's been at the temple all weekend long."

Dante's religious master, Michael Enasvant, was holding a special weekend retreat at the temple in Thailand. Colin had insisted that Dante attend, but he had refused. He had looked his spiritual advisor and lifelong friend in the eyes and lied right to his face. Dante had claimed that important work prevented him from joining Colin. He had been furious, but he had accepted the excuse.

"Are you hungry?" Jude asked through Dante's bedroom door.

"Always," Dante answered, thinking immediately of Emilie.

Jude opened the door and peeked in. "So are we still going out to eat?"

"Absolutely, I'm starved."

"You're in a good mood," Jude commented, but his tone suggested something entirely different.

Dante stared into his closet, trying to figure out what he wanted to wear. "Why shouldn't I be?"

"Because your life is crashing down around you so that you can have a fling with a human girl."

"Emilie means more to me than that, Jude."

"Still? I was hoping you'd be bored with her by now."

Dante turned toward Jude, grinning like the Cheshire Cat. "I'm going to marry that girl, as soon as possible."

Jude sighed irritably. "You can't be serious!"

"Why not?"

There was a hint of sympathy in Jude's eyes. "Listen, I like Emilie. She's good looking and she obviously adores you. She's nice, for a human."

"It was fantastic living with her, but I'm exhausted." Dante rolled his eyes suggestively.

"Listen, why don't you just get a little place and set her up like a proper mistress? Then you can visit her as much as you like and when you get bored, and you will get bored, then you can have her for a snack."

Jude's words hurt Dante more than he cared to admit. He knew that Jude was only trying to protect him. For Dante to believe that Emilie would be seen as anything other than his human mistress was unrealistic. And yet, despite the logic of that conclusion, he remained frustrated. He didn't see her that way. No matter what anybody expected, he wasn't going to use her until he was bored and then kill her. He wasn't a demon, even if he wasn't exactly behaving like an angel. He shuddered, thinking of how horrific it would be to watch the life fade from her bewitching eyes.

"You do realize that your hunting license is designed for that purpose?" Jude asked. He seemed confused by Dante's angry expression.

"I'm well aware of the purpose of a hunting license, thank you. I am Beyowan."

"Really? I was beginning to wonder. You seem to be going native on us here, talking about being monogamous and marrying human civilians. Next you'll be using birth control."

"You just don't understand!" Dante snarled. He locked eyes with his friend and glared at him as though Jude lacked the capacity to comprehend.

"What I understand is that, three months ago, you wouldn't have given a human girl the time of day, forget a marriage contract."

Dante knew it was the truth. He wasn't going to try to deny anything. "So? What's your point?"

Jude threw his hands in the air. "You're the same arrogant, classist bastard who would rather go home unsatisfied from a club than to go to bed with anyone less than worthy of you."

Dante was offended. He wasn't a bastard. "Oh, come on! I'm picky. I've always been picky. Plus we have rules about impregnating changelings in those clubs. I don't want to have to marry anybody. I want to choose my wife."

"Colin doesn't care. He's like a kid in a candy store in those places," Jude remarked reverently.

"Even Colin keeps away from the changelings," Dante corrected. "But he would be happy to marry anyone that could give him a child at this point. That's not the kind of life I want for myself."

"You would have married Tasia," Jude pointed out.

Dante nodded. "I would have. Past tense. She's pregnant, you know," he mentioned, trying to change the subject.

Jude's face brightened. "Really? Weren't you just with her in September?"

"Yes, but don't get yourself all excited. I'm not the father. I'm on the list, though, which still makes me proud. It feels good to be on a paternity list."

"I wouldn't know," Jude grumbled enviously.

"You keep yourself pretty busy in the clubs. You're bound to get somebody pregnant at some point," Dante soothed.

As Dante riffled absently through his shirts, Jude shifted his weight back and forth as though he had something he wanted to get off of his chest. Finally he said, "You know, they've nick-named you 'The Ice Prince' at a couple of the council offices. It seems to be catching on too. It's because you're still unmarried and you treat the women you have sex with like appliances. Why are you such a cold bastard?"

"Quit calling me a bastard, you bastard!" Dante snapped, and they both burst out laughing. "And yes, I know about all of that." He paused and waved his hand dismissively. "That receptionist was a psycho, and I only make reservations at the council offices when I'm feeling desperate. I'm not there to make friends."

"I'm not telling you to be friendly. I'm just saying that you won't have anyone willing to be put on your fantasy list if you aren't at least a little bit nice."

"Oh, I'm nice enough to most of those girls and I've had many back in my bed for repeat performances, so they couldn't have been too offended by my behavior. I just jump out before they get their breath back enough to start talking to me. Plus I've put my name on quite a few lists and I keep getting calls, so there you go... Ice Prince..."

Jude snorted his approval. "You are a dirty animal. I have to respect you for that."

"Thanks...But those days are over for me now. I'm finally ready to settle down." Dante was frustrated to see the cheerful grin fall off of Jude's face. "What's so bad about that?"

"Now you want to marry a little vampire. That, my friend, is what's so bad."

Dante seethed. "Emilie won't be a vampire. She'll be changing for me, not so she can be young and beautiful for the rest of her life. Or so she can run around having sex with everyone and drinking blood like so many other crazy human volunteers."

"Why don't you just live with her for a while?" Jude pleaded. "She's human. She'll start whining and complaining, and then she'll get demanding. She'll probably even start denying you physically. Soon you'll be bored and fed up, and then you can get rid of her and marry a good Beyowan woman who won't want to be bothered with you any more than you'll want to be bothered with her—outside of the bedroom at least."

Dante tried to hide his discouragement at Jude's harsh words. All he wanted was to build a family with his soul mate.

Jude paused introspectively for a moment. "It's going to be so much fun for you, having sex with a fertile human girl."

Dante had to close his eyes quickly as he remembered how wonderful Emilie's scent had been on that night when he had almost abandoned all reason and given in to his instincts. "I think I'm going to keep away from Emilie when she's fertile. I don't have very good self-control."

Jude snorted. "Who does? I pay a premium to get access to the occasional fertile human girl at the council office, but they're usually reserved for you spoiled princes to make more little bastards."

Dante rolled his eyes. Jude wasn't supposed to be having sex with human girls either, but then Jude had never fully embraced religious life. "I keep away from human girls as a rule, so I wouldn't know."

"Oh man, they're fun! So soft and docile. And don't forget the intoxicating scent. Hmmm…I think I'm going to have to make another reservation. There's always such a long waiting list."

"Whatever works for you, my friend. I'm happy with my own human girl. But I don't want to get her pregnant just yet."

"How do you know that she isn't already?" Jude asked, winking at him.

Jude would never let him live down the fact that he was using birth control with a human girl, so Dante just chose to keep quiet about the main reason for his confidence. "She's not, and I'd know. We'll see what happens in this next week, though." Dante turned his attention back to his clothes.

"Are we going to eat or just sit here blabbing all day?" Jude grumbled. Before Dante could answer, he turned and started walking out of the room.

"Just let me change."

"Hurry up!" Jude ordered, closing the door behind him.

Dante sighed heavily. If those closest to him were so against his choice of bride then what would everyone else think? His life was about to get very complicated indeed.

֍

Mondays were always rough, but this one was the worst. After spending the entire weekend with Dante, Emilie was having difficulty returning to her regular weekly routine. She had said good-bye to him that morning and was now taking a lunch break between classes.

She was sitting in the food court waiting for Caroline and was absently playing with the charms on the silver bracelet Dante had given her as a souvenir of their weekend together. There was an elegantly scripted letter *D*, a letter *E* decorated with clear gems, a sun, a turtle, a wine glass, an angel, and more, but she particularly liked the little treasure chest with the heart in it. It was difficult having a secret love. She and Dante had enough challenges in their relationship. Keeping it secret made it so much worse.

She didn't notice Caroline approach. "That's new," she said, looking at her curiously.

Emilie yanked her wrist off the table and stuffed it in her lap. She stared up at Caroline wide eyed, without a hint of a smile.

Caroline laughed uncomfortably and sat down in the seat next to Emilie. "What was that about?"

"Nothing," Emilie replied, trying to wipe the panicked look off of her face. Caroline knew about her relationship with Dante. She didn't have to worry about talking to her…about most things.

"Somebody bought you a present," Caroline suggested. "Somebody whose name starts with a *D*."

Emilie could feel the color rising up her face. "Yes, somebody whose name starts with a *D* bought me a present," she whispered, smiling broadly.

"You be careful with that guy."

"I've told you before, Dante's harmless."

"So you've finally convinced him to take your relationship to the next level?" Caroline asked, smiling devilishly.

"Yes, finally."

Caroline leaned in closer. "So…How was it?"

Emilie smiled dreamily. "Fine."

Caroline shook her head. "The look on your face suggests that it was more than just fine."

"Maybe! But I'm not gonna kiss and tell."

"I'm worried about you. Are you sure you're OK?"

Emilie was confused. "What do you mean?"

Caroline responded by holding her hand out. "Let me see that bracelet."

Emilie brought her wrist out for Caroline's inspection. Caroline pushed the bracelet out of the way and pointed at the bruises that were healing nicely up and down Emilie's forearm.

"This is why I'm worried. What's he doing to you?" Caroline demanded, glaring at Emilie as though she was anticipating some kind of cover up.

Emilie snatched her arm away. She hadn't even noticed the bruises much before. She had asked Dante to play rough with her and he had. How could she explain that to Caroline without making Dante look bad?

"I don't know what to say," Emilie mumbled. She didn't want to appear as though she was trying to avoid the question.

Caroline was obviously getting impatient. "What's going on?"

Emilie smiled uncomfortably. "We played a bit of a rough game. That's all."

Caroline leaned back in her chair, staring at Emilie with a doubtful expression, eyebrows raised speculatively. "A game?"

Emilie sighed deeply. "Yes, a game. Stop looking at me like that. I asked him to play it and he didn't want to hurt me."

Caroline snorted in disbelief. "I've known you for a long time and you've never gotten bruised by any of your other boyfriends. You can't expect me to believe that you've suddenly developed all sorts of fetishes. Dante seems more like the kinky type. There's something not quite normal about that guy."

"It's complicated," Emilie answered cryptically. She was surprised at how perceptive Caroline could be.

"Complicated?" Caroline sneered.

Emilie nodded. She had no intention of going into details.

"Just be careful. You're too emotionally attached to that man, and I'm afraid you're gonna get seriously hurt." Caroline reached across the table and patted Emilie's hand sympathetically.

She wasn't trying to be malicious. She had a legitimate concern. Emilie was in love with a demon. She was in the perfect position to get seriously hurt, both emotionally and physically. But she trusted Dante and had never been happier in her life. "I'm going to be careful, Caroline."

"OK then. Let's get something to eat." Caroline didn't seem completely satisfied. "What were you doing all weekend? I called you a bunch of times, but I just got your voice mail."

"I turned my phone off so I could get some studying done," Emilie lied. She tried as discreetly as possible to avoid meeting Caroline's gaze.

"Funny…you look tanned."

Emilie just rolled her eyes and laughed uncomfortably. Keeping secrets was going to be harder than she thought.

Chapter 15

A couple of days after their return from Hawaii, Emilie sat in class, staring at Professor Ashton. She wanted to see if she could find Dante in his features somewhere. He was a handsome man for his age—over a hundred and fifty. He was in good shape too. Emilie wondered how much camouflage he used or if that was his everyday look. She concluded that Dante must look more like his mother. She didn't see much of a resemblance between father and son. Professor Ashton had light brown, slightly curly hair and blue eyes.

After the lecture, she headed for the exit, completely lost in her thoughts. This was her last class of the day and she was eager to go home. It was December already and final exams were about to begin. There was much to prepare. As she walked past Professor Ashton, she noticed him looking at her strangely.

"Emilie, do you have some time to talk?" he asked.

"Sure. I was just on my way home," she answered, blushing. She had also been thinking about what she would like to be doing with his son.

"Can you meet me in my office? I'll be right there. I'd like to talk to you about something privately."

"Sure," she answered, but the seriousness of his expression concerned her. Was she in trouble in some way? She had become so distracted with Dante recently that her studying had suffered.

Professor Ashton's office door was closed, and she almost stood beside it to wait for him. Instead she gave the handle a try and was rewarded to find it unlocked. With only a moment's hesitation, she walked in, took off her coat, and sat in one of the two chairs facing his desk.

Her memories transported her back to that fateful day when she had stood staring at Dante while he snoozed in the chair across from her. She still couldn't believe that he had purposefully waited for her. She was completely lost in thought and playing with the charms on her bracelet again when she heard a voice from behind her.

"I was wondering if we could discuss your relationship with my son."

The door clicked shut, and she turned to see Professor Ashton hang up his coat on his way around his desk. He seemed to be examining her in a most critical manner. This promised to be awkward. How was she supposed to talk about Dante with his father? She didn't know how much he knew or what she was allowed to say. Keeping secrets was not her forte.

"I have been worried about Dante lately. He disappeared this past weekend and it isn't like him to be so mysterious," Professor Ashton said, sorting through a pile of papers on his desk.

"He left for Bangkok on Monday. He'll be back from Asia on Friday."

Professor Ashton's gaze drifted slowly back to hers. He looked as though he was trying to figure out exactly what she did and didn't know about his son.

"You seem to know quite a bit about his schedule. I wonder if he knows as much about yours," he mused.

Emilie laughed out loud. He was so much like his son. Saying things that had more than one meaning. Without realizing it, she blurted, "Is everything with you demons about sex?" *Oops!* she realized.

A big toothy grin spread across his face. Perhaps his appreciation for her insight would distract him from the insult.

"Has my son switched his religious affiliations without my knowledge?"

Emilie swallowed hard as Professor Ashton ran his fingers over his own angel charm, hanging on a chain around his neck. "Not that I know of, sir."

"He doesn't normally tolerate being classified in that way," he said darkly. "I've known him to put people in the hospital for less of an insult."

Emilie had a hard time imagining Dante being that violent with anyone, but his father obviously knew him better. "I've been careful. He's made his feelings about the subject quite clear."

"It would seem that you know my son a lot better than I first imagined."

The realization clearly made him anxious. She wanted assure him that she wasn't going to put his son in any danger. "I promised him that I wouldn't tell anyone about what he is, and until now I haven't."

"The organization he works for is not the only thing that keeps tabs on his extra-curricular activities. I hope he's made the risks clear to you."

"He has."

"Good." He paused and shook his head. "Have you noticed that my son, who claims to want to blend in with humans and not draw attention to himself, seems to dress in ways that make him stand out in a crowd?"

Emilie had to laugh. "He is colorful in his wardrobe choices at times."

Professor Ashton smiled. "He has an obsession with mythical creatures, especially Chinese dragons."

"I've noticed the dragons."

"He loves all animals, especially ones with sharp teeth or venom, like spiders or snakes. Why do you think he drives a Jaguar? He owns a Viper and a classic Mustang, for that matter, but he really loves his Ferrari Spider. Now that's a machine..." Professor Ashton laughed. "And we can't forget the angels, of course."

He paused in his thoughts, and Emilie shook her head thinking about all of the animals that Dante was deliberately using to define himself and his world. Professor Ashton continued, "Have you noticed that he uses characters or pictographs in foreign languages, both ancient and modern, to describe himself?"

"Yes," Emilie added, amused that she'd never made the connection before. "He wore a shirt with the Japanese character for 'fortune' once."

Professor Aston laughed. "Sounds like him. He has quite a few that mean 'animal,' 'darkness,' 'danger,' and so forth." He paused again and laughed a bit uncomfortably before adding, "He does have a fondness for fertility symbols as well."

Emilie couldn't help sniggering. It was something she could see Dante advertising about himself.

"I have to tell you this story," Professor Ashton began, shifting in his chair. "Once when Jude and Dante were training together, Jude got over-competitive and pulled a bit of a dirty move on Dante, breaking his arm in two places and cracking three of his ribs."

"Wow!" she exclaimed. "Those guys play rough, don't they?"

"They may or may not have been training with weapons. I wasn't there myself. Anyway, Dante almost never beats Jude in a fight. That's one of the main reasons we hired Jude in the first place. While Dante was healing, he went to every public market, in every dangerous city, wearing a shirt with big bull's-eye targets on the front and back. It was only for a week or so, but Jude almost had a heart attack. He already felt horrible for injuring his friend, but Dante wanted to make sure that Jude shared in his discomfort. My son can be evil when it suits him."

"Dante's lucky he didn't get shot."

Professor Ashton snorted. "He's been shot so many times, I've actually lost count." Emilie was about to reply when Professor Ashton asked, "Have you ever seen him in a fight?"

"I was at one once, but I didn't get to see him fight," she explained, trying not to think too much about that terrible night with Ethan.

"He used to compete. Now, mind you, he's not allowed to use his ability in a competitive fight." He paused. "Do you know about his special ability?"

She nodded.

"Even without it, he's faster, stronger, and smarter than men with purer blood and more experience. He still holds some records even though he hasn't competed in a long time. With his ability to move through space he'd be almost untouchable. He's never had a vacant spot in any of his martial arts classes and is highly respected by his peers."

"That doesn't surprise me."

Professor Ashton paused introspectively for a second. "We all have our prejudices, don't we? We all know in our hearts that it's wrong to judge people in these ways, yet we consistently treat others disrespectfully. Color, religion, and social class are still issues for you humans. Class, blood, and family are the issues for us. If you weren't born Beyowan then you're not Beyowan and never will be. Did he tell you about what I am?"

Emilie nodded again.

"Even with his tainted blood, Dante is still arrogant about his birth. I believe that we have more prejudices about class than humans have about everything else put together. Even Dante will occasionally rant about dirty little vampires."

"Dante's tried to explain a few things about Beyowan social structure," she said, trying to sort through a list of questions she would love to have answered. He understood the human perspective and had a way of explaining complex topics in very simple terms. "Dante mentioned a black market for venom. What's that exactly?"

"Do you already know that there are two types of venomous Beyowans?"

"Yes. I know. There's the venom that turns a human into one of you, and the venom that turns one of you into dust."

"Exactly." Professor Ashton obviously enjoyed this topic and dove into it with enthusiasm. "All of our society is built and run on the international cross-species trade in venom. Mostly the venom that turns humans. It has wonderful properties far more useful than turning humans, although you would be surprised how many humans want to change. In droplets it can accentuate humans in ways that give them Beyowan abilities without having to change permanently."

Emilie was curious. "Which Beyowan abilities can humans acquire without being changed?"

"Excellent question. It's absolutely amazing. For professional athletes it can give them speed, strength, endurance, pain resistance, and to a certain degree, even regenerative powers. It isn't detectable on any doping tests, but it does have side effects. It can make some humans much more instinctive, meaning that they become more volatile and consequently more violent. Their instinctive appetites can easily get out of control. It all depends on the human and the amount of venom used. Another serious side effect is often sterility.

"I believe that many myths about the fountain of youth have been based on the use of venom over the generations. Most have to do with drinking water or wine laced with venom. Nowadays taking venom is simple. It's mostly sold in little gel caps mixed with mineral oil, but I've heard it's sold in bulk to the cosmetic and food industries.

"It does wonders for the skin and complexion. It's excellent for shedding unwanted fat and even converting fat to muscle, but it's almost impossible to maintain a venom-induced body. Your increased appetite for food sabotages that fairly quickly. Actually, drinking blood is a very efficient way of maintaining a venom-induced body, but it's difficult to do that unnoticed for long. Some women are thought to be anorexic because they're never seen eating, but it's not always that simple. I'm not trying to belittle eating disorders in humans. I'm just suggesting that not everything is as simple as it appears.

"Venom has military applications as well. It's excellent for Special Forces units. Soldiers are faster, stronger, more aggressive, able to see, hear, and smell better, plus the ability to heal. Unlimited possibilities, really."

Emilie was fascinated. "What about changed humans? Do they acquire any other innate Beyowan abilities, such as travelling through inter-dimensional space?"

"Not really, no. Changelings get longevity and surface abilities like camouflage." He smiled as he said this and the skin of his face flashed bright fuchsia. "They also acquire Beyowan instincts, which many find difficult to control. But no changeling has ever gained powers such as inter-dimensional travel or venomousness. You have to be born with those."

Another thought occurred to Emilie. "You mentioned the military. So governments are aware of Beyowans and trade for venom?"

"Yes, absolutely. We could hardly stay hidden without government complicity. As long as council offices manage their affairs quickly, quietly, and efficiently, plus pay their fees and fines, governments are willing to turn a blind eye. In fact, few of the humans involved are truly aware of the origins of venom. They probably believe it's synthetically manufactured. Human governments, and even organized crime, have been trying for years to perfect such a formula, but thus far their best efforts have been only marginally effective."

"Organized crime? Why would they keep Beyowan secrets?"

"Many human criminals work alongside our kind. As a matter of fact, both species often work together in profitable partnerships. I believe many people owing money to organized crime end up with service contracts at the council offices. Everybody wins, except of course those with uncomfortable service contracts to pay off. You see, many of you want our venom and many of us want access to your bodies and blood."

Emilie was impressed—terrified, but impressed. The market for something like venom must be very lucrative indeed, and Dante had said that venomous Beyowans just sit back and get milked like snakes, selling their venom for profit.

"No wonder Galen was anxious to marry Dante's mother," she mumbled. Then she realized what she had said and quickly covered her mouth with her hand and stared at Professor Ashton, wondering if she'd touched on a delicate subject.

So far he had not seemed at all surprised about the extent of her knowledge of the Beyowan world, but this statement had taken him off guard.

"My son has obviously shared a great deal with you," he whispered, then paused for a moment. "I don't believe many venomous Beyowans have been born since her death." He paused again, his grief evidently still raw. After a moment he drew a breath and asked, "Did you know that venom is hereditary?"

"No, I had no idea."

"Dante's grandfather Dorian was venomous, and Dante's mother, Delilah, was venomous. Everyone was hoping that Dante would be venomous. When it turned out he wasn't, they all blamed my dirty blood, but he still carries the gene. Truthfully, I'm glad he isn't. He'd probably be dead by now if he was. I had a hard enough time protecting him before his ability came in. We had three body guards killed before he was ten years old. Everyone knew that he was heir to a fortune, and I couldn't protect him on my own. If it wasn't for his grandfather, I don't know what would have happened to him. He was always a target for kidnapping. His ransom would have been very profitable. I believe that he developed his ability to travel through mesay as a defense mechanism."

Poor Dante, Emilie thought sadly. *What a horrible childhood.* He had lost his mother at birth. He was brought up by his lower-class father with the help of his grandfather, only to live in constant fear for his life.

Professor Ashton continued, "Once Dante got older, stronger, and could travel in mesay, the attempts against him lessened."

He started digging in his desk drawers for something. Emilie didn't know what to say. She found this all terribly depressing, but also extremely interesting. She felt a pang of guilt for milking Dante's father of all of this information. She didn't know if Dante wanted her to know any of this. Still, she wanted to find out as much as she could. Professor Ashton seemed willing to talk and she was willing to listen.

"Here he is at five years old," Professor Ashton said, handing Emilie a very old picture. She looked at it and smiled affectionately. Dante was the cutest thing she had ever seen, with longish curly hair and big brown eyes.

"He's so adorable," she cooed, handing the picture back.

"This is his mother before he was born," he said wistfully, handing her another picture.

Emilie was very curious to see that one. Even with everything that she understood about Beyowans, she was unprepared for what she saw. Dante's mother was the most beautiful woman she had ever seen. She looked exactly like an Egyptian princess. She had long, dark hair, beautiful golden skin, and dark eyes. She looked proud and happy, with her hands wrapped around her big belly.

"She was beautiful," Emilie said, handing the picture back. Dante definitely resembled his mother's side of the family, but the gold in his eyes and the slight curl in his hair must be from his father.

Professor Ashton looked at the picture, smiled sadly, and whispered, "Yes, she was." Then he tucked the pictures away in his desk.

"I believe that protecting Dante was one of the reasons his grandfather wanted to rush him into the business. Did Dante tell you about his job or how he got Colin in his life?"

Emilie was sure that he was trying to change the subject. These memories must be very painful for him. Dante had trouble talking about his mother for long without getting emotional, and he never even knew her. His father would have far more pain to hide behind his brave face. "No, but I'm sure it's an interesting story," she encouraged.

"I was hoping Dante would choose a life more like Colin's. A peaceful, intellectual, and religious life. Not that I consider myself a religious man, but he wouldn't be at any risk in that kind of life. His grandfather, of course, had other ideas.

"If you think human teenage boys are hormonally driven and easily corrupted, then be thankful you've never met any Beyowan teens. What a nightmare! I would have had to literally tie Dante up if I wanted to keep him in the house, but I would have had to catch him first. I was lucky that he was easily manipulated with guilt and his love for his mother or I would have lost him completely before he hit seventeen."

Emilie could see Dante being a handful. He was used to getting his own way.

"If you want to corrupt a teenage boy, you offer him the standard things: money, drugs, or sex. Dante had money. And drugs are not very effective on Beyowans because their blood cleanses and detoxifies so quickly that it doesn't have a lasting effect. Dante is partial to morphine and cocaine, but he likes to be in control too much to make himself vulnerable through intoxication. So that leaves sex."

Emilie rolled her eyes. She'd immediately come to that conclusion.

"Dante's grandfather threw him a sweet sixteen party that he'll never forget—without my knowledge or consent. When I got him back, I was shocked. He almost collapsed into semi-conscious hibernation. I didn't know what had happened to him. He was incoherent and vomiting blood. He was a complete physical wreck. I thought I would have to have him hospitalized. I didn't know right away that he wasn't vomiting his own blood." Professor Ashton paused and sighed deeply, lost in his memories.

Emilie didn't know if she really wanted to hear any more of this story. She didn't want to think about Dante behaving like a vampire, but she was desperately curious to hear what had happened to him. After all, she wasn't one to judge. Everyone did stupid things as teenagers. She certainly had. It was part of growing up.

"Dante's grandfather was on the Bangkok Council and had many significant problems that Dante's employment contract could resolve. Therefore his grandfather had made him an offer of employment to get him into the business and bought Dante's full cooperation. He went so far as to bind Jude to a contract as well." Professor Ashton rolled his eyes disapprovingly, making it obvious that he thought both Jude and Dante had been naughty, horny little monsters.

He paused momentarily to inspect what Emilie hoped was her well-masked expression. He seemed satisfied and continued. "He showed a sheltered, easily influenced young man the kind of life-style he could have if he worked for the council. Dante's contract contains some of the most generous professional privileges possible. This was not unexpected, but for someone as young as Dante was at the time, it was somewhat unwise."

"Dante has mentioned certain work benefits. Now it all makes a lot more sense to me," Emilie explained, feeling a bit uncomfortable. She didn't like to think about all of the many privileges that he had been exercising for all of these years.

Professor Ashton continued, "Anyway, I figured if he was going to have his grandfather influencing him toward vice then I had to find something to keep him somewhat grounded. Enter Colin."

"I know a bit about Colin."

"I'm willing to bet a large sum of money that Colin doesn't know about you." He paused. "My dear, I don't know what kind of promises my son has made you, but I feel obliged to warn you that he's engaged to be married."

Professor Ashton had said this with sadness in his blue eyes. Emilie felt that he hadn't disclosed this information to be injurious. Perhaps he felt it was the right thing for everyone involved. "I know," she replied. "He told me."

"He did? Now that surprises me." He looked her over speculatively. "Did he tell you to whom he's engaged?"

"No, and I didn't ask," she answered. She didn't see how it mattered. The only thing of importance was the fact that he didn't want to marry the woman.

"His grandfather promised him to Galen's daughter as part of his settlement package when his marriage contract to Delilah was dissolved," Professor Ashton explained.

Emilie now knew exactly why Dante was avoiding this woman. There was no way he would marry any child of the man who had murdered his mother.

"Galen has an illegitimate daughter, for whom he needed to make a profitable marriage. She's his only child. I believe Dante's engagement has saved him from Galen over these years. That and the level of protection he's professionally guaranteed. He was supposed to be married shortly after his fiftieth birthday. He's paying a heavy fine, year after year, to postpone his wedding. It's a good thing that Dante makes so much money. He practically works solely to pay his fines to Galen's daughter.

"Talima will not inherit any of Galen's money, but her bank account is getting bigger and bigger every year that she isn't married to Dante. I think she's happier this way. She's getting his money, and she now has three other husbands to keep her busy. Dante, of course, will never forgive Galen for what he might have done to his mother. Because of my social position, I was never given any say in the decision. I do believe that if Dante fathered a child with Talima, Galen would have him killed before the child's umbilical cord was severed. Then Dante's child would get everything… except a father."

"How awful…" Emilie murmured. "Dante told me about his mother's death and that he wasn't looking forward to getting married. I can see why. It doesn't sound like a wise move for him."

Professor Ashton ruffled a small stack of manila envelopes on his desk and said, "He gets offers on a regular basis. He won't even look at most of them. He could easily find a good wife. He just doesn't want one. Some of the offers are from very good families as well. He's a very eligible bachelor."

Emilie didn't see Dante wanting to be any spoiled princess's boy toy. It wasn't his style.

"Has Dante mentioned marriage to you?"

He was fishing for more information than he was entitled to. "I'm not prepared to talk about that."

"There are a great many things you should consider before you begin making long-term plans with my son," he warned. "Do you know that you'll have to be transformed in order to become his wife?"

"I know what would be expected of me."

Professor Ashton nodded sagely. "It's considered a sin for a Dark Angel to have sex with or drink the blood of a human, but it's absolutely unacceptable to influence a human to volunteer."

"I know this as well, I'm afraid," Emilie said, trying to maintain a conversational tone, but she feared that the discussion was taking a rather negative turn and was trying to figure out how she could politely get up and leave before any other uncomfortable subjects were brought up. On the one hand, she was curious and wanted to know as much as possible about Dante. On the other, she was beginning to feel dirty inside, as though she was betraying him in some way.

"Do you know what he does for a living?" Professor Ashton asked, almost as though he could sense her hesitation and wanted to reel her more securely into the conversation.

"He's a messenger. I even have one of his business cards," she answered confidently.

"Yes, that's it in a nutshell. But do you know what he specializes in?"

"He told me that he gets paid very well because he's 'efficient.'" She suddenly realized that she really didn't know much about what he did for a living. It had never been an issue before.

Professor Ashton laughed softly. "That sounds like something he'd say. He's the best in his field. He could work twenty-four hours a day, seven days a week, and he still wouldn't be able to meet the demand for his talent. There's no one faster or safer. You see, he specializes in the transport of multi-million-dollar shipments of venom. He's the Beyowan equivalent of a drug runner." Professor Ashton glanced up at Emilie to see if he had finally taken her off guard.

Emilie tried to make her face a smooth and unreadable mask. She didn't want to look as though this was at all shocking to her. She even wanted to appear bored, as though she already knew or suspected this. She had known in her heart that Dante couldn't have been a mere letter carrier and felt foolish for not finding out more on her own. In general, people don't earn big bucks for carrying around paper. It would have to be something important—and dangerous. *Ignorance really is bliss*, she thought.

Professor Ashton was waiting to see if he should continue.

"How is Dante any better than the other messengers?" Emilie asked as calmly as she could. She only asked the question so that she could gain a moment to compose herself.

"Most Beyowans with Dante's talent hire themselves out for safer work as assassins, kidnappers, and thieves. Before he entered the business, it used to be difficult to transport venom from one place to another. There was always a scramble to intercept shipments. The fatality rate for both of our species used to be astronomical. There's always someone willing to risk life and limb to steal it. Not every council office has direct access to the stuff and some have to import all the venom they use and sell. It's expensive and dangerous. For example, the Montreal office is not big enough to have its own in-house supply. Dante carries all of their shipments exclusively, as well as many shipments for other offices around the world.

"To him it's just a box. Many other messengers want a cut of the shipment for their own profit as part of their fee. Sometimes shipments show up at their destinations lighter than when they left, or with substituted merchandise. Dante doesn't open his cases. He just carries them quickly and safely from one council lab to the next.

"Dante also couriers the most sensitive documents. He doesn't read them. He doesn't want to know. He doesn't make copies for sale. There's no risk of blackmail or leaked information. He's invaluable to them. The chairman of the council here in Montreal is actually distantly related to Dante through his grandfather, and it's my opinion that he's grooming Dante for an eventual council seat. Dante has his grandfather's shrewdness and his business sense. From the day his grandfather disappeared, they've been holding a seat for him, much to the frustration of many who would see themselves in it. Even at such a young age, many councillors had recognized his potential."

"I can tell that you're very proud of your son," Emilie stated, hoping to terminate the conversation on this positive note.

"I am," he replied. "I'm also very worried about him," he continued. "His involvement with you is obviously more serious than I first thought. I just wanted you to be aware of certain facts before you make any more permanent decisions," he said slowly. He stared down at his desk as he spoke. He looked up and added, "He has the right to marry more than one wife, you understand?"

"Yes, I do."

"I just find it so interesting that you, a young, modern, human woman, would be so open to something like this." Professor Ashton shook his head incredulously. "Can I ask you why?"

"I never said I was open," Emilie corrected stiffly. "I just said I was aware."

His expression changed immediately. "Ahhh. I understand now. You expect him to marry you monogamously. Which implies that you've already talked about this, and which also implies that he's thinking about getting out of his marriage contract with Galen."

Things were going from bad to worse. "You're assuming a great deal. Listen, I should be going." She stood up to leave.

"Please, Emilie. Hear me out. It's important."

"I don't know…"

"You may think you know Dante, but I'm sure he's keeping you in the dark about a great many things."

"I've already demonstrated just how much I know," she replied tersely.

"Yes, you have. But I haven't even begun to touch on the things I believe you're ignorant of."

"Really?" Emilie sneered, sitting down. "Fine then, enlighten me."

"Do you know Dante's real name?"

The confidence faded from her expression as she processed the significance of his question. How could she not know Dante's name? "You introduced us yourself," she argued.

"I had to use his human name."

"What?"

"You see, my dear. He hasn't been as open as you believe."

His condescension was not helping her composure. "What's his name?"

"His Beyowan name is Dante Maxaviel."

"He uses his mother's name?"

"Our world is not patriarchal. Whichever spouse has the higher social standing gets to pass on their family name. There's another matter that I'm sure he hasn't mentioned to you."

"I don't know if I want to hear this."

"He's expecting the results of a paternity test?"

"What am I supposed to say to that?" she demanded.

"There's a very special young lady Dante has always wanted to marry, but her father refuses to allow her to dirty her bloodline with him. If this child is his, he has to marry her...by law. He gets along well with her current husband as well. They've basically been sharing her for thirty years anyway."

Emilie knew immediately to whom he was referring. She had met this woman in the flesh. "This wouldn't happen to be Tasia?"

He looked at her in surprise. "Has he mentioned her?"

"I've met her and her husband, Gavin," she replied. "She and Dante have obvious chemistry."

"Tasia's pregnant."

Emilie felt like she was going to vomit. That was most likely the main topic of discussion between him and Tasia at the ballet. It also explained why Dante acted so guilty when questioned about the last time he had been with Tasia. This was horrible news. She was not willing to share Dante with any other woman, and especially not with Tasia.

"Beyowans don't have illegitimate children with each other, only with changelings and humans. By law, he will have to marry Tasia if he's the father, or he'll be killed before the baby is born."

While she was processing the magnitude of this revelation, he continued, "Has Dante ever mentioned to you what he would have to do to get out of his marriage contract?"

Emilie shook her head, still at a loss for words.

"Has he explained about the expression 'selling your soul to the Devil'?"

"Yes," she answered, feeling trapped and claustrophobic in Professor Ashton's little office.

"You're not the only one who will have to sell your soul for this marriage."

"What do you mean?"

"Dante can't afford to buy his way out of marrying Talima. He signed the engagement papers in blood, and they consummated the agreement."

"What?" Emilie's memories were failing her at the moment. "But he was a baby."

"The arrangements were made in his infancy. The engagement was finalized when he entered manhood. He's committed to Talima. There's only one way out for him."

"Which is?"

"He would have to offer the council something spectacular to get them to pay Galen on his behalf. At the minimum, he would have to spend the rest of his life working like a dog for free, but I frankly don't think they would agree to that. More than likely they would ask him to expand his services."

"Don't be cryptic," Emilie scolded.

"Dante would make a formidable killer if properly motivated. You can be certain this fact hasn't escaped the notice of the council. If he offered to become an assassin and a thief, they might be receptive to such an arrangement. Can you, in good conscience, ask him to pay this price for your love?"

"Why are you telling me this?" Emilie demanded. Alarm bells were sounding in the back of her mind. Dante had mentioned that he was working on a deal to get out of his marriage contact, but he hadn't given her the details. Could this be what he had in mind? Would he really go to this extreme?

Professor Ashton looked apologetic. "I don't mean you any offense. It's just that you need to know what he would have to do for a monogamous life with you. Dante's young, and he's never truly been in love. Believe me, I know what kind of crazy things people are willing to do for love. But one of the saddest truths is that it doesn't always last forever.

"Changelings are almost always sterile, Emilie. You might never be able to give him the child and heir he desperately needs and wants. He's young now, but later, when you're older, he could always take a mistress or another wife, whether you liked it or not. Someone younger, purer-blooded and fertile. Or he could just come to resent you for the rest of your life. Please, think carefully before you make any decisions."

"I would have thought that you, of all people, would have understood how we feel about each other," she complained, trying hard to keep her voice from cracking.

"I do," he replied with surprising gentleness. "That's why I'm compelled to warn you. If I could go back in time, I wouldn't change anything, only because I love my son with all of my heart. But I wouldn't have wished my life on my worst enemy. I almost died changing myself for my love. I had to live in hiding, only to end up watching helplessly as my soul mate died. Dante's grandfather kept me alive after her death just to revel in my suffering as I raised our son without her. I've had to live my life as a second-class citizen in a terrifying world. I'm protected through Dante and my own employment contract, but I've learned to watch my back. What would you do if Dante got bored and divorced you or, worse…got himself killed?"

Emilie was at a loss.

"You'd be just like me, only I have a son to look after me. You might not be so lucky, and you won't get a penny of his money. You could find yourself forced to work for the council. Not that there aren't any number of interesting career opportunities there. But some are less than desirable."

Emilie's memory flashed to the beautiful stranger from the museum and Dante saying that there were a lot of people who would be happy to see him stop working. Now she was beginning to understand just how serious the situation was. If Dante played such a key role in the venom trade, then he would always be at risk. It may just be a matter of time before someone caught him off guard.

She was desperate to get out of Professor Ashton's office. She put on her coat and picked up her things with trembling fingers. "I'll think about what you've said. But I'm not making you any assurances about my intentions," she announced with conviction. She was very close to losing her self-control but wanted to walk out of his office with the appearance of being unflustered.

"I'll see you later," he replied sympathetically, his gaze locked on his desk again. "I know you'll make the right decision."

Emilie walked slowly down the hall, but her thoughts threatened to overwhelm her. She quickened her pace. She needed to reach the security of her home.

As soon as the door clicked shut, tears welled up in her eyes and she began gasping for breath. *What am I supposed to do? How can I live without Dante? But how could I live with him knowing what he had to sacrifice in order to be with me. How can I ask this of him?*

Her phone rang. She had a text message from Dante that read: **Luv u!**

Emilie melted to the floor in tears.

Chapter 16

D ante was asleep far deeper than usual when he was startled awake. The clock read just after four in the morning in Bangkok. The sound that had drawn him from his slumber was the ringing of his phone. He picked it up and checked who was calling. It was Claudia. "Hello," he answered, worried.

"I'm sorry to wake you, sir," she whispered.

"What's wrong?"

"There's someone in the condo," she replied.

"Can you shut off the mesay sensor for me?"

"I'm in your bedroom now. I'll try to reach the panel without being noticed."

"Good, I'll be just a minute."

Claudia had hung up.

Dante sprang out of bed, hurried into some clothes, and grabbed his dart gun. He rushed into Jude's room to wake his bodyguard.

Jude's eyes were open before Dante even entered the room. "What's up?" Jude asked, sitting up.

"Claudia called. There's someone in the condo."

Jude leaped from his bed, grabbed the jeans he'd been wearing the previous evening, and was ready to leave in a heartbeat.

Dante took Jude by the hand and rushed to Montreal. He approached the doorway with caution. It took only a moment of searching to find the culprit rummaging around in the master bedroom. It was Leonard from Gomez's club. *Perfect*, Dante thought. *It'll be a pleasure to exterminate this pest.*

He turned to Jude and said, "Wait here and cover me from the doorway."

Jude nodded.

Dante led them out in the hall outside his bedroom door, then disappeared again to get hold of Leonard. Claudia had been discovered, and Leonard had her cowering in the corner. He was pointing a dart gun in her direction as he inspected Dante's personal possessions.

This was one of the times when Dante wished that he could fire a dart from inter-dimensional space. Unfortunately it didn't work that way. An individual had to be fully emerged from mesay in order to release something or someone. Otherwise, as soon as it left contact with the messenger, it was lost in the bottomless darkness of the portal.

Dante waited for Leonard to be adequately distracted and positioned to best advantage before he stepped out. "Claudia, down!" he ordered, as his left fist connected with Leonard's skull with bone-crushing force.

Leonard crumpled to the floor but quickly rolled over and pointed his dart gun at Dante, who had his own weapon out and ready.

"Looks like we're even," Leonard sneered, but he appeared to be making extra effort to focus his vision.

"Except that you're on the ground and I'm still standing," Dante explained. "Also Jude's in the doorway and you'll never be fast enough to outshoot him."

Leonard snarled and glanced over to confirm Dante's claim. He put his gun down on the floor and slid it in Dante's direction, putting his hands in the air submissively.

"Are you OK, Claudia?" Dante called as he kicked the gun to the other side of the room.

She poked her head out of the master bathroom and replied, "Yes, sir."

"Good."

"Now what shall we do with you?" Dante mused, returning his attention to Leonard.

"We have Eliza Robertson," Leonard announced, smiling maliciously.

"I was wondering how you got in here without setting off the alarm," Dante growled.

"Mr. Robertson was so much more cooperative once we had something he wanted."

"Let's give him to Purson as a gift," Jude suggested.

Dante's cousin was a true demon and indulged in the hunt. Some preferred little risk with their reward, but Purson particularly enjoyed young, strong males, especially changelings. Not that they had any chance of survival, but Purson always wanted as dangerous an experience as possible. Humans were not strong enough to provide an adequate thrill. They starved, dehydrated, or bled out too quickly. Plus they seemed to easily lose their will to live. For these reasons, changelings were highly sought after by extreme hunters.

"That's a marvellous idea," Dante replied. "My cousin knows how to maximize someone's suffering and stretch their physical strength to the absolute boundaries of endurance."

Leonard swallowed hard. Perhaps he was beginning to understand why so few changelings were willing to betray the council. "Aren't you supposed to be an angel?"

"I'm a Dark Angel, and my religion only has rules about humans. Technically, you're a servant of the Devil."

Dante took out his phone and took a picture of Leonard. Then typed:

You have something of mine and I have something of yours. Let's make a trade.

While he waited for a reply from Gomez, he asked, "So where's James?"

"Sid has him downstairs in the office."

"Perfect," Dante said.

His phone bleeped and he read:

My office.

"Jude, Leonard and I are going to drop in on Gomez. You go down and take care of Sid."

"My pleasure."

Dante typed:

Make sure she's ready to go or you'll have to deal with Purson instead of me.

"Mr. Gomez will want us both," Leonard argued.

"Sid wasn't included in the deal I made," Dante explained as he removed Leonard's phone and tossed it to Jude. "Now hold my hand carefully or you'll die a slow death lost in mesay."

Dante opened a mesay doorway and walked quickly to the club. He remained hidden within the threshold as he searched for Eliza, starting at the front and slowly working his way toward the back. He found her standing alone in the corner beside Gomez's large wooden desk, gagged and bound with her hands behind her back. There was a heavily armed man outside the office door, watching the hallway, and there were two men armed with dart guns in the small office with Gomez, guarding the only door in or out. Gomez stood behind his desk, talking on the phone and watching a live feed from the security camera at the front door to the club. An automatic weapon rested within easy reach on Gomez's desk beside a framed picture of his wife.

Dante took a second to plan his strategy. The room was crowded and he was outnumbered. Regardless of Eliza's ability to heal, he didn't want her injured in the exchange. He would have to move quickly if they were both to escape alive.

He lined himself up carefully beside Gomez. Unfortunately his chair was in Dante's way. He would have to come out of mesay and move the chair before he could get his hands on Gomez. He ignored Leonard's confident laughing and unhelpful commentary, took a deep breath, and stepped out. In only a few short seconds, Dante kicked the chair to the right of Gomez, crouched down behind the man, brought out Leonard, sprung up into the air, and toppled Leonard over the chair. As Dante landed, he wrapped an arm around Gomez's throat and used him as a shield as he stepped left, toward Eliza. He grabbed her with his other hand, shoved Gomez forward into the corner of the desk, and disappeared into mesay before anyone could adjust their aim.

After he had quickly verified that Eliza was unharmed, he headed back to his condo, hoping that there would be a happy ending to this incident. If Jude had failed to remove Sid, then James was most likely dead. Gomez would have ordered Sid to kill him and flee.

As soon as Dante entered the office, he saw Jude with James, unharmed.

Dante sighed out his relief and brought Eliza out with him. "How'd it go?" he asked Jude.

"I called Sid on Leonard's phone and mimicked his voice, claiming to have escaped. As soon as Sid poked his head out of the office to confirm, I shot him."

A council-created changeling would have been unlikely to fall for that trick. They were lucky that Sid had been an abomination, and obviously not a very smart one.

"I'm so sorry, Dante," James said with a heavy sigh.

"No, I'm sorry that you had to get caught in the middle of this mess."

Jude had removed Eliza's bindings and she and James embraced each other, leaving Jude and Dante trying to find something interesting in the office to admire.

"Check your Jaguar, Dante. I'm sure they planted some kind of tracking device on it," James added.

"I'm getting a new car," Dante replied. "Are there any vacant parking spots?"

"A couple."

"Good. I'll put my new car in a new spot and they won't be able to track me. Plus I'll do a thorough sweep of my condo and change all my alarm codes."

Dante was so relieved that he had never brought Emilie to the condo. Neither James nor Eliza had ever laid eyes on her and therefore had no information to give his enemy. Gomez still had nothing. In actual fact, he had less than nothing because now he was down one changeling.

His phone rang. Gomez had sent:

We need to talk.

Dante replied by sending the number to the council office. Gomez could make an appointment through proper channels. Dante planned on changing his phone too. "Jude, do you want to stay here or come to the office? I have to speak to Purson and take care of this mess."

"I'll stay and keep an eye on everything here."

"I'll be sending someone back for the car."

"No problem," James replied. "Thanks again, Dante."

He headed into mesay and made his way to the council office. Once he was done with everything, he had to go to work. He had a full delivery schedule, but he would try to visit Emilie on his lunch break. He needed to feel the comfort of her loving embrace.

※

Emilie heard something moving in the darkness of her bedroom. She opened her eyes and saw Dante's familiar shadow next to the bed. She swallowed hard. She didn't know what to say. He was taking off his clothes. She didn't know what to do. She loved him, but her heart was breaking. He slid into the bed and reached for her with his cool, gentle hands. She wanted to be held by him. They didn't have to talk. Emilie rolled toward him, found his face, and kissed him with deep, sorrowful passion. She could tell that Dante was pleased with her response. She made love to him with all of her body and soul, knowing it might be the last time.

Emilie felt guilty for keeping silent, but the truth was that she felt as if she was already leaving him. She just wasn't strong enough to say good-bye. She lay quietly with Dante on top of her, enjoying the feel of his muscular body and savoring his familiar scent. She wished that they could freeze time and stay like this forever.

She knew he wouldn't stay for long. He'd probably snuck away from his friends, and they would eventually notice him gone. She would hold him for as long as she could. No matter what she decided to do, she needed this moment.

Emilie's chest ached and she was having trouble breathing. She feared that she would start crying, thus initiating an uncomfortable conversation. Luckily Dante misunderstood her body language and must have thought that he was getting too heavy for her. He slid off and laid on his back beside her, sighing contentedly. Emilie cuddled up against him because she couldn't bear the physical separation.

Dante rolled onto his side and kissed her while stroking her face and hair. "I wish I could stay," he whispered in his magical voice.

Oh God, I'm going to miss that voice! "I know," was all she could manage. There was a ravenous emptiness swallowing her. She didn't know if she was ever going to feel his lips on hers again. She kissed him more urgently.

Dante quickly pulled away, laughing softly. "Now I really wish I could stay," he whispered more seductively, his eyes glowing softly in the dark.

"Me too."

"I'll be back soon," he murmured as he slid out of the bed.

She watched him get dressed, memorizing every detail of him. Then he came back to the bed and bent down to kiss her good-bye, whispering, "I love you."

"I love you too."

Then he was gone.

She finally released the flood of tears she'd been holding at bay. It was the hardest Emilie had cried since she'd found out about her parents' accident. She felt as if her soul was being ripped out. His scent still lingered in the bed. She could feel his lips on hers and how much passion he inspired within her. She couldn't imagine her life without him. There would never be anyone quite like her angel. *How am I ever going to look him in those beautiful brown eyes and say good-bye?*

Chapter 17

Emilie had asked Caroline to come over, but she didn't know what she was going to say. She knew that she needed to talk to somebody, even if she couldn't tell the whole truth.

When they were settled on the couch, Caroline examined Emilie and declared, "God, you look awful. What's wrong?"

Emilie had never been any good at hiding her feelings. The better someone knew her, the easier it was for them to read her. She sighed dejectedly. "I have a big problem, but I can't really talk about it. It's just too complicated."

"You can trust me. What's wrong?"

"You know how you've been telling me to be careful about getting my hopes up about having a relationship with Dante?" Emilie began. But inside her mind she was thinking, *I wonder if this is really a good idea.*

"Yes. Has something happened between the two of you?" Caroline asked in a tone that suggested she had a lot to say on the subject.

Somehow Emilie didn't get the impression that any of it would be helpful. "You have to promise not to tell anyone about this. Please…"

"You know I wouldn't do anything like that," Caroline insisted, clearly insulted.

"I know. It's just that I promised I wouldn't tell."

"So what's the problem?" Caroline demanded. It appeared as though she was ready to kill Emilie if she didn't get some details fast.

"You know how sometimes the having isn't as good as the wanting?" Emilie asked cryptically.

"So he's no good in bed?" Caroline pried, smiling like a crocodile.

Emilie had to laugh. Caroline was as subtle as a thunderstorm. *No wonder we get along so well.* "No, Caroline. He's fantastic in bed. That's not my problem."

"Is he really?" Caroline murmured. She looked as if she wanted to wring out every sordid detail of Emilie's experiences with Dante, but Emilie just couldn't stand to talk about it. Everything was too raw. "OK…" Caroline encouraged. "Sorry about that…"

"You know I love him more than anything."

"You've always had it bad for that guy."

"I just don't think we have a future together and I don't know what to do about it. Do I stay with him and just enjoy myself or do I let him go, break my heart, and move on fresh?"

"You can't tell me why you don't have a future together?"

Emilie knew that Caroline wouldn't want to advise her with so little information. "No…Like I said, it's really complicated. It would be incredibly difficult for us to have any kind of lasting future together. There really isn't any way to work it out."

"Is he married?" Caroline asked.

"I can't say…"

"He is!" Caroline stood up and jumped up and down in hysterics. "You've got to kick his worthless ass to the curb!"

Emilie had to tell her something. "Caroline, please calm down. He's not married."

"He has another girlfriend then?"

Emilie realized that bringing Caroline into this had been a mistake. She should never have opened this Pandora's box. But how could she get herself out now? "Not that I know of anyway."

"OK, then what's the problem?" Caroline had gotten herself under control and sat with Emilie on the couch again. Emilie got the impression that if there was some foul play on Dante's part then Caroline would easily be able to advise her to get rid of him. But Dante hadn't done anything wrong. In reality he had done everything right. He was wonderful, and he was everything that she had ever wanted in a man. *What the hell am I going to do?*

"You know what?" Emilie croaked as tears crept into her eyes. "This isn't helping. Can we change the subject?"

Caroline's irritated expression quickly morphed into something guilty. "Listen, I'm sorry. I do want to help you."

"I know. You're a good friend. I just don't know if anyone can help me right now."

"Let me try one more time," Caroline begged.

Emilie already regretted dragging her friend into this mess, but seeing the sincerity on her face just made everything so much worse. She owed Caroline the chance to redeem herself even if Emilie would have preferred to drop everything. "OK...Just tell me honestly what you would do in this situation. You're dating a great guy, who you love more than anything, but that you don't see a future with. Do you stay with him and enjoy yourself for as long as it lasts, or do you let him go and move on to find someone with whom to have a lasting relationship?"

"Wow..." Caroline grumbled. "I don't know what to say. In your imaginary situation, do you love him and he doesn't love you back or do you love him and he loves you too?"

"He loves me too," Emilie answered. The emotions the conversation was invoking were overwhelming and she felt as though she was going to lose control at any moment. *I wish I could wake myself from this horrible nightmare. Dante is right, love is Hell.*

"Wow..." Caroline repeated. She stared intently into Emilie's blotchy red face and watery eyes. "Dante told you that he loves you. That's tough...Is there absolutely no hope?"

"We're from two very different worlds. We would have so many problems. We already do."

"If it was just me in love, I might ride it out to see where it went. But if he's in love too, then riding it out might be leading him on, and that really isn't fair to him. You wouldn't want him misleading you about his level of commitment, would you?"

"No, I guess I wouldn't." Emilie reached over and patted Caroline's knee. "Thanks for your honest answer."

"I really don't feel that I've helped you very much. I wish you could give me more information."

"I know. I'm just not ready, and I don't know if I ever will be. Listen, if I do decide to break up with him, can I come and crash at your place for a couple of days?"

"Sure, you're always welcome."

"I might need to hide from my life for a little while to help me get through this."

"I understand," Caroline soothed.

"Thanks."

Emilie knew that she loved Dante too much to allow him to sacrifice so much for her. It was too much to ask of anyone, but she wondered if she would have the courage to do what Caroline suggested, what she knew was right. She would need time to build up her courage and figure a way out that Dante would accept but that would minimize the amount of pain inflicted upon him.

ॐ

Later in the day, after Caroline had left, Emilie got some good news. She wasn't pregnant. *Thank God!* she thought.

It was Friday and therefore no surprise when the phone rang. She felt that she couldn't put off this dreadful task any longer. She took a deep breath before answering, "Hello."

"Hello," Dante's magical voice sang cheerfully.

She wasn't sure where to begin. "How are you?" she asked, her tone uncomfortable and cold.

"Feeling a bit formal tonight are we?" he teased.

Here goes nothing, she thought. "Dante…we need to talk."

"I don't like the sound of this," he said, all humor gone from his voice.

"I'm sorry." *You have no idea how sorry I am…*

"Now I really don't like the sound of this. I'm coming right over."

"OK…" she whimpered. *Be strong,* she chanted.

Dante had already hung up.

He would only be a few minutes, and she was as ready as she could be. She just had to keep it together long enough to get through this, then she could surrender to her sorrow.

Dante appeared in the hallway. Emilie was really going to miss that.

He noticed right away that she didn't get up and run over cheerfully to greet him as usual. "Emilie, what's wrong?" he asked as he rushed over to sit next to her on the couch.

"I don't know where to start."

Dante seemed to want to comfort her in some way but was unsure what she needed from him. He was restless on his side of the couch, but Emilie made no move toward him. She was still organizing her thoughts and firming up her resolve.

"Did something happen to you? What's wrong?" he insisted a bit more firmly this time.

He can probably sense that I'm upset, Emilie thought. She glanced up into his sweet, worried face. "Dante, you should know that I'm not pregnant," she announced.

He smiled. "Is that what this is about?" He sucked in a huge breath and let it out with obvious relief. "I thought you'd be glad. I sure am. It would have been a disaster if you had gotten pregnant. We have lots of time to make babies and—"

"Dante, please stop! This isn't about my not being pregnant!" Emilie interrupted.

"Then what's this about?"

"I don't know how to say this to you, but…I don't think we should see each other anymore." She let the words hang in the air and tried not to look at Dante's shocked expression.

His brow furrowed and he shook his head in disbelief. "What?"

She spoke softly but clearly. "I've been thinking about this for a while, and I don't think we have a viable future together."

"You haven't been thinking about this for very long at all, because I was just here the other night, and you seemed very happy to see me then!"

As the words spilled from his lips, she could see the truth dawning on him. Emilie's overwhelming feelings of guilt made it impossible for her to look into his eyes any longer. She locked her gaze on her hands and waited for his reaction.

"You knew then, didn't you?" he asked resentfully.

She tried to keep herself together. "I'm sorry," she whispered.

Dante growled. "Are you at least going to give me some kind of reason for this phenomenal change of heart?"

He had his defensive, unreadable mask on. He needed to protect himself. She could understand. He had every right to be surprised and every right to be angry. She would be if she were in his shoes. "Dante, we're just too different, and I'll never fit into your world."

"I think you'd fit in far better than you realize," he grumbled.

"I'm really sorry," she muttered. "You were right all along. You tried to warn me from the beginning, and I wouldn't listen to you. It's too much for me, and I just can't do it anymore."

He stared at the floor, tension running through every muscle of his body. "I don't want to be right. I want to be with you."

"We want different things," she explained. "We won't make each other happy in the long run." *I wish I knew what to say to make this easier for you.*

"I've never been happier in my life," he snapped. "How can you say that I wouldn't be happy?"

She didn't want to hurt him. She'd never been happier either, but this relationship was nothing but a train wreck in the making, and it was better for them both to jump off before the impending crash. "I wouldn't be happy," she answered. She almost lost control of herself looking at the pain in his eyes.

"I…I…don't understand," he stammered. "Did I say something? Did I do something? What changed your mind between Maui and today?"

"You would have to give up too much for me. I don't think you understand how hard it's going to be. Your judgment is too clouded."

"I'll give you that," he grumbled. "I can see why they call it 'lovesick.' But tell me, what am I going to have to give up for you?"

"You'll have to be monogamous."

Emilie could sense his irritation.

"I don't want anyone else! Is this about trust again?"

"I guess it is. In my world a cheating husband is a dog. In your world a cheating husband is normal and healthy."

Dante laughed despite himself. "When I think about another man touching you the way I touch you, it hurts me in a way I can't describe. And believe me I've felt a lot of different pain in my days. I know pain. I can only assume that you feel the same way about me. Remember when I told you that everything has a price? That you just have to make a deal to get what you want?" She nodded, and he continued. "There isn't anything anyone could offer me that would make me hurt you in that way."

"How about a child?" Emilie asked tersely. She knew she had him with this point.

He paused for a long time as though scrambling to free himself from the hole he had just dug. "I know what you're trying to do here…" He sighed heavily and shifted restlessly on the couch. "I'm not happy about being trapped like this. Do you think that I didn't know you might not be able to bear me an heir? I've known since before I even waited for you in my father's office. I can't deny that I'd be disappointed if we couldn't have a child together, but it would be a price I'd be willing to pay to spend my life with you—and only you."

Emilie was surprised by his response. She hadn't expected him to have thought this through so thoroughly. Most men thought only about making babies, not about having them. Dante had always been different. She should have expected more from him. She looked into his sincere face and knew that he was telling her the truth. Or at least the truth for now.

"Dante, I'm happy to hear those words from you, and I believe that you mean every word of them. But you're so young, and our relationship is still new and exciting. When we're older and childless, you might feel differently, and you might decide that you want a young, fertile wife to make you feel young and excited again."

He rolled his eyes. "I can't predict the future, but I don't believe our lives will play out that way. You'd have the same risk of your middle-aged human husband running off with a younger woman. Infidelity is the chance we all take with love."

He was right, but that didn't mean he would win this argument. "It's not a risk I'm willing to take with you. You've been careful not to bring this up, but I'm no fool. I know that I'll have to give up being human to marry you. I'd have to live as a second-class citizen in your world. I'd have nothing but you. If you got bored or resentful, there would be nothing I could do to stop you from getting whatever you wanted, whenever you wanted it."

"I wouldn't do that to you, and you know it!" Dante was plainly offended now. "I know in your heart you can't possibly believe I'd ever treat you so contemptuously! I'm willing to sign it in blood too. What's this really about, Emilie?"

Dante locked his eyes on her face and she was afraid that he would see the truth. He was smart enough to know that this wasn't all about his fidelity. He could surely tell she was hiding something from him. She couldn't bring up the fact that he'd have to sell his soul for her. He deserved better, and it wasn't open for discussion. "I don't want to be a vampire," she whispered.

"I don't want you to be a vampire either! You don't have to be a vampire!"

Now he was really angry. *Stupid, stupid, stupid,* she cursed herself. "I'll never be Beyowan," she stated, looking him right in the eyes. She had him again, and he knew it.

"No, you won't, that's true...But it isn't important to me. My father isn't Beyowan."

"This isn't about your father, this is about Beyowan society. You don't get to choose your father, but you do get to pick your wife."

"Apparently not," he snapped, looking very resentful.

Emilie was counting on the fact that Dante wanted to do everything legally and officially as far as his marriage was concerned. Especially if they were lucky enough to have a child. He wouldn't want their child to be illegitimate, so she asked him, "Would you stay with me if I told you that I would never consider changing myself?"

He paused for a long time, thinking carefully about his answer. "I wasn't trying to hide anything from you. It's just too soon to be talking about anything permanent. I wanted to wait for the right moment. Anyway, you might eventually change your mind."

"Time is a lot more forgiving for you. Are you willing to risk it?"

"Probably not," he answered sadly.

Emilie saw defeat written in his eyes. The decision was hers. He couldn't force or trick her into changing, and her remaining human wouldn't be a possibility for him in the long term.

"I'm sorry things couldn't be different. Part of me will always love you," she declared, trying desperately to keep herself together. Her heart was thundering in her chest, and she was sure that he could hear it pounding.

"All of me...will always love you." Dante got up from the couch, preparing to leave.

It would be better if she just let him go quickly. She couldn't keep it together for much longer. This was for his own good. They would both be better off in the long run. She had to believe it. She simply had to.

Emilie wanted to jump up and give him a hug, but she knew it would only make it so much harder for them both. She couldn't afford to touch him. The tentative hold she had on her self-control was shaky at best. At this point the tiniest thing would set her off.

Somehow she managed to say, "Good-bye, Dante. I hope you find happiness."

"I did," was all he replied, and then he was gone.

She knew he could still be standing in the mesay threshold, watching her. It was imperative that she hold it together for a few minutes longer. She sat staring blankly for a few seconds but then sighed heavily. She had to leave. She couldn't stay here. These walls were haunted by too many memories.

Emilie walked to her bedroom, picked up her overnight bag and purse, then slowly made her way to the front door, turning off the lights as she went. She would go to Caroline's and there she could cry until her ribs ached. It was done. It was finally over. She had never felt so empty and alone in her whole life.

ψ

Dante stood in the mesay threshold, watching Emilie. He was in shock. She had taken him completely off guard. There had to be something more. This couldn't just be about his fidelity. He had been faithful to her for their entire relationship. Not once had he betrayed her even though he had ample opportunity to do so, and this made him feel even more angry and frustrated. He was willing to be monogamous. It was one thing for her not to trust him if he was behaving like a cad. It was another thing for him to be honest and pure and be treated like something untrustworthy. It wasn't fair, and it didn't make any sense. Human women were difficult to understand.

He watched her carefully. She seemed to be in control. She seemed to have given this some thought. This didn't seem to be a rash decision on her part, like one of those hormonally driven fits of temper he had heard that human women sometimes experience.

She was preparing to leave. This annoyed him even more because he wanted to see if she was going to say or do anything that would give him some indication of what was really going through her mind.

He could believe that she didn't want to have herself transformed. It was understandable to be afraid. But...she had to change to stay with him. He couldn't spend his long life with her as a human. It went against everything he believed. Plus it just wasn't practical. Protecting her was becoming a full-time job and he couldn't live his life like this for much longer.

Dante would love to have a child. She was right about that, but it wasn't everything. He could live without it. He didn't know how he was supposed to live without her.

He watched her turn off the hall light and close the front door. The realization that he might never see her beautiful face again hit him like a ton of bricks. He was completely unprepared for this moment. He had to take a deep breath just to keep himself under control as he stumbled back to his condo.

He had been so close to having what he wanted. *So close...Emilie was made for me and we're destined to be together. I'm sure of it. How can this be happening?*

God must be punishing him. Dark Angels didn't agree about the existence of soul mates. Perhaps God had introduced Emilie into his life to test his faith. If that were the case, then he had failed miserably. He'd had sex with her and was planning to have her transformed. All that was left was for him to sink his fangs into her body and drink her blood. Then he would have committed every sin possible against one of God's precious children.

Dante couldn't believe it. Emilie was not a test; she was a gift from God. She had to be. Even Michael Enasvant believed in soul mates. How could a man of his years and experience be wrong about something so fundamental?

Dante walked into his condo, dreading having to speak to Jude or Colin. He was in terrible pain, and they would only be insensitive. He felt so alone. A familiar emptiness was clawing its way back into his soul.

Jude looked over at him but didn't say anything. Colin was rest-ing in his room.

Good, Dante thought. *I can't talk to anyone right now.* He needed to calm down. He went to his room and closed the door. He would rest and think. Emilie might yet change her mind. He would give her some time to reconsider her decision. This had to be some kind of mistake. It just had to be, because he couldn't imagine a life without her.

Chapter 18

Emilie knocked on Caroline's door. When Caroline opened it and saw the expression on Emilie's face, she shook her head sympathetically, stepping aside to let Emilie in. Caroline closed the door carefully behind them. Emilie put down her bag and started taking off her coat, but only got it halfway off before she crumpled to the floor, sobbing uncontrollably. Caroline crouched down, trying to comfort her. Emilie wrapped her arms around her friend and wept. She was in so much pain that she could barely draw breath.

"Come on in now," Caroline said. "Let's talk about this. You'll feel better if you get it all out. Keeping these things bottled up only drives people crazy."

Caroline was right. No matter how much it hurt, Emilie needed to let her feelings out so she could start the healing process. "I broke up with Dante tonight," she managed to croak as Caroline helped her to her feet.

"I figured as much," Caroline replied. "Listen, are you staying here because you're afraid that he's going to come after you or something? Does he have a key to your place?"

Emilie sighed miserably. "How many times do I have to tell you? He is...was...not beating me up. It wasn't like that at all!"

"You don't have to protect him anymore," Caroline soothed.

Yes, I do, Emilie thought to herself. She would always have to protect Dante. She would never do anything to put him in danger, and that was why she was here in the first place. "I'm not protecting him. If you want I'll strip naked and show you that I don't have a mark on me. I slept with him on Wednesday and I broke his heart tonight, and he didn't do anything to hurt me."

Emilie drew herself up and stared at Caroline's surprised face, daring her to demand proof. Caroline looked as though she wanted to believe there was more to the story.

Emilie threw her hands up in frustration. "I'm telling you the truth! He may be a bit of an animal, but he never did anything to me that I didn't ask him to do."

She walked over to sit on Caroline's couch. She put her face in her hands and melted into tears once again. Caroline sat down beside Emilie and said, "OK, fine! I don't want to fight with you about this. It's over now and you have to give yourself some time to get used to being on your own again."

Emilie laid her head in Caroline's lap and thought, *I don't want to be on my own. I want to be with Dante. How am I ever going to recover from this?*

ᛝ

Emilie stayed at Caroline's apartment for three nights. On Monday morning she went directly to school. She knew Dante would be working out of town for the week and probably wouldn't try to contact her. He had left one message on her cell phone that she couldn't bring herself to listen to.

Her weekend had been spent wallowing in misery. She had eaten very little and slept even less. Her body seemed to walk around on automatic pilot, going through the motions of everyday life, but she felt as though part of her was missing. She had never realized how much of herself she had given to Dante along with her love.

Now Emilie slowly opened the door to her apartment. It felt as cold and empty inside as she did. She walked in and took off her coat and shoes, then brought her overnight bag into her bedroom. Lying on her pillow was a sheet of paper. Dante must have come back to see her. She was relieved that she had stayed with Caroline. Dante might have easily persuaded her to reconsider.

She walked over to the bed and saw Dante's gold chain with the little angel charm lying on the note. It brought back so many beautiful memories of him. It was the only jewelry he ever wore on a daily basis and was obviously very special to him. Why would he have given it to her now, when everything was over between them? She picked up the chain and ran it lovingly over her lips. It would be a treasured souvenir to remind her of just how close she had come to having a truly magical life.

The note read:

> *You have my love, my heart, and, it would seem, even my soul. Keep this to remind you of me. I'll never forget you. Love, Dante*

Emilie felt sick. She lay trembling on the bed for a moment, tears running down her cheeks. Dante must be feeling the same emptiness in his heart. Had he also given her part of his soul along with his love?

She had always believed that they were somehow connected. It was going to take a long time to find herself again. She only hoped that he would heal from this faster than she would.

He had such elegant handwriting. It would be impossible to forget being in love with an angel. She unfastened the clasp on the chain, wrapped it around her neck, and promised herself that she would only remove it once she felt ready to move on with her life. For now she would allow herself to mourn this tremendous loss.

It will get easier, she chanted over and over. She just had to take one day at a time, because only time could heal her heart. She had to believe it would.

ψ

Jude knocked on Dante's bedroom door and opened it slowly. Dante was lying in bed, on his stomach, in the dark, facing away from the door. He didn't move as Jude came in, but he wasn't sleeping. He couldn't. He was in too much pain.

"Dante, what's the matter with you?" Jude asked, his voice rough with concern.

Dante ignored him. He couldn't talk; too much pain.

"You've hardly moved from your bed since you got home Friday. Did someone poison you? Do you need to go to the hospital?"

Dante ignored him.

After a minute of standing by the doorway, Jude walked over to the side of the bed. He was about to reach out to check if Dante was incapacitated in some way when Dante rolled over onto his back, put his hands behind his head, and stared up at the ceiling. Jude stood in silence, uncertain what to do next.

Dante shot him an irritated look. "Just leave me alone!"

Jude jumped at Dante's voice and stared at him wide-eyed for a second. "What's the matter with you?" he asked with more impatience this time.

Dante returned to staring blankly up at the ceiling.

"We're expected at work. I'm sure your phone has been going off nonstop. Or did you call in sick today?"

Dante took a deep breath and let it out slowly. "I called in sick." Dante finally turned his head to properly acknowledge Jude's presence in the room. "Now can you leave me alone?"

"What's the matter with you?" This time Jude's irritation was plain in his voice.

"I don't want to talk about it," Dante mumbled darkly, then stared back up at the ceiling.

"This has to do with Emilie, doesn't it?" Jude surmised as he headed for the door.

Dante winced at the sound of her name. He felt sick to his stomach. How many days would it take for this pain to go away? He wasn't used to having so much pain for so long. He didn't know how to deal with it. Dante had never loved anyone before, not like this. He had tried not to love Emilie in the first place, but it had felt so good, so right. Now that he didn't want to love her anymore, he was at a loss. *Love really is Hell*, he thought bitterly to himself.

"What part of 'I don't want to talk about it' did you not understand, Jude?" Dante snarled as he rolled back onto his stomach.

Dante could tell that Colin had come to the doorway and was standing with Jude. There was a short exchange between his two friends that he couldn't quite make out, then Jude left and Colin walked into the bedroom.

Dante was immediately uncomfortable with Colin's entrance. Dante thought of Jude as a brother, but Colin was almost like his second father. He had too much respect for Colin to mouth off to him as he could with Jude. Jude also knew not to take Dante too seriously, but "serious" was Colin's middle name. He wouldn't be as easily deterred as Jude either. Jude hated confrontation and knew when to back off and let Dante calm down. But when Colin had something to say, Dante was expected to drop everything and listen attentively.

"OK, Dante. You're going to tell me what this is all about," Colin commanded. "Everybody is getting worried about you now."

Dante sighed. His throat cramped shut and his chest ached. He wasn't ready for this confrontation. He had avoided talking to Colin about his relationship with Emilie since the very beginning. Colin was going to be furious with him for getting involved with her in the first place. In other words, he was going to be completely unsympathetic.

Colin could never understand what it felt like to be in love in this way and especially not with a human girl. He was a shining example of what a proper Beyowan nobleman and Dark Angel should be.

Colin was standing impatiently beside the bed. "Now, Dante!"

Dante couldn't bear to look at him. He closed his eyes and tried to get his heart to stop beating so fast. He might as well get this over with. It wasn't going to get any easier to confess. "Emilie doesn't want to see me anymore," he mumbled, bracing himself for more pain. His throat cramped shut again, but he managed to harness his anger and squash it down into the pit of his stomach. He rolled onto his back, put his hands behind his head, and stared up at the ceiling. He couldn't resist a quick glance into Colin's concerned face. Instead of saying something intelligent in order to gain his friend's sympathy, Dante snarled, "Now don't trip yourself dancing out of the room because I know you'll be happy about this, even if I'm in Hell!" Dante had to close his eyes and hold his breath. He was losing control of himself and really didn't want to fight with Colin. He just wanted to be alone.

He heard Colin draw a ragged breath and let it out slowly. "I'll leave you to think about the situation more carefully. I'm sure you'll come to realize that this is for the best."

"I'm sure," Dante growled sarcastically as he rolled away from Colin.

Colin stood and stared down at him for a minute. Dante could feel Colin's anger pouring off of him. He didn't want to deal with this right now. He couldn't. His own pain and anger were building to almost volcanic proportions. This was a dangerous time for an argument, and he hoped his friend would just leave.

Luckily Colin made the right choice. He paused in the doorway and said, "You need to eat something. You're going to damage yourself if you continue like this." He walked out and closed the door.

Dante knew that Colin would go right to Jude and milk out all of the details of his not-so-secret relationship with Emilie. Hopefully Jude would keep some details secret. Dante wouldn't be able to deal with any of Colin's lectures today.

He closed his eyes and tried to calm down. He couldn't help hoping that Emilie would change her mind. He knew he shouldn't be thinking so optimistically, but he couldn't help it. He had convinced himself that everything was going just great between them and then, out of the blue, this happened. He wished he knew what this was really about. Emilie was hiding something from him, he was sure of it. Maybe he could figure this out before it was too late. He needed to be with her again. More than just his happiness was at stake.

Chapter 19

J ude had tempted Dante out of bed by bringing a still sizzling, two-inch-thick, rare rib steak into the bedroom and holding the plate right next to Dante's face. His instincts had taken over his motor control and he had snatched the plate from Jude's hands, growling like a savage beast.

He now sat at the dining table, wiping up the last of the blood on the plate with a piece of bread. Jude sat across from him, watching with concern.

"Are you just gonna sit there and stare like a statue?" Dante grumbled.

"I've never seen you like this," Jude complained. "And I'm bored out of my mind in here while you brood."

"Well, leave."

"How will I ever hold up my head if I go out and you commit suicide?"

"I'm not suicidal," Dante muttered, rolling his eyes. "I'm just depressed."

"Have you called Emilie?"

"Once, but she didn't call back."

"Why don't you clean yourself up, march over there, smile one of your dazzling grins, and swoop her up in your arms?"

Dante snorted. "I would, if I felt it would get me anything other than slapped."

Jude's eyes went wide. "Sounds like fun to me."

"For a half-breed, you don't understand humans very well."

"I understand them as well as I want."

Just as Dante was about to go off on a rant, his phone rang. He picked it up to see who was calling. It was Soeren Samael, the man watching over Emilie.

"Hello," he answered.

"Dante, I wanted you to know that there's somebody of interest snooping outside the gym where Emilie is writing an exam," Soeren explained. "I'm positive it's Leonard from Gomez's club."

Dante growled angrily.

"Who is it?" Jude demanded. "It sounds like Soeren."

Dante hushed his friend. "I'll take care of him right away," he insisted. "Don't lose sight of him, but don't let him anywhere near Emilie, at all costs. OK?"

"Fine."

Dante put his phone away and turned to Jude, who was pacing across the floor impatiently. "Want to have a little fun?"

Jude smiled brightly. "Yeah!"

"Let's go hunt ourselves a changeling."

The two men made their preparations to leave, then Dante extended his hand to Jude.

Dante had to give Gomez credit. If someone was planted in front of the gym for the entire exam period, almost every student at the university would walk by at one point or another. It was a slow but efficient way to find someone. It was December in Montreal and therefore freezing cold outside. No man could stand outside for an entire day. Hopefully Leonard had just arrived and was waiting to see if she exited the gym.

Soeren would have told him if Leonard had actually gotten anywhere near Emilie, so it was safe to assume that he didn't realize she was in there. Dante was familiar with the area and knew where it would be safe to emerge from mesay without being noticed. He and Jude went over their strategy on the way and were all set to go as soon as their feet hit the pavement.

Jude circled around to come out as close to Leonard as possible. Jude smiled cheerfully as Leonard recognized him and started walking quickly away. He crossed the street and continued on a public route, hoping to avoid a scene. Dante followed close behind Leonard, hidden in mesay.

Leonard took out his phone and started talking. Dante was behind him and unable to read his lips but assumed he was calling for help. Having someone as dangerous as Jude on your tail would be disconcerting for even the bravest man.

At first Dante was concerned that Leonard suspected that Jude was not alone. If he stayed on public streets, it would force everyone to behave. As Leonard ducked into a deserted alley, Dante scanned their surroundings and sighed out his relief. It would have been most frustrating to watch a foe escape, but Leonard had just given Dante the opportunity he was waiting for. As Leonard broke into a run, Dante came out of mesay in front of him and smashed him on the skull with the butt end of his dart gun before he had the chance to change directions.

Dante picked up the phone. "Leonard is currently unable to answer your call. Please leave a message after the beep. Beep!" He dropped the phone and ground it into the pavement with the heel of his shoe.

"What do we do with him?" Jude asked, staring down at the unconscious man.

"He won't be out for long," Dante replied.

"Can we take him to Thailand for a chase?" Jude suggested. "This was too easy and I'm all excited now."

"You're such a demon," Dante scolded. "You know I can't allow that."

Jude made his sad puppy face. "Please…"

"Jude!" Dante hissed. "This time I'm gonna give him to Purson as a thank you gift for his understanding and support."

"Fine. It's the right thing to do and will score you bonus points, which you're really gonna need."

"Can you make your way back on your own?"

"Sure."

"I'll drop this package at the office."

Leonard stirred and moaned. Dante viciously kicked him in the head to ensure he remained unconscious for the journey through mesay. He didn't want to lose his prize. If given the choice, Dante would prefer to starve in mesay than to be Purson's plaything.

He picked Leonard up, tossed him over his shoulder, and headed for the office, coming out at the front entrance. Instantly guards converged on him, pointing their dart guns. Dante smiled sweetly to the receptionist on duty and announced, "Would you be so kind as to call the chairman and mention that I have a special delivery for him."

The guards backed off as the woman picked up the receiver and spoke to Purson's assistant. Then she put the phone down and smiled. "He's expecting you in his office."

Dante opened a doorway and went through. As he came out, the mesay alarm hardly sounded before it was silenced. Purson stood up and smiled warmly, examining the still unconscious body of Leonard.

"Did Gomez ever register his changelings like I suggested?" Dante asked.

Purson's grin widened. "No, I don't believe he did."

"Excellent!" Dante exclaimed, then dropped Leonard like a sack of potatoes onto the carpet. "This is for you, my old friend."

"Really?" Purson cooed. If it were possible for him to flush with pleasure, he'd be as red as a beet. He walked around his desk to have a closer look. Leonard was regaining consciousness and was gingerly probing the scabby gashes on his scalp.

"This is most unexpected," Purson cheered.

"This one was sniffing around where he was unwanted," Dante explained. "You've been more than generous to me, sir, so I felt I owed you this little favor."

"Thank you, son," Purson replied. "It won't be forgotten."

"Have fun," Dante said, extending his hand to his cousin, who took it enthusiastically.

"Indeed I will."

Dante left the office with the knowledge that he had rid himself of a most troublesome enemy, sent Gomez a harsh message, and pleased the chairman of the council, who held Emilie's fate in his hands. If only he could celebrate with the woman he loved. He hadn't even taken a peek in to see her. Hopefully it wouldn't be long before he thought of a way back into her heart.

ω

Emilie heard someone knock at the door. Dante's magical voice called her name from the other side. She got up to open it, but somehow it was much farther away than usual. He was waiting for her, if only she could get to the door. She was absolutely desperate to see him again, but every step she took brought her no closer.

Dante called her name again. His voice sounded uncertain, as if he was about to turn and leave. She tried to answer him but found that she couldn't speak. If she didn't get that damn door open soon, he would leave. She started to run and finally reached the door only to find it locked. She searched her purse for the key. How her purse happened to be over her shoulder was a mystery, but she knew the key was in there somewhere. She could feel Dante's presence on the other side of the door. She wanted to call out to him, to tell him that she was doing everything in her power to get the door open, but she still couldn't speak.

Finally she had the key in the lock and opened the door. Dante, dressed all in black, was striding magnificently away from her down a long dark corridor. He was so beautiful. She could hardly breathe watching him. She reached out and tried desperately to call him back. Then he disappeared into thin air and was gone. *No!*

Emilie woke up with a start. Another dream. The misery she felt knowing that Dante would never again be a part of her life was a dull pain underlying her existence, but it was especially intense in her dreams. Her heart pounded and tears flowed down her cheeks. She would never get over him if he haunted her dreams. There, she was free to love him without restraint, fear, or pain, and he loved her in the same way. But something always kept them apart.

She allowed herself to cry for a while. She tried to reassure herself that the pain would ease with the passage of time.

She looked at her clock and sighed miserably. It was the middle of the night. She needed to get more sleep if she wanted to retain enough information to pass her final exams. There was no point in studying until her eyes watered if she wasn't going to get any sleep.

She decided to get up and review for a while. The material would surely lull her to sleep again.

Chapter 20

F inally Emilie's exams were done for the semester. As she made her way out of the gym after writing her last exam, she saw a stranger leaning against the wall. He seemed to be searching for someone. She didn't recognize him, so she switched her attention to making sure her coat was zipped and her hat securely covering her ears. The wind was bitter cold, and even though it wasn't a long walk back to her apartment, it seemed like miles when you had the winter wind stinging your face.

She was eager to get packed for her trip to Vancouver for the holidays. She longed for the milder temperatures and could almost smell the familiar scents of cedar and sea salt in the air. She also looked forward to visiting her dying grandmother in the hospital. Every moment was precious, and she intended to make the most of the time they had together. Lost in thought, Emilie didn't noticed the stranger walk up beside her.

"Dante sent me," he began.

The sound of that precious name was like a dagger in her heart. "Why?" she demanded.

"There's a problem at the council office," the man said, looking gravely serious.

"Who are you?"

"I'm a good friend of his."

A friend with no name, she thought. Then something dawned on her. Dante had warned her to be watchful for scouts. He had said that they might be sent to make sure that he hadn't divulged any confidential information. Her instructions were to play as dumb as possible, because they would do everything to try to trick her into exposing any knowledge she had about the Beyowan world.

"Dante's in trouble and wants you to come meet him at the office."

"Where and what's the office?" she asked.

"You know, the council office," he said, winking.

"I don't know what you're talking about."

"Really?" he asked. He seemed almost disappointed.

"I think you have the wrong person," Emilie growled and began walking off at a quicker pace.

The man followed along behind. Of course, he yanked her into the very first alleyway they passed, clamping his hand over her face.

"You know I could do all sorts of things to you if I wasn't so afraid of Dante." He paused and gave her a long sniff. "Does he drink your blood?"

Emilie furrowed her brow and shook her head, trying to figure a way out of this mess. She could almost see a hint of the fangs in his mouth extending.

"What a waste…"

Ethan had been a changeling scout of the council and she had barely escaped from him. Dante wouldn't be coming this time. This realization was only escalating the sense of despair rising up in her soul.

"Why don't you call him?" the man suggested. "I'll take my hand off your mouth so you can call him. But if you scream, I'll snap your neck just enough to keep you alive long enough for me to thoroughly enjoy you."

His fingers slipped cautiously away. "There now," he urged. "Give him a call. He'll be here to protect you in a heartbeat."

"What are you talking about?" Emilie sniffled. "It's Wednesday, and it's the middle of the night in Thailand or China. How can he get here in a heartbeat when he's halfway around the world? Is he really here in Montreal? I don't understand…What am I supposed to say to him?"

"Are you sure you don't know what I mean?" he asked, pressing himself closer to her. "He could come and save you from me."

"You're not a very good friend of his, are you?" Emilie asked, her voice quavering. She was tempted to call Dante. She didn't like the look in this man's eyes.

As he was about to answer, a handsome young man walked into the alley. "Is there a problem here?" he demanded.

The man holding Emilie stepped quickly away. "No, I was just leaving."

"Good."

As the scout passed, he shot the other man a scathing glance. "Are you OK?" the handsome man asked.

"I don't think so," Emilie replied.

"Do you need some help?"

"Who are you?" she asked. "I've seen you around campus."

"I'm a student too," he explained. "My name is Soeren. I just wrote the physics exam. And you?"

"I'm Emilie," she said, extending her hand. "It's so nice to meet you."

Soeren smiled and shook her hand. "Listen, if you're OK, I've gotta run. I'm meeting my girlfriend and I'm running late."

"Sure," Emilie said. "I'll be fine. You go ahead. Thank you so much for interfering on my behalf."

Soeren nodded politely and left. Emilie poked her head out of the alley and watched him walk toward the metro station. There was no sign of the other man.

On her way back to her apartment, she thought about the scout. She wondered if the council office was waiting for her to call Dante to report this incident. Perhaps the scout had been rough with her because he was trying to throw her off guard so she would panic and make a mistake. Obviously Dante hadn't told them about the breakup. Or maybe he had, and they wanted to make sure she was free of secrets before leaving her to her own life.

Then there was Soeren. If she didn't know better, she would have thought he was Beyowan. He was too good looking to be human, with his milk-chocolate skin, sparkling hazel eyes, sensuously full lips, and short curly black hair with a hint of red in it. A changeling scout would have been bolder with a human man. This one had fled the scene without a single protest. Perhaps they worked together.

Although, she did remember seeing the physics students filing solemnly into the gym to write their final. The gym often held students from more than one class at a time. His story certainly fit, but there was something a bit off about the whole situation.

One way or another, she was glad he'd arrived when he had, and hopefully there wouldn't be any more scouts from the council office testing her knowledge. She was now even more anxious to leave Montreal. It would be good to get away from everything. Perhaps she would even leave her dreams of Dante behind.

ψ

Dante was beginning to settle into his old routine. Life without Emilie was difficult, but if he distracted himself with work, the days seemed to pass by uneventfully enough.

He was waiting in the Bangkok lab for his last shipment of the day and had plans to drop Jude in Egypt for a visit with his father, then spend the weekend at the Maxaviel Venom Palace in Thailand. Most venomous members of his family lived together in a secure facility known as the MVP. His Ferrari Spider was housed in their garage, and he was looking forward to racing it around the track against some of his cousins in their super cars.

His phone rang and he pick it up, concerned. It was Soeren. "Hello," Dante answered.

"Hi," Soeren replied brusquely. "I'm at the airport in Montreal. I've lost Emilie."

"Really?" Dante was unsure how to proceed with this unusual turn of events. He didn't want the council aware of the breakup. Emilie was safe as long as she belonged to him, and he needed it to stay that way, at least until his license expired in the late spring.

"Did she mention any plans to you?" Soeren asked.

"She might be visiting her dying grandmother for Christmas."

"That makes sense," Soeren said, his voice sounding much more relaxed. "But as far as we know, she doesn't have any airline tickets."

"She never lets me spend any money on her," Dante grumbled. "She's probably flying stand-by in order to save money. She didn't get her exam schedule until late and the ticket prices were already unaffordable."

"Do you want me to follow her?"

"No," Dante insisted. "It's not worth it. She'll spend some time with friends and family and be back to start her new semester in January."

"True enough," Soeren agreed. "I'll take the opportunity to spend some time with my own family."

"Say hello to your mother and sister for me."

"My sister would be happier if I brought you home with me," Soeren replied. "She's still hoping to marry you."

"Your mother would never allow it," Dante argued with a chuckle.

"True," Soeren agreed. "But that hasn't stopped Senika from fantasizing."

"Have a good time, Soeren."

"You too, you rogue."

Dante put his phone away, smiling. Senika Samael was a high-ranking princess and married to a venomous Enasvant prince. She was young and potentially fertile. There was a huge line of childless noblemen hoping for the opportunity to father a child with her. Her mother's fertility played a key role in her desirability. She'd had five pregnancies over her lifetime, which was unheard of for most Beyowans. Senika was the only legal child to survive.

Soeren had been fathered by a human and was a nephilim. He was fortunate that Senika had not felt threatened by his birth. Many illegitimate children met with unfortunate accidents arranged by jealous legal siblings. Perhaps her mother had pleaded for Soeren's life. The siblings shared their noble family name, which made them more than half siblings. They were family. Females were generally more tolerant of illegitimate siblings. It was theorized that their maternal instincts made them more sympathetic to their parents' feelings. Males were much more likely to feel threatened and territorial. Senika was fortuitously married and extremely busy working in her father's family business, building her own fortune that Soeren could never touch.

Dante shook his head. Beyowan family politics were complicated indeed. His thoughts returned to Emilie and the life he had hoped to build with her. Those feelings were still too raw. He redirected his thoughts. Maybe he should consider Senika as a possible bride. It would be a good match, but he had never wanted to be matched. He wanted a family.

Chapter 21

Emilie had thrown herself completely into her studies, desperate to keep her mind occupied as much as possible so that she wouldn't have the time or the energy to miss Dante.

It wasn't working very well, and not just because of her dreams. Christmas was fast approaching, and she found herself reminded of him everywhere she went. He had been her angel, and there were angels everywhere. It was absolutely horrible.

Caroline was the best friend imaginable and had been trying everything humanly possible to distract and comfort her. Caroline had gone home to Vancouver to be with her family for the holidays, and Emilie had decided to join her. She had sat all day long in the airport, waiting for a stand-by seat to become available.

It was great to be back in Vancouver. The weather was predictably cold, foggy, and spattered with drizzle, but everything felt like home. Best of all, there was nothing to bring back memories of Dante, except the ever-present, inescapable Christmas angels.

Christmas was also the time when she missed her parents the most, and although Caroline's family did everything possible to make her feel like part of their family, it just wasn't the same.

Emilie's parents' ashes had been scattered in the forest on Whistler Mountain. They had been such avid skiers and would have wanted their final resting place to be somewhere so beloved. It was essential that Emilie make the trip up to visit them, at least in spirit.

The long, winding drive up into the mountains gave her some time to ponder. Of course the main focus of her thoughts was her relationship with Dante. She went through their brief relationship with a fine-toothed comb. The more she thought about it, the more she felt that with their problems aside, they would have been good for each other. She loved his sense of humor, his intelligence, and his thoughtfulness. No other man had ever taken her as seriously, listened to her as an equal, or treated her with such respect. Dante knew just what to do to make her feel good in every aspect of her life. If only things could have been different. If only he had been a regular human man. Or if only she had been like him. She would have been willing to give up being human for him, even if change-lings didn't live as long as Beyowans. She could still expect to live another hundred and fifty years. The information had been dis-closed because he had unconsciously wanted her to be prepared.

Love doesn't last forever, the professor had said. At this particu-lar time, Emilie was actually counting on it. She expected her love for Dante to eventually fade, but so far it hadn't. If anything, she seemed to have an ever increasing sense of regret over her decision to leave him. Had she really thought the situation through all the way? Or had she overreacted when Professor Ashton had dumped all of that information into her lap? He had chosen his arguments strategically and had fanned all of her insecurities. Perhaps she should have had an open discussion with Dante and maybe they could have worked through their problems together.

Emilie sighed heavily. One way or another, she couldn't have lived with herself if he'd had to sell his soul to the council in order to get out of his engagement.

No, she consoled herself. *I've made the right decision.* They had so many obstacles in their way. None of their friends had wanted them to be together. It would have been only a matter of time before something had driven them apart. He wasn't human and lived in a crazy world. There was no other choice.

By the time she arrived in Whistler, she had resolved to live her life without him. No matter how much it hurt.

Emilie's visit to Whistler served a dual purpose. She had to com-mune with the spirits of the dead, and she had to lift the spirits of the dying. Her mother's adoptive mother lived in the critical-care wing of the local hospital. She was ninety-two years old and dying of terminal liver cancer.

Emilie knocked on the door of her grandmother's room and opened it. Emilie was saddened to see how old and frail her grand-mother had become. The woman in her fondest memories had been younger and so full of life.

"It's so good to see you again," her grandmother exclaimed as cheerfully as anyone could in her situation.

Emilie walked over and stood next to her grandmother's bed, trying not to look too distressed. "It's good to see you too, Grandma," she replied, bending down to give her a hug and kiss. Her body had grown gaunt and pale in the few short months Emilie had been away. Even her hair had changed; it was as white as snow and thin enough to expose the scalp. But her grandmother's eyes still held the same strength of spirit.

"How have you been?" her grandmother asked.

"I've been better," Emilie answered evasively. "How about you?"

"I'm dying," she answered with a derisive snort. "How do you think I am?"

Emilie was pleased to see that her grandmother had managed to retain her sense of humor through this trial. Her body may have changed, but inside she was still the same.

"I don't want to talk about my health or myself," her grandmother continued. "Tell me what's new with you. What's happened to make your face so sad?"

"Not too much is new, Grandma. I've been working hard at school. Montreal is fun, but I've missed Vancouver."

"Have you met anyone special?" her grandmother inquired.

Emilie laughed. Some things never changed. Her grandmother had always been very interested in her romances. "I did have someone very special, but things didn't work out between us," she answered, feeling her throat tighten up.

"Did he give you that?" her grandmother asked, pointing at Dante's necklace.

Emilie reached up and ran her fingers over it tenderly. "Yes, he did."

"Well, I know that you aren't religious, so it had to belong to someone else."

Emilie smiled. It would be difficult to explain Dante's religion. Her grandmother might be fascinated to hear that she had been dating a real angel. "My boyfriend is religious. Well, he's not my boyfriend anymore," she corrected herself.

"Why isn't he?"

"It's complicated," Emilie started. She pulled a chair up next to her grandmother's bed and sat down. "We didn't have a future together."

"Wow! You only got to Montreal in September. You get serious fast, don't you?"

"He was the serious one," Emilie clarified, smiling wistfully. "He kept talking about getting married. I wanted to take things slow."

"So he wanted more than you were prepared to give him?"

"No...I think I would have married him, eventually."

"Really? Then why didn't you stay with him and see where your relationship took you?"

"Because we were from different worlds. He would have had to give up a lot to be with me."

"How did he feel about that?"

Emilie realized that she had never given much thought to Dante's feelings about what was involved in the breaking of his engagement to Talima. "I never really asked him."

"Why not? If he was the one to make the sacrifices then shouldn't it have been his decision and not yours?"

Emilie swallowed uncomfortably. Her feelings for Dante were too raw to get into a discussion like this. "I don't know, Grandma. It's my life too. I didn't want him to come to resent me later on."

"Was he the resentful type?"

Emilie didn't have the answer to that. Dante didn't seem like a bitter person. He was light-hearted and easygoing. He was content with a relatively simple life for someone who could have anything he wanted. "I didn't know him that well."

"I see." Her grandmother paused for a second, then said, "What was so different about his world?"

Emilie snorted. She didn't know where to begin. "He was an important man from an old family with lots of money and power. They wouldn't have approved of me."

"Really?" her grandmother said doubtfully, patting Emilie's hand. "I'm sure they would have accepted you as soon as they got to know you a bit better."

"That's sweet of you to say, Grandma, but I don't think it would have worked out that way. Where he comes from, a person's social position is very important."

"Where does he come from?"

"It's a long story, but I guess you could call him of Egyptian descent," Emilie estimated, thinking about Dante's mother.

"I would have thought him a Muslim, if he was from Egypt. That angel charm seems Christian," her grandmother said, furrowing her brow.

"Umm…He really wasn't either, Grandma. His religion is a bit complicated."

Her grandmother nodded and said, "All religions are."

True enough, Emilie thought.

"What would he have to give up to marry you?"

How could she explain this? "He would have had to make a lot of difficult sacrifices."

"You don't seem so sure. What did he tell you?"

"It wasn't so much what he had said as what someone close to him said."

"Really? Was this person a reliable source?"

"I think so," Emilie answered, almost under her breath. Something frightening was creeping into her consciousness. Something she hadn't considered. Could Dante's father have lied?

Dante had alluded to the fact that his father was overprotective of him. She had never actually confirmed anything with Dante, a fact that was now causing her a considerable amount of distress. It would kill her to find out that she had thrown away a chance at happiness for nothing.

It couldn't be possible. She just couldn't believe that Professor Ashton would have lied to her. It was possible that he had taken a risk. Maybe he had hoped that their relationship was young enough that she would decide to just walk away. Which, in fact, was exactly what she had done. Tears welled up in her eyes. *What if I've made a terrible mistake?*

"I'm sorry, Emilie. I didn't mean to upset you."

"It's not your fault, Grandma. I have to accept responsibility for my actions. It's just that I loved him…I still love him." Her voice trembled with the emotion she had been trying so desperately to suppress.

"Is it really too late for you to talk to him? Maybe you could still work things out?"

Her grandmother's voice was so soft and hopeful that it actually made Emilie feel worse. "It's definitely too late," she said. "I told him that I didn't want to see him again. I can't just call him up and say that I need to talk."

"Why not?" her grandmother demanded. "He might be happy to hear from you. Maybe he misses you as much as you miss him."

"I don't know. He has a busy and complicated life. Maybe he's even forgotten about me. I doubt we would have been able to work it all out even if we tried. It would probably make everything worse to see each other again."

"You'll never know if you don't try. What's the worst that could happen?" Emilie's grandmother asked carefully. "He could say that he's over you. Would that change anything for you?"

"I don't know. It's too painful to think about. Can we please change the subject?" Emilie pleaded.

"OK, dear. I didn't mean to pry into your personal life," her grandmother replied, perhaps sensing that the conversation may have gone too far.

"It's OK. Why don't you tell me what you know about my mother's birth mother?" Emilie suggested, desperate for any new topic.

Her grandmother adjusted herself slightly in the bed. "Really? I don't know very much. What did you want to know?"

Dante had made jokes about her having a changeling in her family. Could there be any truth to it? "Was my mother a C-section delivery?" she asked.

"I really don't know."

"Was she a big baby?"

"Yes, I believe she was. Why are you so interested in all of this?" Her grandmother was looking at her strangely. "I'm just curious," Emilie answered innocently. "Did she, by any chance, have teeth when she was born?" she asked, feeling a bit silly.

"Yes, she did." Her grandmother looked surprised. "Did your mother tell you about that?"

"I'm sure she did."

"We found it very strange, but they fell out and normal teeth grew in."

"Did she...bite people?" Emilie asked sheepishly.

Her grandmother threw her a scathing glance. "We just thought she was teething."

Emilie couldn't believe it. *No*, she thought to herself. *My own mother*. It wasn't possible.

There was one way to know. "What did you know about her real father?"

"Nothing," her grandmother answered sadly. "We think the poor girl had been raped."

Someone might have been out hunting without a license. But how was it that she survived that kind of attack? Dante had said that his kind didn't have to kill someone to get blood. It was possible that she had been raped and left alive or simply left for dead. Maybe her attacker had been interrupted before he was finished.

But all Beyowans were born Beyowan. Emilie's mother had been human. It was a ridiculous idea. Wasn't it? And yet, her mother had often been mistaken for her older sister even with a forty-year difference in their ages.

Emilie couldn't believe that she was actually entertaining such fanciful ideas. Her imagination was running away with her. She laughed it off and changed the subject.

♨

It was New Year's Eve, and Caroline had insisted on going out to a club to celebrate. As she watched Caroline and their friends dancing together, Emilie thought about what she would resolve to do differently this coming year. She was going to have to be more careful about what she wished for. Sometimes the wanting was better than the having.

If she was lucky enough to find love again, she resolved to be completely open with him. There would be no more second guessing of hasty decisions.

Caroline made her way toward Emilie through the crowd. "How are you doing?" she asked sympathetically, taking the vacant seat next to Emilie.

She pasted a cheerful grin on her face. "I'm OK."

"Liar," Caroline accused.

Emilie smiled and patted her friend on the shoulder. "I'm trying."

"Isn't it getting any easier? It's been almost a month now."

"No, I think it's actually getting a bit worse."

"Really?"

"Since I talked to my grandmother, I've started to second guess my decision to breakup with Dante. I should have talked to him."

"You're better off without him," Caroline blurted.

Emilie sighed heavily. "I don't understand why you can't accept that he was never physically abusive to me. He was different from other guys, I'll give you that, but he was only rough in a playful way."

"Whatever...I'm still standing by my opinion of him. I think he's an intimidating, kinky pervert. Granted he's absolutely, positively gorgeous, but a pervert nonetheless."

Dante would have gotten a laugh out of that description of him, and he would have found some witty response. Emilie couldn't afford to ruin all of her relationships, so she chose not to get into an argument with Caroline about Dante's strengths and weaknesses. She just stood up and headed for the dance floor. "Let's go dance. I need to burn off some energy," she called over her shoulder.

"Sounds good to me!" Caroline exclaimed, heading in the direction of the DJ's booth. "I'll get the DJ to play some of our favorite songs."

All of their friends welcomed Emilie enthusiastically. She was beginning to find everyone's pity somewhat tiresome. She took some solace in the fact that when she was dancing, she could close off her mind and just lose herself in the music.

After a few songs, Emilie heard Caroline call to her. "You're going to have to tone it down a notch or two or you're going to be harassed by half of the men in the club tonight."

Emilie had been so internally focused that she hadn't noticed what she was doing, or anyone's reactions to her. Maybe a break and a drink were in order. The last thing she wanted was the attention of anyone in the club. She shouted over the music, "I'm going to get a drink! Do you want something?"

"No, I'm good for now, thanks!" Caroline shouted back. "Watch out for that guy at the bar. He's been watching you like a hawk for a while now. I don't know what it is about you that attracts these enormous gorgeous guys. If you ever figure it out let me know so I can try it out for myself."

Emilie sniggered as she looked toward the bar to see who Caroline was referring to. The smile quickly slid off of her face when she found him. He was definitely Beyowan. He was too tall, too broad, and too beautiful to be human. Plus he was well dressed and, judging by his even bigger companion, who was looking around nervously, he was a nobleman out with his bodyguard. The very last thing she needed was to be targeted by some demon out hunting without a license.

She was grateful that she wasn't fertile this week. Dating Dante had forced her to pay more attention to her cycle. At least this stranger wouldn't be all over her like a rash. She was going to make every effort to avoid him, and hopefully he would leave her alone.

Emilie went to the bar and tried to put as much distance between herself and the Beyowans as possible. She was leaning against the bar, watching the bartender pour her drink, when she heard an eerily resonating voice behind her say, "I was wondering about your necklace."

Emilie's heart sank to her shoes. She turned and looked into some of the most beautiful blue eyes she had ever seen. The man attached to them was as tall as Jude but not as powerfully built. He had short sandy-blond hair and was dressed in impeccable style.

She couldn't help being impressed. *It must be instinctive,* she thought, *having your hormones so easily manipulated by a beautiful person of the opposite sex.* Too bad he wasn't the same species. Her first instinct should have been fear. "Why do you ask?" she replied, looking him up and down suspiciously.

He seemed confused and distracted. "That symbol has a special meaning where I come from. I find it odd that someone...like you...would be wearing one."

Dante had told her that she was beautiful enough to make other Beyowan men need to verify her scent to be sure she was human. Perhaps this was why he was so confused. Her looks, grace, and the angel around her neck had led him to believe something that wasn't true.

"Someone like me. What does that mean?" she asked innocently.

He didn't know how to respond. He hadn't had enough time to figure out how to react to her humanity. An uncomfortable grin stretched across his face. "Are you a Christian?"

"No, are you?" she answered, smiling at him knowingly.

He looked her over carefully, probably trying to figure out if she knew what he was. Perhaps it was all the alcohol she had consumed over the course of the evening, but she was feeling a bit more confident than she should, playing this game in a crowded human club. He was, after all, a demon, but he was in her world and would have to tread lightly in such a public place.

"No," he replied. "I'm not religious, but where I'm from that symbol is worn by people that follow a different religion." He wore a rather familiar dazzling grin as he reached a long finger over to touch the charm around her neck.

Emilie didn't want him to get any ideas about where else his fingers would be permitted to wander. "Where are you from?" she asked, leaning back against the bar. His family tree hadn't started growing on this continent. Plus he wasn't talking about where he lived. He was talking about his world.

"I'm from Los Angeles," he answered, mirroring her grin.

Good answer, she thought. "What are you doing here?"

The stranger was trying his best to close the distance between them. He was probably accustomed to receiving a warmer reception from human girls. "Just visiting," he replied innocently, glancing toward his friend, who was watching them with a worried look on his face.

"I didn't mean what are you doing in Vancouver. I meant what are you doing here, in this club?"

At this point, he almost had her pinned to the bar. He smiled and rolled his eyes angelically. "I'm just enjoying a change of scenery and having a little fun. There's no harm in that, is there?"

Emilie had to laugh. Beyowan men were as charming as they were beautiful. She hadn't met very many of them, but they all seemed to be highly intelligent. Plus many of them had special abilities, so she would have to be prepared for the unexpected.

"It all depends on what kind of fun you're *hunting* for," Emilie clarified, holding her drink out in front of her in an attempt at making him take a step away from her.

He closed his eyes and snickered softly. She had just let him know that she understood exactly what he was and what he was up to.

"I wasn't sure what I was hunting for, but I'm starting to get a clearer image," he answered with a more determined look in his eyes.

She had to get away from him quickly. He was probably a spoiled nobleman, used to getting what he wanted, and she didn't want to put herself on the menu. As sad and unhappy as she had been feeling of late, she was far from suicidal. "You need to keep in mind that some game is more wary than others. You may need to choose your quarry carefully."

A huge grin stretched across his face. His eyes roamed over her body so erotically that she could almost feel it on her skin. She instantly understood that she was only making matters worse for herself. Instead of being warned away by her remarks, he was being further stimulated by her intellect. Every woman could tell when harmless flirtation was getting out of hand, and Emilie had serious alarm bells sounding in her mind. She didn't want this man waiting for the bar to close so he could try to separate her from her friends.

"Sometimes stalking more wary game makes the hunt much more exciting and heightens the anticipation for the hunter," he purred. "Otherwise the kill can be anticlimactic." He ran the backs of his fingers sensuously down Emilie's arm from her shoulder to her elbow.

She suppressed a shudder. He was getting too resolute for her taste. "Sometimes getting caught hunting without the proper license can be very unsatisfying as well," she cautioned, trying to warn him with her eyes and her body language to keep his hands to himself.

His grin turned far more malevolent. "Who said that I was unlicensed?"

His voice sounded much too confident, eroding what was left of hers. If he did have a license then she could be in serious trouble. Then she remembered something pivotal. Dante had told her that his license protected her from others of his kind. She didn't know if he still had a license, but she could at least try to bluff her way out of this situation. Emilie ran Dante's angel charm along the chain. "Some licensed hunters don't want to share their game with others."

The Beyowan smiled nervously and glanced around the bar to see if he could find anyone watching them. He looked at her in confusion and said, "You have a very dark Angel in your life. I would be careful taking anything for granted if I were you."

Emilie was relieved to see a hint of disappointment in his eyes and she hoped he was going to abandon his pursuit of her. "I'm still alive," she countered.

"For now," he warned, looking her hard in the eyes. He was probably confused about why she knew so much about his world. "I don't believe your guardian angel is watching over you tonight. He's most likely off hunting other game. Perhaps you'd like to experience a different hunter."

"I know what to expect from men like you, and I wouldn't trust you to let me walk away from you."

He laughed. "I can see your point. Not that it will make any difference, but some of us have better control than others." He ran his eyes over her suggestively.

Emilie was flattered, but it made her heart ache to think about her angel. She desperately wished that she was back in Montreal, in bed with him.

"I'm dying of curiosity. Can I have your angel's name?" the Beyowan asked. "Perhaps I know him."

"I thought all of you little princes were related," she answered, smiling sweetly.

He shook his head in disbelief. "In many ways that's true, unfortunately. I didn't realize that any princely Angels lived here in Vancouver."

Emilie realized that she had accidently informed him of her angel's social class. Dante was considered a prince because he was a legal child of noble blood. Now she really had this man intrigued. "No more twenty questions," she scolded. "You're not going to get his name out of me unless you have the ability to read minds."

Her admirer was obviously disappointed. "I wasn't lucky enough to be born with any abilities. Does your princely Angel have any abilities?"

Emilie brought her hand up and made a zipped lip gesture. If she said anything more then he might be able to deduce Dante's identity. "What's your name?"

He shrugged. "You must know that I would only lie. Plus we all have our own human names. You might not even know your angel's real family name."

Emilie nodded, but the fact that she didn't react may have led him to believe that she did know his name.

"Come on now," he pleaded. "You have to give me *something*."

"Maybe you should call the council office and make some kind appointment. It would be safer for you," Emilie suggested. It would be great if she could spare some other girl a grisly death.

The man snorted and wrinkled his face up in disgust. "If they had anything half as tempting as you at the office, then I would be there instead of here."

"Aren't there any good clubs for your own kind here in Vancouver? I'm sure you could find someone willing to put up a good fight."

He threw his head back and laughed. Then he ran his eyes over her erotically again. "Not many mistresses are so open-minded and understanding." He paused thoughtfully for a second. "I can see why you're still alive."

"You're very sweet for such a dangerous animal. I hope you find something fun to play with tonight," Emilie said as she worked her way around him, trying to get back to Caroline and her group.

He smiled broadly. "Thank you. But I would advise you to change your name and go on an extended vacation." Then he turned and headed back toward his bodyguard.

Hopefully he would leave to pursue other opportunities. He was smart enough to realize that if any girls disappeared from this club then she would be able to describe him to the authorities. Even if he was licensed, he would still need to be as discreet as possible.

The stranger watched her dance for a while longer, then he and his friend got up and left. A huge wave of relief washed over her as he disappeared.

Unfortunately her thoughts had stuck on Dante, and she wondered what he was doing tonight, or who he was with. One way or another, it was no longer any of her business. As much as it hurt, she wished him well. He deserved to be happy.

Chapter 22

Anew year had just begun and Dante was working as many hours as he physically could. The small amount of spare time he allocated for himself was dedicated to his martial arts students and to his own training. As he dressed after an unusually vigorous session, he contemplated dropping in at the temple in Thailand for a little solitary prayer.

Jude had an appointment for a workout of a different kind and had already left. Dante winced. He still couldn't stomach the thought of touching any other woman. Getting back to work was one thing, getting back into that aspect of his old life would take some time.

It had been a long day here in Bangkok and he would have to go to his mansion to change before going to the temple. He couldn't show up there in his venom-running gear, not that anyone was unaware of his career choices; he would change his clothes out of respect. After tightening his utility belt, he removed his phone from a pocket to check for calls. The message light was flashing. Upon further inspection, he found a text from Gomez. Dante growled out his frustrations. *How did that man get this number?* he silently asked the device in his hand.

The door on that part of his life was supposed to be closed. Purson had found and exterminated the mole at the Montreal office, cutting Gomez off from his source of information. So badly that it had affected his club revenue.

Purson had made an example of the changeling in question. Now many others were afraid to frequent the club lest they draw the ever-watchful eye of the council. Plus after the kidnapping of Eliza Robertson, many didn't trust Gomez. He had crossed lines that human partners were not supposed to cross. The Robertsons were protected and Gomez had seriously over-stepped, but it had cost him dearly in the end.

Dante had even heard rumors that other crime lords were circling like vultures, waiting for Gomez to make a fatal error. The tentative hold Marquez had on the city was dependent on how Gomez ran his business. Marquez was likely to be very upset with the current state of his affairs, and Gomez would bear the brunt of his anger.

Out of curiosity he opened the message and read:

I have something you want. To get it back, you'll have to bring me something I want.

He scrolled down to find a picture of Emilie, tied and gagged. Her long dark hair partially hid her face, but she was wearing a sweater he recognized as one of her favorites.

Dante's heart leaped into his throat. Soeren hadn't reported her arrival back in Montreal. They had left her alone only for an instant and now Gomez had her. Dante had wanted to respect her wishes and keep his distance, giving her time to realize that they were meant to be together. Now he would have to look her in the eyes and see how much the woman he loved wished she had never met him. *How I am supposed to do that?* he demanded of himself. *And how am I supposed to get my hands on pure venom?*

He took a deep breath and tried to calm himself. His emotional turmoil was interfering with his reasoning, and he needed to focus on a solution to this crisis. First, he couldn't ignore the message. It had been sent almost an hour ago. He typed:

Working on it.

That should buy him some time. Next was the problem of the venom. *What are my options?* he asked himself. He could walk into the venom palace and purchase pure venom from the source, but such a thing would surely be reported as suspicious. Purson would find out and would guess it had to do with Emilie, and then she would be exterminated like any other pest.

Dante didn't have any upcoming shipments of pure venom, only processed industrial grade venom and fatal venom for darts.

He could steal some from any of the labs he had access to. *No, I can't do that,* he scolded himself. *The labs are run twenty-four hours a day. Security is far too tight. I'd never get away with it, and I'd ruin my reputation. Plus Purson would find out, and as soon as I freed Emilie from Gomez, she'd be dead anyway.*

Dante had to find a way to get Gomez what he wanted without putting Emilie at even greater risk. He growled out his frustration. It appeared that his hands were securely tied. No matter which path he chose, it led to the same unpleasant place.

One option stood out in his mind. He pulled out his phone and dialed his cousin's office. With almost half a day's time difference, it was early in Montreal, but like most ambitious people, Purson worked long hours and was likely to be in already.

Luckily he was, and Dante was put right through. "Good morning," Purson sang cheerfully into the phone.

Dante wasn't entirely sure if he wanted to divulge this sensitive situation to his cousin but knew he would likely find out one way or another. Perhaps it would be better to come forward from the get go. The risk was that Purson would lose patience and want Emilie dead. Given the choice, Dante would prefer that she be killed by Gomez than by the council. "I have a big problem," Dante muttered with considerable reluctance.

"I don't like the sound of this," Purson said. "Maybe you should come in to the office, where we'll have more privacy."

"Good idea."

Dante hung up and made his way out of the gym and toward the main entrance of the Bangkok Council Office, where he could safely open a mesay portal without setting off the alarms. It only took a moment before he was back in Montreal and sitting across from his cousin.

"So let's have it," Purson urged.

"Gomez has my mistress," Dante admitted and winced at the angry expression spreading across Purson's face.

"Your mistress *again.*"

"I know, I know…"

"Couldn't we just let him have her?" Purson argued. "I'll let you pick out another one, free of charge."

"I don't want another one!" Dante insisted, then instantly regretted the tone he'd used to speak to such a dangerous man.

"I see," Purson purred. "So what do you propose we do about this?"

"Can I buy some venom to give him?" Dante asked, wincing again.

"Your mistress is nothing but trouble," the chairman growled. "You know what Gomez is planning to do with it, don't you?"

"Couldn't we give him something inferior, with little or no chance of success?"

"There are simple tests to gauge the quality as well as the type of venom. He's sure to check it before he hands over your mistress."

"You're right, of course," Dante admitted. "Listen, I could have tried all sorts of underhanded ways of dealing with Gomez behind your back. I don't want to make a mess of my life, but I don't want my mistress dead. Isn't there anything we can do to get Gomez off my back once and for all?"

"I'm grateful that you came to me," Purson soothed. "There may be something we could do that would be mutually beneficial."

"I would appreciate anything you could do," Dante muttered, eyes locked on his shoes. Being in such a vulnerable position was excruciating and he hoped he would never experience anything like this again. Unfortunately he knew that he would probably be back here in a similar situation in the coming months. He had allowed himself to postpone dealing with the pain of his loss by clinging to the hope that Emilie would eventually come back to him. Now he had to deal with the reality that she was forever out of reach, and unless he could figure out a tempting bargain to secure her freedom from the council, he would be forced to kill her once his license expired.

Purson proved his resourcefulness and had all of the arrangements completed in a remarkably short amount of time. Just enough time for Dante to go back to Thailand to pick up Jude and to go to Miami to collect Rodney, who had jumped at the chance to be included in another of Dante's meetings. Dante was desperate to get Emilie back, but he wasn't stupid. Going in to face Gomez alone was insane.

Jude was furious with the whole situation and was doing little to keep his anger to himself. "I can't believe Purson agreed to this nonsense," he complained. "This bromance the two of you have going on is getting nauseating."

"Shut up, Jude," Dante warned. "I'm not in the mood."

"Is anyone gonna tell me exactly what we're doing?" Rodney asked, glancing back and forth between the other two men.

"We're going to see Gomez about an exchange. That's all," Dante soothed.

Age and experience may not have been on Rodney's side, but he was no fool. His jaw muscles bulged and he nodded his head thoughtfully.

"Listen, if you want out, I'll understand," Dante said.

"No," Rodney assured him. "Sounds like fun." A menacing grin spread across his face, his eyes reflecting his excitement. "I've been looking forward to flexing my muscles in a *real* fight."

Jude laughed heartily and slapped Rodney on the back. "You're gonna do great in this business."

The three men grew serious as Purson approached with a small medical carrying case in one hand. "Here you go," he said. "I'm charging you for this, understand? Regardless of the outcome."

Dante nodded and handed the case to Jude, then extended a hand to each man. They would be dropping in on Gomez unannounced. The council was sending a van full of security officers, just in case there was a mess to clean up.

Dante did a preliminary scan of Gomez's club while hidden in mesay. His reconnaissance had served two purposes. Firstly, he needed to know if Emilie was being held in the building, which she wasn't. Secondly, he wanted to know how well fortified Gomez's club was. Fortunately it was too early for anyone but the minimum of staff to be in.

Dante briefed his companions of the situation and then brought them all out of mesay inside the front door. As soon as they had feet on solid ground, Dante barked, "It's gonna get ugly in here. Anyone who values their lives should leave now or forever hold their pieces!"

A young human male dressed in a cheap suit approached, looking irritated. "You sure know how to be discreet, don't you?"

"I don't react well to threats," Dante growled.

"We expected you to arrive alone," the man explained.

"Fools."

"Your weapons," the offended man demanded, extending his hands.

"You've gotta be kidding, right?" Jude hissed, flashing him with his eyes.

"Do you take me for an idiot?" Dante roared, fangs fully extended. The glow from his eyes was so bright it forced the human to shade his eyes.

Even Rodney took a step back, seeing how truly ferocious his normally light-hearted martial arts master could be when provoked.

The man recovered quickly and smiled. "Do we have a deal or not?"

Dante stuffed the case in Jude's direction and barked, "Fine. I don't have the patience for this garbage. Tell Gomez to keep her." He extended his hands to both Jude and Rodney, who jumped to attention.

"Wait!"

Everyone looked down the hall to see Gomez standing outside his office door. "I was beginning to doubt that you would come."

"I'm here," Dante growled. "Can we get this unpleasantness over with?"

"This way please, gentlemen," Gomez insisted.

Dante tried not to show his relief as he marched down the hallway, deliberately making his body language as confident and powerful as possible, even though he felt like curling into a ball and weeping like a child. He dreaded having to look into Emilie's tear-stained face. He couldn't bear to see her fear or, worse, her revulsion.

"So," Dante growled. "Where is she?"

"After the episode we had with Eliza Robertson, I didn't feel it would be prudent to leave her within easy reach."

Dante nodded. It made perfect sense. Why risk having your bait snatched?

"First things first," Gomez insisted. "What did you bring me?"

"I need assurance that my prize will be returned alive," Dante said, holding the case closer to his body.

Gomez switched on a monitor, displaying Emilie with her entourage. From the look of her surroundings, she was being held in another small office. There seemed to be a filing cabinet off to one side of the chair in which she was bound, and a crooked print in a cheap, gold, metallic frame hung on the wall behind her. At least two armed men were in with her; their faces hidden behind scarves to disguise their identities. Something didn't look quite right about her face, but it was probably swollen from crying and possibly from injury. It was difficult to tell because the lighting was poor and her long hair hung in her face, masking her features.

"See. Everything's fine."

"This could be a recording," Dante argued. "I want to speak to her."

Gomez seemed to have anticipated this demand and had already taken out his phone. "Jackson, let our guest say a few words."

The woman on the screen was passed a phone but didn't look into the camera.

Gomez handed his phone to Dante, who took it eagerly. "Hello."

"Dante?" a familiar voice begged.

"Are you OK?"

"I'm fine..." she began, but the phone was snatched away from her.

There was so much Dante wanted to say to her, but he handed the phone back. Her voice hadn't sounded quite right, but it never did over the phone. Plus it had been weeks since he had spoken to her.

"Here," Dante urged, passing the case to Gomez. "Your turn."

"How very kind," Gomez purred, taking the case with the same eagerness Dante had shown the phone.

The venom had been brought in the same glass tube in which it had been frozen. It was imperative to freeze pure venom as soon as possible to maintain its potency.

"It might still be frozen," Dante warned. "I haven't had it in my possession for long."

"Of course," Gomez said, slipping on a latex glove and removing the tube from the ice packs. "I was hoping you might get some fresh from the source."

Dante laughed. He didn't have a close enough relationship with any of his relatives with venom of this type. To ask such a favor would have been highly unusual and would have been met with some resistance. "Sorry. This was the best I could arrange on such short notice."

Gomez looked as if he might have a few words about how much notice Dante had been given, but wisely kept his comments to himself. He inserted a hypodermic needle into the tube, drawing out a sample of the precious liquid. He then dropped some venom onto the test strip laid out on his desk.

Dante held his breath. He had trusted Purson to provide him with something passable. Perhaps his cousin had tricked him so that he could be rid of Emilie once and for all. The test strip would tell Gomez which venom was in the tube. The color intensity and speed at which the results came to light would indicate the quality of the venom.

Dante craned his neck toward Gomez's desk, trying to catch a peek at the developing results. Gomez held up the strip for Dante to see. The bloodred blot in the middle meant that it was the right venom. But Beyowan eyes were far more sensitive than humans or changelings, and Dante had noticed something odd on the test strip. There was a slight iridescence to the red dot, possibly on an ultraviolet spectrum, undetectable to the human eye. Could Purson have laced the pure venom with fatal venom? Even the smallest amount of fatal venom would contaminate the sample and make transformation impossible. *Perfect*, Dante thought. Both Jude and Rodney were half-breeds and probably hadn't noticed anything odd about the sample. They made no hint of it if they did.

"There you go," Dante said, anxious to finalize the transaction and leave before the deception was discovered. "You have what you want. Now give me Elizabeth." He didn't want to give Gomez time to have his technicians run a sample of the venom through more sensitive testing equipment. The machines would surely detect what the eye had missed.

Dante also meant to test if Gomez knew Emilie's real name, knowing he wouldn't skip a chance to gloat about uncovering more of Dante's lies, but Gomez was silent. Dante clung to the slim hope that Emilie's real identity was still intact.

Their backs to the group, Gomez whispered something to one of his human associates, who ran off to carry out his orders.

"So, seeing how you've won this round, how about you tell me how you found Elizabeth?" Dante probed.

Gomez grinned like the Cheshire Cat. "Even though the council removed my last informant, I still have a few options available to me. So I had someone search through the changeling registry to find her name."

Dante had to harness all of his control to keep from bursting into laughter. *Changeling...* Gomez believed that Emilie was a changeling? Surely someone in his employ would have been able to tell the difference. Something was wrong here. Dante glanced at Jude, who was looking as confused as Dante felt.

"That was very smart of you," Dante encouraged.

Gomez seemed pleased with the compliment and, like many evil villains, appeared to be eager to explain his genius. "I was given a phone number and made arrangements to meet Elizabeth, claiming to have a special job for her," he continued. "And the rest is history."

Dante could scarcely draw breath. They didn't have Emilie. They had someone pretending to be Emilie. But why? What was going on here?

Any way Dante ran the facts through his mind, he came to the same result: Purson. But what was his cousin trying to accomplish with this ruse?

Gomez turned the screen back on and said, "Now, let's just be sure the quality of this product is up to the standards I've been expecting."

On the screen, Dante could see Gomez's human associate approaching the bound and struggling impostor.

Gomez watched Dante with ever increasing concern over his obvious disinterest. "Your skills at bluffing have certainly improved."

"Do whatever you want," Dante growled. He was tempted to just take Rodney and Jude and leave, but his curiosity got the better of him. If the woman was human, she would survive a prick with the needle. If she was a changeling, even the smallest amount of fatal venom would prove fatal. The larger the quantity of the venom simply ensured a quicker, less painful death.

The unfortunate girl almost instantly began to howl, confirming the fact that she was a changeling.

"You are a much colder man than I expected, Mr. Ashton," Gomez growled, obviously miffed at Dante's apathy. He must have been expecting more begging and pleading. "I was hoping that you would at least be as upset about the death of your woman as I was about Sid and Leonard."

"She's just a woman," Dante argued. He was sorry to see any creature suffer, but she was a pawn of Purson's. Her fate was not his responsibility.

"I'm leaving," Dante announced, reaching back for Jude and Rodney.

In an instant, Gomez and his two remaining human associates had drawn out their dart guns. "Step away from the messenger or your ashes will be lost in space," Gomez warned.

Jude and Rodney were forced to comply.

"You've played me for the last time, Mr. Ashton," Gomez hissed. More humans poured into the room and grabbed Jude and Rodney, removing their weapons.

"You're the one who doesn't realize his place in this world, Mr. Gomez," Dante retorted, scrambling to find a way to get Jude and Rodney out unscathed. His right hand came up and innocently brushed across his nose, then came down to the pocket of his trousers, quickly pressing the panic button hidden within as a man grabbed him by each arm, another checking him for weapons. The panic button was found and handed to Gomez.

"What's this?" he asked.

"The last nail in your coffin," Dante explained.

Gomez shook his dart gun, stressing the fact that it was squarely facing Dante. "But I have you."

"Not for long." Dante opened a mesay doorway and disappeared as Gomez fired into the empty air. He reappeared behind his target and clamped both arms around Gomez to keep him from being able to use his arms. Plus he made such an excellent shield.

The walls and floor were awash with human blood. Jude and Rodney had made short work of the humans. Purson's men had stormed the front door and could be heard tidying up the rest of the club, distracting the remaining humans from the happenings in the office.

"Drop the dart gun, Gomez," Dante snarled into the man's ear.

Gomez laughed but fired just as Rodney turned to come to Dante's aid. Luck would have it that Rodney had taken a step, leading with his right leg and was hit in the shin bone of his left, just above the top of his boot. So much room for error, and yet fate was horribly unkind to such a promising young man.

Dante howled out his rage and squeezed Gomez within an inch of his life. "Drop the gun or I'm going to pop every organ in your body one by one."

Gomez complied.

"Why don't you kill him?" Jude roared, stepping over Rodney's ashes on his way over.

"I'm a Dark Angel, Jude. Remember?"

"Can I kill him? Please…"

"No. Let's give him to Rodney's father as a gift."

Jude burst out laughing. "Oh, God!" he exclaimed. "What a fabulous idea!"

"Mr. Gomez," Dante explained, "Rodney's father is the chairman of the Miami Council Office."

"What?" Gomez choked, close to tears. "You never said he was of noble blood."

"I introduced him as the son of a nobleman, but I used his human name, you simpering fool," Dante snarled. "His father is Ronan Xaphan, and Rodney was his only son."

Gomez swallowed hard and closed his eyes. He had probably come to realize that the Xaphan family name was the second-highest-ranking noble bloodline and Rodney's family members would be out for vengeance. Gomez could look forward to experiencing new and creative definitions of agony and despair.

Purson's men had finished with the interior of the club and now arrived to relieve Dante of his burden. Before releasing Gomez, Dante commanded, "Take this one to the council office and call Ronan Xaphan. Rodney was killed, so make sure he's delivered alive."

The black-clad security officer growled ferociously, took a Taser from his utility belt, and walked over to Gomez. "I assure you he'll be treated with kid gloves until Ronan comes to collect him."

"Excellent," Dante purred as Gomez, now sobbing like a child, dropped to the floor, twitching to the sound of an electric discharge. "If you boys don't need us, I'd like to have a few words with Purson."

"This was one of the easiest jobs I've had the pleasure to handle," the officer declared, handcuffing an unconscious Gomez.

"We're done here. The cleanup crew is already on their way to wash these people from existence."

Dante nodded to the man, extended his hand to Jude, and opened a mesay doorway.

It was a short walk to the council office hospital emergency entrance. "Jude, can you find something to do while I have a word with Purson?"

"Sure, man," Jude answered. "No worries."

Dante marched purposefully to his cousin's office and told the assistant it was imperative that he see Purson as soon as possible. Distressed by Dante's angry tone, she scanned her eyes over her screen as if checking Purson's agenda for the morning, picked up the phone, and announced, "Sir, Dante Maxaviel is here to see you. He says it's urgent." She hung up the phone and smiled in relief. "The chairman has been expecting you. Please, go on in."

I bet you have, you bastard, Dante thought bitterly as he walked in.

The chairman rose and extended his hand in casual greeting. "So how'd it go?"

Dante was too upset for pleasantries. He wanted answers. If he took Purson's hand, he risked yanking the limb from its socket. "You're a fiery demon, Purson," he accused. "What the Hell was that?"

"Please, have a seat," Purson insisted, his voice velvety smooth.

Dante staggered and shook his head. "Get out of my brain, Purson. I'm already too worked up and might do something rash."

The chairman had a special ability most beneficial to a man of his position. He controlled people's minds. Each individual reacted differently to his probing, but Dante had never experienced the full force of Purson's determination. His head was beginning to throb, fighting his command.

Purson growled, "I said sit!"

"You've humiliated me enough for one day," Dante muttered through gritted teeth. "You'll have to kill me."

Purson released Dante's mind. "Come now, son," he soothed as Dante staggered as if struck. "Sit down and I'll answer all of your questions."

Dante wiped the blood dripping from his nose, straightened up to regain what little remained of his dignity, and took his seat.

Purson passed him a box of tissues, concern etched into his features. "You're tough as nails, son," he murmured. "I'm actually sweating."

Despite his anger, Dante smiled at the compliment.

He'd always had a close relationship with Purson and his current feelings of betrayal left a bitter taste in his mouth. "I'm gonna pack my bags and leave Montreal."

"Don't say that."

"I expected Gomez to mess with me, Purson. But you? That was underhanded. We're family."

"Your mistress is safe and sound in Vancouver, Dante," Purson soothed. "It troubles me that you don't know this."

"So you were testing the closeness of my relationship with my mistress?"

"Partially," Purson explained. "Why didn't you call her?"

How could Dante explain that he didn't want to scare Emilie half to death if nothing was wrong? She would only rejoice over her decision to leave him. He also didn't want to seem as if he was making up excuses to call her. She might feel he was trying to work his way back into her life instead of letting her move on with it.

"You haven't been in contact with her for quite some time," Purson continued. "Is there a problem?"

"How do you know that?" Dante hissed, but quickly regretted it. "Of course you do. What am I saying?" he added quickly, rubbing his hand across his face in frustration.

"I sent someone out to test her."

"Really?" Dante asked, eyes wide. This was serious. If Emilie had failed the council's test, she would surely have been brought in.

"She did well, son," Purson said. "But I'm worried about this situation."

"It's only January, I still have months left on my license. She's still mine."

"She is," Purson agreed. "But you know what has to be done, right?"

"I know," Dante murmured past the lump in his throat. "Can I count on you to leave her alone now?"

"Yes," Purson answered. "Unless of course either of you gives me reason to suspect something."

"Gomez is out of the picture now so hopefully there won't be any more nonsense from the humans."

"Getting rid of Gomez was my primary reason for this little episode," Purson admitted.

Now Dante was even more confused. "What?"

"I couldn't exactly do anything to him personally. It would be viewed as a conflict of interest."

"I guess, but he didn't know his place. Aren't you within your rights to put him in it?"

"Marquez is responsible for disciplining his men."

"Did you tell Marquez that you were having trouble with Gomez overstepping?"

"I did, but Gomez is Marquez's sister's husband."

Dante was glad that he hadn't targeted Gomez's wife in retaliation. "She's about to be widowed. Will that come back to haunt you?"

"This is why I used you," Purson explained. "Gomez started something personal between the two of you. You've followed protocol at every step and reported everything. So this incident will be seen as something that has been building between the two of you and my hands remain spotlessly clean."

Dante's heart sank into his shoes. "Will everyone know about Emilie?"

"Only you and Jude know what really happened. Everyone else is dead," Purson soothed. "I've already filed complaints stating that you were approached over the sale of pure venom for the purpose of illegal transformations. That's all anyone will need to hear. Your reputation will stand for itself and you'll be perceived as a hero for putting yourself at risk to protect our species from exposure."

"Won't Ronan want an investigation into his son's death?"

"Rodney's death was most unexpected," Purson noted gravely, pausing out of respect for the dead. "Rodney will be given a hero's funeral. But again, you've done well. By giving Ronan his son's killer, he'll be able to satisfy his grief through the torment of the guilty party. He'll have his closure, and he still has his daughter and grandchild to comfort him."

Dante was beyond relief. Beyowans loved to gossip and this would be worthy news. *"Dark Angel goes into murderous rage over human mistress's abduction."*

"Are you still angry?" Purson inquired.

"I'm calming down," Dante muttered. "Where did you find that girl?"

"It's unfortunate that she didn't make it out. She was a valuable asset, but casualties are to be expected in any war, regardless of how small," Purson began. "I tried to find someone with the right bone structure for their camouflage to work well enough to fool both Gomez and you. I gave her some recordings of Emilie's voice so she could mimic it. Then I fed one of Gomez's spies the information I wanted him to have."

"So Emilie is fine?" Dante asked.

"Yes," Purson explained. "But you have to kill her, or I will."

"Don't rush me," Dante muttered, rekindling his previous hopes for reconciliation between the two. "You owe me one for today. Leave Emilie alone and I'll take care of everything."

"She's all yours, but I'll be watching."

Chapter 23

Emilie opened her eyes and saw something move in the darkness of her bedroom. At first she was frightened, but it didn't take her long to realize that it was Dante. He was getting undressed. She was so happy to see him. She watched him take off his clothes amongst the dark shadows of her room, his eyes slightly glowing red. As he approached, she pulled back the covers and patted the spot next to her, crooking her finger at him. She yearned for his touch so badly that she could hardly wait for his naked body to slide into the bed with her. The sound of his soft laughter sent shivers over her skin and her nose could just detect the familiar fragrance of his cologne.

Then she remembered that he wasn't in her life any longer and tried desperately to hang on to the image of him in her mind, but he was already fading out of her imagination. It just wasn't fair. Why couldn't she have been woken out of sleep by the spectacular orgasm he was sure to have given her? At least she could have some pleasure with her pain.

The time on the clock informed her that, not surprisingly, it was the middle of the night.

When she had returned to Montreal with Caroline, she had tried to get back into a regular routine. At least she was doing fantastically well in school this semester. Dante had distracted her from her work last year, but the advantage of being tormented by dreams about him was that she was able to get more studying done. Still, she had been avoiding Professor Ashton like the plague. How could she face him? She kept hoping the pain of losing Dante would get easier so that she would have the strength to see his father. Maybe she could find another professor to be her advisor and help her with her thesis.

It would be difficult to make a change like that in the middle of the year so she resolved to look into it come spring. Maybe she could finish her master's degree at the University of British Columbia. Being back in Vancouver had been therapeutic, and her grandmother's health was deteriorating rapidly. It would be good to spend more time with her before it was too late. She was the last of Emilie's immediate family.

Montreal had lost its appeal. It was just cold and lonely here. She sighed heavily and slid out of bed. Today was Valentine's Day. *Great,* she thought miserably. *Another painful, empty day full of horrid, loathsome angels.*

Fortunately the upcoming holidays would be easier. The Easter Bunny wasn't going to be an issue. She clung to the hope that by her birthday in April, she would be able to go a whole week without any dreams about Dante. Right now, she would read until her eyes stung and then try to catch a few more minutes of sleep before she ran to class.

ॐ

Dante lay in his bed, feeling numb and empty. He stared blankly up at the ceiling.

Jude knocked at the door and opened it slowly. "Colin and I are going to Reds tonight. You really should come with us. It's Valentine's Day. This is the biggest party night of the year. It's been over two months now. You should be feeling fairly…needy…by now."

Dante's couldn't bear the thought of touching any woman other than Emilie. But he hadn't touched a woman in a long time and had a lot of pent-up sexual energy. Maybe it would do him some good to get back into the fray. There would be a lot of women out for Valentine's Day. Perhaps he needed to adjust his attitude and stop thinking about what he'd lost and focus on what he could find.

"Fine! I'm coming," Dante announced as he got up out of the bed.

"Really?" Jude asked, then quickly corrected himself by adding, "I mean…of course you are! I'll give you a minute to get ready and change." Jude walked off, leaving Dante's bedroom door hanging open as he hollered enthusiastically down the hall to Colin. "He's coming!"

"Good! It's about time!" Colin yelled back from his own room.

Dante headed into the shower. He smiled to himself and shook his head. *I can do this*, he chanted to himself over and over as he undressed.

A couple of hours later, Dante sat at the bar, staring into the bottom of his empty glass. The party in the club was going full tilt, but he just couldn't get in the spirit.

A bit more than five months had passed since he'd last been here. A small blink in time and yet it contained some of the most significant moments of his life. He had experienced the most joy and the most pain of his existence.

Out of the corner of his eye, Dante noticed Jude walking toward him from the back of the club. "You haven't been sitting here by yourself doing coke, have you?" Jude accused, looking into Dante's eyes with concern.

Dante shrugged. "No, I don't want to get too aggressive tonight. I have enough restless energy as it is."

"No kidding! Now come and dance with us. There are some interesting people here you might want to meet."

Dante just rolled his eyes doubtfully.

Jude smiled and leaned in closer. "Gavin Mamona's little sister is here. She's only twenty-two. What a cute little thing. You've had his wife. You may as well take his little sister for a ride."

Dante was curious to see her again. A devilish grin slithered across his face. The last time he'd been here, he'd been trying to forget Emilie with Tasia, but…Gabrielle? "She's too pure-blooded for the likes of me. She'll be after Colin…and even he might not measure up."

Jude smiled crudely. "She's been dancing with Colin and asking about *you*."

Dante laughed. "Has she?" he whispered, almost to himself. He downed his last two shots, got up, and headed to the dance floor with Jude trotting alongside him, smiling like a fox in a hen house.

As Dante approached the dance floor, he searched the faces to find his quarry. The last time he had seen Gavin's younger sister was at the last cotillion, when Gabrielle and the other young ladies from noble families had been introduced to Beyowan society.

Dante was taken off guard by how much she'd changed in such a short period of time. Gavin's father, Garin Mamona, must be very busy indeed, brokering marriage offers for this fine young woman.

Dante smiled. He wouldn't be submitting any. He didn't have a shot with Tasia, and she wasn't as upper-crust as Gabrielle Mamona. Dante had always preferred a challenge and only targeted women who were his social superiors. Maybe he would not only get the privilege of bedding Gabrielle, but he could get even luckier if she became pregnant in the process. Garin would be positively seething. Dante and Garin had a history, and it was anything but good. At one time, Gavin and Dante had been almost as close as brothers. Almost. But even at the peak of their friendship, Gavin would never have wanted Dante for a brother-in-law. That just made the game all the more tempting to Dante.

"Here he is," Jude said cheerfully to Gabrielle. "I told you he was around here somewhere. Dante, you remember Gabrielle?"

"Yes, but I wouldn't have recognized her. She's grown into such a fine young woman," Dante answered as he ran his eyes over her suggestively.

Gabrielle seemed pleased with his attention. She smiled back and ran her own eyes speculatively over him as well. Dante leaned in to kiss her, unsure of how he would be received. She kept smiling, but parted her lips for him at the last second. He decided to take the opportunity to greet her a bit more sensuously than was normally considered polite.

He was encouraged by her response as he pulled back slowly, gauging her reaction. She was still smiling, but he thought he saw something else in her eyes—a spark of interest perhaps? He felt emboldened, but he wasn't naive. He needed to be careful with this magnitude of a challenge. He was out of practice and didn't want to make any mistakes.

He greeted all of the others in the group politely and then tried not to pay too much attention to Gabrielle while he danced with everyone else. He probably wasn't emotionally ready for this type of game, but physically was a different story entirely. He tried not to think about how long he'd gone without sex. He had a reputation to uphold, and a woman like Gabrielle would require controlled focus.

But it didn't take long for Dante to get bored. He had never enjoyed the tedious small talk that often accompanied dancing in council clubs. He excused himself from the group and walked toward the bar. He was anticipating a long wait for Norma, the bartender, to get a chance to serve him. After all, it was the busiest night of the year at the club, but he wasn't in any hurry. In his peripheral vision, he noticed Gabrielle following him. Knowing his face was hidden from view, he grinned devilishly.

Physically, she didn't resemble Emilie, which was good because he couldn't have handled that. With her high-heeled shoes on, she was only a couple of inches shorter than he was. She had a spectacular hourglass figure, with broader shoulders and childbearing hips, making her waist tiny in comparison. Her skin was a rich medium brown, and she had greenish hazel eyes with dark, shoulder-length hair. Gabrielle was more than just cute, she was stunning.

Dante wondered how much experience she had in bed with rogues like him. Her father would be doing his best to encourage her toward eligible men of exceptional breeding. She was too young to be out of her father's sight for long, which brought to mind a couple of important questions. "So what are you doing here in Montreal?" Dante asked casually as she took the seat next to his at the bar.

"My dad is here on business. He thought it would be fun for me to tag along."

A mischievous gleam shone in Dante's eyes. "You mean Garin didn't trust you to stay home on your own?"

She smiled broadly without comment.

"Does Garin know that you're here tonight?" Dante asked. He needed to know whether or not her father was going to charge in at any moment to retrieve her.

"No," she replied. She shot him a suspicious look, as though she was wondering if he was going to inform her father of her whereabouts. "He got stuck in a late meeting. He thinks I'm out shopping."

Dante smiled. This wasn't good news. There wasn't anyone here in Montreal on the same social level she was. Her father hadn't asked her to tag along in order to show her off to any potential husbands. Garin wouldn't risk her wandering around Montreal, getting attached to anyone too far below herself. "The stores are closed now," Dante said. "He'll figure out what you're up to soon enough."

Gabrielle gave him an unconcerned shrug.

"So what are you doing here?" he asked more specifically.

"I'm here for the same reason you are, I assume…" she answered, batting her eyelashes at him with suggestive playfulness.

He suspected that she didn't have much experience in the art of clubbing Beyowan style. She was being flirtatious, but Dante was concerned about her intentions toward him. He didn't want to waste a lot of time with Gabrielle, especially if her father might arrive at any minute.

In truth, if he took her upstairs into one of the playrooms, Garin would be forced to wait until Dante was done with her. No matter how rich you were or how pure your blood was, you couldn't barge into any of the occupied rooms. It just wasn't acceptable, and every council club around the world had the same rules. But Dante didn't relish the thought of looking Garin in the eyes afterward. Perhaps she was worth it. He certainly was curious to find out.

He would have to be on his best behavior with Gabrielle. If she came out of their room bloodied and crying, Daddy would be annoyed. If she came out flushed and smiling dreamily, Daddy would be really angry. Dante wanted to make her father furious.

"What I meant was," he purred, flashing her a dazzling smile, "what are you doing *here*…with me?"

She appeared a tad uncomfortable with his bluntness but remained composed. "I'm just curious," she replied mischievously.

He nodded his head. "Curious about me?"

"Yes." She ran her eyes over him. "Tasia has mentioned a few things about you."

Dante had to laugh. This could either be really good for him or really bad. "What exactly did Tasia say?" he asked, cocking his head.

"She said to keep away from you."

He laughed again. This was definitely good for him. "Did she happen to say why?"

"Yes, she did," Gabrielle answered, smiling coquettishly. "But I'm not going to betray her confidence."

He flashed her his sad puppy dog look and whined, "That's not fair. She doesn't have to know." Beyowans were incorrigible gossips, and he could tell that she was itching to divulge all of Tasia's secrets. He decided to bait her to see if he could convince her to be more forthcoming. "Did Tasia tell you that I'm an animal in bed?"

Gabrielle pretended to be shocked. "Are you?" she inquired.

With Tasia I am. With you…we'll see, he thought. "It depends. I can be, if I'm properly motivated."

She seemed intrigued. Dante was wondering where this conversation was headed when the DJ started playing the song that he and Emilie had danced to back in October, when they had been just friends. Visions of that night flashed through Dante's mind. His chest started to ache and he suddenly felt nauseous.

"Are you OK?" Gabrielle asked, looking him over with concern.

"I'm fine," he replied, trying desperately to smile through his pain. "I just hate this song."

Gabrielle was happy enough to let it slide. "So you're still not married yet," she said.

"Nope. I like being a bachelor," Dante lied. "What about you?"

She made a sour face. "I'm too young to worry about breeding."

He nodded his head in understanding. "You're way too young," he agreed with an evil edge to his voice. That fact wasn't going to deter him or any other man in the building.

She tittered behind her hand, obviously basking comfortably in his attention. "You have nice hair," Gabrielle murmured. "I like it longer like this. It suits you."

His heart seized in his chest. It was bad enough to have Emilie's song playing in his ears but to have Gabrielle mention his hair was making him feel worse.

Norma finally came over and said, "Sorry it took so long. What can I do for you guys?"

Gabrielle asked, "Do you serve any food here?" She turned to Dante and ran her fingers playfully into his hair from his temple up over his ear. "Are you hungry?"

He felt as if he had been punched in the stomach. He closed his eyes and saw Emilie's beautiful face smiling at him. He answered in a haunted voice, "Always…" *What am I doing here?* he asked himself. *I still love her.*

Dante took a second to compose himself and then took Gabrielle's hand out of his hair as gently as he could. It wasn't her fault that he was an emotional wreck. He looked into her confused eyes and said, "I'm sorry, Gabrielle. But I have to go. It was nice seeing you again." She was about to protest, but he was already up and practically sprinting for the exit. "Goodnight, Norma," he called over his shoulder as he bolted for the coat check.

He was almost out of the club when Jude came rushing up and grabbed him by the shoulder. "Hey! Where are you going? Gabrielle said that you were leaving. She looked so disappointed. I thought things were going well between the two of you."

"I can't do this," Dante answered, his voice trembling. He was far too agitated for an argument.

"Oh, it's been a while, but I'm sure you'll remember if you give yourself half a chance," Jude sneered, slapping him on the shoulder.

"That's not what I meant, Jude. I'm not ready yet."

"What's your problem, man?"

"I think I've had too much coke. I'm feeling violent," Dante lied.

Jude wasn't buying that excuse. "I'm sure Gavin wouldn't appreciate you bloodying up his sister."

Dante snorted. "Like I've ever cared about what Gavin Mamona thought about anything. But Garin is going to show up here any second, looking for his daughter."

"I see. Well, maybe you should leave then. It might be safer for you. You and Garin have never gotten along very well. Do you want me to come too?" Jude glanced longingly back into the club.

"No, you stay with Colin. He may need help getting home," Dante joked.

"OK. See you later."

"Have fun!" Dante called over his shoulder as he walked through a mesay doorway on his way home. He intended to curl up in bed and wallow in self-pity. *God knows it's been working so well these last two months,* he thought sarcastically to himself.

Chapter 24

Dante inhaled a deep breath through flared nostrils. The night air was ripe with the mingled scents of many creatures, but the unique scent he was searching for still eluded him. Dawn was fast approaching. The darkness outside would soon be waning, but inside his soul, it had become impenetrable.

Dante was angry with God. The only woman he had ever loved had been torn from his life, leaving his soul open and bleeding. The only logical reason for his current suffering was that God was punishing him for having sex with Emilie and planning to take away her humanity. Satan himself had been cast from Heaven for refusing to give up the love of a human woman.

Dante was so confused and bitter. Why would God give him a human soul mate unless it was some kind of cruel test of faith? His own mother had been bound in love to a human man. She had transformed him into a changeling with her own bite. Perhaps she had been denied entry into Heaven for her sins. Not all Dark Angels believed in the bonding of soul mates. Some believed that being joined to a soul mate was one of the highest rewards to be bestowed upon mortals. Others considered a human soul mate a reminder of the difficult choices faced by the forefathers.

What added insult to injury was the fact that he had finally made an effort to move on. He had tried to get back into his world and do what was expected and encouraged for a man in his position. And God had made him suffer for that too. As soon as he was about to lose himself in the comfort of another woman's body, he had to be reminded of Emilie. Not just reminded—tormented. It was as if she was haunting him.

He couldn't eat, he couldn't sleep, and he couldn't lead a normal life. He was in Hell, and he wasn't even dead. Yet...

He couldn't stand another three hundred years of this.

He had gone home from Reds and stayed in bed for two straight days. It hadn't helped, but it had never helped before. Nothing helped. Jude and Colin had tried everything to console and encourage him, but no light could penetrate the darkness building within him.

Then Dante had come to a decision. If God was going to put him in Hell, then he might as well embrace the life of a demon.

Something moved in the trees and drew Dante's attention back to his task. He was excited to be hunting on his land in Thailand. He was ravenous, and every fiber of his being felt alert and sensitive. The Bangkok Council Office had notified him that one of the perimeter sensors had been tripped by humans trespassing on his land. This was his second night out alone in the jungle. Yesterday he had found nothing, but today he was feeling more hopeful. He was dressed in black and armed only with a hunting knife, primed and ready for the kill.

Another deep breath brought with it the faint smell of smoke. A wicked grin cracked his face. Tonight would be lucky after all. He followed the scent, keeping his eyes and ears open for anything.

It didn't take him long to find their camp. He picked his way slowly and quietly through the underbrush, careful to stay downwind of his prey. Not that he expected them to have the ability or the common sense to smell him, but he wanted to be absolutely sure to catch them unaware. *Stupid humans!*

He hadn't eaten in three, almost four days and felt almost reckless with anticipation. He could see their camp. They must be inexperienced hunters because it didn't appear that they had caught anything yet. *Good,* he thought, *more animals and less humans.*

There were three of them, asleep around the misleading security of their fire, uninvited on his land. Dante smiled. He snuck up on the camp and hid behind a dense clump of underbrush. He growled, and they woke. *Good,* he thought, *come and get the helpless animal, you overconfident fools.* He growled again, louder this time. The poachers got up, shined their flashlights in his direction, and tried to assess the risk to their group. They were well armed, but that didn't make it an even match.

They were coming out to investigate, and Dante was ready. He backed through the underbrush, leading them away from the meager safety of their fire. He wanted to split them up and take them down one at a time. He popped in and out of mesay, making noises here and there to confuse them and send them in different directions, then jumped up into a tree to wait as footsteps headed his way. He flattened himself along a branch and lay still, waiting.

He had never done anything like this before in all of his life. He had only ever had fresh human blood combined with sex, and he hadn't killed anyone in the process. He had always kept a tight rein on his instincts, all the while allowing the woman's blood to fuel the fire of his passion without losing control over his body. Tonight he would surrender to his most basic, primal instincts. Tonight he would revel in violence and celebrate the extermination of a human life. Dante trembled with excitement. The context may be different, but the pleasure of the act would be the same.

A man dressed in military fatigues walked into sight, carefully scanning the surroundings with his flashlight in one hand and his rifle in the other. Although he didn't look in the one place danger lurked—up. *Good*, Dante thought, *humans are so stupid*. The poacher was almost within striking distance, and Dante began calculating the trajectory necessary for his attack.

The man stopped almost directly beneath Dante's branch. Without a second thought, he sprang. The man looked up too late, dropped his flashlight, and brought up his rifle. He screamed in surprise and managed to fire a single shot, but his fumbling had thrown off his aim. In a heartbeat, Dante had him pinned to the ground. Dante viciously slammed the poacher's skull into the earth, knocking him unconscious. Then he jumped up, picked up the flashlight, and turned it off. The jungle was dark and still except for the sounds of the other two men desperately calling to their companion.

Dante returned to his prize. He couldn't afford a struggle with this first victim, so he took out his hunting knife, picked up the poacher's head by the hair, and shoved his blade quickly into the back of his neck, severing the man's spine. His body would be alive long enough to bleed. Fangs fully extended, Dante bent his victim's head to one side and bit him hard on the neck. Blood filled his mouth. It was warm, rich, and felt good running down his throat.

He closed his eyes and savored his meal while listening to the other men stumbling in the dark. Neck wounds bled fast and made for satisfying feeding, but they were messy. He didn't have the experience necessary to swallow so much blood neatly.

One of the other men was heading his way. Dante reluctantly withdrew from his prey and jumped back up into the tree to wait. He wiped his face on his sleeve as he crouched, watching carefully. The other man's flashlight illuminated the grisly remains, causing him to rush headlong toward the dead man on the ground. *Stupid human*, Dante thought. *You really should be more cautious. Most predators don't easily abandon their kills. You should be expecting at least a show of aggression.*

He readied himself again. The second poacher called out to the last man and then put down his rifle to examine the corpse. Dante almost gave his hiding place away stifling a laugh. This one would be easier than the first. He sprung gracefully out of the tree, grabbed the man by the head, and twisted himself around as he fell. The man's body was picked right up off of the ground and his neck snapped as he flipped over Dante, who landed hard on his back and rolled on top of the poacher as soon as the body hit the ground.

Dante jumped up quickly and turned off the second man's flashlight. Again he was alone in the dark with a kill, but this time he wasn't very hungry. He was starting to feel slightly intoxicated. Human blood had that effect on him, and he had drunk on a completely empty stomach. His lip curled in a distasteful grimace as he examined the bodies on the ground. The first would already be cooling. How unappetizing, and the second just didn't inspire him. Dante decided to wait for the last man. After all, he couldn't afford to get careless.

He planned on fully enjoying this last kill. With this one, he would be able to relax and take his time. Footsteps were headed his way. Humans never made enough effort to be quiet hunters. They relied too heavily on the efficacy of their weaponry.

Dante ducked behind a shrub and listened. The third man came crashing into the small clearing under the tree and saw the bodies of his companions, broken and bloodied on the ground in front of him. He stopped and flashed his light around anxiously, the smell of fear billowing off of him. Dante smiled dreamily as he gave the man time to check his friends and fully recognize the situation in which he found himself. He was alone, in the dark with a killer, and he was going to die.

Dante growled. The poacher looked up in terror and flashed his light in Dante's direction. He stood up quietly and growled again as he stepped into mesay. The poacher raised his rifle and sprayed the underbrush with bullets, but Dante was already gone. He stood in the mesay doorway right behind the poacher, laughing softly to himself. He drew his hunting knife and stepped out quietly behind the man. The poacher stumbled forward toward the spot Dante had just vacated, flashing his light around wildly.

The light is so beautiful, Dante thought. *It's the only thing separating this fool from the darkness.* Losing the security of the light would make the game more interesting. Dante growled behind the man and walked back into mesay. The poacher jumped in panic and spun around, uselessly spraying more bullets.

The weapon would also need to be removed. That would leave hunter and hunted together with what they had been born with. He waited until the poacher was walking in a straight line again to step out behind him. He shoved the man with all of his might and sent him sprawling face first into the weeds. Dante quickly stepped over him and picked up the flashlight, then disappeared again as the man rolled over and pointed his gun around in the dark.

Dante came out of mesay a little ways away to enjoy the sense of despair growing within his prey. The poacher lay in the underbrush, trembling in terror. He cast desperately about for his flashlight. He was still armed and dangerous, but that would soon be rectified.

The poacher cried, cursed, and prayed while Dante laughed quietly. *Don't worry little man,* he thought, *your pleas may be falling on deaf ears at the moment, but you'll soon be able to express your disappointment to God in person.*

Dante lay flat in the underbrush and growled again. Another spray of bullets whipped by, making him wonder how much ammunition the man had on him. At this rate, it wouldn't be long before he ran out, which would save Dante the trouble of disarming him.

The poacher finally decided to get up and move. He was blind in the darkness of the jungle, but Dante had perfect night vision.

His quarry was trying to make his way back to the fire. Dante followed quietly, trying to decide what to do next. He was getting bored and sleepy. The intoxicating effect of the blood was already wearing off. He either needed more blood or he needed to go to bed. Dante decided to end this game quickly and go home to rest.

He stepped into mesay and came out behind his prey. His quarry sensed him this time, but it was to be expected. You take away one sense and the others start working more efficiently. The man turned to shoot, but Dante was too close. He grabbed the rifle barrel and yanked it out of the man's hands, sending him sprawling into the dirt once again. Dante casually tossed the rifle into the jungle. The poacher quickly righted himself, scrambling on the ground like some kind of bizarre crab.

Dante loomed over him and growled again, deliberately making his eyes glow bright red. He wanted this human to know the purest fear before he died. He wanted to look his quarry in the eye as he killed him.

"What the hell?" the man mumbled in a language Dante understood.

"How does it feel to be hunted?" Dante asked.

"Please don't kill me. I have a wife and children at home," the man begged.

This only made Dante angrier. Conversation was not part of his plan. "You're a lucky man," he replied, genuinely envious. "But you're stupid." Dante growled a low and rumbling growl deep in his chest. "If you were smart, you'd be in bed with your wife tonight."

"They need me," the man pleaded.

"I should be in bed with a wife of my own, but instead I'm here in Hell, paying for my sins. Now you have to pay for yours."

"Who are you to judge me?" the man demanded.

"Did you read the signs as you crossed into this land?"

"Yes," the man answered, his voice trembling.

"What did they say?"

"Death awaits anyone who trespasses on this land," the man recited in terror.

"Allow me to introduce myself. I own this land. I'm Death." Dante sprang forward just as his quarry brought up a knife. Dante curved his body just in time, but felt the blade slice under his left armpit and around his rib cage instead of piercing his chest. Dante landed hard on the man and brought his knees up into his chest, breaking his ribs and knocking the wind out of his lungs. The knife fell as Dante grabbed his prey's head and twisted it viciously around.

Dante closed his eyes, took a long, deep breath, and smiled. He was injured and should be suffering, but the nerves of his skin were tingling tantalizingly, stimulating other appetites. It had been far too long since he had enjoyed the feel of a woman's nails on his skin. He would have to take care of that as soon as he cleaned up this mess and made himself presentable.

He got up and stared down at the dead man on the ground. Dante's hunger had not returned; as a matter of fact, he suddenly felt a wave of nausea wash over him. He'd taken too much blood on an empty stomach, combined with too much excitement. He stumbled over and vomited. He knelt in the weeds, heaving and groaning for a few minutes until he could get up again.

He looked at the body on the ground and gagged. Now he'd completely lost his appetite. The warmth of the bed back at the hunting cabin beckoned him. He walked into mesay and arrived at the poachers' camp. After a quick check for any caged animals, he put out their fire as best he could. The peace and tranquility of the jungle without humans enveloped him, and he stood in the still-ness of the moment to savor it.

A movement startled him. Out of the corner of his eye, he thought he saw someone. He listened carefully, but heard nothing. *Man, I'm jumpy*, he thought. *I need some rest.* Dante quickly disappeared.

Back at the hunting cabin, he went right to the bathroom. What he saw in the mirror made him gasp. Staring back at him was a wild man with matted hair full of dirt and twigs. His face was streaked with mud and blood, eyes red and savage. He was a stranger, a demon. Dante thought of his friends and family and felt deeply ashamed of himself. The thought of his mother's spirit watching him as he took such pleasure from killing helpless humans made him feel sick.

He fell to the bathroom floor and barely got his head into the toilet in time. He heaved miserably but was already pretty much thoroughly purged. He remained on the cold tile floor, feeling wretched. He wasn't a good angel and he wasn't a good demon. He was nothing...

Rising unsteadily to his feet, he began stripping off his clothes. He turned on the shower then stood in front of the mirror to admire his injury. He lifted up his arm and turned his body to see how far the slice went. It wrapped around and down in a beautiful arc from the front of his pectoral muscles, around the back of his ribs, and under his shoulder blade. He hissed to himself as he touched the skin tenderly. No ribs were broken, but he was cut through to the bone. The wound had been bleeding for a while, but his body had already started repairing itself. It oozed as he probed, but it was going to be fine.

Dante stepped into the shower and let the water run over him. He braced his hands on the wall and hung his head in the water, feeling dirty inside and out. He remembered feeling similarly soiled after the first time he'd had sex with Emilie. He groaned. Thinking about her was not going to improve his current state of mind. He turned around and bent his head back into the water to wash the blood, dirt, and weeds out of his hair. As he ran his fingers through it, he couldn't help recalling the sensation of Emilie's hands in his hair. Again...

Why couldn't he stop this? Why wouldn't this pain heal? He was determined to shave his hair down to his scalp as soon as he got home. Problem solved.

As another wave of nausea washed over him, he crouched down and put his face in his hands. He leaned his back against the wall and let the water run over him. He emptied his mind and focused on his breathing, then stood up and started washing himself from head to foot, scrubbing mercilessly.

He had come to a decision. He would go to the temple to pray. He needed to make peace with God.

Chapter 25

E milie heard a knock at her front door. She hadn't buzzed anyone into the apartment building and she wasn't expecting any visitors. She had been so completely wrapped up in the editing of her paper that she hadn't even realized the time. It was late, almost eleven o'clock on Wednesday night. Who could be at the door at this hour?

She had managed to survive Valentine's Day and had almost made it to the weekend without any dreams about Dante. She felt as if there might actually be a light at the end of this long, dark tunnel. There was another knock, louder and more insistent this time. Emilie went to the door and peeked through the peephole only to find Colin standing impatiently out in the hallway.

"Emilie, it's Colin. I know you're in there," he called. "It's important. Please open the door."

She couldn't begin to imagine what Colin wanted with her. It would have to be serious to make him, of all the people in this world, come to see her. She was overcome with curiosity and opened the door.

She was immediately struck by the anxious expression etched into his handsome features. "I'm sorry to bother you, but we're a bit desperate," he whispered.

"What's wrong?"

"Have you by any chance heard from Dante lately?" he asked with a look of hope in his haunting blue eyes.

"Come in," she insisted. "Please, tell me what's going on."

"Well, OK. But just for a minute," he replied as he reluctantly stepped inside and stood awkwardly in the entrance. "I don't want to bother you."

She closed the door. "What's happened to Dante?" Her voice cracked with undisguised emotion, and she felt tears welling up in her eyes.

He passed a critical eye over her body and then proceeded to inspect the disastrous state of her apartment. "You look almost as bad as he does."

"Thanks so much, Colin," Emilie responded sardonically. "It's great to see you too."

He stared at her for a moment in confusion, then the truth of her situation dawned on him. "You still love Dante, don't you?" he asked, his face hard and accusatory.

"I'll love him forever. I think he's my soul mate," she murmured. Unwanted tears dripped down her cheeks and she tried discreetly to wipe them away. She stood proudly in front of this person who had never hidden his disapproval of her relationship with Dante.

Colin snorted disdainfully. "You humans use the term 'soul mate' as though it was synonymous with 'convenient.'"

Emilie didn't have the strength to deal with this kind of criticism. She had set Dante free and Colin, of all people, should be thanking her, not berating her. "There was nothing convenient about my relationship with Dante. We loved each other despite all of the cultural, religious, and species differences that we faced. We have been connected since the first day we met, like magic."

Colin stood in the hall staring at her, his face a smooth and unreadable mask. He shook his head slowly and sighed. "Dante said that you were his soul mate too. But for us, it means something different, something much more serious."

"Why are you telling me this?" she growled. "Did you just come here to mock my pain?"

His smooth expression softened slightly, and he said, "I'm sorry. You seem to be as emotionally volatile as Dante."

"I will not stand here and allow you to lecture and criticize me. Why don't you just tell me what happened to Dante?"

"Just let me ask you one more thing. Am I correct in assuming that you broke off your relationship with Dante in order to protect him?"

Her throat seized shut with emotion. It was excruciating to discuss her feelings. She looked up into his cold blue eyes and explained, "It's what his father wanted, and what you and Jude wanted too. He was going to have to give up so much to be with me. I thought I was doing the right thing for everyone concerned."

"It was noble of you to give him up, considering how much he means to you. Maybe the two of you are a better match than I first suspected." Colin paused briefly, then continued, "Dante is missing." He let the words hang in the air for a few seconds while he silently debated telling her more. "Dante has taken this breakup very hard. Harder than we ever expected. We thought that after a few weeks he would snap out of it and realize it was for the best. We tried everything we could to cheer him up, but nothing has worked. He's been absolutely miserable, and just when we thought it was finally getting better, it actually got worse."

Colin's face was wrought with worry. "He's locked himself up, on and off, for the past two and a half months. He just works and broods. He hasn't been eating very well…if at all. We've been worried that he'll lapse into semi-conscious hibernation if he continues much longer. He seems almost delirious at times, talking about his definitions of Heaven and Hell. He keeps saying things like God is punishing him for his sins. As his spiritual advisor, I can say with all honesty that I've never seen him like this. I'm really worried he's going to harm himself, or someone else," Colin admitted. "He's been gone now for almost three days without a word."

Emilie had been listening so intently that she hadn't realized she had unconsciously reached for Dante's angel around her neck.

Colin saw her do it and appeared surprised. "I was wondering what had happened to that. It's not like Dante to be without it. Did you know that his mother bought that for him before he was born?"

"No, I didn't," she managed to croak. She squeezed the little angel tighter in her hand as fresh tears ran down her face. She didn't want to admit that Colin's revelations had only intensified her pain. Any progress she had made in the last months had, in a matter of minutes, been completely negated.

Colin returned to Dante's situation. "He disappeared sometime in the early morning two days ago and hasn't been answering his phone. We've left him many messages. We figure he's probably somewhere with no cell phone service, but we're being discreet in our inquiries because if word gets out that he's out on his own and vulnerable, I hate to think of what might happen to him. He's always been such a target.

"Even more than that, though, we're afraid he's going to hurt himself. If he lapses into semi-conscious hibernation while he's travelling inter-dimensionally, he could get lost or trapped. It would be close to impossible to find him." Colin locked his gaze on Emilie's as though trying to drive in the message that this information was confidential and that it had cost him dearly to be so forthcoming.

"I want to help."

"Jude and I would really appreciate anything you can do, but you must be careful. Dante's hurting. Please, don't make anything worse for him. Do you have my phone number?" Colin asked, glancing toward the front door. He was anxious to be on his way.

"Let me get my phone."

Colin gave her both his and Jude's numbers and made her promise to call if she heard anything. As Emilie closed the door behind him, she struggled to formulate a plan of action. Dante could be anywhere in the world. Even if she could find him, what could she possibly say to him?

There was no point continuing with her schoolwork, she was far too distracted. She slowly readied herself for bed, then lay in the dark, thinking of Dante's situation. Her bleakest thought was that she may have cost him his life. Imagining him wandering lost through inter-dimensional space in some kind of hunger-induced delirium—because of her—was excruciating. She couldn't let herself believe it had happened. He was too smart to be so careless and was probably just hiding somewhere, trying to sort out his thoughts without everyone fussing all over him.

She had ended their relationship in order to protect him. He was supposed to be moving on with his life without her. She had expected him to lose himself in his family, his work, his friends, and his religion. He wasn't supposed to be suffering like this. Had she really underestimated his feelings for her so completely?

She was miserable without him, but how could she possibly ask him to take her back now? *Maybe we can work things out,* Emilie thought hopefully, then shook her head. It was more likely that when he came back from wherever he'd been hiding, he'd have worked her out of his system once and for all.

How could she be so selfish? She didn't want to hurt him any more than she already had. Colin's plea haunted her. "Don't make anything worse."

If she spoke to him again, there was no way she would be able to lie to him. It still amazed her that she had done it the first time. Turning off her phone and staying over at Caroline's was probably what had saved her.

There was still a message from him on her phone that she had saved. She could finally listen to it, but it wouldn't contain any useful information about his current whereabouts. On the one hand, she longed to hear his magical voice, but on the other, it would be like a dagger in her heart.

Her pain squeezed her throat shut, and tears leaked down her cheeks. She curled up into the fetal position and clasped Dante's angel to her chest. If only he was here with her now. Her sorrow would dissipate quickly in the comfort of his strong arms.

Chapter 26

E milie didn't know when she had fallen asleep, but she knew she was dreaming.

She was still in her apartment, lying in her bed, but now Dante was with her; his body spooned up against hers. She tried to stay with the dream, not wanting to wake up alone with her pain. Her attention was focused on Dante, enjoying his memory. It was all she had left of him. In a futile attempt at fighting back fresh tears, she sucked in a deep, ragged breath. Her senses seemed particularly heightened. She could smell him. She could feel him touching her. She could hear him breathing quietly next to her. Her tears were tickling her face and she wanted to bring her hand up to wipe them away but was afraid that her movements would bring an end to this marvellous dream. So she lay still, clinging to her false reality.

But in the end, it was too much. Before she lost him completely, she had to touch him one last time. His hand was resting against her side and she twined her fingers into his. "Dante, I love you so much," she whimpered as she gave in to her sorrow and waited for him to disappear.

"Hmmm…I love you too," his magical voice replied, deep and gravelly with sleep. His warm fingers squeezed hers, and she suddenly realized that she wasn't dreaming at all.

She turned and wrapped every possible inch of herself around his body. She couldn't seem to get close enough to him. She sobbed uncontrollably as she kissed his shoulder, his neck, and his face, finally pausing to look him in the eyes to see if he was truly real.

Dante smiled.

"I thought I was dreaming," she squeaked, trying to regain her composure.

He pulled her tightly into his arms, hugging her hard against him. She could barely breathe, but she didn't care. He was real.

"What are you doing here? Where have you been? Everybody's been worried sick about you," she growled, pushing herself away from him.

He laughed.

The sound of his laughter was unbelievably wonderful to her ears. She could feel fresh tears welling up in her eyes just listening to him, just looking at him. Nothing had ever or would ever feel as good to her as long as she lived.

"Slow down. Give me a chance to answer you," he said, pulling her down into the bed and spooning himself against her again.

She felt so safe in his arms. The pain was starting to ebb away. While she waited patiently for him to start explaining, he rubbed his face in her hair and kissed her neck. Her need for answers was being overshadowed by a more instinctive need. Her body had been aching for him for so long. Emilie wanted desperately to surrender to her desire, but they had serious issues that required resolving. She didn't want to have this pleasure only to lose him again right away. She couldn't survive it a second time. "Dante, I'm waiting," she insisted.

His hand was wrapped around her breast and she quickly brought it up to her lips. She kissed his fingers playfully as his lusty purr vibrated in her ear. He was undeterred and continued kissing her neck, rubbing his fingertip along her lips. She closed her eyes, enjoying the feel of his finger on her mouth and the familiar smell of his skin. He took advantage of her parted lips by slipping his index finger into her mouth. She ran her tongue over it, sucking gently. He responded with an enthusiastic growl, pressing himself more firmly against her. With every ounce of determination in her heart, she pushed his hand away. "You're distracting me. We have a great deal to talk about here."

He let out a deep sigh and rolled onto his back. "OK, OK. Let's talk instead…" His voice trailed off bitterly as he stared up at the ceiling.

She rose and sat cross-legged next to him on the bed. She reached over and turned on her bedside lamp. The brightness forced her eyes into a squint, but he had to shade his completely with his arm. Despite his irritated blinking, he looked fantastic. He was wearing a dark green long-sleeved button up shirt with black trousers. "Let's start with what you're doing here in the first place?"

"I had a little talk with my father." Dante growled deep in his chest. He had spat out the word "father" as if it was a curse. He rolled onto his side, propping himself up with his arm. "I felt guilty about taking off on everybody. They'd all left me a hundred angry messages on my phone. I just needed a bit of time away from them all." He paused, adjusting himself more comfortably on the bed. "I've been having a hard time with all of this." He looked up at Emilie with shame burning in his eyes. "I've had stuff to work through my system. I've done things..." He sighed, locking his gaze on the bed. "When I finally went to the temple to think and pray, I checked my messages and called people back.

"Speaking of guilty responses, my father told me about the... conversation...you had with him in December. He told me it was his fault that you had made your decision to end things with me. He said you were trying to protect me. I was so angry I was afraid I would say or do something stupid, so I just hung up and went right home to my place to clean myself up so I could come here to confront you about this whole mess.

"At the condo, Colin told me he'd been so worried about me that he'd actually come over here to see you. He confirmed what my father had said. Colin said you looked awful." Dante smiled up at Emilie. "As if you could ever look awful. Then he told me you still loved me."

He had such a happy, satisfied grin on his face that she wanted to jump on him and smother him with kisses right then and there.

"He told me you said I was your soul mate." He paused as a wave of emotion swept over his face. "I became even more determined to come here to talk some sense into you." Dante grew more serious as he continued, "I had to see you again. I had to set things right between us. I got here ready for a fight, but you were asleep." He looked up at her, smiling shyly as though he felt he had somehow intruded on her privacy. He had, of course, but she was overjoyed that he had stayed. "You were so beautiful." He sighed, reaching his hand up to brush her cheek. "I could tell you'd cried yourself to sleep because you were still sniffling." He paused and laughed softly to himself. "You had your hand around my angel and you were too peaceful for me to wake.

"But I couldn't bear to leave you," he added, his voice harsh. "So I crawled into bed with you, and I've been waiting here ever since. I knew I had made the right decision because the first words out of your mouth were that you loved me. I knew it! I've always known in my heart that you wanted us to be together as much as I did." He patted her thigh with his strong hand.

"So you understand that everything I said to you when I ended things between us was all an act? You know I didn't mean any of it?" she whimpered, her eyes begging him for forgiveness.

"I figured as much. But it feels good to hear the words coming from your lips," he replied with relief. "Speaking of those lips…" Dante sniggered, sitting up next to her. He wrapped her in his arms and rolled her back onto the bed with him on top of her. "…I have some unfinished business with them."

Emilie looked up into his beautiful face as he brought his lips to hers. She had dreamed of this moment so many times. Finally it was real. She parted her lips eagerly.

It was wonderful to have him back in her life. But the hopelessness of their situation crept unwanted into her consciousness. There were serious questions to be asked and answered before she could completely relax in his arms. "What are we going to do?" she whispered between kisses. "I can't let you sell your soul in order to marry me."

He stopped kissing her immediately. His face hovered over hers and he stared down as though some kind of realization had just dawned on him. Then he kissed her hard on the mouth and rolled off, lying on his back again. "So that's what this was all about," he muttered. "Who told you I would have to do that?"

"Your father," she answered with guilty hesitation. "He told me that you would have to offer something irresistible to the council to get out of your marriage contract. He said you would have to become a thief or, worse, an assassin."

Dante's features became angrier than she had ever seen. His jaw muscles were tight and twitching, and his eyes glowed bright red. "He's really lucky that he's my blood. Otherwise…" Dante growled menacingly as if indulging his imagination. "And here I thought I couldn't get any angrier with him. I can't believe how much he's interfered in my life. Now I can see why you were driven to leave me in order to protect me from myself."

He sucked in a ragged breath and let it out slowly, obviously trying to calm himself. As he sat up next to her, he spoke as gently as he could, "You should have come to me with this. I promise you that I never had any intention of hiring myself out as an assassin or a thief. I love you, but I don't think I'm capable of living another three hundred years robbing and killing."

She saw nothing but honesty and sincerity in his eyes. He wasn't just telling her what she wanted to hear. The realization that all of their pain and suffering could have been avoided if only she had been open with him threatened to overwhelm her. "So you're not going to sell your soul for me?" she asked, her voice quavering.

He hesitated. "Do I have to answer that exact question?"

Her guilt was instantly replaced with anxiety. "You are, aren't you?"

"It's my choice!"

"It's my life too! I couldn't live with myself, knowing you had to do something like that for me."

"I have to get out of that marriage!" he stated with determination as he pulled her into his arms and down on the bed again.

"Isn't there any other way?" she whimpered, cuddling against him.

"No," he replied flatly. "Emilie, I'm going to do it with or without you. It's not about you. This is for me."

"Galen is going to have you killed!" she countered, voicing her deepest fear.

Dante growled under his breath as he realized that his father had given her information about this part of his life as well. "It's only a matter of time before he does anyway. I'd rather enjoy what's left of my life. I can't put this marriage off indefinitely." His voice was soft and gentle, as though trying not to make the situation sound as grave as it was.

"So I can't say or do anything to stop you?"

"I'm afraid not."

"I can't just sit around and wait for you to get killed. I love you too much." She reached over to stroke his cheek and then ran her fingers lovingly into his hair.

He leaned into her hand, closed his eyes, and let out the most heart-wrenching sigh. He lifted his hand and covered hers, locking it into his hair. "God in Heaven…You have no idea how much this feeling…this simple thing…has tormented me."

Emilie saw the rawness of his suffering in his brown eyes and regretted causing him so much pain.

"I can hardly believe how amazing it feels to have your fingers in my hair again." He let go of her hand and leaned into it, smiling sorrowfully. She couldn't even bring herself to smile because she felt so guilty. Instead, she continued to stroke him, watching as his face became more peaceful.

Dante took a deep breath and sat up. "If I told you that I had cancer and had six months to live, what would you do?"

She didn't think it was a fair question. How could he be so cruel? It wasn't the same. Or was it? She wouldn't leave him if he had cancer. She would want to make his last days as happy as she could. "You're evil!" she hissed.

He was looking far too victorious for her taste. "Galen may not be able to kill me that easily. You may be stuck with me for a very long time," he announced with a confident smugness.

"Oh, now that would be torture!"

"Listen, in order to get out of my marriage, I do have to go before the council to make a bargain. I'd like to have your support. It would help me a lot."

She took a deep breath and let it out slowly. "I guess so. But I don't like the sound of this. What exactly are you planning?"

He lay back down and hugged her hard. "If you want to spend your life with me, you'll have to live with some uncomfortable truths. The council is a dangerous but necessary organization. There has to be some order in the chaos that is our society.

"There's good and evil in everything. The documents and packages I carry almost always hold someone's life in the balance. I know that I'm contributing to many deaths, indirectly. Am I responsible? Maybe. But that's between me and God. It's not for anyone else to judge. I believe I'm doing the best I can with what I've been given.

"There's a fine line between good and evil. I think it depends on what side of the line you're looking from. You stand on the good side. As you walk toward me, where does good stop and evil start?

Isn't it a matter of perspective? What about necessary evil? Is evil ever necessary? I've been wrestling with these questions all of my life. It's easier for you. Ignorance is bliss. Humans are so unaware of the many evils going on in their everyday lives, and they seem to prefer it that way. We Beyowans have to live with evil a little more intimately. Maybe we've also become desensitized.

"I'm going to have to make a difficult decision. I have to offer the council something. There's no other way. I might indirectly cost even more people their lives. You and I and God may not be completely happy with that decision, but I consider it a necessary evil. I'll ultimately be judged for my decision, but it's the lesser of all the evils in terms of the options available."

"What exactly are you talking about here?" she asked nervously.

"I can't tell you, and I won't be able to tell you either. I have a plan and you're just going to have to trust me to make the best decision, under the circumstances, about my future. I love you, and I want to be with you, and only you, for the rest of my life. I'm willing to pay a heavy price for that privilege." He brought one of her hands to his lips. "Are you?"

There was uncertainty in his eyes, then, as if he couldn't bear to hear her answer, he looked away. Emilie felt as though she could become an assassin herself if it meant she could be with him forever. How much evil would she be willing to accept into her life to get the happiness she wanted? It should be a difficult decision, but it wasn't. This time she would be completely and totally honest with him.

"I'm willing to do whatever it takes," she replied. "I understand that the decision is yours. I'm going to trust and support you." Emilie spoke with more confidence than she actually felt. She was nervous about committing herself to his plan without knowing what he intended.

"You're willing to do whatever it takes?" he verified, his desperation evident in the quavering of his voice.

"Yes!"

"Are you willing to give up being human?" That familiar, smooth, and unreadable expression had returned to his face. He was preparing himself in case she didn't give him the answer he wanted to hear.

"I thought a lot about this after talking with your father. I've always known that you would eventually ask me this question. I've known since the day you told me your parents' story. I believe it's one of those necessary evils that you just mentioned. I'm willing to do it if it means we can be together."

He wrapped her up into one of the biggest hugs ever. "Are you absolutely certain? This isn't a decision to make lightly. You can't change your mind about it later."

He was looking so deeply into her eyes that she knew he would be able to see any doubt she was trying to hide. She needed him to understand how serious she was, but she was concerned about the details. "I'm positive, but how are you going to arrange to have me changed into a vampire?"

Dante let go of her as if she had suddenly burned him. "Please… please don't ever call yourself that. I'm not going to marry a… vampire."

"I'm sorry," she soothed. "How are you going to have me… changed?"

He seemed to come to the realization that he may have over-reacted and took a slow, cleansing breath before continuing. "I'm going to buy the venom and pay for you to be transformed, in the best way possible, under complete medical supervision."

He was making every effort to sound as reassuring as possible, but Emilie still had concerns. "Is it going to be expensive?"

"Yes, it is. But don't you worry, I can afford it, and it's worth every penny." He smiled tenderly.

"Is it going to be painful?" she asked without any effort to disguise her fear.

Dante couldn't bring himself to meet her gaze for more than a second. He must have been feeling sorry for what she was going to have to endure for him. She was afraid that he might be tempted to tell her some comforting lie so that she wouldn't be afraid.

"Yes, it is," he said quietly. "But I'm hoping to have you sedated for the worst of it."

Perhaps his hesitation stemmed from his own fear that if he told her the truth, she would change her mind. Both of them were still hurting from their breakup. Emilie would have to pay a heavy price to be with Dante, but he wouldn't be able to marry her if she didn't change first. He couldn't force her or trick her into it. She had to give herself willingly. The only reason he had walked away from her on that terrible day when she had ended their relationship was because remaining human was not an option, and there wasn't another compromise either of them could live with.

Speaking of which, she thought. There was one thing in particular she was unwilling to compromise on: Dante's fidelity. She needed to have something cleared up before they could start celebrating. "Are you the father of Tasia's baby?" she asked with dread.

He stared at her as if she had just slapped him. "How much did my father tell you?"

"He told me a lot," she replied resentfully. "It was a lot to process all at once, and you know how well I handle information overload."

He laughed uncomfortably. He knew very well. "Remember my little chat with Tasia at the ballet?"

Emilie nodded, trying not to think too much about the woman.

"She told me about her pregnancy and that I *wasn't* her baby's father. I've known all along. I was just on the paternity list out of consideration. Gavin is the baby's father. There wasn't ever any doubt, but my father was extremely disappointed. He's been bugging me to get married and have a child since I turned forty."

"He did say that he was hoping you would have a baby before he died." She slid closer to him and whispered, "We'll make this work. We'll both have to do things we'd rather not, but we'll have our fairy tale ending, even in your dark world." She needed to feel his arms around her. She needed to feel his love.

Dante hugged her hard. "I know," he replied and brought his hand up to caress her cheek. He brought his lips to hers and Emilie knew she'd never be able to live without him ever again, no matter what it cost either of them.

He pulled away from her reluctantly and said, "You have to promise me something." He took her face in his hands and looked her hard in the eyes. "You have to promise to talk to me about anything that upsets you. Anything! You can't hide information from me and you can't take it upon yourself to protect me from things— ever again. Is that clear?"

She smiled sheepishly and nodded her head. Tears leaked from the corners of her eyes and his face softened as he wiped them away.

"So are we in this relationship forever?" he asked.

She understood that he needed some sense of permanence in order to be able to leave her apartment again. "Are you asking me to marry you again?" she teased.

He paused carefully before answering. "I guess in a way, I am." Before she could protest, he continued, "You have to understand that I won't be able to protect you for long with you being both human and apart from me so much of the time. It's only a matter of time before somebody decides to use you to get to me. It's an extremely dangerous situation for you to be in. I've only just gotten you back in my life, and I don't think I could survive losing you again."

Emilie laughed uncomfortably. They had only known each other for a short time, and they had just gotten back together. She knew in her heart that they were meant to be together, but that didn't mean they had to rush out and get married right away. They should be able to take their time. She also couldn't afford to take time off in the middle of her semester to transform herself, plan a wedding, and go on a honeymoon. "Couldn't we just live together for a while? Then we could be together and you wouldn't have to worry so much."

Dante snorted. "Are you really happy being my mistress?" he asked harshly.

She hadn't thought about it that way, but if she lived with a Beyowan heir, she would be seen as his human mistress. He wanted more from her. He had been telling her so from the beginning, and she wanted to be taken seriously. The way other Beyowans treated her as though she were nothing more than a passing fancy of his bothered her immensely. "I don't want to be your mistress," she grumbled. "But I'm not ready to get married yet. It's too soon. I have school. Couldn't we wait a little while?"

Dante sighed and glanced away pensively. "Can I at least consider us unofficially engaged, and we can see what happens this spring? Maybe we can settle everything as soon as your semester is finished and before the fall semester begins." He paused to read her face. Then his own brightened and he added, "It would give me a chance to make a more formal proposal at another time."

Emilie couldn't help but smile. He was so romantic. A few short hours ago, she had thought that she would never see him again, and now she was going to commit to spending the rest of her life with him. Somehow, she wasn't surprised.

Dante's expression changed to something more mysterious. "Let's try to be married before my birthday," he declared. "I really don't want to have to pay that woman another penalty to put off my marriage to her."

Emilie had to laugh. "I know about that too. You've had sex with her too," she growled, thinking of Tasia again.

Dante snorted. "Oh, I have sex with her every year. Did you think I just mailed her a check? I am a messenger after all."

"What if I'm not ready by your birthday?" she challenged, but she wasn't entirely serious, only curious.

"Then you pay the penalty and I won't have sex with her," he answered, looking entirely too serious.

"How much will it be?"

"It's been increasing every year I put off the marriage. This year it will be about a quarter of a million dollars."

Emilie whistled. "That's expensive sex."

"Tell me about it," he grumbled. "But it's a matter of principle for me. If I'm going to pay that much, I expect something in return. It's not like I'm just taking her out for dinner."

"You're a dog…"

His eyes narrowed and he growled playfully. "Wouldn't you expect something for a quarter of a million dollars?"

She had another personal question that had been nagging at her. "Why didn't you just marry her, then turn around and divorce her? It would have been cheaper and easier."

He shook his head. "That was a matter of principle for me too, but it sounds like sage advice. Perhaps I'll do it this year, if you don't marry me first."

She shot him a dirty look. "OK, you win. We can be unofficially engaged, but don't you rush me." She punched him playfully in the arm.

Dante glared at her in mock anger, rubbed his arm, then grabbed her and rolled on top of her. He held her hands above her head and spread her legs apart. Before she could say or do anything, he kissed her hard on the mouth. Without thinking, she struggled with him, but he growled deeply and pressed her harder into the bed, reminding her of who she was dealing with. He ground his pelvis hard into hers and she made a little whimper into his mouth.

He stopped suddenly and rolled right off the bed, laughing darkly to himself. "Listen, I should get going. I've not eaten very much lately. I'm not really feeling like myself. As I've mentioned before, I have problems with control when I get too hungry. I accidentally ate some kind of monkey or lemur this morning," he admitted, shuddering with revulsion. "It wasn't very good at all. Very gamey."

"How do you accidentally eat something?" Emilie asked, afraid of the answer.

"You'll understand better once you've gone through your change. We run mostly on instinct, and when we're really hungry, it's much harder for us to control our feeding habits. I was sitting on a bench outside the temple, lost in my own thoughts. I think this creature was curious about me and got too close. You know what they say about curiosity."

The malevolence in his tone made her shiver. *What have I gotten myself into here?* she wondered. But she was still too elated about their reconciliation to allow any negative thoughts to dull her mood.

"Couldn't you stay for a little while longer?" she begged. She stood up, made him sit on the bed, and climbed into his lap, facing him. She put her hands on his shoulders and shoved him back onto the bed.

"Maybe for a few minutes," Dante purred, then rolled on top of her again.

He ran his face along her neck, breathing deeply. He was a hungry demon, and she didn't know which of his appetites was currently engaged. She couldn't stop her thoughts from straying to him devouring that poor creature. She couldn't imagine him snatching some animal out of the trees and draining the blood out of it or gnawing the raw flesh off of its bones. Dante was always so civilized. And then she remembered another time he'd had trouble with his instincts. She had found herself lying underneath him, wondering what he was going to do to her. He certainly hadn't been in complete control then.

"Dante...are you going to bite me?" she stammered, feeling herself going rigid under him.

He just laughed, obviously finding her discomfort amusing. "Do you want me to?" he purred into her neck, rubbing her gently with his teeth. "I don't have to drive. I can afford to get a little intoxicated."

"What does that mean?"

"I haven't had much human blood in my life. For some reason it affects me physically, especially when it's warm and fresh," he explained, laughing softly again.

He was so naughty, and he knew how uncomfortable she was. "Ummm...will it hurt...much?" she asked nervously.

"Yes..." he answered, sniggering. "And no," he continued more seductively. "There's a fine line between pain and pleasure. I could do other things to your body at the same time. You might really like it."

"You've done this before then?" she asked, even though she already knew the answer. She just wasn't ready to stop talking yet.

"Yes, I have," he purred evilly.

She could tell that he was just teasing her and enjoying it. She loved his sense of humor, even if it could be a bit dark at times. Her feelings of joy over their reconciliation suddenly overwhelmed her and she burst into tears, clinging to him as tightly as she could.

He went silent and seemed at a loss as to what to do. "I was just kidding," he whispered. "I would never..."

"I've been so miserable," she interrupted.

"Me too."

"I don't think I've ever hated Christmas before."

"Really?" he asked, encouraging her to continue.

"You have no idea how many angels made me cry," she croaked and buried her face into his shoulder.

He held her tighter and kissed her hair. "I had a young, socially unattainable yet sexually available woman run her fingers through my hair in a club and I sprinted for the exit as though she had set my head on fire."

Emilie didn't like to think about her angel with other women, but she had set him free. She couldn't blame him if he had spent every day they had been apart in the arms of a different woman. Obviously it wasn't the case. Even if it shouldn't matter, she was still relieved.

"I can top that one!" she exclaimed, remembering something special. "I had a Beyowan prince try to pick me up New Year's Eve in Vancouver."

He sat up and looked her over curiously. "Did you get his name?"

"No. But he wanted yours."

"How did he know about me?" he inquired, furrowing his brow.

"I didn't give him your name, but I was wearing your angel. He probably thought I was Beyowan until he got close enough to smell me. Then he assumed I was somebody's mistress."

"I can't wait to make you my wife so everyone will stop thinking of you as my mistress," he growled. "It really irritates me."

"It kinda bugs me too," she admitted as she unclasped his angel from around her neck and reached up to fasten the chain around his, where it truly belonged.

He played with the charm between his long, elegant fingers, then clasped her face in his hands and kissed her.

"We're together now," she said, slipping her arms around his waist.

"I couldn't be happier," he added, deepening his kisses.

"I can think of a way to make you happier," Emilie murmured. She leaned back onto the bed and brought Dante with her.

Coming Soon:

Book Three in the *Love is Hell* series

A Coin For The Ferryman

Even though Emilie Latour and Dante Ashton have known each other for only a short time, they are determined to build a life together. The price for this privilege is high, and each has serious sacrifices to make in order for their dream to become a reality. Unfortunately time is running out for the couple since Dante's hunting license is about to expire, and the chairman of the Montreal council is anxious to be rid of Emilie.

Dante has been carefully guarding a secret that he plans to use to secure Emilie's freedom from the council and to rid himself of his unwanted fiancée. But Emilie also has a dark secret that not only threatens Dante's love but even her life.

For more information about the books in the *Love is Hell* series, please visit soniabranchaud.com.

Made in the USA
Charleston, SC
15 November 2012